BOSTON BOLTS HOCKEY:
HOCKEY BOY

BRITTANÉE NICOLE

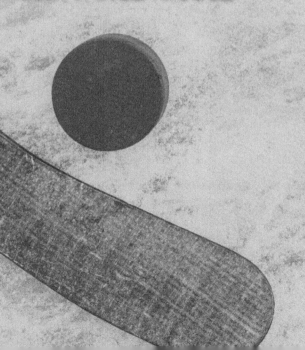

CONTENT WARNING

This book contains adult themes including discussions about depression and depressive thoughts.

SAVE THE DATE

GUESTS WHO HAVE RSVP'D SO FAR...

LANGFIELD FAMILY

Beckett Langfield &
Olivia Langfield
Children:
Winnie
Finn
Addie
June
Maggie

Gavin Langfield &
Millie Hall (Ford Hall's
Daughter)
Children:
Vivi

Brooks Langfield &
Sara Case

BOSTON BOLTS

Cade Fitzgerald
(Goalie Coach)

Tyler Warren

Daniel Hall

Camden
Snow

FRIENDS OF FAMILY

Ford Hall & Lake Paige

"DOWN BAD" PLAYLIST

01	STILL INTO YOU	PARAMORE
02	FABULOUS	ALLY BROOKE
03	NEXT TO YOU	JOHN VINCENT III
04	ALL MY LOVE	NOAH KAHAN
05	RIGHT WHERE YOU LEFT ME	TAYLOR SWIFT
06	I WANNA BE YOURS	ARCTIC MONKEYS
07	WHAT IF I WASN'T DONE LOVING YOU?	FLY BY MIDNIGHT
08	MASTERMIND	TAYLOR SWIFT
09	PARIS	THE CHAINSMOKERS
10	FEATHER	SABRINA CARPENTER
11	ROOM FOR 2	BENSON BOONE
12	I CAN DO IT WITH A BROKEN HEART	TAYLOR SWIFT
13	SOMEONE TO STAY	VANCOUVER SLEEP CLINIC
14	CRAZY IN LOVE (FEAT. JAY-Z)	BEYONCÉ, JAY-Z

DEDICATION

To all of us who wear our hearts on our sleeves, who feel the need to be bright and shiny for everyone else.

Sometimes it's okay to sit in the dark, to protect your heart, to dim your sparkle and save it for you.

And sometimes you're lucky enough to find someone who will sit in the dark beside you, hold your hand, and provide the warmth you need until you're ready to step back into the sunlight.

FOREWORD

Author's Note

Dear Reader,

With each book I write, the world I build becomes more connected and complex. While Hockey Boy is the first book in this series and you can absolutely read it as a standalone, you will see some character overlap and since I know many of you enjoy the easter eggs I hide and prefer to read in order, here is a suggested reading order as it comes to this world:

Revenge Era: Ford Hall and Lake Paige
Mother Faker: Beckett Langfield and Olivia Maxwell
Pucking Revenge: Brooks Langfield and Sara Case
A Major Puck Up: Gavin Langfield and Millie Hall
Hockey Boy: Aiden Langfield and Lennox Kennedy

All of these books take place in the Boston Billionaire World so you will see or hear about those characters as well.
I hope you enjoy this world as much as I enjoy writing it.
XO,
Brittanée

CONTENTS

CHAPTER 1
AIDEN

"I THINK HE'S CRASHING." The voice is distant and muffled.

My heart will go on.

"Get his heart rate." Another voice I don't recognize.

The power of love.

"You need to help him, *please.*" Lennox. She sounds so sad. Oh, Lennox, don't be sad.

Because you loved me.

"Is he singing a Celine Dion medley?" *Beckett?*

"Aiden, *please* wake up."

It's all coming back to me.

I remember my first kiss like it was yesterday. Lennox Kennedy. Strawberry ChapStick. Soft lips and an even softer accidental nipple swipe. Nervous laughter. A vow that our friendship would remain intact no matter what.

"Never have I ever kissed someone," I whispered.

It was our thing. One of us said it, and the other was obliged to do it. Never Have I Ever mixed with Truth or Dare. The game was so very us. She'd started it—she was always pushing the envelope, always getting us in trouble. But that night, I was the instigator. I had been dying to kiss her. The word crush had never been so accurate.

The sensations that bubbled up inside me when I thought about her threatened to decimate me if I didn't let them out. I was walking around with an anvil on my chest, in a constant state of fear that I'd say the wrong thing and lose her.

The spark of competition lit in her eyes at my statement, though, and I knew I had her.

She held me back with a hand to the chest, her eyes wide and swimming with a mix of fear and wonder. "I'll kiss you, but you have to promise this changes nothing."

It changed everything, but I nodded anyway. I'd have said anything to get her mouth on mine.

Lips pressed together, she let out a disbelieving huff. "I'm serious. Friends forever. If either one of us changes their mind, no matter what, and no matter when, all we have to do is say *shamrock*, and the other person can't get weird."

"Shamrock?"

She giggled. It was light and airy. "'Cause you're the Leprechaun."

I should have worried that my nickname in hockey would forever remind me of this moment, that shamrocks would become a curse rather than the good-luck charms they were touted as. Even if I had been concerned, it wouldn't have mattered. I wanted to feel her lips more than I wanted to preserve my heart, so I nodded. "Fine. Got it."

"Aiden, I'm serious. If one of us says it, nothing changes."

I settled a hand against her cheek, rubbing my thumb along her soft skin. "Lex, I swear, nothing changes."

I inched closer, my attention darting between her lips and her blue eyes. My heart pounded out an unsteady rhythm. God, she was so pretty. I was dying to taste her. And when she licked her lips and let out a soft sigh, I knew I'd promise her anything.

Oddly enough, the last word she said to me before disappearing from my life was shamrock. Though I suppose she didn't even speak the word. It was via text, and it destroyed my life.

That *was* the worst day of my life. Until today.

As the beeping gets louder and her sobs continue, I will my eyes to open. But as she utters the next words, I wish I'd never woken up.

"Dammit, Aiden. I can't do this again. *Shamrock.*"

Six Months Earlier

"Stop fidgeting." Jill sets her hand on my arm, as if that will stop me from moving. If I'm not singing, then there's a song playing in my head, and I can't help but bop to it, even if it's just my fingers drumming the beat against my knee.

I turn to my fiancée and force a smile. How long have I been forcing smiles? Years, at least. Happiest guy in the room. Faking it till I feel it, or something like that.

"Are you nervous?" She studies me as if she thinks she can read my expression.

I'm surprised she cares enough to even ask.

"You won't embarrass me, right? This is the most prestigious wedding planning company in Boston. They have a years-long wait-list. We're lucky the Langfield name bumped us to the top."

Ah. My stomach sinks. Of course she isn't actually concerned about my state of mind. She just doesn't want me to humiliate her. That's more like it.

I have to bite back a laugh at the absurdity of this. At the stereotype we're literally personifying. A rich boy marrying the wrong woman—a woman who only cares about appearances and definitely doesn't care about him. But at least I know that going in. Can't get hurt if I know what to expect.

"I'll be fine. Been playing my part in this dog and pony show since I was a kid. I know how to behave."

She fiddles with the oversized rock on her hand. I almost considered buying a small gemstone, maybe a plain band only, just to see if she'd still say yes.

In the end, I was too nervous to risk it. I need my brothers off my back like I need nothing else in this world. They're far too focused on the way I reacted when I discovered Lennox Kennedy was back in Boston. I had to do something to shut them up. And this makes sense. Jill and I have been together for three years. She may be difficult at times, but I know how to handle her—for the most part, at least. And I know what to expect when it comes to her. The fewer surprises in my life, the better.

The door swings open, and a burst of energy zaps through the space, electrifying the air. A pink flash darts past me, the breeze she creates causing the hair on my arms to stand on end. As the woman settles into the seat across from us, all the air in the room goes to my head.

"I am so sorry I'm late," she says, her focus fixed on her phone. "It's my first day. You'd think that alone would inspire me to be here early, but no, I need to make an entrance." Her tone is full of self-deprecation. "I swear I'm trying to be better about that. The good news is that since you're my first couple ever, I will want to make a grand entrance into high-society weddings with you. So yay!" With a clap, she shifts in her seat.

All that air forced into me is suddenly sucked out, stealing the breath from my lungs.

As if the woman could ever not make an entrance. She dips her head and studies a sheet of paper in front of her. And then her widened eyes tell me she's just seen precisely who her first client is. "The future Mr. and Mrs. Aiden Langfield." Lifting her head, Lennox Kennedy locks eyes with me.

I swear the world stops. Just like it did for the three years we were together.

And the years before that, when I was just learning that I liked girls. That I really fucking liked Lennox Kennedy.

I don't have the first clue why the universe is taunting me, but in this moment, I don't even care. The smile that curls my lips as we stare at one another is genuine. The strong beat of my heart—pounding to the rhythm of "Crazy in Love" by Beyoncé—tells me precisely what I have to do.

At the top of that list? Dumping my fiancée the second we walk out of the office.

Rule 1:
Don't fall for
the groom.

9:55AM

Sara Bestie for the Restie
Online

Good Luck today Bitch!!! Love you!

Seen

Ahhhh thank you! I am so nervous, but excited to finally get to do what I know I can kick ass at!

Seen

Well, you will kill it!!!! Brunch Sunday right? Or should we celebrate tonight

Seen

I'll text you! Gotta go....almost time for my meeting

Chapter 2
Lennox

AIDEN LANGFIELD IS GETTING MARRIED. Aiden Langfield, who I haven't spoken to in over ten years, is getting married. And I'm planning his wedding. Tell me the universe doesn't have a wicked sense of humor.

Kind of like mine. Sarcastic and loud.

"Jillian Murgo," the woman sitting primly beside my Aiden says.

Not your Aiden, Lennox. You can't be territorial over a man you haven't even spoken to in a decade.

"Of course." I paint on the perfect smile. The one I've perfected over the last twenty-nine years. The one my family expects me to wear to uphold our reputation. "What an exciting time. Tell me about yourselves. How'd you meet? What's the proposal story?"

Did he tell you that I was his first kiss? That he promised I'd be his only kiss? That we once meant everything to one another?

Aiden's lip quirks into what I know is his true smile, as if he can read my internal ramblings, but he tamps it down quick.

"Oh, where to even begin?" the woman next to him says. Her voice is slightly nasal, just like her face. Seriously, her schnoz could give Pinocchio a run for his money.

"Yes, where?" I place my hands on the desk in front of me,

keeping my eyes on her. If I look at Aiden, I'm liable to have a heart attack.

Aiden Langfield is getting married. The only man who ever held even a tiny piece of me—the jokester, the romantic, the man I truly believed at one point would be my endgame—*married.*

How did we get here? My internal voice suddenly sounds like thirteen-year-old me, and judging by the venom in her whispered words, she isn't happy with what I've done with our life.

"We've been together for almost three years," she explains, nudging the man next to her.

In response, he gives her a wide-eyed look that I interpret as *what do you want me to add?*

Hmm. Interesting.

Though I'd find it more interesting if she wasn't wearing a goddamn emerald on her finger the size of her nose. Damn. How much money do hockey players make these days?

Yeah, Aiden Langfield comes from money. So do I. Our families' ridiculous wealth was a topic we bonded over early on. It may seem annoyingly cliché to be upset that our families each have more money than a small country, but with money comes strings. Not like Pinocchio strings either. These pull so taut they make it impossible for a person to even control their own actions. They're the kind of strings that will twist you in so many ways you won't recognize the person you've become when they're finished with you.

And they do eventually finish with you. Once you say no. Once you decide to live for yourself. Once you've—*Okay, I've obviously gotten sidetracked.* Jill is still talking—mostly about herself and what she envisions for her wedding.

Hers. Not *theirs.* It's obvious this is her show.

"And it has to happen next month."

"Excuse me?" I say, forcing my attention from her to Aiden.

A warm smile spreads across his face. What the hell is wrong with this guy? He keeps giving me these dopey smiles. Did Jill drug him? Maybe that's how she got him to propose.

Oh, Lennox, stop being a conspiracy theorist. I can practically hear my mother's groan.

"I'm not sure if you're aware, but my fiancé is the Boston Bolts' star center." For the first time today, she actually looks at Aiden, acknowledging his existence, like he's worth something. It's in this moment that I hate her. Aiden Langfield is many things, and yes, he *is* one of the best players to ever play in the NHL, but his worth—his value—has absolutely nothing to do with what he can do with a hockey stick and a pair of skates.

As if he can sense the tension mounting in my every cell, Aiden clears his throat and sits straighter. Then he speaks to me for the first time in over a decade. "I start training full time in August."

The gravel in his voice causes a full-body shiver.

"We need to be married by the end of July at the latest," Nasal Nancy says.

So what if I don't ever intend to call her by her given name? Let me live.

Holding back a sigh, I pull up the calendar on the computer in front of me. Finding a venue, a caterer, a photographer, a band, and a DJ on such short notice will be nearly impossible. Never mind that it's all for my ex-boyfriend. Freaking fantastic.

"Will that leave you enough time for a honeymoon?"

Jill shifts in her seat, putting space between herself and Aiden. "Not much. But I'm a dedicated hockey wife—or soon to be." Her smile is saccharine. "Hockey makes Aiden happy, so watching him play is honeymoon enough for me."

I snort. "Better you than me. The last thing I'd be doing on my honeymoon is watching."

Jill sucks in a harsh breath, the sound making my stomach plummet. I slap a hand over my mouth. Shit. I really need to work on my brain-to-mouth control. I've never been good at keeping my every thought from escaping through my lips.

Aiden chuckles, instantly easing the tension in my shoulders. Damn, I haven't heard that sound in years. This boy's laugh is certainly worth my heated cheeks and the thread of embarrassment working its way through me.

"How did you end up working here?" he asks, planting his elbows on the armrests of the chair and lacing his fingers in front of his torso.

Nine Inch Nose forces a smile. "I'm sure she has better things to do than get into her life story with a couple of strangers, Aiden. It is a Sunday. We're lucky she could squeeze us in at all."

I shrug. I could talk about myself all day. "I don't mind." Tossing my hair over my shoulders, I straighten. "I was born on November sixteenth. Makes me a Scorpio. I'm an only child, so I was eternally lonely growing up, and even as an adult, I get to deal with my parents' dramatics all by myself. When I was five, I fell off my bike and decided then and there that sports would never be my thing." Lifting my gaze to the ceiling, I tap my finger against my chin. "Hmm, I obviously like pink." A laugh bubbles out of me. Of course I do. My hair is bright magenta, as is the stone pendant around my neck. My nails too, and my shoes. "Had my first kiss at fourteen—" I home in on Aiden when I say that last part.

His dark eyes are sparkling, and his lips are quirked up on one side.

Feeling brave, I cover one-half of my mouth and add, "Lost that V-card shortly thereafter." As my heart rate skyrockets, I drop my hand and rush out the rest. "Went to college, met my bestie—Sara— graduated." I force an exaggerated pout. "Had to leave my bestie and then went on to try out several jobs before I became your wedding planner."

Finally, I suck in a breath and relish the way the oxygen floods my system.

Aiden's full-on grinning.

Not Your Average Nose is staring at me like I have three heads. "That's...great," she says, though the way her lip curls on one side makes it clear she really thinks otherwise. "So what do you think for a venue?"

Wishing I had a gallon-sized mimosa right about now, I fill my lungs and force my fake smile to widen. "How about I take the day to scope out a few locations, and we can tour them tomorrow? If this wedding is going to happen next month, then we need to hit the ground running."

Aiden smirks. "I'll make myself available."

"Oh, I'm sure you'll be busy with hockey stuff," I suggest. Because really, the last thing I need is to spend more time with my ex-boyfriend, the former love of my life, while planning his fucking wedding.

His eyes don't leave mine as he replies. "Nothing is more important to me."

CHAPTER 3
AIDEN

"SHE WAS COLORFUL," Jill says.

Technically, she isn't wrong. Lennox is as bright as a rainbow, even without the pink hair, pink lips, and the pink dress that hugged her curves perfectly. But Jill's snarky tone belies the sentiment.

It's a dig. A slight.

My blood heats, and anger clouds my vision. For three years, I've swept nearly every negative comment this woman has made under the rug, whether she was talking about my teammates, my brothers, or other women. But I can't when it comes to Lennox.

"We used to date," I say as I hold the door open and follow her to the elevators.

"Excuse me?" She sneers, her lips curled in a way that matches her ugly personality. "You barely acknowledged her when she walked in."

Smiling, I shake my head. "I was speechless. She's always done that to me. Steals the words right along with my breath."

The elevator opens, and I step in. When I turn, ready to push the button for the ground floor, Jill is still standing in the hall, her mouth wide open. How the hell did it take me this long to realize I couldn't go through with marrying her? To see how vapid she really is? There's not a thing I like about her. *Not one.*

Fuck, that's depressing.

I hold the elevator open, but when she doesn't step in, I grab her hand and tug her through the open door. "We should go somewhere to talk."

Jill smooths her hands down her black dress and runs her tongue over her teeth. "Right. We've got wedding plans to discuss."

I choke on a laugh. "I just told you my ex stole my breath away, and you think we're going to talk about a wedding?"

"Our wedding," she chides, lifting her chin and narrowing her eyes on me in challenge.

"No, Jill. Maybe it was your wedding, but nothing about this was ever ours."

I watch the numbers above the door change as the elevator descends, and with each floor we pass, I feel lighter. Like when I step out of this stainless-steel box, I'll finally have the strength to walk away from this woman, this relationship. To step into the damn sun.

I turn to her and give her a genuinely remorseful frown. "I'm sorry, Jill. This isn't working for me anymore. The wedding is off."

As the door slides open and sunlight from outside the floor-to-ceiling windows of the lobby hit me, my entire body relaxes. The pressure that's engulfed me, tightening like a boa constrictor, killing me slowly, vanishes, and I'm ready to step forward.

Until Jill hits the emergency button, and the door slides shut.

My heart lurches as the warmth of the sun is extinguished. "What the hell?"

"You're done?" she screeches, clutching my shoulder and pulling me back. "What the hell does that even mean?"

Tensing, I spin and take her in. She's pretty on the outside, there is no denying that, but she's an ugly person on the inside. And the sneer she's aiming my way is proof of all the awful things my brothers and friends have been pointing out for years. Dammit. I've wasted so much time. Mine and hers.

I take a deep breath, ready to apologize. We were engaged—technically maybe still are?—and she deserves an explanation.

"Years ago, I fell in love with the woman you just met. I gave her my entire heart, and I never got it back. It was selfish of me to think I could give you something I no longer own. You deserve a partner who will make you happy and will feel the way I did for Lennox."

Her expression morphs into one of disbelief. "Are you fucking kidding me? We've been dating for three years, and you just—" She throws her hands up in the air with a huff. "What? One look at her, and you're done? She's fucking pink, Aiden. *Pink.* You think your family hates me?" Hands on her hips, she tilts her head and lets out a condescending scoff. "I can't imagine your father's reaction to that oversized pink pig upstairs."

A red cloud of rage edges into my line of sight. I've never wanted to hit a woman—never even considered it—until this very moment. I squeeze my fists at my sides. "That woman upstairs has more class in one pink fingernail than you have had in your entire existence. And not that it matters, because it's the thing I find least interesting about her—but she's a Kennedy—as in Kennedy records, Kennedy properties, Kennedy diamonds..."

Her beady eyes grow wider with each word, and her mouth drops open.

A sick sense of satisfaction hits me. "You catch my drift, I see. My family would love it if I ended up with her, but not because of her last name. They'd be thrilled because the only time in my life that I was ever truly happy was when that woman was smiling at me."

Her jaw goes rigid and her nostrils flare. Then a loud *ha* echoes off the stainless-steel walls. "I did not waste three years dating you for this." She points from herself to me with one sharp nail. "You think I'm in love with you? Please. You are a fucking puppy seeking the crumbs your brothers throw at you. They don't care about you. That woman upstairs doesn't care about you." She points at the ceiling. "And I never cared either. You were a mark." The smile that stretches across her face is cruel. "An easy one, at that. I've been dating

Vincent Lukov for years. But he doesn't make the kind of money you do. So we made a little plan. I'd go after one of the Langfield boys to secure the lifestyle we need. Honestly, I wanted Gavin, but Vin worried I'd actually fall for him since he's got big dick energy, and let's be honest"—her eyes drop to my crotch and she scoffs—"you don't."

Throwing my head back, I roar with laughter. Fuck, it's amazing to not feel guilty anymore. Vincent Lukov is a scab of a man. A winger for New York and the nephew to my old coach—a man who used to be my uncle until my aunt found out he'd been cheating on her for years. The entire Lukov family sucks and the best thing to come out of my aunt's divorce was the fact that Vincent is no longer family.

"That why you needed a monthly break from my dick? Honestly, thank you." I press my palms together and bend slightly. "The less time my prized jewel spent near your slutty, scheming self, the better. Good luck with Lukov. Without the money you figured you'd take me for in our divorce, it'll be just you and him and his mediocre salary. But don't you think it's odd, Jill, that the man you think cares so much for you was willing to barter you? I'd never let a woman I love be touched by another man, let alone encourage it." I lean in close. "But you? I don't feel a damn thing for. So have fun."

I hit the button to release the emergency stop, and as the elevator door jolts open, I stalk out, my head held high and a smile on my face. I just lost 150 pounds and three years' worth of pent-up anxiety.

Life is only going to get better from here.

Rule 1:
Don't fall for
the groom.

Dearest Lennox

Chapter 4
Lennox

"NO FUCKING WAY," my best friend Sara says from her spot across from me.

Beside me, Millie tsks and adjusts the blanket that's covering a sleeping Vivi. "Try using *ducking* if you need to use that language."

"Sorry." Sara cringes, then shakes her head. "But how is she going to plan Aiden's wedding? This is ridiculous."

Beside her, Ava, the quietest of the bunch, bites her lip. "I couldn't do it."

With a small frown, Hannah nods. "No way could I watch the man of my dreams marry someone else, let alone plan the magical day."

My girls and I are all brunching it up, like we do every Sunday. With booze, of course. What's brunch without a Bloody Mary or mimosa?

Breakfast.

And who the hell wants to settle for breakfast?

Especially today. Regardless of the brave face I've donned, I wholeheartedly agree with my friends.

This is why I rushed here, even though I originally told them I couldn't make it since I was meeting with my first official client. I've been working for the company for two months and have overseen a few wedding planning sessions, but this is my first solo gig.

The universe is clearly fucking with me. What are the chances that I'd be assigned to plan Aiden Langfield's wedding?

Sara pushes my drink toward me, brows raised.

With a chuckle, I take a sip, giving in to her silent request.

We've known each other since college. Sara works for the Boston Bolts' PR team. Yes, the same Bolts Aiden plays for, along with his brother Brooks, who's engaged to Sara. She's got long blond hair that she'll likely dye blue when the season starts, because she's obsessed and supportive.

The rest of the girls are new friends, all introduced to me through Sara.

Millie, while technically the youngest of us all at only twenty-four, is mom to Vivi, the nine-month-old snoozing in her arms. She's engaged to Aiden's brother Gavin, who is forty-two. Vivi was a surprise neither of them saw coming, and while they aren't her biological parents, they rolled with the surprise and have created the most loving little family.

Millie and Gavin also happen to be my neighbors. Their penthouse apartment is next to the smaller unit Sara lived in before she and Brooks got together. When she moved out, I moved in, though she didn't technically know that at first.

Across from Millie is Hannah, a petite brunette who comes across as quiet to those who don't know her. In reality, the girl is snarky and holds her own like no other. The quality is necessary, really, since she runs PR for the baseball team the Langfields own, the Boston Revs. I've just started to get to know her, and so far, I'm a fan.

Rounding out our little friend crew is Ava, the tall redhead who always wears calming colors and never raises her voice or has a bad thing to say about anyone—unless we bring up Tyler Warren, the left winger for the Bolts, who has bad boy basically tattooed all over him. The man has an uncanny ability to get under this sweet one's skin.

"Yeah, it's not ideal." I down the rest of my mimosa, then hold it up and smile at our server, who is collecting drinks from the bar.

The dark-haired man with an easy smile, striking blue eyes, and muscles far too large to be hidden under that black shirt, shakes his head. "Should I just leave the bottle?"

"Now we're talking." Grinning, I scan the table, only to find my friends wearing varying looks of unease. "What? It's been a long day." It's only one, but it seriously feels like I've survived three Sundays already.

"Of course it has," Sara snaps. "The love of your life asked you to plan his wedding."

My chest gets tight, but I ignore the pain and shoot her a glare. "He's not the love of my life. Stop being so dramatic. He was my childhood sweetheart. It's been over for a decade."

When the waiter returns with the bottle, I slide him my card.

"Don't you dare," Sara hisses.

I shoo the hottie away. I'm not ready to close the tab, but if I don't give it to him now, we'll fight about the check at the end.

"What did she do?" Ava asks, darting a look at me, then Sara.

My best friend harrumphs. "She gave the server her card."

Millie rests her hand on top of mine on the table. "You don't have to do that. Gavin told me brunch is on him."

Sara rolls her eyes. "He bought it last week. Why can't we split it like normal people do?"

"It's my love language. Let me love you," I whine, bumping her shoulder with mine.

Hannah snorts. "You can love me over at Nordstrom if ya want."

Clasping my hands in front of me, I beam. "Now that's my kinda sugar baby. Come to mama." I hold out my arms and shimmy.

Hannah blows me a kiss.

Millie giggles. "Whatever. I'm getting next week."

"You don't have to do that, you know," Sara says, her expression pensive. "We'll love you even if we buy our own mimosas."

And I love her for reminding me. As a Kennedy, money is my most sought-after commodity. My value is directly linked to what I can offer, and while I still have the means, I'd like to spoil the people who have never made me feel that way at all.

CHAPTER 5
AIDEN

Gavin: How'd wedding planning go?

Beckett: He probably burst into song in the event planner's office. Did you jump up on the desk? What did you sing? Wait, don't tell me. Britney Spears Toxic?

Brooks: Lol

Gavin: Aiden?

Beckett: We're just teasing. Seriously, how did it go?

Brooks: Oh, shit. Guys. Sara just texted. Apparently, Lennox is Aiden's wedding planner.

Beckett: No ducking way.

Gavin: I feel like this deserves a real fuck.

Beckett: I tried. Damn autocorrect doesn't know it's duck, not duck.

Beckett: Duck.

EVEN THOUGH I hate every one of them right now, I can't help but snort at their antics. God, they were so right about Jill, and it pisses me off. They've always looked at me as the idiot little brother. Lots of eye rolls and scoffs. Silly Aiden, Goofball Aiden, Happy Aiden. They clearly don't think much of my intelligence, and it's obvious they think I have no real emotions. Most of the time, I let their comments slide. It's better to just be Happy Aiden.

Easier.

People like Happy Aiden.

They don't take him too seriously, so no one digs deep. I prefer it that way. If they uncovered even a layer or two, they'd discover how very depressed I've been on and off for years.

A man with everything he's ever wanted. Who greatness comes easy to. The guy the world smiles and laughs at. If they're going to laugh, I might as well laugh with them.

But right now, there's no faking that I'm okay.

I am not even remotely upset about Jill. I suppose that's not completely true. I am pissed that she almost got one over on me, but I'm not upset she's gone. Even so, I don't exactly want to go home. Her stuff is all over my place, and I don't want to risk running into her if she's there.

But I can't crash with any of my brothers because then I'd have to admit that yes, they were right. Jill is toxic.

So instead, I go to the one place that always brings me peace. My personal sanctuary.

The rink.

A sense of calm washes over me the moment my skates hit the ice. From a young age, I've known two things with complete certainty: that I was destined to be a hockey player, and that Lennox Kennedy is the love of my life.

For ten years, I've focused on only one of those things. I pushed the other out of my mind completely. What's the point of knowing something so definitively if it's completely out of reach?

All along, I've understood that no woman would compare to her. That I would never feel as comfortable, as at home, as infatuated, or as cared for as I did when she was mine.

But I couldn't have her, so all of those facts became irrelevant.

I may be the funny Langfield, and the world may assume that because of my humor, I'm not very bright, but I'm quite possibly the smartest, because I managed to successfully put her out of my head.

For years, I didn't think about her. My brothers may think I pined for her, but unlike them, I have a healthy sense of self-preservation.

Beckett pined for his wife, Liv, for over ten years, even while she was married to another man. He walked around miserable, day in and day out, snapping at everyone in his proximity, all because he couldn't put Liv out of his head.

Gavin—fuck, the guy fell for his best friend's daughter and then stayed away from her for an entire year, even though he could think of nothing but her. Then the idiot almost lost her again.

And Brooks? Jesus. Anyone could see that Brooks and his fiancée, Sara, were meant to be, but he settled in the friend zone without a fight, then stared at her like she was a damn ice cream sundae on a hot day.

Me? Lennox Kennedy owned me. So the moment she said shamrock and ripped my heart out, I knew the only way I could move on was to forget she existed.

What I didn't realize was that forgetting her meant I'd be giving up my heart. So I've been walking around with a hole where that organ used to be for the last decade. Day in and day out until she waved at me last season, and I slammed into the plexiglass. Flat on my back, I went, almost knocked out cold.

And since then? Fuck, since then, I can't get her out of my goddamn mind.

She's been my every thought for months. My heart pounds at the mere mention of her.

It was beyond idiotic to propose to Jill. Even if I hate her for what she did, I'm no better. I used her to fill a hole in my life, and if it hadn't been her, it would have been another woman who didn't deserve to be my second choice.

Because any life short of one spent with Lennox would be half a life.

Now that I've acknowledged the truth I've been running from, the real question is, what the hell am I going to do about it?

I press my skates deeper into the ice, forcing myself into suicides. This move is pure torture most of the time, but today, after just a few passes, I'm locked in completely on each movement. If not, I'll be tempted to fly into the wall in order to force my mind to go blank. My lungs constrict, desperate for more oxygen. My legs burn with each stride, and my mind goes numb.

At the sound of my name, I'm pulled from my trance-like state. Sweat drips down my body despite the cold arena, and my chest aches as I come to a stop.

"Aiden." Daniel Hall, my right winger, skates toward me. "Jesus, I said your name fifteen fucking times. Why the hell are you doing suicides on a Sunday?"

Flattening my palms against my knees, I drop my head and pant out a few ragged breaths. As I straighten, Hall tosses a water bottle at me.

"Here, you need that more than I do."

I twist the cap and take a few seconds to breathe before guzzling it down.

He points to the boards, and with a nod, I follow him off the ice and onto the bench.

"I ended things with Jill."

God, it feels so good to say it out loud. Like a weight has been lifted off my shoulders.

"Holy fuck." Sliding his hand through his dark hair, he studies me, his lips tipped down in a concerned frown. "You okay?"

I allow myself to really sit with that question. For so long, when

asked even the most surface-level questions about myself, my immediate response has been to joke around, to laugh, to smile, to hide the
pain, the melancholy, that constantly plagues me. Bury the negativ-
ity. People ask because it's polite, not because they actually want me
to open up and say that no, I'm not feeling particularly great. Or that
I woke up that morning and thought, *why the hell am I here? What
am I doing with my life? Do I even want to get out of bed?*

I settle my elbows on my knees and survey the ice. More often
than not, I am okay. But in this moment, I remind myself that it's okay
that right now I'm not.

"Ya know, I'm really not."

I turn to Hall, not sure what to expect. He's only twenty-four, and in
general, he's a happy guy. Fucks around a bit too much, but that's what a
lot of the rookies do. I don't judge him for it. The only time he's truly
serious is when he's on the ice. Though right now, his hazel eyes hold more
understanding than I thought him capable of. Is it possible that beneath
his playboy persona, there's a layer of him I've yet to see? Yeah, I wouldn't
be surprised, knowing that so few have ever seen beneath the mask I wear.

He settles a hand on my shoulder and squeezes. "Okay."

Instantly, some of the tension eases from my body, and a relieved
breath slips out of me. "Okay."

"You want to talk about it?"

I roll my neck. "I only want to say it once. So call the guys. Let's
get this over with."

Hall perks up. This is where he shines. Social situations. He pulls
out his phone and gets to work summoning the guys who are still in
Boston for the summer. There aren't a ton of us. Most skip town as
soon as the season is over and head back to their families, the small
towns where they're treated like heroes, their wives who miss the shit
out of them while they're playing hockey for ten months out of the
year.

Brooks and I grew up here. Boston is our small town, and we are
gods here. Hall too. He grew up nearby, in a small town in Rhode

Island where his dad still lives with his new wife, Lake Paige. She's one of the biggest pop stars of our generation, and though it sounds bizarre, she used to date Daniel's brother.

I suppose it's about as bizarre as showing up to a wedding planning appointment with my fiancée, only to discover the love of my life on the other side of the desk.

I cough out an uncomfortable laugh, garnering Daniel's attention. He shows me War's response. My left winger says he'll meet us wherever we want.

Tyler Warren—also known as War—is an absolute beast on the ice and in person. Though he grew up in Canada, he moved to Boston when he was in high school and played hockey with Brooks there and in college. He was first drafted to another team, but after a couple of years, he made his way back to Boston. Pretty sure the man has more Boston swagger in his pinky than the rest of us have in every cell combined.

I give Daniel a nod. "Where we meeting?"

"The Pad?"

I shake my head. My family owns Boston sports, and with so many players under their care, it made sense to purchase an apartment building for the guys to reside in. Both Gavin and Brooks live there, but Jill wanted a penthouse. Since the penthouse unit at the Pad, as Hall and so many of the guys lovingly call it, is reserved for the coach—now Gavin—that wasn't an option. Though my building is arguably nicer than the Pad, I would have killed to live with all the guys.

Normally, I'm more than happy to hang out there, but seeing as how Sara sublet her apartment to Lennox, it's not a good idea.

"Ground Zero?"

With a nod, Daniel focuses on his phone again.

Ground Zero is honestly the coolest thing my two oldest brothers have done since they took over both teams. The bar is located below the Langfield corporate offices and can only be accessed from the underground tunnels that connect the stadium, the arena, and the office.

The best part about the bar is that it's a players-only place. So the only people getting in are those we invite. That's what I need today. Privacy. Shelter from the media, strangers, and my ex-girlfriend.

I don't know who'll show up or what I'll tell them, but when Daniel stands, I follow him, unwilling to fake it any longer.

CHAPTER 6
AIDEN

SINCE THE BOLTS are in the offseason and the Revs aren't playing today, the bar is closed. As luck would have it, I have a key, so Daniel and I step into the dark space and flip on the lights. The brick walls are covered in sports memorabilia, and the space is filled with dark pub-style tables, along with ping-pong and pool tables. A large bar spans the back wall.

I suck in a breath as I pass last year's Stanley Cup championship photo. I proposed that week, and in that photo, I'm wearing the biggest fucking smile as I hold up the cup with my guys surrounding me.

Even then, I searched the crowd for Lennox. Though I didn't find her, I knew she was there with both my brothers' fiancées, Sara and Millie.

"Want a beer?" Daniel asks as he rounds the bar, ready to play bartender.

I shake my head, not interested in numbing this empty feeling. I need to feel it. Need to let it bleed out. I've been faking happiness for so long. Today, I'd rather sit with my real emotions, even if it's uncomfortable. "Just club soda."

With a nod, Daniel gets to work. I settle at the bar and am taking my first sip when my favorite seven-year-old appears in the doorway.

"Bossman," he hollers over his shoulder. "Why have we never come here before? This place is awesome."

"Huck, don't run so fast," my brother yells from the tunnel.

Finn, who Beckett lovingly nicknamed Huckleberry Finn when he met the kid three years ago, is technically his stepson. My brother married Finn's mother Liv, and in addition to Finn and his two sisters, they have twin baby girls.

Finn ignores Beckett and barrels into the bar, a big smile on his face. "Uncle Aiden!" he cheers. Halfway to me, he stutters to a stop and eyes the pool table. "This place is *so* cool. Wanna play with me?"

It's impossible not to smile when this kid is around, regardless of how bad my day has been. I hop down from my barstool and am holding a fist out to Finn for a bump as my brother enters, a car seat in each hand.

With a nod to me, he sets his daughters down on either side of him. "Huck, sit over here. You can play a game on my phone while I talk to Uncle Aiden."

Finn sticks his bottom lip out and looks from Beckett to me and back again, like he's formulating an objection.

"What did I tell you about that face?" Beckett says, as if he's talking to a forty-year-old rather than a seven-year-old.

With a stomp of his foot, Finn huffs. "That big boys don't pout."

"And what are you?" Beckett asks, brows lifted expectantly.

Finn rolls his eyes. "A big boy."

Laughing, I clap Finn on the shoulder. "I'll play with ya after I talk to the guys, okay?"

A small smile lifts his lips as he looks around. "What guys?"

Daniel leans over the bar. "Me for one, big man. How ya doing?"

War appears then, with my brother Gavin behind him. Gavin took over as coach for our team this past year, and in that time, his role as fun older brother has shifted into something more. He's always been a friend—I'm friends with all my brothers—but I've come to respect him more than I thought possible over the last several months. He navigated a difficult situation with an impressive amount of grace when he replaced our head coach. But I'm most proud of how he stepped up when a little girl was left at his doorstep. He became her father, knowing full well that she wasn't his biological child.

"No Vivi?" I ask, peering around War for Gavin's little girl.

He shakes his head. "She's with Millie and the girls for their weekly brunch date."

I nod. Lennox is probably with them. That would explain why Brooks knew I had seen her for the wedding planning appointment.

As if my thoughts conjured him, Brooks saunters in, his face buried in his phone.

"Let me guess," War says, reaching for Brooks's phone. "Texting Sara about how much you miss her face?"

Brooks's goalie reflexes kick in, and he pulls the phone to his chest before War can snatch it from him. "At least I have someone to miss," he chirps.

War rolls his eyes, but as he takes a seat at the bar and turns to me, his expression is sincere. Daniel is already in full-on bartender mode, taking orders and pouring drinks.

I sigh, doing my best to ease the tightness in my chest. Any minute, the guys will settle, and I'll have to speak.

Gavin drops down and fist bumps Finn, who's now focused on a game on Beckett's phone. "You brought the kids?" he says to Beckett as he straightens.

Beckett shrugs. "I thought this was a team meeting."

Smirking, Gavin shoves his hands into the pockets of his dress pants. "Oh, team meeting, eh?"

Brooks rubs his hands together, his green eyes lighting up. "I love team meetings. Especially when they aren't about me."

From behind the bar, Daniel surveys the group with a wary frown. "What is happening?"

I snort. "You tell me. You called them."

He points to Brooks. "No, I called him. *He* summoned them."

With a nod, Brooks settles back in a booth, his legs splayed out in front of him.

Hit with a wave of unease, I shift on my stool.

"Figured after that wedding planning appointment, it was time to launch into Operation Dump Jill and Win Over Lennox." He runs a hand over his face. "And as much as it pains me to say this—"

"Beckett is the matchmaker," Gavin finishes for him as he slips onto the stool beside me.

My oldest brother is wearing the cockiest grin as he stands with his arms crossed in the center of the room. "Finally," he booms, "you've all come to your ducking senses. Can I just say that I appreciate the support and acknowledgment? It hasn't been an easy couple of years—"

Gavin slaps a hand over his face and sighs. "We didn't give you a ducking Oscar, Beckett. There's no need for an acceptance speech."

In the booth across from Brooks, War chokes on his beer, the bottle he's holding to his mouth shaking. He sputters for a minute, then drags the back of his hand over his mouth. "Holy shit, I forgot how much fun your brothers—"

"Duck!" Beckett and Gavin growl in unison.

It's too late. Finn's spidey senses are activated, and he's in our space, having abandoned Beckett's phone on the table across the room. "Do you prefer Venmo, or do you want me to have my uncle take it out of your salary cap?"

Bottle dangling from his fingers, War blinks at my nephew.

Summer in Boston has proved to be too warm for the denim-on-denim getup Finn has favored for most of the last year. Now he's sporting a pair of Under Armour shorts and a Boston Revs T-shirt. Naturally, he's become a fan of Beckett's team. But he still has a gold chain around his neck and about a dozen friendship bracelets on his wrists.

"What's he talking about?" War asks, scanning the group.

Shaking his head, Brooks chuckles. "How have you never fallen victim to the swear jar?"

War sets his bottle on the table. Leaning back, he digs his wallet out of his pocket. "Oh yeah. Sorry, little man."

Finn scowls. "The name's Huck." He looks him up and down, his eyes narrowed, unimpressed. "Though only my friends call me that, and I'm not sure you're my friend."

Gavin chuckles, and Beckett breaks out in a proud grin.

"You realize you're turning him into a mini you, right?"

Beckett simply lifts his chin like he couldn't be prouder of the kid. They may not be blood, but my brother loves Finn just like he is.

"A mini Bossman?" Finn muses, his glare still on War. "Excellent. Now pay up. The fine is a thousand bucks, but I'm willing to offer you a deal since you look like the type who'll need it."

Brows jumping into his hairline, War gapes at him, his expression screaming *is this kid for real?*

I merely nod. Yeah, he is. Kid is awesome, but he's about to take War for his yearly bonus.

War and Finn negotiate, Finn signaling for my teammate's phone, probably to get things set up on Venmo.

Thankful for the levity Finn's antics have brought, I clear my throat. "I appreciate you all showing up."

Beckett frowns. "You call, we come."

"Well, he called." I wave at Daniel, plastering a smirk to my face out of habit. Deflecting with humor is my MO. "But thanks."

Gavin turns his stool so he's facing me. "What's going on?"

Heart in my throat, I spin my glass of club soda on the bar top, unable to look at the guys. "I ended my engagement."

"Thank fuck," War shouts, startling me.

With a shake of his head, Finn holds War's phone out to him.

"Fine. Let's call it an even five, and you go over there and put on earmuffs, kid."

Beside me, Gavin drags his hand over his mouth, stifling a laugh.

Beckett has tuned out the chaos. Frowning, he steps closer. "You okay?"

My chest tightens at the edge of concern in his voice. "Yeah, I will be."

"Is it because of Lennox?" Brooks gets up from the booth and wanders closer, keeping his words soft.

I shrug. "Yes? No? I don't know. Did I know the moment she stepped into that office that I couldn't go through with it? Yes. Did I ever really want to marry Jill? No."

"So why'd you propose?" Daniel asks, elbows on the bar as he studies me.

Shifting on my stool, I lift a shoulder and let it fall. "Thought it was time, I guess. You all were relentless about Lennox, and I wanted to get you off my back."

I look from one brother to the next. They're all watching me, but not one of them looks the least bit ashamed.

"It's only because we care. Jill was bad news," Gavin says.

"You don't know the half of it," I mutter.

"Tell us," Beckett implores.

So I do. I give them all the embarrassing details. The shameful ones. How Jill used me, how Vincent Lukov made a fool out of me. Despite the rotten feeling that settles in my stomach, the anvil on my chest lifts, and a lightness I haven't felt in years trickles into me. Fuck, it feels good to no longer live in this darkness alone.

With every word, my brothers' faces turn angrier. War's jaw clenches, and Daniel scowls. These men have my back. These men have me. Knowing that only eases my trepidation further.

"I'm going to lay Lukov out every fucking game," Daniel mutters, straightening and gripping the edge of the bar.

"He won't make it past game one," War promises. "His career is over."

Gavin's silence is its own support. As our coach, I'd expect him to tell his star wingers to stand down. Instead, he drops a hand to my shoulder and gives it a squeeze.

I roll my neck, then take another sip of my drink. "I can fight him myself."

"But you shouldn't have to," Brooks fumes. "He was coming after our family, not just you. Fuck, I hate them."

I stare at the brother I've always been closest with. He's the biggest of us all, but he's also the most gentle. That all went out the window last year when he found out that our former coach, Sebastian Lukov — who was not only our uncle by marriage, but is Vincent's uncle too— was secretly dating Sara. He failed to tell her he was still married to our aunt though. At the time, Brooks and Sara were nothing more than friends, though Brooks had been pining for her for years. The fallout from it all was a shit show and it still remains a sore spot for Brooks. The guy isn't rational when it comes to protecting the woman he loves. I get it. I'd be the same way. But I don't want my brother to end up in jail for protecting me.

"What I need more than your muscles," I tell him, "is your silence."

Brooks frowns, his brows pulled low. "What?"

"I don't want to answer questions. And I don't want your women trying to 'fix' me." With a sigh, I drop my elbows to the bar. I can already imagine how awful it'll be when they find out about Jill. Sara might be worse than Brooks when it comes to protecting those she loves. "Just give me the summer to figure this out. To lick my wounds."

"I don't lie to Sara," Brooks says on one side of me, spinning his beer bottle on the bar.

Gavin's already shaking his head. "Not lying to Millie."

"Come on." I hang my head. "I'm calling team confidentiality."

War snorts. "Oh, like Brooks kept our last team secret so well."

Brooks adjusts himself and grimaces. Yeah, after we were all sworn to secrecy, he told Sara about how the group of us ended up with blinged-out dicks.

Gavin shakes his head. "Nuh-uh. I don't have a glitter dick. This doesn't apply to me."

Huffing, I throw my head back.

Beckett takes a step closer and studies me. "This means a lot to you?"

"Yeah." I sigh, running my hand through my hair. "She didn't only cheat on me—I was a goddamn mark. Give me a few weeks to come to terms with that before you tell all your girls, and they're all over me. It's embarrassing."

Beckett nods. "Fine."

"Hey, you don't speak for us," Gavin tosses back.

Beckett merely glares at him, his green eyes hard. "I said fine. Get on board. Every one of you has had secrets in the past, and I've kept them. We'll do the same for Aiden. That's what we do."

Brooks's shoulders droop, but he nods. "Yeah, okay."

Lips pursed, Gavin looks from brother to brother, then finally focuses on me. "This is a bad idea, you know. They're going to find out, and then they're gonna be all over this."

I grit my teeth. That's what I'm worried about.

Rule 1:
Don't fall for
the groom.

Dearest Lennox

Chapter 7
Lennox

My dearest Lennox,
I know you are probably very angry with me. But please know I have only the best intentions, and I love you.

EYES SQUEEZED SHUT, I will myself not to cry. I've had this letter from my grandmother for two weeks already, and still, I can't get past this first sentence. When my phone buzzes, I let out a breath of relief and use the interruption as an excuse to fold the letter up and stuff it into my bag. Don't need Aiden and his bride to show up and discover me blubbering over my grandmother's last words to me.

> Mom: You know you can't hide forever.

Me: I'm not hiding. I'm in Boston. Out and about. I live at 2018 Langfield Way, in apartment 16 B. Come visit.

Mom: Don't be sarcastic.

Me: I'm not. We can have tea and cookies and chat all about your ridiculous obsession with my dating life.

Mom: Your father and I only want what's best for you. And we didn't write the trust.

Hands balled into fists, I scream. I know they didn't write the trust. I know exactly who did. And I know word for word what it says. Doesn't make it any easier to understand or accept. What was my grandmother thinking?

If I could force myself to read this damn letter, maybe I'd get answers, but it's the last piece I have of the one person who loved me unconditionally, and I'm not ready to shatter that memory of her.

I blow out a slow, uneven breath as my heart pounds wildly in my chest. My hand shakes as I lift the phone back up, contemplating a response.

It's fine. I don't need their money. I don't need the trust. As long as this job goes well, I'm fine. I can stand on my own two feet. Fortunately, I'm living rent free in the Langfield building. If I just squirrel away as much as I can until they cut me off completely—

Ugh, even the thought of it gives me the hives. I know I said that money like my parents have is stifling, but it also provides shoes, and I really freaking like my shoes. But what choice do I have? I can't do what they're demanding.

An image of the kind of man my father would propose hits me, and a shiver runs down my spine.

"Nope. No can do. No shoe is worth *that*."

A woman nearby grabs her child and steers him away from the crazy woman in pink who's talking to herself about shoes.

Defeated, I spin and check the time on my phone. Where the hell is Jill? I emailed today's schedule to both her and Aiden. This is our first stop, and they're late. This venue is in a park. There's a carousel that would make a cool backdrop for photos. I can already picture all the wild hockey boys in tuxes, making fools of themselves on the bright-colored ponies.

It's a perfect spot for Aiden.

Not that I haven't considered Jill. We could set up an elegant tent, keep the details classy, with pops of fun. I'm quite proud of this option, as was my boss when I mentioned it to her.

My top priority now is to impress her with my skills rather than my name, since soon, my family will make it clear that I've got nothing to back it up. I won't have the ability to attract event contracts the way she probably hopes I will. I can't offer up family parties as more business. It's just me, my big, bright, pink personality, and the shoes I already own. *Hopefully that's enough.*

I bite my nail as I scan the park, searching for the happy couple, and jump out of my skin as a strong hand lands on my shoulder. "Hey, Lex."

Shit.

Shit, shit, shit.

Lex.

That single syllable, said in *that* voice, transports me back to every moment that ever existed between us.

A word whispered between kisses. A moan. A plea as he sank inside me for the first time, his eyes holding mine, so concerned. His brows furrowed as he studied my every expression, making sure that it was good for me too. Making sure it didn't hurt too much.

Aiden Langfield was the sweetest boy that ever existed. He loved me enough in those few years to last me a lifetime.

That's what I tell myself, at least.

"Lex," he says again, softer now, his brow furrowed in that familiar way.

Oh shit. I blink myself ten years into the present.

A hard swallow, a step back so that I'm out of his grip, away from his scent, and distanced from his mouth to ensure that I won't mount my lips against his.

"Lennox," I remind him.

A smile splits his face, that damn dimple winking at me. "We playing that game?"

"What game?"

"The one where you and I pretend we don't know one another. The one where we pretend I don't have a nickname for you?"

I suck in a heavy breath, fighting the dizziness that overtakes me. The bright summer day grows hazy as my head spins. Where is the air, and why won't it make it to my lungs?

"Was I supposed to tell your fiancée that we used to date?"

Flinching, Aiden steps back. I miss the heat of him immediately. "I told her."

"You what?" I ask, my heart lurching painfully and my jaw dropping in surprise.

Aiden zeroes in on my lips for an instant, then forces his attention back up, holding me captive. "She could tell."

"H-ow?" I stutter.

"I stopped talking. You stole my breath." He stuffs his hands into his pockets, shoulders rounding, and grins. At first glance, I'd say his expression is shy, but Aiden doesn't do shy. "And since I never stop talking, she knew something was up."

Stomach sinking, I hold up my hands. "Is that why she's not here? She thinks I'm going to come after you?" My heart rate picks up as I search the park for the obnoxious woman. I've been dreading being in her presence again, but suddenly, I'd do just about anything to make her materialize. "Aiden, I'm not interested in you. You need to tell her." I push closer, pressing my palms against his chest, and give him a push.

Stumbling backward, he lets out a surprised laugh. "Gee, thanks."

"I'm not joking around." Panic floods me. "I need this job. Do you have any idea what a big deal this wedding is for me?" I spin, unable to face him anymore. "Fuck," I whisper.

This is so bad.

So, so bad.

"This was supposed to be my fresh start," I mutter to myself, gnawing on the side of my thumb.

Such a bad habit. We raised you better than this. My mother's voice echoes in my head. I close my eyes, willing the criticism away.

"Lex." Aiden is in front of me now. His voice is a calming whisper as he settles his palms on my forearms. Though calming is not how I'd describe his effect on me. Aiden's touch has never been anything but electrifying. In this moment, it's an explosion on my skin that risks breaking the chains I've bound tightly around my heart.

I push away from him and lower my focus to the ground between us. I can't look him in the eye. "*No.* Don't *Lex* me. What did you tell her?"

He clenches his fists at his sides like he's fighting the urge to reach for me. But that's absurd. Why would he want to reach for me when he has her?

His *fiancée.*

"Where is she?" I hiss.

"Why are you so upset?" He swipes his hands through his messy curls, his caramel eyes warming.

Dammit. *Caramel eyes? Really, Lennox?*

That's lovey-dovey shit. I don't do lovey-dovey. Not anymore. Not since him.

God, since him.

Shit. I'm spiraling. With a shake of my head, I pull my shoulders back and lift my chin.

"I'm upset because I'm good at my job, Aiden. I spent hours picking out venues. Do you know how hard it is to find a location classy enough to host a Langfield wedding on such short notice? Do you have any idea how many phone calls I made? How good I am at this job? This place is amazing." I turn and wave at the carousel. "Picture this, it's July twenty-eighth, and the sun is sinking in the sky, peeking through the trees. Your guests are seated in white chairs in that clearing." I point to an open green space, a perfect circle for friends and family to gather. "White and yellow flower petals line the aisle. Green flowering vines run the length of the chairs. A flower wall stands as the backdrop. You're standing at the altar with your brothers, waiting for your bride to arrive."

Aiden tilts his head, his expression going soft as he looks at the space, as if he's picturing the scene I'm describing.

"The music starts up, a soft guitar maybe, or even a violin," I whisper. "Then one by one, bridesmaids walk down the aisle. They'll wear something made of chiffon, light and airy. And just as the sky turns the color of sherbet, she'll appear."

Aiden's lips lift like he's picturing his bride appearing in front of him. For a moment, I imagine what it would be like to see him standing there, his dimple popping. Hell, who am I kidding? Aiden would be in tears.

My throat gets tight at the vision.

Imagining a future I'll never have with the only person I ever saw at the end of the aisle. The only person I've ever wanted everything with.

I'd forgotten that dream.

Put it out of my head.

When Aiden turns to me, his eyes are watery, just like I imagined they would be. There's warmth there too.

And fuck, if I look too closely, I'd probably believe I can see love too.

I choke on air. Suddenly, there's so much of it, it's suffocating. I cough, breaking his gaze.

"Jill," I say.

She must be behind me. Why else would Aiden be wearing such a look of genuine affection, such a blissful expression? It was a look of warm love, pure and simple. It's one I remember well from the nights he held me in his arms and promised me forever.

It may have been cheesy, but we were seventeen, and I believed every word.

I think if I'd let him, he would have kept every promise he made.

He was that good. All the way to his core. And we were that in love.

"She's not coming." The words come out soft, but they hit me hard enough to bowl me over. He says them again, more intimately this time, as he gently grasps my arms and holds me still.

"Because she doesn't want me to plan her wedding." I deflate. It's time to accept that I'm going to lose this job. I let out a weary sigh. "I understand. I'll turn all the information I've collected over to one of the other planners." I dig out my phone and once again take a step back from the man who continues to get too close for my battered heart.

"This job means a lot to you?" Aiden asks, dipping his head to catch my eye.

I've never been good at hiding my emotions. I live my life loudly. Boldly. I wouldn't know how to stop, even if I wanted to. The entire point of not agreeing to my father's ludicrous demands is so that I can remain me, not stifle more of myself.

I straighten my shoulders. "I just need a win, ya know?"

Aiden nods. "So let's plan a wedding."

I almost laugh. "What?"

"You need a win, and I'm happy to help you get it."

"Aiden," I chide, my heart hammering against my sternum. "Jill obviously isn't comfortable with me planning your wedding."

He shakes his head. "No. That's not it at all. Jill isn't coming. I'm planning it."

I stare at him, all rational thought escaping me. "You're planning the wedding?"

He grins. It's wide and easy, and I want to sink into it. His smile burrows beneath my skin, making me warm, even though we aren't touching. "You don't think I could plan a spectacular wedding? Come on, Lex. This is my calling."

My heart lifts at the teasing in his tone. "Thought that was hockey, Leprechaun."

The grin that sank beneath my skin works its way straight to my heart as the expression morphs into a smile so wide his eyes are all squinty. "So you do remember the nicknames."

I roll my eyes. "Of course I do. I gave that one to ya."

Eyes dancing, Aiden cups his mouth like he's wiping away his smile. "So tell me more about these venues."

CHAPTER 8
AIDEN

Beckett: Aiden, how are you feeling today?

Gavin: Did you just ask Aiden about his feelings?

Brooks: It's a valid question.

Gavin: When he shows up at your house and asks you to have a slumber party so you can stay up all night and talk about your feelings, I don't want to hear it.

Brooks: LOL

Beckett: Sounds like you have experience with this…

Brooks: I definitely do.

Beckett: 🙇

Gavin: Same. Come to think of it, you're owed an Aiden serenade.

Beckett: What? Who said anything about singing?

WITH A CHUCKLE, I tilt my head and study the ceiling, running through songs that would be fitting for Beckett. He feels like an Aerosmith guy. I make a mental note to rework "Pink" and type out a reply.

> Me: No pillow talk tonight. Sorry, big bro. I'm heading over to War's.

I slip my phone back into my pocket as I knock on his apartment door, an overnight bag in hand. I snuck into my apartment today and grabbed a few things. Fortunately, all my belongings were as I left them. As far as I could tell, Jill hadn't been back. Maybe she went to New York to be with her loser boyfriend. Whatever. If I keep moving and don't think about it, I'll be fine. That's my MO. Put on a smile, and it will all be all right.

I tap my knuckles against the door in a jaunty little rhythm, and a moment later, War appears, a little out of breath.

"Someone here? I can come back." I thumb toward the hallway. Sara won't turn me away if I show up at Brooks's place to wait until whoever War is with leaves.

He shakes his head, his blue eyes widening. "Nope. Just me."

I stalk in and throw my bag down on the black leather couch. The second it lands on the cushion, I pick it up again. Leather couches in hockey players' apartments probably aren't safe. Too easy to wipe down.

With a huff, War eyes the way I hold the bag a few inches over the couch. "I never bring women back here."

I roll my eyes. Other than Daniel, War gets more action than anyone on the team. Hell, he probably gets more than Daniel too. He's just quiet about it. He'll disappear randomly and without a word. One minute, we're playing pool, and the next, he's texting from the bed of some stranger, telling us to have a good night.

"Fine. But you better give me a sheet to cover it with tonight." I drop my bag on the floor and head to the fridge for a beer.

"You can stay in the bedroom."

I freeze, one hand wrapped around an ice-cold bottle, the other twisting the cap. "Dude, I get that it's probably been a few hours since you got laid, but I'm not that desperate." Coughing out a laugh, I hold up the beer. "Seems like you need this more than me."

War snatches the bottle from me with a grumble. "I'm not fucking sleeping with you."

"Good, 'cause I'm not fucking *or* sleeping with you."

He eyes me. "I got a place in Cambridge."

Frowning, I take him in. The ripped jeans and the black T-shirt. The piercing blue eyes and the almost permanent scowl. "What? Why?"

He sips his beer and leans back against the counter. "Good schools. More grass. Easy access to the city."

"Good schools?" I toss my head back and guffaw. "What are you, Beckett?"

War shrugs. "Everyone was settling down. Two of your brothers got married and had kids."

I snag another beer from the fridge and pop the top. "Gavin isn't married."

Setting his beer on the quartz counter with a *thunk*, War glowers.

"Okay, fine, he's practically married. Still, they're a whole freaking decade older than us."

He kicks one leg over the other, crossing them at the ankles. "Brooks will be next."

Can't really argue that. And he's probably dreaming of the day he can knock Sara up.

"And you," he adds.

"Are no longer getting married." I hold up my ring finger to emphasize the point. Though I guess men don't wear engagement rings. Why we don't, though, I have no idea. If I had been with the right girl, I'd totally have wanted to wear a ring.

Lennox's sparkling blue eyes haunt me. The softness in her

expression when she looked at me this afternoon. The wistfulness of her voice as she described the perfect wedding. *Our* perfect wedding.

She could tell me the scenario is one she planned for Jill till she was blue in the face, but I knew without a doubt that when she was describing her vision, she saw me standing at the altar, but she was the one walking down the aisle.

It's the same thing I saw.

My dreams have never included Jill. She was a reality I settled for because, for years, I've believed that there was no way Lennox ever would be.

War's dark laughter brings me back to the present. "Yeah, you'll be married by the end of the year."

I shudder. "Fuck no. Did you not hear me last night? Jill sucks." I take a long pull from my beer.

War's normally icy-blue irises warm. "Not to her. To Lennox."

I roll my neck, pushing away the hope that is probably lighting up my face. "Yeah, no. We've barely spoken in ten years. Definitely not getting married anytime soon."

Pointing a finger and circling it in the air, War laughs. "See? You can't even deny that you want it. Anytime soon, eh?"

I keep my face straight. Neutral. I can be cool. *I am cool.* Cool as a cucumber.

"You all right?" he asks, studying me. Apparently, I am not cool as a cucumber.

"I'm fine." I take a sip of my beer. Of course I'm not fine. I didn't want to wake up this morning. I lay on my back in bed for far too long, willing myself out of bed. Wondering whether anyone would truly miss me if I didn't. Then I remembered I make them all smile, so yeah, they'd probably miss me. That's what I'm good for.

I smile now to show just how very fine I am. "So Cambridge, eh?"

War drops his focus to the floor, and suddenly, I'm not the one hiding something. "Yeah, Cambridge."

"There a girl?"

He scoffs, grabs his beer, fiddles with the label. "A girl?"

"Yeah, a woman who made you want to find a place in a good school district. Near a safe park, all that stuff."

War pushes off the counter and stalks toward the bedroom. "Here, I'll show you the bedroom."

"Oh, there is so totally a girl," I say, jogging after him.

The door to War's apartment flies open, and Brooks walks in like a man on a mission. "Why did Lennox just walk into my apartment to tell me she spent the day planning your wedding?"

"No *hi how are you*? No knock to signal your arrival before you barge in? What happened to your manners? I know you've got them." I fold my arms across my chest, ignoring the way my heart is galloping at the knowledge that Lennox is in this building right now, talking about our afternoon.

Behind me, War laughs. "It's your apartment now, Leprechaun."

"Right. And like you've ever allowed doors to stop you from barging in where you're not wanted," my brother scoffs.

I hold up my hands and let those words—where you're not wanted—roll off my back. Mostly. "Gentleman, please. Remember, I'm the broken one here. I'm sad." I stick out my bottom lip the way Finn did last night.

War smacks the back of my head, sending me stumbling.

Brooks barks out a laugh. "I'm grabbing a beer, and then you're going to start talking."

"I guess the tour can wait until later," I mumble, heading toward the couch. I might as well get comfortable if I'm going to get yelled at.

My brother settles beside me while War takes the leather chair.

Brooks lifts his chin. "Does that have one of those massage things in it?"

With a moan, War closes his eyes and reclines. "Yeah, it does."

"Oh Jesus, don't have a fucking orgasm in my chair," I whine.

"Your chair? Glad you're making yourself comfortable." He keeps his eyes closed and laces his fingers over his abdomen, as if he doesn't care one way or the other how the rest of the conversation goes.

"Start talking," Brooks says, leaning back against the couch cushion.

"What is there to talk about? I told you I wasn't going to tell anyone about the breakup yet. Why are you acting weird?" I try for defensive, hoping it will get him off my back.

"I agreed to keep your breakup to myself because it's really no one's business, but I won't let you screw over Lennox—"

"Watch yourself," I say, straightening. "I would never do anything to hurt Lennox."

"Wasting her time planning a wedding that isn't going to happen isn't exactly helping her," War throws out, though his eyes remain closed.

"I don't plan on wasting her time. I showed up to tell her that I would have to cancel the contract, and I intended to ask her to lunch since she'd done all that work setting up the appointments, but when I got there, she seemed so—" So *not* Lennox. The girl is fire and sure of herself. She never shows weakness. But today? Fuck, today she seemed broken. I hated every second of it, and I would have done anything to fix it. So I did. "She seemed lost."

"Lennox seemed lost?" Brooks asks, resting his elbows on his knees.

"Yeah. Like she needed this job, and it really mattered to her."

Leaning back again, Brooks runs a hand through his hair. It's grown a bit wild since he cut it last season and started a challenge that led to half the league being practically bald. It was all for Sara. Of course it was. My brother would do anything to make that girl smile. "She does seem a bit different."

This time I'm the one who leans in close. "It's not just me? I'm worried about her. Something's going on."

Brooks nods. "Yeah, I'll talk to Sar."

War cracks one eye open. "You two sound ridiculous."

"Sorry for interrupting your nap." With a long pull of my beer, I turn back to Brooks. "Give me a few days to figure out why this gig means so much to her. Then maybe I can help her out of whatever she's gotten herself into."

"Aiden," Brooks says, his tone full of disapproval. "You haven't been in a relationship with the girl in ten years, and the last time you were—"

I hold my hand up. I don't need to go back to that time. "This isn't about that."

"You aren't using this time with her to reacquaint yourself?" War asks, both eyes finally opened and locked on me.

"No, I—"

"You aren't thinking that if she spends a little time with you—planning your nonexistent wedding—that she'll get jealous and remember all those feelings she had?"

Lips pressed together, I shrug. "I mean, when you put it that way..."

"It's a bad idea," Brooks grumps.

War sits up straight and leans forward. "I actually think it's pretty brilliant. And I know just the wedding you can actually plan in the meantime."

Rule 1:
Don't fall for
the groom.

Dearest Lennox

Chapter 9
Lennox

"OKAY, I have thirty minutes. Tell me everything," Millie says as she rushes into my apartment, the baby monitor in one hand and a glass of red wine in the other.

"I like how you roll," Sara says from beside me at the kitchen island, pointing to Millie's road soda.

Millie grins and tilts the monitor back and forth. "Gav's putting Vivi to bed, and then we're having sexy times. This is just my lubricant." There are hearts in her eyes as she gushes about what a turn-on it is when Gavin is in dad mode.

"I hate you all," Ava whines, covering her face.

I push a glass of white wine toward her and give her a reassuring smile.

"Thanks," she murmurs.

Hannah is in the corner, seated on a barstool against the wall, her knee up as she taps the screen of her phone. "Fucking Jasper Quinn." She slams the phone down. "I need wine."

"I'm so happy my boys are all being good tonight." Sara grins as she rounds the counter with a glass held out to Hannah.

"Please, you've got all those rookies starting this season. Your life is gonna suck."

When Hannah sticks her tongue out at Sara, she merely shrugs and rolls her eyes. "Then I'll tell my big, bad fiancé to glare at them, and he'll do my job for me."

"That's cheating." Hannah takes a big gulp of wine. As she sets her glass down, her eyes brighten. "Actually, do you think you could get your big, scary fiancé to talk to my rookie? He would totally shit his pants and fall in line."

I laugh. "Are we all talking about the same fiancé? The one known as Saint? Good Boy Brooks?"

Millie bites her lip to hide her laugh.

"Hey," Sara hisses. "Only I get to call him good boy now."

Ava chokes on a mouthful of wine and slaps a hand to her lips.

"Rein it in, girls. Rein. It. In." I settle on my stool and sigh. "Let's talk about me, because that's what I like to do."

Hannah's laugh is so loud it echoes around the space. The sound makes me feel at least a little lighter. She's tiny, but everything about her is loud. In different ways than I am, though. Where I'm bright, she's aggressive and outspoken. Even her laugh has a bark to it. I kind of adore her.

"Jill didn't show—"

Sara slaps a hand down on the counter. "That witch." She turns to Millie. "Seriously, she isn't fit to be a Langfield girl. We need to get rid of her."

Millie purses her lips. "I don't love her either, but my days of meddling in other people's relationships are over."

Hannah eyes her, her cheeks going pink. "You ever meddle in your brother's love life?"

"Stop trying to get her to set you up with Daniel." Sara nudges her in the arm. "She's talking about how she tried to torpedo her father's relationship with his wife."

Millie sticks her tongue out. "Feel free to take Daniel for a ride any day," she muses. "But I'd make sure he wraps it up, because that boy is gross."

"*Millie*," Ava chides, her eyes wide with shock.

With a smirk, Millie lifts a shoulder. "My brother is a manwhore. My father slept with my other brother's girlfriend. I seduced my dad's best friend. We have no scruples."

Hannah throws her head back and full-on belly laughs again.

Scanning the room, I grin. I love these girls.

"So you were saying," Ava prods, holding her glass in my direction.

"Right. Me." I shimmy my shoulders at Sara, and she sticks out her tongue at me now. "As I was saying, Jill didn't show. At first, I freaked out, because holy hell, I need this job. But Aiden swore they weren't firing me. That Jill just couldn't make it. So he and I visited all the venues I'd lined up. It was totally fine."

I keep the very real unfine moments to myself. The moments where Aiden looked at me. Or how when his fingers brushed against mine as we both reached for the door of the last restaurant, literal sparks shot up my arm. Or how I spent the day practically rewriting the past, pretending that I was scoping out wedding venues with Aiden as my groom and not as my client.

It's unhealthy. I realize that. But I'm already delusional, so why not? I've been ignoring the ticking time bomb strapped to my chest for months, so I might as well enjoy the fantasy until the bomb goes off. Until the day Aiden marries Jill. Until the moment my father drags me, kicking and screaming, out of my apartment.

"Not to change the subject," Ava starts.

The room instantly goes silent, and every eye is trained on her. This girl never asks for attention, so if she's got something to say, we'll all listen.

"Josie's birthday is in two weeks, and I was hoping you could help me plan a party," she says, tucking a strand of red hair behind her ear.

Heart clenching, I straighten and grin. "Of course."

Josie is like the sixth member of our girl gang. Seventh, I guess, if we count Vivi. She's fighting leukemia and has been a resident at the children's hospital for months. She's also in the foster system. After she was admitted, her foster parents abandoned her, and when the

Langfields caught wind of the situation, they stepped up to pay for her treatment and her hospital stay.

Ava, the head of charitable relations at Langfield Corp, fell in love with Josie while she was at the hospital for a team visit, and the two formed quite the bond.

Our girl group stops in to visit her on Sundays after we have brunch, but Ava is there far more often.

With a hum, I tap a finger against my lips. "What does one like to do for their ninth birthday?"

All eyes turn to Millie.

With a playful roll of her eyes, she giggles. "I might be the youngest, but I'm a long way from being nine. How am I supposed to know?"

"Because you're the only mom in the group," Hannah replies with a smirk.

Millie's cheeks turn rosy. "Oh. Right. Well, is she a fan of Lake?"

"Who isn't a fan of Lake?" Sara asks, her voice a little too loud. The girl is obsessed with Lake Paige.

I wave a hand at Millie. "She sure wasn't for a while."

Millie lets out a light huff. Lake married her father last year, and she's now like a hundred million years pregnant. Or maybe that's just how it feels to me. Pretty sure she's due this month.

"Lake and I are good now. Better than good. And with her so close to giving birth to my baby brother, she and I have spent a lot of time together recently."

Ava reaches across the counter and squeezes Millie's hand, her eyes going misty. "I love that the two of you have worked through your issues. Family is so important."

At the emotion on her face, my throat gets tight. Why do I suddenly feel like sweet, quiet Ava and I have a lot more in common than I ever imagined?

Ava is a pastel angel, floating through life with a gentle smile for everyone she comes into contact with. Even her work is for the benefit of others. And she spends her free time supporting her friends and visiting a little girl in the hospital.

But who shows up for her?

I vow in that moment to be a little easier on her. And to make this the best party ever.

"Do you think Lake would be willing to make a video for Josie?" I ask Millie before turning my attention to Ava. "And can we take her out of the hospital at all?" I'm thinking a picnic under a light pink tent, a low table surrounded by vibrant multicolor pillows. Colorful hanging lanterns, deep magentas and teals. Maybe chocolate fondue and fruit, along with a variety of cakes. And pizza. Because who doesn't love pizza?

"I can talk to Maria," Ava says. Maria is our line of communication to Josie.

"Okay, let me know. I'm going cake tasting with Aiden tomorrow, so I can scope out birthday cakes too. What's her favorite flavor?"

"So long as it's pink, she doesn't care," Ava says with a grin.

"Cake tasting with Aiden?" Sara's grin is evil behind her wineglass.

My stomach twists. "And Jill. Obviously. It's their wedding."

Sara nods, but that stupid smile remains. "Obviously."

"I hate you," I whisper-hiss.

The girls all devolve into giggles, and soon I'm joining them. Because I don't hate them at all. And despite the anvil sitting on my heart right now, they're the good that keeps me smiling.

CHAPTER 10
AIDEN

WITH AN AGREEMENT TO meet at the arena tomorrow and a plan for helping Lennox without having to lie to her, I push War and Brooks out the door.

Once they're gone, I head out myself. On Gavin's floor, a group of guys are lounging around the communal space, controllers in hand and beers on the table in front of them.

Training doesn't start for another month, but several of the guys who've been home with their families are in town for Camden Snow's birthday. The forward rarely travels home to Vegas because of a tragedy that plagued his family years ago, so we'll celebrate here.

Because that's what we do—we support each other. We're the only family some of these guys have. For others like me, who are lucky enough to have big, overly involved families, we're bonus brothers.

"Hey, bro," Hall calls from the couch, controller in hand. "Wanna play?"

Camden nods a silent greeting, then turns back to the game.

"Nah, I'm going to stop by Gavin's. You guys going out tonight?"

With a shrug, Hall leans back against the cushions and focuses on the TV. "Maybe. We'll probably stay here, but if we change our minds, I'll shoot you a text."

Nodding, I head toward my brother's apartment. As I pass Lennox's door, I force myself to keep my eyes forward. Laughter from inside has me pausing, though.

My heart squeezes at the sound. Who's she laughing with? Is she dating someone?

I glance back at the guys, cataloging who's here and who's missing. Has she been hanging out with one of them?

Nah, they wouldn't.

Right?

Shit. Why wouldn't they? None of them know how I feel about her. Hell, they think I'm engaged. There's no way they'd even consider that I have a thing for her.

She *is* available. She doesn't belong to me.

My blood pressure spikes at the mere thought of anyone touching her.

A burst of laughter startles me. The responding giggles, though, calm my racing heart. I let out a long breath and flex my hands. That is definitely a group of women.

Saying a silent prayer that she isn't laughing about some other guy, I keep moving forward before the guys notice that I've stopped in front of her door.

When I reach Gavin's door, I don't even bother knocking. "Hello," I call as I push the door open.

"Ever heard of knocking?" Gavin growls from the kitchen. He's holding a bottle of red wine in one hand and a glass in the other.

"Perfect timing. I'd love a glass of wine."

The door to their bedroom opens, and Millie appears.

"No wine. You're not staying," Gavin says without taking his focus off his fiancée.

She rolls her eyes, but her face lights in a smile. "Hey, Aiden. How are you?"

"Don't ask him about his day," Gavin grouses. "We're having sex.

I've waited all day. My baby is finally asleep. You've had your girl time. It's my time now."

Laughing, I stride over to him and snag the glass from his hand. I take a slow sip, then shoot Millie a grin. "Man is grumpy when he doesn't get attention, huh?"

"We've been in a little bit of a drought this week," she replies, slipping beneath Gavin's arm and squeezing him.

"We aren't discussing this with my brother."

"Good idea," I tease. "I'd rather not know about how depressing sex is when you get older."

Millie guffaws, smacking a hand to her mouth, probably to keep from waking the baby. Gavin just glares at me.

"Anyway," I say with a dismissive wave. "You're going to thank me when I tell you why I came to visit."

"Doubtful," my brother grumbles.

Millie smacks him in the stomach. "*Gav.*"

"Yeah, *Gav*," I mimic. "Seriously, though, come sit down and let me tell you all about the wedding I planned for you today."

"Weren't you with Lennox this afternoon planning *your* wedding to Jill?" Millie's eyebrows knit together as she studies me.

"Yeah, no. I'm not marrying that money-grubbing woman."

Millie gasps, blinking rapidly, then zeroes in on Gavin. "Why don't you seem surprised?"

He gives her a sheepish smile. "You know, little brother, you may just be onto something. Peaches, weren't you just saying you didn't have time to plan a wedding?"

"*Gav.*"

"Or is it that you just aren't ready to get married—" Gavin looks away, but not before his face falls. "It's okay if that's the case," he says, his attention locked on the baby grand piano in the corner. "I know I still have work to do."

Millie steps in front of him, sets her hands on his cheeks, and tilts his head until he's forced to look at her. "Gavin Langfield, I can't wait for the moment I'm your wife. If I had the time to plan, I'd marry you tomorrow."

"Tomorrow would be nice," I say, "but July twenty-eighth would be preferable. All the potential venues are available that day."

Gavin shoots me a glare, but Millie smooths her thumbs over his cheeks, and the expression immediately softens. "Would that make you happy, Peaches?" He grasps her wrists. "We can go to a justice of the peace tomorrow, but I think your father would kill me if he didn't get to walk you down the aisle."

Millie pops up on her toes and presses a kiss to my brother's lips. "You make me happy, Coach. July twenty-eighth sounds perfect."

"Did we just set a wedding date?" Gavin murmurs as he palms Millie's ass.

"I think I'm gonna head out." I throw a thumb over my shoulder, but neither is paying me any mind. "I'll let you know about the venues, though. Tomorrow, we're cake tasting. Chocolate or vanilla? Or something crazy like lemon meringue?"

"*Out*," Gavin growls as he lifts Millie into the air and pulls her legs around his hips. Then he's practically sprinting toward their bedroom.

Millie's giggles echo around the space. "Vanilla with peach filling, please," she whisper-shouts.

"Sure, guys," I say as their bedroom door clicks shut. "I'll just let myself out. You're welcome, by the way. I'm happy to do the wedding planning. Have a good night." I head for the door, but halfway there, I spin and dart to the kitchen, where the half-full bottle of red wine sits and snatch it up. "Tip for all my work."

Rule 1:
Don't fall for
the groom.

Dearest Lennox

Chapter 11
Lennox

"YES, Mom, I'll be there. Send me the info, and I'll handle everything else," I say into the phone as I scan the park for Jill and Aiden.

"Your father wants to introduce you to someone, so make sure your hair is back to its natural color."

With a laugh, I roll my eyes, though she can't see the latter. "Mom, I'm not dying my hair for dinner at the club."

During my next scan of the park, I spot Aiden. He's laying a blanket out on the grass in the spot I showed him yesterday. The place I suggested the ceremony take place.

I head in his direction, my heart rate picking up.

"Lennox—"

"Sorry, Mom," I cut her off before she can bring down my mood. "My client is just arriving. I've got to go."

At the sound of my voice, Aiden looks up from his task and his face lights up. "Hi, Mrs. Kennedy," he singsongs.

Thank God I already hung up, or my mother would be calling me back with a completely different set of demands and questions.

"Aw, she didn't want to talk to me." Aiden juts out his lip in a perfect pout.

I snort. "You know she never liked you."

He clutches his chest in mock offense. "Go easy on me, Lex."

"Please," I scoff, pocketing my phone. "When you have a daughter, I can guarantee you'll hate any boy who sneaks into her bedroom nightly."

Aiden's dimple pops. "It was just so I could kiss you good night."

For a moment, the world fades away, and I can feel the way his lips would ghost against mine, the heat of his breath between kisses as he whispered how he just needed a little sweetness before bed. *"Please, Lex. Just another minute."*

My grandmother caught us one time, and I swear she grinned at me for a week.

"And so I could give you your nightly peony." He bites his lip shyly, the same damn way he would when he'd hand me my favorite pink flower. Did he give them to me because I love pink, or do I love pink because he'd given them to me?

Blood rushes to my face, likely turning me my favorite damn color, and I force the memories to fade. With a step back, I peruse the park, looking for Nosy McGee.

"Where's Jill?"

"Just me today," Aiden says.

A wave of giddiness washes over me despite my best efforts. Spending more time with Aiden is dangerous and stupid. We're planning his wedding to *her*, not catching up on old times.

"So you decided on this venue?"

Aiden plops down onto the blanket and looks up at me. The way the sun lights his brown eyes is almost magical. "Nah, let's book the beach."

A frown tugs at my lips. It's not that the beach location wasn't gorgeous. I wouldn't have shown him it yesterday if it wasn't a perfectly acceptable option. But it didn't feel like Aiden. Then again, what the hell do I know? The Aiden I know was a kid who lived to pull pranks, laughed his way through life, and was obsessed with making me smile.

This Aiden is a hockey star engaged to someone else. The dedication his career requires likely leaves little time for joking around the way he used to. It was juvenile to think he'd want to have wedding photos taken on the carousel—that he'd want his wedding in a park.

Not befitting of a Langfield or a Kennedy. I can hear the muttered words in my mother's voice.

God, why does the idea that Aiden has changed so much over the years, that I don't know him anymore, make my throat burn?

I grab a pair of sunglasses from my purse and cover my eyes before they give me away. "If this isn't the venue choice, then what are we doing here?"

Aiden leans to one side and snatches up a basket I hadn't noticed. "Lunch."

Pulse spiking, I take half a step back. "Lunch?"

That damn dimple pops again as the boy smiles. For someone I no longer know, the expression is so familiar. That simple look is all it takes to set me at ease. "You can't expect me to eat dessert before feeding me lunch."

A laugh breaks free, making me feel instantly lighter. "I didn't realize I was feeding you." Even as I argue, I drop onto the blanket beside him and settle in.

Aiden opens the basket, pulls out two sandwiches, and hands one to me.

I pull it from its plastic bag, and when I lift the corner to inspect it, I snort. "Peanut butter and Nutella?"

Tapping his sandwich against mine, he grins. "Just like old times." With a giant bite of his sandwich, he watches me.

"You realize this is pure sugar, right? We're loading up on sugar before taste-testing cakes?"

Aiden shrugs. "I'm like Buddy the Elf. Sugar is an important part of each one of my food groups." He pulls an orange soda from the basket and offers it to me.

I bite my lip to hide my smile. We enjoyed many picnics just like this when we were kids. Drinking orange soda and eating peanut butter and Nutella sandwiches while staring up at the sky, hiding from our families. Heads touching as we dreamed about the future.

I unscrew the top to the soda and take a sip, carefully avoiding looking at Aiden. Somehow sitting on a picnic blanket eating peanut butter and Nutella sandwiches with our thighs touching feels more intimate than any sexual encounter I've had in the last decade. "Is Jill meeting us at the bakery?"

Aiden knocks his knee against mine and grins. "Nah, it's just you and me today."

A shiver slides up my spine. "Jill doesn't want to pick out the cake?"

"Jill doesn't eat cake," he says matter-of-factly. He tears off another enormous bite of his sandwich. "How are you liking living in Sara's old apartment?"

The way he turns the conversation from his fiancée to me so easily should raise alarm bells. With any other man, I'd be concerned he was hitting on me, be concerned he's a cheater, but none of those bells are ringing.

Because this is Aiden. Though *this* Aiden is mostly a stranger, there's no doubt that he is an honorable man at his core. So instead of questioning his motives, I relax and take a bite of my sandwich.

Leaning back, I enjoy the warmth of the sun against my skin. "Honestly, it's amazing. It's like being in college again. Sara is always around. Her friends have become my friends. They're the best. There are always people to work out with in the building's gym. And the eye candy—" I nudge Aiden's shoulder and waggle my brows. "It's an all-around good time."

He huffs out a laugh. "Usually, I'm all for sugar, but you should steer clear of that particular candy."

"I'm more of a sampler, anyway. Just a lick here or there will hold me over. I don't have a sweet tooth like you."

Aiden sucks in a sharp inhale and proceeds to choke on his sandwich. Face turning red, he coughs and pounds his chest. "You cannot," he says, gasping, "hook up with the guys on my team."

Nerves skitter through me at the demand. "What?"

"By eye candy, you mean the guys in the building, right? They're all players."

I break out in a wicked grin. "I know. They play for the Bolts."

"Lennox," he groans, his face still red, beads of sweat forming at his hairline.

"Wow, pulling out the full name."

Aiden sets his sandwich down on its bag and runs a palm over his face. "Unless you want me to beat up every single guy I play with, you have to promise me that you won't go near them."

"Aiden," I laugh, even as a thread of unease curls through me. Why does he sound like he's jealous? Why does the thought that he would be make me dizzy?

"Lex," he says, his expression more serious than I've ever seen. "Promise me."

I glance away. Shit. If we continue down this path, I'm liable to mount him. "I don't sleep around, Aiden. I won't go near your players, promise."

"That's not—" He sighs. "I wasn't saying that you do."

I plaster on a fake smile, ready to move on from this conversation. "I forgot to tell you—I signed you and Jill up for dance classes. The first one is tomorrow."

Aiden frowns, his brows pulling together. "Lex, I'm sorry if—"

Dammit. Why can't he just let it go? With a hand on his arm, I give it a slight squeeze. "It's fine. I know. This is a little awkward, huh?"

Aiden's focus lowers to my hand, and I immediately let go.

His voice comes out a bit raspy when he replies. "Not awkward, just different."

"It's been over ten years. It'd be weird if it wasn't a little strange, right?" I say lightly. At least I hope it comes out lightly. Nothing feels all that light right now.

As we sit side by side like this, it's like time is unraveling. The years apart are revealing themselves through every word spoken.

When his brown eyes settle on me, I'm eighteen again.

Aiden angles closer and swipes a thumb over my bottom lip, his skin warm and rough. "You had a little chocolate," he murmurs. With his attention fixed on me, he brings that thumb to his mouth and slides his tongue against it.

My entire body warms in a way that surely has my face and chest burning as pink as my hair.

"So you were saying something about dance lessons?"

"This one is incredible." Aiden stabs the small piece of chocolate cake in front of him with his fork and brings it to my lips. "Here, try."

Without thought, I open. When the flavor registers, there's no stopping the moan I release. That cake is fucking orgasmic. Aiden's left dimple pops again, and then he's sliding my coffee toward me.

"God, that's incredible." I bring my coffee to my lips and take a slow sip to wash down the cake. "But so were the last four. Seriously, how are you going to pick one?"

He leans back in his chair, posture relaxed. "Already know what the bride wants, so we're all good."

The cake I was sure was already clear of my throat makes a reappearance and chokes me. Because we're planning Aiden's wedding. To Jill. *This is not a date, Lennox.* We're not getting to know one another again. I'm planning my ex-boyfriend's wedding to another woman.

Fortunately, before I have a breakdown right here in the middle of this bakery, a woman with a hot pink bow in her hair walks by, snagging my attention. The pop of color reminds me of my other assignment for today. "Oh, I need to see if they can make a cake for Josie."

Aiden straightens, his eyes brightening. "Ava's Josie?"

Relief floods me at the successful change of topic. "Yes. Her birthday is coming up, so Ava asked me to plan a little party."

"How'd you end up in this job anyway? I know I asked at our first appointment, but I was a bit distracted, and I'm not sure if I ever got an answer." The way he says it, in an almost flirtatious way, his eyebrows raising as if we're sharing some unspoken secret, leaves me thoroughly confused.

"Sounded like a fun job." I shrug and scrape at the crumbs on my plate with my fork, going for nonchalant. "I still haven't quite figured out what I want to do with my life, so I've been testing out one career after another. I figure that I'll eventually like something enough to stick with it. Kind of like taste testing these cakes. I like to try a job or a city out for a bit, take a few bites."

"What do you think of this one so far?" The smirk he gives me is knowing. Like it's obvious that I both hate and love this job because of him.

I lift a shoulder, focusing on my plate. "It's okay."

Aiden swipes a hand across his face. "Come on, you get to hang out with me, eat copious amounts of sugar and—" He scans the bakery, humming. "Actually," he says, grinning again, "I think that's reason enough to make this job awesome."

Laughing, I pick up my fork and stab it into the chocolate cake that I'd like to box up and bring home, since this is the closest I've come to an orgasm that wasn't self-induced in over a year. Does this count as non-self-induced? Someone else made it...

Aiden leans in, his arms settling on the table. "What are you thinking about right now?"

"Orgasms," I reply without doing any thinking at all.

Shit.

He rears back, and his eyes flare.

Shit, shit, shit. Choking on air and embarrassment, I snatch my coffee from the table and tip it back. Though maybe it's better if I just choke to death right here.

"I'm just going to—" I point to the bathroom and then book it before I mortify myself further.

> Me: I'm going to need you to come to the bakery and light it on fire so I can sneak out the bathroom window.

> Sara: Wait. Did you lock yourself in the bathroom?

> Me: I can hear your sarcasm and judgment from here.

> Sara: Impossible.

> Me: Okay, Judgy McJudge Pants. I need you to not be so smart right now and HELP ME.

> Sara: tell Momma what's wrong.

> Me: I hate you.

> Me: But really, I love you and I need you because I just told Aiden I was thinking about orgasms while we were eating cake.

> Sara: Told you that place is awesome. Can you bring a piece of carrot cake home? It's Brooks's favorite, and I love it when he licks it off me.

> Me: Sara.

> Sara: What?

> Me: I JUST TOLD MY EX-BOYFRIEND I WAS THINKING ABOUT ORGASMS WHILE I'M PLANNING HIS WEDDING TO SOMEONE ELSE. CAN YOU NOT TALK ABOUT YOUR AMAZING SEX LIFE FOR ONE MINUTE?

Sara: Wow, all caps. That takes a lot of work. Aiden probably thinks you're having a lactose reaction to all that chocolate.

Me: I hate you.

Sara: Love you. Don't forget the carrot cake!

Breathing deep, working to steady my pulse, I survey the bathroom door, then study the tiny window. I'm pretty positive my ass would *not* fit through it, but it may be worth trying if it means avoiding Aiden. Then again, if I get stuck in the window, that would only ratchet up the humiliation.

Dammit. I pull my shoulders back and don my *I don't give a shit* face, then head back to the table, letting my hips sway the whole way.

Aiden's got his face buried in his phone, so I make a quick stop by the counter to place an order for Josie's cake. Once the pink musical perfection is ordered, I force myself back to the table so that we can place the order for his wedding cake and get the hell out of here before I make a bigger ass of myself.

"You almost ready?" Rather than sit, I collect my things, making it clear it's time to go.

"Sara told me to remind you to get the carrot cake." Aiden holds up his phone, shaking the screen a little, wearing an eager grin like he knows there's a hidden message there.

I groan. "I ordered her stupid carrot cake. And don't ask unless you want to know the kinky shit she and your brother get into."

Aiden presses his lips together and looks off to one side, thoughtful. "What kind of kinky things involve carrot cake?" Then he shakes his head. "Never mind. Don't answer that."

"Which flavor did you choose?" I ask as I follow him to the counter.

"Vanilla with peach filling."

I have to hold in my resigned sigh. I was certain he would choose the chocolate. Clearly, I don't know the adult version of Aiden even half as well as I thought.

He chose a venue I never would have imagined he'd like, and now he's ordering a cake that I'm pretty sure he's allergic to. Let's not forget he's marrying a woman who isn't me.

And somehow, I'll have to be okay with it.

As the owner boxes up Sara's carrot cake, I lean over the counter and whisper, "Can you throw in a slice of chocolate cake too?"

CHAPTER 12
AIDEN

"TO THE WINDOW," I shout.

"To the wall," Daniel replies as the biscuit flies in his direction.

"To the left, to the left," War sings, but Daniel is already rushing forward.

"Wrong song," I holler as he slaps the puck into the empty net.

"If you'd stop changing what the songs mean, then I'd know where to be," War grumbles, skating past me to get the puck so we can line it up again.

"If we don't change it up, then people will figure out what we're saying," I point out.

"Not even I can figure out what you're saying half the time," War groans, shaking his head. "Believe me, no one is going to remember the lyrics you make up and know what play to expect."

"Except you. You need to." I swipe the puck from him. Then, in my best Lizzo voice, I start the next play. "I do my puck toss, check my stick." I aim for Daniel, who is already on the move. "Playboy, how you feeling?"

He grunts, ready with a slap-shot. "Feeling good as hell!"

"Not sure why you're feeling so good taking shots at an empty net," Brooks booms from behind us.

War spins to face him. "By all means, give us something to hit."

Propped up against the boards, Brooks shakes his head. "We've still got a month before preseason starts. Let's grab lunch instead."

"Nervous you can't handle us?" Daniel throws back, lifting his chin.

Brooks merely chuckles. "We all know I can handle any one of you. But I promised Sara I would take a real break."

"And whatever Sara wants," Daniel starts.

"Sara gets," War finishes.

I laugh. My brother is so whipped, and he doesn't even care.

"Exactly," he says. "Now, are you going to stay here and sing, or can we grab some food?"

Both of my wingers look at me. They're my closest friends, but here, in this arena, they know I'm in charge. It's a responsibility I relish and, quite frankly, need. While everyone else is happy when the season comes to an end, especially after a grueling Stanley Cup run, I find myself coming out of my skin.

Darkness settles in far too easily when I'm not busy. I meet with a therapist annually—a team requirement—who has suggested that I stick with the activities I enjoy, even when I don't feel up to it. After Lennox appeared earlier this year, I went from annual therapy sessions to weekly. Though I canceled this week's appointment, I am following my other routines—namely avoidance and hockey. "Yeah, let's grab food."

Half an hour later, we're seated at a round table at a local pub.

Brooks bumps me with his elbow. "How was the cake tasting?"

My chest tightens as memories of yesterday flood me. Outside of being on the ice, I feel more comfortable sitting beside Lennox than anywhere else. "It was interesting."

War spins the amber bottle in front of him slowly. "Interesting?"

With a long pull of his beer, Brooks leans back in his chair. "Heard Lennox hid out in the bathroom. She and Sara kicked me out of my own apartment last night so they could eat cake and talk. There were a lot of whispers and giggles before that, though."

I can't help the smirk that spreads across my face. "She may have mentioned something about orgasms. Her face went beet red, and then she disappeared into the bathroom."

"How the hell did orgasms come up in conversation during a cake tasting for"—War air quotes with his hands—"your wedding to another woman?"

I smirk. "I asked her if she was having a good time. Instead of responding, she stared off into space, so I asked what she was thinking about." I chuckle. "And that's the answer she gave me."

Laughing, Daniel taps his beer bottle against mine. "See? You still got the magic touch."

"It's the glitter dick," War says with a smirk.

Daniel immediately deflates. A bunch of us went out and got piercings before Daniel joined the team, and he's been jealous of it since he found out.

I nearly chickened out, but the only way to get out of it was to give him a truth. And the question he asked? Yeah, there was no way I was admitting the truth. So a Jacob's ladder it was.

I shift in my seat, remembering the pain of the entire ordeal.

War clears his throat. "When did you and Lennox break up?"

"Right before college." I avert my gaze and pick up my beer to give myself something to focus on.

"Why?" asks Hall.

Such a damn good question. It's one I still can't answer. How did I go from being Lennox's whole world to being no one in the blink of an eye? How did she go from someone whose every thought I could read to a stranger I'm conning into spending time with me? We were best friends first, and now we're acquaintances at best. It's ridiculous how the universe plopped her back into my lap like this. What are the odds that she'd become best friends with a woman who would later become my brother's fiancée?

Slim to none, that's what. Yet I'm not surprised at all.

Lennox Kennedy was always meant to be mine. My soulmate, my better half, the person who made even my darkest moments feel light.

But saying all of that would raise a hell of a lot of flags, especially when it comes to the depressive thoughts that plague me. Thoughts I'd never share with my guys. So I affect my most casual response and shrug. "Why does anyone break up after high school?"

War smirks.

"Aw, Lep," Hall says. "We have more in common than I thought."

We don't.

I'm not a playboy, and I never could be. I'm a one-woman man. Namely, Lennox's man. But allowing them to believe that nonsense is easier than explaining the unexplainable. That I have no fucking clue why Lennox broke my heart, and I'm too scared to ask her.

Brooks rolls his eyes. He, more than anyone, knows I did not do the breaking up, but he'd never spill that secret. He's a gentle giant who is always the most intuitive person in the room.

Apparently, my feelings aren't the only ones he's considering, though, because his next words have the blood in my veins running cold. "Sara hasn't asked me point-blank about your feelings for Lennox or the wedding, but when she does, I won't lie. So what the hell is your plan?"

"I just need a few more days," I grumble.

A few more days with Lennox. Hanging out, reminding her of the past, reminding her that she once loved me. At least I think she did. I know I loved her.

Love her.

Fuck. I'm so screwed.

"And then what?" Daniel asks.

My brother smirks. "Yeah, then what?"

I roll my eyes. "Cocky doesn't look good on you."

A dark chuckle rumbles out of Brooks. "Just tell her soon."

Rule 1:
Don't fall for
the groom.

Dearest Lennox

Chapter 13
Lennox

"THE KINGSTONS WANT a big band for their wedding. From the research I've done, it looks like Seven is the next "it" band. Do any of you have a connection that can get us in contact with them? I know it's last minute..."

I don't look away from Serena as she lays out what is an almost impossible task, but I can feel the scrutiny of every person sitting at the table.

Seven shot to stardom after they played at a birthday party for Melina Rodriguez—Lake Paige's best friend and fellow pop star.

It's rumored that both Kennedy Records and Hall Records are trying to sign them, but the band leader isn't interested in "selling out."

If I was at all involved with my family business, I might have some insight, but seeing as how I'm avoiding phone calls from my father and my cousin, I've got no idea where they stand with Seven.

Even so, I say, "I'll see what I can do."

Every head nods, as if the whole team expected that response from me. My chest grows tight. Dammit, maybe they really did hire me for my connections. If that's the case, then I won't be worth much.

My entire life, I've been valuable only because of my name, connections, and what I can provide.

Though I could ask Millie to help, since her father owns Hall Records, I'd rather try on my own

"How is the Langfield wedding coming along?" Serena asks.

Once again, all eyes land on me, and a bead of sweat runs down my spine.

"They've decided on the Seaport Hotel for the reception. We're working through the rest of the details this week and should have them solidified by Saturday."

She nods once and closes her binder. Just as I let out a breath, relieved that the meeting is over, she looks up at me. "Let me know when you have the number for Seven."

Lips pressed together, I nod. Come hell or high water, I need to get her that contact.

"Let's get the chiffon one," Millie says, pointing to the computer screen in front of us.

"Yes, definitely chiffon," Ava agrees.

I hit *add to cart* and then type in the next item on our list. "Edible glitter."

Ava scrunches her nose. "That seems messy."

With a giggle, Millie bounces Vivi on her knee. "Kids are messy, Ave. Besides, the party is outdoors, and Josie deserves all the sparkle."

With a concerned frown, Ava nods, relenting to the pressure.

I add a variety of colored sprinkles to the cart. "I ordered the cake yesterday."

"Oh, right. Aiden mentioned you were going cake tasting. How was that?" Millie's eyes sparkle as she regards me. Stares at me is more like it. What the hell? Does she know about the orgasm thing?

Oh my god. I will kill Sara if she told her. My stomach bottoms out. Shit, would Aiden say something to Gavin? He wouldn't, right?

"What's wrong?" she asks, her eyes dulling. "Did something happen?"

"No," I say, drawing out the word. "It went well. Though he ordered a vanilla cake with peach filling." I shudder at the thought.

"What's wrong with peach?" Millie asks, straightening and hitting me with a frown.

"Nothing if you're a savage and like baby food in your cake."

Ava covers her mouth, but a giggle slips free.

Brow cocked, I eye her. "I'm right, aren't I?"

Eyes widening, she schools her expression, her cheeks going pink, and shakes her head, clearly trying to remain impartial.

Millie huffs. "It doesn't taste like baby food."

"If you say so." I hum. "Personally, I'm a chocolate girl, but for a wedding, I could be convinced to go with red velvet."

"Whatever." Millie drops a kiss to Vivi's head. "What's next on your wedding checklist?"

Absentmindedly, I scroll Amazon for party supplies. "We've got dance lessons tonight."

"You've got dance lessons?" Ava chirps.

Keeping my attention on the computer screen, I say, "I scheduled them for Aiden and Jill, *obviously*, but I guess Aiden wants to surprise Jill with a dance, so he asked me to stand in as his dance partner."

On one side of me, Millie squeaks.

I finally give up ignoring her. "What? Just say it."

Millie merely lifts her shoulders innocently. "I didn't say anything."

"But you wanted to. You want to know why I'm helping my ex-boyfriend plan a wedding to another woman, right? You worry that I'm spiraling. That I'm imagining them walking down the aisle together after having just pledged their undying love and then sharing a passionate kiss in front of all their friends and family."

"I don't really see Jill pledging her undying love to anyone," Millie says evenly.

I roll my eyes. "You know what I meant."

With a sympathetic smile, Ava squeezes my arm. "It's okay to admit this is too much. Surely one of your coworkers could take over the planning."

"She can do this," Millie says, her chin lifted in assurance. "Or she could admit her feelings to him. Then maybe he'd admit his."

With an annoyed huff, I push the computer back. "No one is admitting to feelings. I'm planning this wedding because I need this job. I'm going to impress the hell out of my boss and take on other high-profile events so I won't need my parents' money, or anyone else for that matter—"

I snap my mouth shut. Dammit. What is with me word vomiting my thoughts like this? Panting, I force myself to look at my friends. Millie and Ava are staring at me with looks of compassion but, thankfully, no pity.

Millie speaks first. "Of course you can do it. I didn't mean to say you couldn't."

"You didn't."

"I get wanting to stand on your own two feet, though I must admit that accepting my family's help is why I'm finally in the studio recording my own album."

I deflate. "My family isn't like yours," I say, chest tightening. If only... "My parents don't want to help me become the person I long to be. They want to use me as a prop for business deals. I'd be married off to whichever man makes the most financial sense to my father, and I'd be expected to dutifully appear at events each and every time my mother demands."

Ava nods. "You need to do this so that you can prove you can."

I smile. She gets me. I have no idea what her real story is, but there's a pain lingering just below the surface. A seriousness that keeps her smiles small and her eyes dull. Like she's living half a life—

too afraid to step completely outside the lines someone else has drawn for her.

"But first I need to get contact information for Seven so I can woo them with my sparkling personality."

"Didn't they perform at Melina's party?" Millie asks.

With a grin, I point to her. "That's the one."

"I got you, girl. I'll work a little magic when this one goes down for her nap, and I'll text you if I get anywhere."

My stomach flutters. Is accepting her help considered cheating? Or would it be stupid of me not to, since she's offering? With a deep breath in, I decide it's the latter.

"Only if it's not too much trouble."

Millie shoos me as she stands and bounces Vivi. "Never. Now tell me more about this wedding you're planning. I want to know everything."

CHAPTER 14
AIDEN

"THIS REALLY ISN'T what I envisioned you'd want to practice," Lennox whispers out the side of her mouth as we watch some of Boston's finest fifteen-year-olds jam out to the Cha-Cha Slide.

A kid in the middle of the pack breaks out into the moonwalk mid-Cha-Cha.

This dance studio showed up on my FYP when I was scrolling TikTok, and I knew I needed to see it in person, so I canceled the lessons Lennox booked and brought her here instead. "That right there." I nudge her arm and tilt my chin in the kid's direction. "I'm telling you, the bride is going to love that."

I've been extremely careful with my words when talking about the wedding. I have no interest in lying to Lennox, but I want to spend time with her. And I want to help her plan a wedding, since she apparently needs the win. So long as I word things right, I'm doing a fantastic job of keeping my word and being helpful to my brother.

My comment about the bride is the truth, anyway. Millie is going to laugh her ass off when we do the Cha-Cha Slide at her wedding. I'm sure of it.

"If you say so," Lennox mutters.

I snag her arm and pull her toward the class. "Come on, it's dancing time."

The woman I spoke to when I called and asked if we could sneak in on a class was thrilled at the prospect of having the star center for Boston's hockey team show up. I normally don't like to use my status to my advantage, but I'll do just about anything to win over Lennox.

From what I've seen in the last few days, the girl needs to remember how to smile again. She needs to loosen up.

What better way to do that than with some good old-fashioned dancing?

It doesn't take long—after some deliciously sinful moves on my part—before Lennox is laughing. I glide across the room like I'm wearing a damn pair of skates, pulling her with me, and she's lit up, her cheeks pink with pleasure.

"We're bringing the team next time," I tell the dance instructor at the end of class.

"You made the night of every kid in that room," Lennox says when we're on the sidewalk outside the studio. Her lips tip up in a smile as she assesses me.

For a moment, I'm sixteen again, sweaty after the homecoming dance and excited to get Lennox home. Anxious to feel her skin beneath my palms after having had to keep my hands off her while the chaperones watched on.

"You made mine," I say, unable to resist cupping her cheek.

Her skin is soft and hot beneath my fingers as I brush my thumb back and forth. Her tongue slides across her lips in a way that has me biting my own. When her eyes flare, it takes everything in me not to lean forward and kiss her. But now is not the time. Not when we're standing outside, surrounded by sweaty teenagers waiting for their rides. Not when she still doesn't know that I'm free to kiss her.

"So what now?"

Lennox blinks, like maybe she was also lost in the moment. Like maybe all she could think about was what it would feel like to have my lips on hers.

God, one can hope.

"Um, I'll probably—" Her phone rings, cutting her off. "Sorry, give me a second." She pulls the device from her pocket and quickly answers. "Hey, Mills." Her eyes dart in my direction. "Yeah, we just finished. What's up?"

Despite my best effort to stay positive, a thread of disappointment works its way through me. She's likely making plans with Millie, which means my time with her is coming to an end.

"Really? Right now?" She bites her lip and scans the area around us. "That's crazy, right? Yeah, I guess. I'll think about it. Thank you. Seriously, I owe you big. All right. Love you, bye!"

As she slips her phone back into her pocket, I can't help but move closer, like a moth to a flame, risking the burn of rejection because I can't stay away. "What's going on?"

She bites on her pink nail, her blue eyes swimming as she works through whatever it was Millie had to say. Lips pursed, she finally meets my gaze. "My boss wants to hire a specific band for one of her clients."

I press closer, thankful that she's letting me in. "Yeah?"

She nods as if she's coming to a decision. "They're virtually impossible to get a hold of, but Millie found out that they're performing at a wedding in Boston tonight. It's a surprise."

Warmth floods me, and there's no stopping the grin that splits my face. "So we're crashing a wedding?"

Lennox's laugh is light, even as she shakes her head. "What? No. That's crazy."

"But you need to talk to these guys?" I duck my head and zero in on her.

She looks away, worrying her lip again. "Yeah, I really need this win."

I've yet to discover why this job means so much to her, but it doesn't matter. If she needs it, then I'll make it happen. No questions asked.

"Lex," I say softly, waiting until she gives me her full attention. I wouldn't do what I'm about to do if getting this band didn't clearly mean so much to her. But once the words are out, she won't be able to say no.

Her blue eyes settle on me, and once again, the thrum of tension settles between us. "Yeah?"

"Never have I ever crashed a wedding."

The way she licks her lips as a full smile graces her pretty face lets me know that I've just tapped into the competitive side of Lennox.

My Lennox.

The years fall away, and suddenly, I'm standing before the girl I dared to kiss me so many lifetimes ago.

She huffs out a laugh and grabs my hand. "Okay, Hockey Boy. You win."

Electric lava races through my veins as she pulls me away from the building. I haven't won her over yet, but in this moment, I know I will. Because I haven't felt this alive, this happy, in years.

"We've gotta look the part."

"Aiden, you are not buying me a dress."

On the way to the wedding venue, I pulled into the mall parking lot and dragged her inside. At the first department store we came to, I snagged a couple of dresses off the rack for her, as well as a suit for me, then herded her toward the dressing room.

I handed the kid standing in front of the rooms a fifty and told him to get lost. He probably thinks Lennox and I are fooling around in here, but really, I just can't handle the idea of anyone being near while she's trying on dresses. Call me possessive; I'm fine with it. I'm not the least bit ashamed of how possessive I am of my time with Lennox. Of her.

BOSTON BOLTS HOCKEY: HOCKEY BOY   101

"I'm buying a dress regardless, so you might as well pick one you like," I say, straightening my tie in the mirror.

"Aiden," she huffs, the puff of air from her mouth sending her pink hair flying.

"Personally, I'd go with the blue one, since it matches your eyes."

"You just want me in Bolts colors." She's standing outside the stall next to mine, hands on her hips and a mix of annoyance and excitement flashing in her eyes.

I smile, a hit of anticipation coursing up my spine. "It's only the best."

With a boisterous laugh, she spins and slams the door to the changing room.

"I'll grab shoes for you," I holler, striding out. "Still an eight and a half?"

When I return, she's waiting for me, wearing the blue dress that matches my tie, looking absolutely fucking gorgeous. "You remember my shoe size?" she asks, wearing an apprehensive frown.

Chuckling, I kneel at her feet and hold out the pair of silver shoes I picked knowing they'd match any of the dresses in the room. I grasp one ankle, relishing the feel of her skin beneath my palm, and look up at her. "I remember everything, Lex. When it comes to you, every detail is tattooed on my brain."

She sucks in a breath, her eyes widening, as I secure the shoe.

"You're unforgettable."

She doesn't respond, but her swallow is audible.

I have to look away before I let every other truth slip out. Truths like *I miss you* and *I love you*.

With both shoes strapped, I get to my feet. "Ready to crash a wedding and convince a band to be your bitch?"

Lennox's loud laugh echoes off the dressing room walls.

My heart flips in my chest in response. Making her smile is an addiction.

We stride into the wedding venue like we're meant to be there. "I'll grab drinks. You go scope out the band," I offer.

She nods, and then she's gone. The wedding is a bit ostentatious. The tables are covered in glittery gold tablecloths with vases filled with peacock feathers. Servers weave through the space carrying champagne flutes on trays, making sure no one has an empty hand. I make my way to the bar and order. While I wait, I prop myself up against the edge of it and take in the scene. Within minutes, I'm approached.

"Hey, would you mind?" the woman asks, holding up her phone.

I nod and give her a practiced smile. I'm recognized just about everywhere I go. "Sure, happy to take a picture," I reply, holding out my arm so the woman can hop in for a selfie with me.

Her lips turn down in a frown. "I meant can you take a picture of my friend and me?"

Face heating, I hold out my hand. "Of course." Quickly, I take the requested photo, going above and beyond by being sure to get several angles for them.

"Well, that was embarrassing," a sultry voice purrs in my ear.

I turn to find a pretty brunette standing very close to me. I back up a step and give her the same practiced smile I gave the first woman. "Yeah, not sure what I was thinking."

She slides closer and pulls her shoulders back, putting her chest on display. "No, I meant that she should be embarrassed for not real-izing she asked the best center to ever play the game to take her picture without realizing who he was."

Surprised, I survey her, this time wearing a genuine smile. "You know hockey?"

"Guilty," she says, licking her red lips.

"I'm Aiden." I offer her my hand.

She takes it, pushing closer again. "Oh, I'm very aware of who you are."

"Right." I laugh, a niggle of unease worming its way through me. "And you are?"

"Very interested."

I shake my head, neck heating. "Sorry. I'm here with someone." With that response, I can't help but scan the space, searching that someone out. When I spot her, I point her out so that this woman knows I have an actual date, hoping that'll discourage her from pursuing me and I won't have to outright shut her down. "She's right there."

Of course, at that very minute, Lennox pulls a piece of paper from the bodice of her dress and passes it to the lead singer of the band.

The woman beside me hums, her tone full of amusement. "You sure she knows she's here with you?"

"Excuse me." With a nod, I pick up the drinks I came for, then head in Lennox's direction.

As if she can feel me approaching—fuck, I hope she can sense me the way I sense her—she turns, her lips twisted into a big grin. Though an instant later, the expression sours.

"What's wrong, Hockey Boy?"

I take a deep breath, my tie suddenly a little too tight. "What did you give the singer?"

Her smile returns. "My number."

Gritting my teeth, I remind myself that I have no claim over this woman. Not yet. "Your number?"

"Yeah. Hopefully he'll text me when they're done with their set. I'm pretty sure he thinks I handed him a song request, but unless he thinks I'm asking him to sing that song about Jenny, I doubt he'll belt out a series of numbers into the mic."

The tension in my jaw instantly dissipates, and a bark of a laugh escapes me. I doubt anyone else would understand Lennox's rambling, but she and I speak the same damn language. I get her, and she gets me. "Can you imagine how many people called that number when that song came out?"

"I always wished it was my number. How cool would it be to answer the phone singing 867-5309?"

My chest expands at the joy radiating from her. "Well, while you were flirting with lover boy up there, I was made a fool of not once but twice."

Brows shooting to her hairline, Lennox plucks the glass of champagne from my hand. "Oh yeah, how?"

"First, a woman asked me to take a picture. I thought she wanted a picture *with* me, but it turns out she just wanted me to take a picture of her."

Lennox covers her mouth like she's trying not to spew champagne, her eyes glittering in the overhead lights. "*No.*"

I nod. "Yup. Then another woman approached me. She actually did know who I was, and when she hit on me, I told her I was with you. Then the two of us watched you give your number to that guy." I thumb over my shoulder at the stage.

Lennox's eyes go wide, and then she's peering around me. "Where is she?"

My heart stutters. Is she jealous? The old Lennox would be. If another woman so much as breathed near me, she would be ready to knock her out.

"Why?" I challenge, keeping my cool. "You going to go over there and set her straight? Tell her I'm taken?"

Stepping back, she holds up a hand between us. "I mean, you are. Though not by me."

Frustration mixes with the jealousy still coursing through me after she gave her number to Seven's lead singer. I step in so close that my lips brush against her ear when I speak. "Or maybe you could show her that I'm taken."

Lennox sucks in a breath. "H-how?" she stutters.

"Dance with me." I grasp her waist and pull her into me, almost causing her to spill champagne all over the both of us. "Come on, Lex. Never have I ever danced with a pretty girl at a wedding."

Her body relaxes, but she rolls her eyes and brings her drink to her lips, refusing to give in. "Ha, nice try. You're a serial monogamist. There's no way you haven't danced with a beautiful woman at a wedding."

"Keeping tabs on me?" I tease.

Her cheeks go pink, and she huffs. "No. What? Ugh."

"Come on, Lex. Dance with me," I beg, wrapping my arm around her hips and pressing my body against hers.

She tucks her chin and seems to be considering the way our bodies are touching before swallowing thickly, like she's scared to get too close to me. Like she knows if she does, she won't be able to hold herself back anymore.

Good. That's how I want her.

"Fine. I'll give you another one," I whisper.

Then, with her gaze locked on mine, I tell her the truth. "Never have I ever gotten over you."

Rule 1:
Don't fall for
the groom.

Dearest Lennox

Chapter 15
Lennox

WHAT IN THE ever-loving hell is happening? Aiden watches me, his golden eyes warm, and I feel like I'm lost in this moment, my world turning upside down. Maybe it's because he's so close. I'm steeping in his scent, absorbing the heat of his body.

"What?" I whisper, still shocked by his admission.

Aiden lets out a shaky breath—

"Lennox?"

I practically jump out of my skin at the sound of my name behind me. Aiden remains steady, his fingers tightening on my hip possessively as the lead singer of Seven—Ryder, I've discovered through the research I've done since Serena asked me to get into contact with them—approaches.

"Hi, yes. That's me." I take a step away from Aiden, forcing him to release me.

"You wanted to talk to me?" Ryder holds up the piece of paper I handed him. He's wearing a tight white button-down with the sleeves rolled up to his elbows, exposing a tattooed forearm that I work hard not to comment on.

"Yes." I take a deep breath, and then I launch into my spiel, selling myself and the Kingston wedding. This is the perfect opportunity to ignore the feelings swirling inside me because of Aiden's confession.

Ryder nods along, and with a glance at Aiden, he says, "I've got to get back up there, but I'd like to hear more. Can you stick around for a bit and have a drink with me after?"

"Absolutely, thank you so much." Excitement skitters through me as he turns on his heel and jumps up onto the stage again. "Ah," I hiss, bouncing in my heels. "Did you hear that?" I ask Aiden. "He's going to talk to me. I think I can really pull this off."

"Of course you can. So about that dance?" Aiden's expression is serious as he surveys me.

Thank god Ryder interrupted us. It gave me the time I needed to see clearly just how out of control this night has become. I shouldn't be here with my ex-boyfriend. He's marrying someone else. As much as it hurts, I need to come to terms with it. It's inappropriate of me to use their wedding as an excuse to spend time with him.

With a deep breath, I plaster on my best professional smile. "I think it's probably best if you go. I'm going to sit and take some notes for my boss until Ryder is done. I'll probably even have time to come up with some fun ideas for your wedding."

Aiden reaches for me. "Lex."

I pull back before he can make contact and shake my head, swallowing down the emotions that threaten to pour out of me. "I think we got a little carried away this week. This job means a lot to me. I need to focus. *Please.*"

Aiden's brown eyes bore into mine, full of determination. For a moment, I worry he'll continue to push. But then the light leaves him, and he deflates. "How will you get home?"

My heart pangs at the concern he has for me. "I'm a big girl, Aiden. I'll be fine."

Jaw locked, he gives me a jerky nod. "Call me if you need me." His eyes roam over me for one breath, then another. "*Please.*"

"Of course," I murmur. *Please, god, make him leave before I beg him to stay.*

Angling in, he brushes his lips against my cheek. I hold my breath, knowing that it would only take one whiff of his scent to make me lose my mind and have me leaning into this moment and getting lost in him.

This is cold feet. Nothing more. I'm a comfort to him when he's nervous about the future. And dammit if my heart can't handle watching him walk away. So when he brushes past me, I force my attention to the stage, 1,000 percent focused on my job. And the rather good-looking singer whose eyes are laser-focused on me.

CHAPTER 16
AIDEN

Me: I told Lennox how I feel.

Brooks: Shit, really??

Beckett: Proud of you.

Gavin: What did she say?

Me: She told me to leave

Brooks: Shit, sorry.

Beckett: Where were you?

Me: At a wedding.

Gavin: Whose wedding?

Me: I don't know. That's not really the point.

Beckett: How do you not know whose wedding you were at?

Brooks: Are you high?

Me: No. We crashed the wedding. But like I said, NOT the point.

Beckett: Okay, I'll bite. What's the point?

Me: I think she likes the wedding singer

Beckett: Is this a prank text? Are we supposed to be guessing movie titles? So far, I've got Wedding Crashers and The Wedding Singer.

Gavin: Epic movies, though anything Vince Vaughn does is hysterical.

Beckett: The one where he got locked up in Thailand, not so much.

Brooks: True. Major downer.

Me: Focus! No, this isn't a movie game, although that does sound like a fun time.

Me: What do I do?

Gavin: I'm still confused about what's going on.

Me: Lennox's boss wanted her to talk to some band. I guess Millie found out they were playing at a wedding tonight. Lennox and the lead singer are probably having drinks, and she's likely falling for him. I should go back, right?

Gavin: Millie says you're an idiot.

ANOTHER CHAT POPS UP, and when I see Millie's name, I groan.

Millie: I did not say you're an idiot.

Brooks: I'll say it. You're an idiot.

Sara: Hey, guys. What are we talking about?

Beckett: Aiden finally told Lennox how he feels and that he's not getting married, but now Lennox is hanging with some wedding singer, so she told Aiden to leave. That sum it up?

Sara: OH MY GOD. AIDEN! You aren't getting married?!?!

Beckett: Duck.

Me: Beckett...

Beckett: I'm really ducking sorry.

Gavin: 😂

Sara: Wait, you all knew??

Sara: Brooks Langfield, you are dead to me. Aiden, spill now.

Me: I haven't had a chance to tell Lennox yet, so you have to keep this to yourself.

Sara: Ah, shit. Okay, talk to me.

As my phone vibrates in my hand and Sara's name flashes on the screen, I can't help but stew over the events of the last couple of hours. If only I could go back to the dressing room, when I had Lennox's undivided attention. Everything was perfect until I had to insist on taking her to a wedding so she could meet Ryder. What the fuck kind of name is Ryder anyway?

"It's a perfectly good name," Sara replies, her voice barely audible, since I'm still gaping at my phone.

I bring the device to my ear. "I guess I said that out loud?"

"You did," Sara sings.

Brooks chuckles in the background.

"Duckhole," I grit out, referring to my asshole brother.

"Good boy," Sara coos. "Now tell me what happened?"

My jaw is clenched so tight that my head pounds as I dive into all the details, starting with the moment Lennox stepped into that office last weekend and how I ended things with Jill and discovered she'd been cheating on me throughout our entire relationship.

"That bitch," Sara hisses. "Dammit. I saw her in New York last season. I thought it was suspicious, but then I got distracted and totally forgot to mention it. I'm so sorry, Aiden."

I sigh as I climb out of my Uber and head for the lobby of the Langfield building. "It's fine. Honestly, she doesn't matter. I should have listened to all of you when you told me to dump her years ago. The cheating was the icing on top of her awfulness."

"True," Sara agrees.

I hit the button for the elevator. "What if she falls for him?" My heart cracks a little as I force the question out.

"Him who?" my brother asks.

Sara scoffs. "Ryder. Stay with the story, Brooks."

"Who's Ryder?" he asks.

"The guy in the band," Sara hisses.

"He's got arm tattoos." I let out a dramatic sigh as I step off the elevator onto my floor. "And he can sing. Probably better than me."

"Definitely better than you," Brooks agrees.

"Oh my God, you are so not helping." Sara huffs, the sound crackling through the phone. "Aiden, you're you. No one else can be you. You make people laugh with your absurd songs. You do ridiculous things like plan a wedding that's not happening just to make her smile—"

"Oh, the wedding is totally happening. It's July twenty-eighth, and it's for Gavin and Millie. Save the date."

"Oh," she squeals. "That's fun!"

Brooks grunts, closer to the phone now. "Can the two of you focus?"

"Right." She hums. "You have a bedazzled penis. Not many people can say that."

"He very well could have one too," Brooks teases. "I mean, he's got forearm porn."

I scoff. "Who said anything about forearm porn?"

"The tats. It's what Sara calls it. It's in her books."

"It's true. Forearm porn is totally a thing, but you can't ride a forearm." Sara's tone is a bit too seductive for this conversation.

Shuddering, I ask, "Ride a forearm?" Why am I even asking?

"Yeah, like I ride your brother's—"

"Crazy girl, you finish that sentence, and we're going to have a problem," my brother grumbles.

I snort. "Okay, I'm hanging up now."

"What? *No*. We were just getting to the good part."

Inside War's apartment—my apartment now, I guess—I slide off my shoes. "The good part?"

"Yeah. When you tell me about the grand gesture you have planned."

I survey the empty space. The quiet is impossibly loud now that I know just how bright life could be with Lennox in it. Memories of her pink hair and bright smile pummel me, one after another. The way she lit up at the park as she painted a picture of a beautiful wedding. The awe in her expression as she watched me buckle her shoes.

"You're right," I whisper, more to myself.

"I know I am."

"I'm going back to the wedding."

"*Yes*," Sara cheers. "Oh shit, wait."

"What?"

"She just texted."

My heart jumps, and all the breath leaves me. "What did she say?"

"She's coming home, and she needs to talk. Brooks, you gotta go."

"Why do I have to go?" my brother grumbles. "Stop pushing me toward the door. I don't even have shoes."

Her laughter is so loud I have to pull the phone away from my ear. "Your brother is on the way. Aiden, don't worry. I got you." She screeches the way she does every time Brooks tickles her, and then the phone goes dead.

Trepidation washes through me. Am I really leaving my fate up to them?

Rule 1:
Don't fall for
the groom.

Dearest Lennox

Chapter 17
Lennox

"OH MY GOD. He almost kissed me," I yell as I stumble over the blue silk train of my gown into Sara's entryway.

Sara's blue eyes pop, and her jaw falls slack. "Ryder almost kissed you?"

Mid–shoe removal, I pause and frown at my best friend. "Wait, how do you know about Ryder?"

From the couch, she shrugs. "The hot singer from the wedding you crashed?" She looks away from me then, avoiding my stare.

"Yeah," I say, stomach sinking. "How do you know about him?"

"From you."

"Me?" I suck in a breath and toss off my other shoe. "What do you mean from me?"

"You called me from the Uber and told me all about him and his sexy forearm porn."

I stalk toward her, my bare feet thanking me for being released from their confines. "I did?" *Am I losing it?*

"Yeah, you told me that your boss wanted you to convince him to play at a client's wedding and that he had sexy arms."

"I remember saying that to my conscience, but I have no memory of talking to you."

I yank my purse from my shoulder, set on checking my call log, but Sara grabs my hand and pulls it into her lap. "I am your conscience. Now tell me, what the hell did you do when Ryder almost kissed you?"

I shake my head, confused. "Ryder didn't almost kiss me. We chatted after his set, and he asked me out for drinks this weekend."

"Are you going to go?" she asks, her tone almost judgmental and so unlike my friend who's always got my back.

"No, I have that family party this weekend and—" I shake my head. I've completely gone off topic. "That's not why I came over here."

Sara smiles, her eyes too bright. Too knowing. What the hell does she know? "Well, then, why did you come over here?"

"Because *Aiden* almost freaking kissed me."

"*Oh.*" Sara claps and bounces in her seat, though she quickly tries to temper her reaction. There's no use trying to swallow that smile, though. It's so bright that it lights up the room. "Really? Did he now?"

"Yes," I hiss. This conversation is making my head spin.

"Well," she chirps. "That's something, isn't it?"

My stomach twists at her strange reaction. Sara was unwittingly the other woman in a cheating scenario not all that long ago. Why isn't she furious with Aiden?

"Stop smiling like a lunatic. I'm planning his damn wedding, and he almost kissed me."

Sara pats my hand, her smile placating. "The two of you have history, and Jill is awful. This could be fate stepping in and making things right."

"I'm not JLo. This is not *The Wedding Planner*. This is real life, Sar. I can't *kiss* the groom."

My asshole best friend leans over, scoping out my derriere. "You definitely have JLo's ass. Actually, yours may be better."

"Saraaa." I throw myself back against the cushions. "I'm being serious."

With a huff, she tosses her hands up. "So am I. Grade-A piece of ass. I've seen you shake it. Aiden would be lucky if you let him anywhere near that ass."

The door flies open as she utters that last word. "Sara." Brooks groans as he throws his keys into the little pumpkin bowl on the table in the entry. Yes, a pumpkin. In June. My best friend is so basic. "What have I told you about discussing anal and my brothers in the same sentence?"

"But it's not my anus," Sara whines.

Brooks darts a look at me, his green eyes bugging out.

Of their own accord, my cheeks clench. "Don't look at my anus like that."

Brooks scowls. The bastard is a giant, but most of the time, he's like a big, sweet teddy bear. Right now? He's all ogre. "Will the two of you stop saying anus?"

"Bro, weird." Aiden appears in the doorway, making my heart jump. "Who the fuck says anus?"

"I told you to stay upstairs," Brooks grits out, roughing a hand down his face.

Sara points to her fiancé. "And I told you to go to his apartment. What are you doing back here? I was just getting to the good part."

"What's the good part?" Aiden asks. He drops his shoulder to the doorframe and crosses one ankle over the other, then zeroes in on me.

My face heats at the memory of the last time he was looking at me like this. How he licked his lips. How the world around us went still. How he almost freaking kissed me.

Heart lurching, I jump off the couch. "I've got to go."

"Wait, what?" Sara hops up too. "Brooks, I'm going to kill you."

Clutching her arm, I fight back tears. "Don't kill him. It's me. I have a long day tomorrow. I've got to go home and dye my hair anyway."

"Why?" Aiden straightens, his jaw hardening.

With a shrug, I let out a caustic laugh. "You know the Kennedys.

Can't have their daughter showing up to a family event with pink hair."

"Len," Sara says softly, reaching for me.

Sidestepping her, I shake my head. It's official. The day has caught up to me, and my emotions are taking me off-guard. "I'm okay." Head down, I beeline for the door. "I'll see you guys tomorrow." I breeze past Aiden, silently praying he doesn't follow and knowing I'll never be that lucky.

CHAPTER 18
AIDEN

NO FUCKING WAY are we doing this again. I let her walk away without an explanation once. I'm not going to make that mistake again. And I've had just about enough of the lack of communication.

I know what I want. Lennox Kennedy. That hasn't changed in the last decade.

"Where are you going?" Brooks moans as I step out into the hall.

The elevator dings, signaling Lennox's departure. Dammit. "To talk to Lennox."

"Yes," Sara cheers.

I spin and offer her a smile. "Did she say anything about what happened with Ryder?"

Approaching the door, Sara eyes me ruefully. "Only that he asked her out on a date."

Anger floods me, and I clench my fists at my sides.

Sara rushes forward and grasps my forearm, trying to hide a smile. "She didn't say yes."

I blow out a breath. I can't get ahead of myself. Just because she didn't say yes to him doesn't mean she'll say yes to me. But I have to try. "Wish me luck," I mutter as I stride down the hall.

"You don't need luck when you have a fancy peen," she shouts as I head toward the stairwell.

My shoulders shake with laughter.

My brother picked a good one.

I take the stairs up to Lennox's apartment to give myself time to think. I contemplate popping into my place and grabbing a bottle of wine. In the end, though, I figure that's a bit presumptuous. It's possible she won't even answer the door or that she'll slam it in my face when I tell her the truth.

When I reach the top floor, I consider going to Gavin's apartment instead, but before I can chicken out, I force myself to knock on Lennox's door.

When she opens it, she's in nothing but a robe. Her pink hair is up in a ponytail, and her face is wiped free of makeup.

It takes effort not to stumble back. The woman is absolutely gorgeous.

Blue eyes blink several times, and then she sighs and steps back so I can come inside. "You don't listen well, Hockey Boy."

As I step over the threshold, I can't help but smirk. "I've been told that a time or two."

I glance around the apartment, taking in all the changes she's made since she moved in. Sara and Lennox both have loud personalities, but their tastes couldn't be more different. When Sara lived here, she hung artwork with soothing sayings all over the place, and there was a candle on every surface. The place was cozy.

Now, there's a bright pink glowing sign above the bedroom door that reads *This Is Where The Fun Happens*.

On the counter is a big jar filled with coins and labeled *Here for a good time.* Purple and pink sequined pillows line the couch, and a shaggy white rug sits beneath a glass coffee table covered in magazines. It's like a room at a sorority house. Though I suppose my penthouse would probably look like a frat house if not for Jill's presence.

In Cincinnati, I bought a beer bottle opener that hangs on the wall and when you pop the top off, it drops and makes its way through a maze. If the top makes it all the way to the end, it sings one of many Britney Spears songs. It was awesome.

Jill stopped me before I even got a nail in the wall to hang it. Now it's in Daniel's apartment. I should really get that back.

Lennox sets a small box on the counter. A box with a photo of a blond woman on it. "You really are dying your hair?"

Ignoring me, Lennox sashays to the kitchen. "Want a drink?"

As she pulls two wineglasses from the cabinet, I snatch the box off the counter and silently watch her, waiting for an answer.

She sighs. "I have to attend a family event this weekend. The pink has to go." She sets the glasses on the counter, then turns back for the wine and bottle opener. I take both from her, pop the cork, and fill each glass halfway.

"Why are you still changing yourself for your family?"

With a tilt of her head, she hits me with a glare. "Seriously? I understand that most people don't get it, but you? I didn't think you'd changed that much." She stalks over to the couch and slumps into it. Then she tugs the chenille blanket thrown over the back down and covers her legs, hiding herself beneath it.

"I'm sorry," I say, a lump forming in my throat, and settle into the oversized chair beside the couch. "That came out wrong. It's just— you're perfect, and I hate seeing you change yourself for them."

"You need to stop saying stuff like that," she whispers, wearing a pained expression.

I stare her down, unblinking and confused. I'm just being honest. "Why?"

"Why?" she mutters with a shake of her head. "The engaged man asks me why he has to stop being so sweet." Her quiet words get progressively louder as she picks at the blanket. "I don't know, Aiden. Maybe because I'm your wedding planner, and you're marrying someone else."

I scoot to the edge of my seat and slide a coaster closer. With my wineglass settled there, I run my palms down my thighs and focus fully on her. "I'm not."

Her eyes narrow. "You're not what?"

"I'm not marrying someone else. I ended the engagement."

"Shit." She covers her face with one hand and slumps into the cushion. "Please tell me you didn't make a rash decision because of what happened tonight. This"—she motions between us with her pink-tipped finger—"can't happen."

"Why?"

"Why?" Shrieking, she hauls herself to her feet and paces. "You can't end your engagement because of an almost kiss. You can't..." She stops and tips her head back, slamming her eyes closed. Then she spins and glares at me. "I needed this job. I told you I needed this job. You promised that you understood."

I stand so I'm facing her, though I give her the space she so obviously needs. "Why do you need this job? Why are you dying your hair? What is going on, Lex? If you tell me, maybe I can help."

She lets out an obnoxious squeak-snort sound. She clearly thinks I'm an idiot.

She's not wrong, but I am also dedicated to fixing this. Fixing us. Fixing the issue that has her acting like a robot for her family.

"Fine, you want to hear what a disaster my life is? Want to hear what you signed up to deal with because you are a lunatic who *ended* his engagement and probably cost me my job?"

"Lex," I plead, stepping closer and reaching for her.

She holds up her hand. "Nope. You asked. But don't say I didn't warn you." She paces back to the couch and snatches up her wine. "You know that my parents and I have never seen eye to eye. They've always wanted me to be the perfect wife for a banker or hedge fund brat or lawyer. Definitely not an athlete, and certainly not you,

Hockey Boy." She eyes me dismissively, mimicking the way her mother surely would. "And while I was okay with never having their approval, because, let's face it, I'm not one to conform. I didn't realize that I'd be cut off if I didn't follow their rules."

My stomach sinks. "They cut you off?"

Eyes closed, she takes a sip of wine. "Not yet, but there's a deadline."

"A deadline?"

"My grandmother died last year," she says softly, blinking back tears.

Dammit. I want to pull her against my chest and keep her there forever, comfort her and keep the world from hurting her. "I'm sorry, Lex. I didn't know."

Lennox was always close with her grandmother. She was the only person in her family who wanted her around just for her.

"Apparently, I can only access my trust if I'm married by the time I'm thirty. If I'm not, then my father becomes the trustee, and he's made it clear that he'll withhold it if I don't marry someone of 'Kennedy caliber.'"

"That's bullshit," I seethe. "You can't marry a man you don't love."

Lennox eyes me. "Obviously, which is why I never intended to get married."

The flippant way she spits out that fun fact is a punch to the gut, but I keep my face impassive. "So you'll just lose everything?"

"Which is why I need this job. Even before my grandmother got sick, my father was frustrated with me for bouncing from one job to the next. It's just"—she looks away from me, and when her blue eyes turn to mine, they look so lost—"I don't want to settle. I want to have a life worth living. Maybe that's the spoiled brat in me, the privileged girl who had everything. But I want to create a life that's right for me. A kind of life that makes *me* worth it."

The way she says the words—the heartbreak in them—is so familiar. I hurt for her. Dark emotions linger inside me, loom over me, even on the best days, making me question my worth too. But while I have hockey and an awesome family to bring light into the darkness, Lennox is struggling to find her calling, and clearly, her family is nowhere near as supportive as mine.

I stalk toward her and press my palm to her cheek. Without hesitation, I speak the words she needs to hear, the words I so often wish I'd hear. "You are worth everything, Lex."

Her eyes fall shut as she lets out a heavy breath. "I think you may be one of the very few people who have ever believed that."

"I don't just believe it. I know it. Sara does too," I urge, brushing my thumb over her cheek. When she opens her eyes and fixes them on me, I add, "And the girls, they all care about you."

A hint of a smile tugs at her lips. "I'm so thankful for the people in my life now, but they're all settled. They have careers or family." She lowers her focus to a spot on my chest, her expression falling. "I've just got me."

"Do you like this job?"

"I do. But then you had to go and screw it up." There's no malice behind her words. She just sounds sad.

Stroking her cheek, I give her a partial truth. "Jill was cheating on me. I was a mark. She didn't want me, just my money."

Lennox pulls back, her eyes going wide and her mouth falling open. "What?"

"That's why she hasn't been coming to appointments with me. I found out in the elevator after our first meeting."

"Oh my god, Aiden." She splays a hand over her heart, the move making it hard not to fixate on the peek of cleavage exposed where her robe crosses over her chest. "Are you okay?"

Stuffing my hands in my pockets, I rock back on my heels. "It's embarrassing that I didn't see the truth, but yeah, I'm okay."

"So the wedding planning?" She nibbles at a pink fingernail, searching my face.

"You said you needed the job." I shrug. "So Gavin and Millie are your bride and groom. We're going to make it the best wedding ever so that your boss sees how awesome you are."

"*Aiden*," she says softly, her eyes going misty.

A lump forms in my throat, but I swallow it down. "What?"

"You did all of that for me?"

"I'd do anything for you, Lex. So tell me what needs to be done so you can access to your trust."

With a shake of her head, she steps back from me again.

All I want is to reach for her, hold her, but I keep my hands where they are.

"Unless you are offering to marry me, I don't think there's much we can do."

My heart trips over itself at the prospect, but then it's up and running. "Okay."

Mouth ajar, she scoffs. "I was being sarcastic."

"Why not? You need a groom, and I was supposed to be one. Maybe it's fate," I tease, though in reality, I can't help but believe that's exactly it.

She rolls her eyes, but a laugh slips out. "Be serious."

"I am. I want to help you, and honestly, you'd be helping me out too."

Frowning, she studies me. "How?"

"My brothers have been worried about me since things ended with Jill. Honestly, even before that. This will get them off my back. It will get *everyone* off my back."

And it's the perfect opportunity to be close to her again. To win her over. This might be my best plan yet.

"It won't be real, Aiden. You want marriage, babies, the white picket fence. I don't want that stuff." The words are so sincere I almost believe her.

I give her an easy shrug. "I just got out of a really bad relationship. I get that this would be fake."

"Do you? Can you promise you won't fall in love with me? Because I'm not built for long-term commitment."

"I won't fall in love with you," I promise.

And once again, I'm not lying. I can't fall when I'm already on my ass in love. I've been in love with her since I was fourteen years old, and there is no chance in hell I'll allow someone else to take this role, fake or not.

Worrying her lip, she scrutinizes me for a long moment without a response.

"Lex, I'm offering this as a friend. That's all. It would be beneficial to us both."

"But you said you never got over me." Her voice is soft this time. Almost like she's nervous to have brought that up.

"It was the heat of the moment. You were in a pretty dress. Reminded me of prom. I got carried away." It's true. Dancing with Lennox at a wedding. Being able to hold her. Spending all this extra time with her. It's dangerous and yeah, I played my cards too early. I'll do better. I *have* to do better. I find her eyes. "I can do this Lex. For the both of us."

"But what if one of us catches feelings?"

I try not to let my heart lift at that. *One of us.* Like she's concerned she could be the one who falls. Those simple words give me hope.

"See?" she says, throwing a hand up. "That's what I mean." She circles a finger in the air, gesturing to my expression.

I scrub a hand down my face. "I have no idea what you're talking about."

"You almost kissed me tonight," she says, her tone far softer now. "Be honest. Have you continued planning this wedding in hopes that we'd grow closer again?"

"I did it for you," I say, taking half a step closer. "Because you needed this. I'd be doing this for you too. I understand what this is, Lex. And I understand what's it's not."

Crossing her arms over her chest, she lifts her chin and doubles down. "We're going to have to kiss, Aiden. We'll have to act as though we're in love. But it won't be real."

I shrug like it's no big deal. Like memories of her lips on mine don't run on repeat in my head like an old film, highlighting the way she used to taste, the feel of her body against mine, the sound of her whimpers when she'd ride me, clothes on, while we made out for hours.

Her eyes are narrowed, but her tongue peeks out and slicks across her lips, leaving a sheen of moisture.

I can't help but track the movement, and I have to stuff my hands into my pockets again to keep from reaching for her. The air between us is charged as she takes another breath and slowly steps closer. She presses a hand to my chest, the heat of her palm soaking through my Oxford, and slides it up and around my neck. I'm frozen, stunned stupid, as she pops up on her toes and practically devours me in one fell swoop.

For the first time in more than a decade, Lennox Kennedy's lips are pressed against mine, and every moment that's taken place since the last time we were in this position evaporates.

I'm eighteen and in love again. She tastes like strawberries, which is so very on brand for her. I nip at her bottom lip because she tastes so fucking good, and it's the moan that slips from her throat that pulls me back.

Fuck, I want to run my hands all over her body. I want to pull her close and never let her go. But if I don't stop kissing her, I'll only prove her point. So I step back and run my thumb against my lips, swiping away her kiss rather than going in for another.

Pupils blown wide, Lennox sways. On instinct, I grasp her hips to steady her.

She looks up at me and blinks. She *fucking* blinks. Then she clears her throat. "You're telling me you can handle doing that without catching feelings?"

Hands in my pockets once more, mostly to appear unaffected, but also to relieve the tightness in my crotch, I lift my chin. "Can you handle it?"

She coughs out a breathy laugh. "Obviously, I'm completely capable. I'm just worried about you."

I shrug. "I'm fine. And now that we got that out of the way, it'll look more natural when we kiss at the party."

She blinks those stunning blue eyes at me again. Still affected. Still dizzy from our kiss. I fucking love her like this. "The party?"

"When we tell the world we're back together."

Face lowered, she presses her fingers to her temples and scoffs. "You were just engaged to someone else. No one will buy that we're engaged now."

My heart leaps. She's right. Damn, this just keeps getting better. "You're right. So we'll have to sell it. We'll date publicly for a few months. Then when the season starts, I'll propose. Everyone already thinks I'm in love with you, so no one in my family will be surprised that we moved so quickly."

Her expression goes stony, but there's pain and a little disappointment in her eyes. "See? This is a bad idea."

I press my hand to her shoulder and squeeze, ignoring the zap that hits me when I do. "It won't be real, Lex. I can do this. How long do you have to be married before you inherit the trust?"

Please, god, let it be ten years. Fuck, a lifetime with her wouldn't be long enough.

She lurches back and paces once more. She's always thought through her problems like this. Like me, she's not one to sit still. "There isn't a set minimum. Probably just long enough for the trust to be turned over to me. At that point, we can get a quick divorce and move on from this insanity."

I hide my grimace with a hand over my jaw, as if deep in thought. "But we'll need to make it believable so they don't contest the marriage, right?"

Lennox hums as she picks up her wine and takes a sip. "Yeah, I guess. And the wedding would have to happen before my birthday in November."

"Of course."

Her shoulders sag. "You say of course like this isn't a big deal."

It isn't a big deal. It's brilliant, really. We'll have to sell this marriage, and the only way to do that is by spending time together. Holding her, kissing her, showing her what it's like to be loved by me. Reminding her of just how good we can be together and how a healthy relationship isn't something to fear.

"It's just a few months," I say, trying to ease her concerns.

I can practically see her thoughts racing as she flips through her options. When she reaches the conclusion I've already come to—that this makes the most sense if she wants her trust—she finally meets my gaze.

"No one can know." She says it almost like a taunt. Like she thinks I can't keep this secret. Silly woman. For years, I've been keeping my thoughts to myself on all kinds of topics, happily playing into my reputation as the happy-go-lucky idiot.

I can do this.

I nod. "Not even Sara."

For the first time since I showed up here tonight, she genuinely smiles. It's a little evil, but I'll take it.

"Definitely not Sara. She didn't tell me when she was fake dating your brother, so there's no way I'm letting her in on this. Besides, it will drive her nuts trying to figure it out."

A low laugh rumbles out of me. "You two have a weird friendship."

"True." Her smile vanishes and is replaced by a tremulous frown. "One more rule."

A wave of dread hits me at her serious tone.

"If either of us changes our mind, or if you catch feelings, this ends, no questions asked."

"What if you catch feelings?" I counter, rubbing my fingertips over my lips again, reminding her of who pushed whom away.

"Then I'll say the word, and the fake engagement is over."

Pain slices through my chest at the thought, but I keep my face neutral. "Got it."

"If either of us says—"

I cut her off. I don't need to hear the damn word. "Got it."

"You know the word?"

I know the fucking word. Jaw hardened, I give her a succinct nod and mutter the two syllables I never wanted to hear again. "Shamrock."

She walks toward me, gaze determined, and sticks out her hand. "Okay, Hockey Boy, you've got yourself a fake fiancée."

CHAPTER 19
AIDEN

"YOU SEEM HAPPIER TODAY," Robert says as I sit across from him in his office.

During the season, most of my therapy sessions are done over Zoom, but when I'm in town, he expects me to make the trek across the city to visit him. I'd like to say it's because of my dazzling smile, but he sees through the façade, and he doesn't let me fake it, so more often than not, I'm subdued when I see him.

I nod. "What's there not to be happy about? We won the Stanley Cup, I've got a few weeks off, and my health is good." I tick off all the events that should contribute to genuine happiness yet don't make my heart rate pick up the way they probably should.

Not one of those items has much impact on my mood. My smile can be attributed to only one thing. The one thing I can't talk about with anyone but him.

"And you got engaged?" Robert prods, though his expression is hesitant. Probably because he expected that to be the first item on my list. "Have you and Jill started planning the wedding?"

"We actually broke up." I rub my palms over my thighs, though I can't help the way my lips quirk at the thought of being done with her.

Based on Robert's concerned frown, my reaction isn't the right one. "And how do you feel about that?"

Leaning forward, I bob my head. "Good, I guess."

Robert's already giving me a concerned look, and it's only going to deepen when I tell him about Lennox. I've never mentioned her before, and now that I think about it, maybe that's why I've still got so many unresolved issues.

So I start at the beginning. I give him a rundown of who Lennox is to me. I don't shy away from sharing my feelings with him, and I even detail the marriage pact and my plan to win her back. The more I tell him, the lighter I feel.

"Are you feeling worried about what the repercussions might be?" he asks gently as our hour comes to an end.

Sitting back, I shake my head. "I've got this under control."

The truth is that so long as I can be the person Lennox needs— the fake fiancé, the friend—without showing her how truly attached I already am, this will be fine.

Or it will be a disaster. But at least I'll be smiling while it lasts.

Step one of my plan is to show Lennox how chill I can be around her. What better way to do that than in a steamy hot tub?

"Knock, knock," I sing while tapping against her door.

"You've got the wrong door," she yells from the other side.

Chuckling, I tap louder. "Come on, it's your fake—"

I don't get the words out before she's swinging the door open and yanking me inside. "Are you insane? Someone could have heard you," she hisses.

The smile I've been sporting falls as I take her in, and my mouth goes dry. She's got a hot pink silk robe pulled tight around her waist, and her full breasts are spilling out, obviously free beneath the smooth fabric, her pebbled nipples enticing me almost as much as her bare legs.

She was dressed in a robe the other night, but it was the thick bathrobe kind. There were no nipples poking through the fabric, and her cleavage was barely on display.

Fuck.

Lennox always has had a great rack, but somehow, every time I see her, she just gets prettier.

I thumb toward the door, trying to catch my breath. "Was going to invite you up to the roof." I raise my eyes to her face, hoping that avoiding her luscious curves will make it easier to speak. But when those soulful blue eyes lock on me, my tongue gets even more tied.

God, she's gorgeous.

This was a terrible idea.

"The roof?" She frowns.

I choose to focus on her skepticism rather than how much I just want to say fuck it and drag her into her bedroom. That would obviously be a terrible idea.

"There's a hot tub up there. Gavin had it installed after we won the Cup."

Lennox perks up, her expression brightening. "Seriously? Hockey Daddy has been holding out on me? I had no idea."

I shake my head. "No."

Her smile grows. "No?"

"No, you cannot call my brother Hockey Daddy."

With a flourish, she spins, her slinky robe flaring out and giving me the tiniest peek of her ass, and heads toward her bedroom. "Don't be jealous, Hockey Boy." In the doorway, she grasps the frame and tilts her head back. "Single dads aren't my kink."

She disappears into her room with a loud laugh, leaving me standing in the middle of her living room with my jaw wide open.

"Wait, where are you going?" I yell. I'm not sure if I've been dismissed or if I'm supposed to stay here.

Lennox giggles. "I'm getting my suit."

And I'm back to smiling again.

"How was your day?" I ask as we settle beneath the bubbling water. The weather is mild, and despite the light pollution, the sky sparkles above. It's a perfect night.

Lennox leans her head back and moans in a way that makes my dick perk up. Thank fuck we're the only people out here. If any of the guys saw her like this, I'd have to murder them.

"God, this feels good." She lifts her foot and presses it against the steady pressure of water coming from one jet. "My day was okay. Just went to work and did a little more planning for Gavin and Millie's wedding."

"Oh yeah? Planning it without me now?"

She rolls her eyes as she laughs. "Figured you were done planning now that you got what you wanted."

I drape my arms over the back of the hot tub and sink a little lower. "And what's that?"

"Never mind that," she says, waving her hands under the water. "How was your day?"

I allow her to change the subject without argument. We both know why I was helping her plan the wedding, so there's no sense in revisiting that conversation. "It was okay. Got a skate in this morning. Hit the gym after, had lunch, saw my therapist, then took a nap."

"You see a therapist?" Lennox asks, gripping the bench on either side of her thighs. There's no judgment in her tone, just genuine interest.

I nod. "Annual visits are a team requirement. I just turned it into a weekly thing."

She's quiet, thoughtful, and interested, so I find myself continuing.

"Sometimes, after a game, I'd find it hard to breathe, and not just after the losses. The wins were often worse. The heaviness would settle in, and then I'd get angry at myself for not *being* happier." I shrug. "Don't get me wrong, I can smile along with the best of them. I'd never drag my team down."

The genuine concern in her eyes makes my chest go tight. Needing a break from her scrutiny, I let out a long breath and dip my head beneath the water. Why am I sharing all of this? I want to show her I can handle our arrangement. Instead, I'm proving to her that I'm the kind of person whose feelings she'll to tiptoe around. I breach the surface and smile. "Anyway, tell me—"

"Don't do that."

I blink the water from my eyes and rake my fingers through my hair to get it out of my face. "Do what?"

"Don't hide yourself from me. Don't make yourself smaller, or happier, or *anything-er*, than you are. If this is going to work, I need you to be real with me. If you need something, tell me. If you feel a certain way, express it. Promise me you won't be anything but real when it's just us."

My stomach twists at the request. Total transparency? If it's possible, then I'll do it. I'll do anything she asks. "Fine. What I need right now is for you to take my mind off this conversation."

"*Aiden.*" She tilts her head and gives me a disapproving frown.

I hold up my hands. "Lex, I'm being serious. I'm new to this sharing the real me thing. Unless you want me to shut down or to break out in song—both coping mechanisms, I'm told—I need to change the subject. Please. It can be anything; just talk."

For a moment, she blinks at me, her lip caught between her teeth. "Shit," she breathes out. "My mind literally went blank."

I cough out a laugh. "Seriously?"

"Yeah, like there's nothing in here." She taps on her head. "Nada."

I suck in a harsh breath, willing myself to focus on her and not the emotions we've dredged up. The emotions now swirling beneath the surface, threatening to pull me under.

I've never told anyone about my depression diagnosis. Never admitted that I see a therapist weekly. The guys would be concerned about all the pressure they put on me during games. There's a good chance they wouldn't trust me to be center. Sometimes I wonder why they do. If they should—

"Breathe," she says, pushing off the edge of the hot tub and coming to sit beside me. The warm water sloshes over my torso as she settles so she's facing me.

Obediently, I suck in a lungful of air. I didn't realize I was holding my breath. As I exhale, I stare into her blue eyes. Once again, there's zero judgment. Just empathy.

"I'm right here with you," she says, placing a hand on my chest.

Swallowing thickly, I shift so I'm facing her, one leg pulled up on the bench, and grasp her thighs, needing to ground myself to her. To calm myself. I don't expect her to climb on top of me. To straddle me. But when she does, my brain short-circuits in a completely different way.

"Is this okay?" she mumbles, eyeing me cautiously.

Settling with my back against the jets, I grip her ass and pull her closer, hugging her to my body. "Yes."

She loops her arms around my neck and hugs me back. The simple move pulls a sigh from deep within me. In the past week, Lennox has kissed me. She's danced with me. She's spent countless hours planning a wedding with me. But this is the first time she's hugged me. And unlike our kiss, which was meant to prove something, this is just for us. For me. She's holding on to me, her head cradled on my shoulder, our bodies pressed tightly together. My very being shifts as our hearts beat a steady rhythm in time. A door that's been locked up tight for years creaks open in my chest. I relax into the embrace, letting go of all the worries weighing me down, and breathe, enjoying this moment with my old friend.

"I read a good book today," she murmurs, her breath skating across the damp skin of my neck.

I think my heart is beating louder than her voice.

"Oh yeah? What's it about?"

"Promise not to make fun of me?"

"Lex," I say softly, leaning my head back.

She snuggles in closer to my neck, and fuck if I don't love having her cuddled right there. If she weren't using the move to hide from me, I'd let her stay there forever.

I rub a hand up and down her back. "I'd never laugh at you. Only with you."

Straightening, she hits me with a smile that's like an electric shock to my heart. On the heels of that, my breath is stolen from me. Holy fuck. Clearly, I didn't get a good look at her when she got in the hot tub. I never got to truly see her bathing suit, and then when she crawled into my lap, I was too focused on my panic attack to appreciate the breasts that are spilling out of her hot pink top.

Don't look at her tits.

I suck on my teeth and force my attention to remain on her face. "Tell me about the book."

She shifts back like she's going to climb off my lap.

I grab her thighs, keeping her where she is. "Where are you going?"

Giggling, she points to her stuff. "I read on the Kindle app on my phone. I thought I'd pull up the book and read it to you. See if you can really keep a straight face."

Oh fuck. She's going to read to me? Is it like porn? Am I going to get hard in this hot tub? Yes, if Lennox is reading porn to me while wearing that tease of a swimsuit, chances are I'm going to be a rock beneath the bubbles. Maybe she'll sit back on my lap while she reads to me...

A guy can dream, right?

"Let me set the scene," she says, leaning over the edge of the tub and drying her hands on her towel. Once she's got her phone, she sits back down on my lap.

I have to bite my cheek to keep the huge smile from spreading across my face. She didn't even pause to think about whether she should sit here or keep her distance. Climbing into my lap was her natural inclination.

"Okay, set the scene," I prod.

"They broke up because he was a jerk."

I nod, taking in the stars visible in the night sky.

"He's not *really* a jerk. He's actually very swoony, but he acted like a jerk because he didn't believe her."

Chuckling, I drag my hands up and down her thighs. "Got it. He's a jerk. We should always believe the girl."

She narrows her gaze on me. "When you love her? There's no question."

I sober. "Of course. Keep going."

She relaxes against me, her body so soft and warm. "He sees her out on a date with another guy. Actually," she hums, twisting her lips to one side, "that makes it sound like it wasn't on purpose, when in reality, he knew they were going to be there."

"So he's a stalker?" I waggle my eyebrows.

She shrugs, but her eyes light up like she finds the idea of it hot. "For her."

Now we're getting somewhere.

She looks down at the phone, her face illuminated, and begins to read.

"*'Does his touch set fire to your skin like mine does?' he grits huskily into my ear, his breath sending a shiver of betrayal down my arms. With his left hand still on my hip, he presses against me and trails his fingers up my bare arm, and I have to hold back a whimper.*"

I ghost my fingertips over her thighs, making circles as she reads, and keep my focus trained on her lips as I memorize every word that spills from them.

"Do not let him know he's affecting you," she continues reading, but her eyes jump up to mine.

I grin. Am I affecting her? God, I hope so. My cock pulses at her proximity. It takes Herculean restraint not to rock against her.

"'Do you possess his thoughts like you do mine? Making it impossible for him to work, to breathe, to fucking sleep at night without dreaming of your taste?' His tantalizing voice dances against my skin as he brushes the barest of kisses against my shoulder, and my legs clench together as I squeeze my eyes shut."

Lennox inches forward, and when she sucks in a breath, I know she's discovered how hard I am. Instead of darting away, she freezes and drags her attention up to me. In the light of her phone screen, her blue eyes are dark, her pupils almost eclipsing the irises completely.

"Keep reading," I tell her, all the while squeezing her thighs and rubbing her oh so gently over the head of my cock. If the kind of obsession she's reading about is what turns her on, then she's in luck. I've always been that guy when it comes to her.

Obsessed. A bit crazy. And determined as anything to make her mine.

Rule 1:
Don't fall for
the groom.

Dearest Lennox

Chapter 20
Lennox

"SO LET ME GET THIS STRAIGHT," Sara says, dropping a blob of concealer onto a sponge." He showed up at your apartment and told you he ended his engagement with Jill right after he left your office? *Swoon—*"

"Total swoon," Hannah agrees, fanning herself with a magazine.

"Yes, total swoon." Dabbing the cool liquid concealer under my eyes, Sara arches a brow. "And then what? You decided eleven years apart was too much and expressed your love for one another, and now you're back together?"

I clutch her wrist and tug, stopping her from attacking my face with her sponge. "First off, cool it with the jabby hands. Second, no. Obviously, that isn't what happened."

Blue eyes narrowed, she huffs. "Then please explain how you went from freaking out that Aiden almost kissed you to bringing him *as your date to* your family's party tonight."

Hannah sucks in a breath and tosses her magazine onto the bed. "He almost kissed you?"

Lips pursed, I assess her, then Sara. "He did kiss me."

The girls scream in surround sound, making it impossible to tamp down the giddy excitement that bubbles up in my chest at the reminder of Aiden's kiss. It was nothing like it used to be. Aiden Langfield has become a master with his mouth.

Don't get me wrong—when we were teenagers, I was certain his kisses would be the best of my life. But adult Aiden has the lips of Adonis. Plump and soft, with just the right amount of pressure, and a teasing tongue. Don't even get me started on the way he nipped at my bottom lip before pulling away. I practically orgasmed on the spot, and that is not how I roll.

I'm not difficult to please, but I am always in my head, always juggling a million thoughts, which can make it hard to focus and actually orgasm.

But that's a story for another day.

My attempt to show Aiden that he absolutely could not handle a fake engagement-slash-wedding to yours truly backfired spectacularly when the only person who got lost in that damn kiss was me.

And last night in the hot tub? There was an intimacy there that even a kiss couldn't convey. Aiden's vulnerability awoke a protective instinct inside me. It was impossible not to fall a little for him then, and if I'm not careful, I'll be halfway in love before we even go on our first fake date.

"How was it?" Sara drops onto the bed beside me, apparently giving up on my makeup.

"Ugh, it's been so long since I've been thoroughly kissed," Hannah says, her tone airy as she falls back against my pillows.

I don't even have to lie when I reply. "It was perfect. And so incredibly weird. It's been over a decade, and somehow, it felt like the most natural thing. He was sweet and told me about how Jill cheated on him—"

"Seriously?" Hannah bolts upright. "That chick is the worst. I'm so glad we don't have to deal with her calling for her specialty teas and all the dietary requests she pretended were for Aiden. Like girl, the boy lives on orange soda. We know he isn't drinking green kombucha."

I snort. She's not wrong.

"And then what happened?" Sara prods. She's like a bear sniffing around a campsite for scraps. She won't let go of this until she's gotten every morsel out of me.

I shrug, buying myself an extra couple of seconds while I figure out how to spin the next part so I don't slip up and clue them in to the fake relationship. "I told him about the party, and he offered to come." See? Perfect. That is an absolutely truthful statement. "He knows my family, and he knows how difficult my relationship with my parents can be. We're going as friends," I add, trying to act nonchalant.

I don't mention how he almost brought me to orgasm in the hot tub just by rubbing me on his lap. Or how I nearly cried when I got to the end of the chapter, and he said he was tired and wanted to head to bed. He was so damn hard beneath me, and when he stepped out of the hot tub, there was no hiding it. Especially because the man had to be a gentleman and wrap me up in a towel before he covered himself.

But he didn't let us go there. Which is good. Obviously. Because this is *fake*.

My best friend is not easily persuaded. Especially because I'm terrible at hiding my emotions. That's one of the reasons I rarely try. So the effort I'm putting in now probably makes it more than obvious that I have feelings for my ex-boyfriend. Feelings, mind you, *I'm* not supposed to have.

"You can't even look me in the eye when you say that," she deadpans.

Hopping off the bed, I snatch the sponge from her hand and the makeup bag from beside her. "Whatever. It's a crazy situation, and I don't know what to think." I stroll into the bathroom to finish getting ready. "Two days ago, I was planning the man's wedding, and now I'm going on a date with him."

"So you admit it's a date?" Sara sings.

I practically jump when she appears in the mirror. What the

fuck? Has she been practicing sneaking up on people? She's as stealthy as a midnight burglar.

"Hannah, can you take this lunatic home with you so I can get dressed in peace?"

In the other room, Hannah laughs. "I'm actually late for a meeting." She appears in the doorway, bag slung over one shoulder and a magazine pressed against her chest. "Jasper, the idiot, was caught on camera with not one but *two* strippers last week. I've arranged for him to meet with the Revolutionary Society today for afternoon tea. Gotta clean up that reputation somehow."

Sponge pressed to my face, I eye her reflection. "The Revs have high tea?"

Hannah tosses her head back and snorts. "God no. The Boston Revolutionary society—*not* related to baseball."

With that, Hannah is gone.

For several heartbeats, the room is silent. I get back to work on my makeup, though I'm on edge. I know my best friend, and she's not letting our conversation go. Once the apartment door clicks shut, signaling that Hannah is officially gone, Sara spins and gives me her most intense gaze. She's trying to read me. See inside my brain. She could probably do it too if I let her. It's going to take some Jumanji shit to keep her spidey senses at bay.

Ignoring her scrutiny, I continue working, surveying all the imperfections my father will find within seconds of my arrival. There's not much I can do about my hair or my size, so I focus on the things I can control.

"I feel like you're hiding something."

I open the mascara and flutter my lashes wide. "When have I ever hidden anything? I'm an open book, Sar."

A haughty laugh echoes through the bathroom. "For a month, you hid that you were living in *my* apartment."

I almost poke myself in the eye with the mascara when I glare at her. "Judgmental doesn't look good on you."

"I'm not trying to be judgmental." She softens, propping a hip against the counter and facing me. "I'm asking you to trust me. I'm your friend, and if you want to talk about whatever big emotions you're feeling, I'm here."

My heart aches at her sincere expression. "I'm focusing on enjoying the moment. Avoiding too much thinking. God, if I think too much about who he was to me and what any of this could mean, I'll probably live in my head for the next year."

It's the most honest I've been with her all day. What Aiden and I are doing is dangerous. If we get caught, I could lose everything. If I fall for him again, I risk my heart. But the scariest part? If he falls for me again, I'd break him, and Aiden is the last person in the world I want to hurt. I did a number on him years ago, and while he's better off because of it, I have no intention of ever hurting him again.

Especially after seeing just how fragile he is.

"You know he's crazy about you, right?"

Trepidation rolls through me at the words. They're meant to ease my burden, yet they have the opposite effect. Because, yeah, that's what I'm afraid of.

"You ready for this?" Aiden's voice is soft as he offers me his hand. His curly light brown hair falls onto his forehead as he helps me out of the car.

"As I'll ever be," I quip, tearing my gaze away from his hazelnut eyes and the innocent way he assesses me.

I paired a flowing, pleated light-pink floor-length chiffon skirt with a white silk halter that accentuates one of my best assets: my cleavage is absolutely on point tonight.

With a breath in to settle my nerves, I lead Aiden up the stairs toward the oversized Victorian housing tonight's festivities. Ahead, each time the doors open and guests filter in, music floats across the porch.

The party is for my cousin's thirtieth. My boss caught wind and asked who was handling it. Unfortunately, I didn't have an answer. She gently requested I find out. No pressure or anything.

As Aiden reaches for the door, I tug on his hand. "Should we discuss our story?"

He arches a brow. "People don't know our history?"

Unease swirls inside me. "I'm pretty sure everyone heard about the great Aiden Langfield's proposal to his longtime girlfriend right before winning the Cup."

Grasping the door handle, he chuckles. "I've got it handled."

"How?"

Aiden brushes the back of his fingers against my cheek. "Trust me, Lex. Everyone in that room will know the only woman I have eyes for is you."

I'm not sure if it's his words or the intensity of his gaze, or maybe the way his lips tip up when he realizes that he's left me speechless, but every single thing about this moment has my brain screaming *shamrock* over and over again. Everything about this man spells trouble for my heart, and I have a feeling tonight is the beginning of my downfall.

"Ready?" he asks softly, his hand traveling down my jaw until he grips my chin.

In response, I lick my lips. There's no stopping the reaction.

His smile is wicked. "If my girl wants a kiss, all she has to do is ask," he teases, dipping in close.

And then his mouth is on mine. *Fuck*. Why is he so good at this? His lips shouldn't be so soft, and his tongue shouldn't know precisely how to slide against mine to make my kitty purr. But here we are. I'm about to walk into a family party I've been dreading for days, yet I'm happily preparing to maul my fake date. Clutching the lapels of his suit jacket, I pull him closer, deepening the kiss.

"Excuse me," a nearby voice mutters.

Aiden pulls me closer, out of the way of the door. I reluctantly break the kiss, and as I pull back, Aiden wipes that thumb against his lip again, chuckling. I should be bothered by the way he's always wiping away my kisses, but I'm too busy searching for oxygen. When my head stops spinning, the pink lipstick smudged on his face registers. Cringing, I wipe at it as well.

"Sorry," I say. "It's a stain, so you might need to wash it in the bathroom."

Aiden grins that schoolboy grin, and my heart skips like it's a rock floating across the water, creating life-changing ripples. *What is happening to me? I don't do heart flutters. I don't do* love.

"It'll sell the relationship. My new girlfriend can't keep her hands —or *lips*—off me." With a wink, he pulls the door open.

Right. Because this is all to sell the relationship. The flirting. The winking. The earth-shattering kiss...*fake.*

I swipe both sides of my mouth, straighten my back, and step inside with my head held high, pink hair and all. This night is going to be an epic disaster.

CHAPTER 21
AIDEN

PARTIES IN GENERAL are where I excel. I'm a fun guy. The life of the party. My toes are already itching to boogie, and my shoulders twitch along with a beat I know I can crush. But I happily remain plastered to Lennox's side. Proud doesn't begin to describe how I feel to be on her arm. Her hair is pulled back with wisps of light pink hair framing her face, the color making her blue eyes look practically electric.

She scans the entryway, likely searching for her parents, though I'm not sure whether it's because she wants to get this meet-and-greet over with or because she's working out a plan for avoiding them all night. I'm game either way. This is Lennox's show, and I'm just along for the ride. Honestly, I'd follow her to the gates of hell. I can guarantee even that would be more enjoyable than any night out I've suffered with the devil herself on my arm over the last few years.

"My cousin Nick is at your nine o'clock. We'll want to say hi to him at some point. His wife is well-known as a gossip, but she has absolutely nothing on him. Every person who wishes him a happy birthday will hear the story of how besotted you are with me."

Lips twitching, she looks up at me. I have to work hard to hide my smile. She's teasing me because I kissed the life out of her outside and she doesn't know what to do with herself now. She thinks this is all an elaborate game. If that's the case, then I'd happily play it for the rest of my life.

"One juicy story coming up," I tease, pulling her back against my chest so that her ass is flush against me.

As a surprised gasp escapes her lips, I run my nose against her bare shoulder and press soft kisses all the way up her neck until I reach her ear. "Let's start with a little show and tell," I murmur with a nip of her lobe.

She melts into my embrace, and when I spin her to face me, she whimpers. Once again, the element of surprise works in my favor. This time, I cup her face and kiss her, allowing my desire for this woman to speak volumes in the crowded room.

Unlike yesterday's kiss, or even the one we shared moments ago, I allow myself to get lost in this one. Why not? It'll only make it more realistic. That's a poor man's excuse, for sure, but I own it. Because right now I'm selling our love story to the masses. Showing them precisely how gone I am for this girl so that not a single person can question Lennox when she finally tells them she's agreed to become my wife.

I don't allow myself to even focus on *those* words. I don't allow myself to get attached to the possibility that she'll ever truly be mine.

But I do let myself enjoy the hell out of her lips against mine.

Pulling back an inch, I lick my lips, giving us both a second to breathe. "Think they're watching?"

Lennox blinks, shaking her head. "Huh?"

A low chuckle slips out of me. "Your family. The birthday boy. You think we gave him enough of a story to run with, or should I take you over there and tell them how madly I've fallen for you?"

"Right." She lets out a soft, almost sarcastic laugh. "Yeah, I think they got their story."

I tear my gaze from hers and immediately catch her father glaring in our direction. There's no stopping the smile that spreads across my face. I always loved pissing off Jackson Kennedy. He never liked the idea of his daughter dating an athlete, but I think what he hated more was how happy I made her.

Or maybe it was the way I kissed her. He certainly doesn't look happy right now.

This power dynamic is one I'm familiar with. I grew up surrounded by people like her father. Walking over *to* him, shaking *his* hand, and acknowledging that I need his approval is what is expected.

Ordinarily, I wouldn't play these games. Beckett and Gavin are much better at keeping up a façade in these situations. I'm the entertainment. The puppy. People approach me. If they don't, then I don't interact with them. I couldn't care less what these people think they can do for me or my family.

But when it comes to Lennox, I'll gladly play by the rules.

With my hand on her back, I guide her forward. "Let's start with your father. He looks absolutely thrilled to see me."

An unladylike snort leaves Lennox. God, I love the sound.

The house is larger than it looks from outside. Against one wall, a bar has been set up, and a line has formed. To the left of it is a DJ.

The Kennedys have certainly thought of everything. I wouldn't be surprised if an up-and-coming musician is slated to perform tonight. That's how these things normally go. Since this event is being thrown by the head of Kennedy records, I have no doubt the talent will be impressive.

Heavy gold and black curtains are draped along the walls, creating a speakeasy-type vibe. As we make our way toward Lennox's father, the room goes silent. Every eye is locked on us, waiting to see what the Kennedy family heiress will do.

Lennox believes that she is a stain on her family's reputation. In reality, they fear her because she can't be controlled, and they have no fucking idea what she'll do right now.

Her mother, Tia, is standing next to Jackson, but she still hasn't noticed us. That's probably a blessing. If Jackson Kennedy considers me an annoyance, Tia Kennedy doesn't believe I should even breathe

the same air as any member of their family. It's a wonder Lennox is so kind and caring, with a mind of her own, unwilling to be molded into what they consider the perfect daughter.

"Hi, Mom," Lennox says, gently grasping the woman by the shoulder.

As she turns toward her daughter, a smile tugs on her lips. It quickly falls, though, when she catches sight of me.

"Mrs. Kennedy, you look lovely," I say, biting back the foolish smile I'm itching to break into in order to cut through the discomfort of this moment. It couldn't be more clear how unwanted I am in this space.

"Yes, well, hello, Aiden. Lennox, I didn't know you were bringing a friend with you tonight."

Lennox clears her throat, but before she can respond, I butt in.

"Not a friend, Mrs. Kennedy. As you know, Lennox and I could never *just* be friends."

It may not be wise to irk them so early in the night, but when Lennox breaks out into a surprised smile, instantly twisting her lips to cover it, I know I'm playing this right.

"Jackson," her mother says, her voice tight. She tugs on his arm, drawing him into the conversation. Or maybe she just needs an anchor so she doesn't fall to her knees in despair over her precious daughter being seen with the likes of me again.

"Princess," he says, taking Lennox in.

"Hi, Daddy," she says.

It's odd, the way they greet one another. For all the shit I've given my parents for being too busy when we were kids, my family has never been stingy when it comes to affection. My mom hugs us, my brothers and I hug each other too. Hell, hugging is my favorite thing to do, and I'm not going to change for these people. Maybe that's all Jackson Kennedy ever really needed—a nice, big Aiden Langfield-style hug.

So when he holds out his hand to me, I can't resist. I pull him in, and this isn't a one clap bro hug. No, I grip him around both arms so he can't escape my embrace and then I do a one-two step. There's no stopping the dance moves when the mood strikes.

The snort behind me is obviously from Lennox.

"It's good to see you, Mr. Kennedy," I say in his ear, and then because he's so damn tense, I plant a big kiss on his cheek. "It's been too long."

As I pull back, Lennox's shoulders shake with laughter, though she's got a hand clamped over her mouth.

Though I expect to find her parents wearing angry or otherwise passive expressions, I'm surprised to find them smiling. Though it's not *at me*. It's clearly at someone right behind me.

I glance over my shoulder, and as I'm turning back to the Kennedys, prepared to go into the story of how Lennox and I are back together, the man's face registers. Heart lurching, I spin and come face to face with the musician who asked my fake fiancée out on a date this week.

Somehow, I know that this won't bode well for me.

"Ryder," Jackson says in a far friendlier tone than he's ever used with me. His smile is wide as he shakes the musician's hand.

"Thanks for the invite." He glances in Lennox's direction, and his eyebrows raise, not like he's surprised to see her, but like he's excited.

Tia is smiling now too. Dammit. This just went from not good to a fucking disaster.

"I'm just happy that you finally said yes. I do believe you've met my daughter," Jackson says, practically grabbing Lennox by the arm and pushing her in his direction.

One side of Ryder's mouth kicks up in a lazy smile. "Yes, I have."

Lennox, oblivious to the way her parents have clearly used her to lure the singer here, smiles warmly.

I hate it.

"You didn't tell me you were coming tonight."

"Didn't know I was." He assesses her parents quickly. "But then I realized you'd be here."

A red flush creeps up Lennox's chest, and yeah, I'm over all of this.

"That she is," I interject. "With her boyfriend." With a hand on Lennox's hip, I tug her back against me, pulling her hand from Ryder's.

"Boyfriend?" the guy has the gall to question, his brows furrowing as he looks from me to Lennox. The expression morphs into a scowl as he turns to Jackson. "I wasn't aware."

Lennox straightens and lets out an uncomfortable laugh. "It's new." She tries to pull free, but I tighten my hold on her, splaying my fingers possessively across her stomach.

"But serious," I add, holding her close. I nuzzle into her, dropping a kiss against her neck.

"What's serious?" a male voice asks.

Lennox's cousin, the birthday boy, Nick Kennedy, saunters up. "Holy shit, it's Aiden Langfield." The guy hands his drink to a woman I'm guessing is his wife and swipes his hands against his suit. "Dude, you're like the best player Boston has ever seen."

Grinning, I give him my full attention. Lennox uses the excuse to extricate herself from my grasp, so when he holds out his hand to shake, I have no option but to let her go completely. I absolutely hate it.

"Aiden's a big fan of hugs," Jackson Kennedy mutters.

The birthday boy's smile grows larger, and he opens his arms, waiting.

"I do like hugs," I offer, allowing him to lock me in a tight embrace. The dude then legitimately lifts me off the ground.

"Nick, *be careful*," his maybe wife yells.

He sets me down, a sheepish grin on his face. "Sorry, I'm your biggest fan. Is this my surprise, hunny?" He spins in her direction and points at me.

She shakes her head. "I had no idea that your idol was coming tonight."

"Your idol?" Lennox asks, breaking into a huge smile.

"Ya hear that, Lex? Apparently, I'm not just *your* idol."

The birthday boy's eyes sharpen. "Who's Lex?"

I pull Lennox close again. "That'd be my girl, right here."

"Wait, I thought you were engaged," Nick says, a confused frown marring his face.

Six sets of eyes settle on me, five of them full of suspicion. "I *was* engaged." I straighten. "Lennox was actually our wedding planner."

"You plan weddings?" Nick's maybe wife asks. She's got a ring on her finger, and he called her hunny, so I'm thinking I've nailed this description.

"She's a rock star," I boast, jostling Lennox. "You should have had her help with this event."

"I would have if I'd known," she says, cringing a little sheepishly. "Let's talk later. We're working on an event at the hospital that I'd love your help on."

Lennox is giving her a tight nod as her father steps in front of Nick's wife. "Lennox will probably be too busy helping me now that Seven is signing with our label, right, princess? His only stipulation is that you help with the tour plans." He's speaking about Lennox—practically to Lennox—but smiling at Ryder. His daughter is nothing more than a prop he can use to get what he wants.

The thought has my gut roiling.

"We can chat about that later," Ryder says, his focus aimed solely at Lennox. "I'd love to hear about how you went from his wedding planner to his girlfriend."

Lennox ducks and pushes a pink wisp of hair behind her ear. "It wasn't like that."

"It actually was," I cut in, stealing the group's attention again. I lift Lennox's hand to my lips, drawing her attention too. Hers is the only one I actually want. If the entire room faded away, and for the rest of my life, she was all I could see, I'd be a happy man. It'd be an incredible existence.

With my focus solely on her, I speak the truth. "When she walked into the office for our first appointment, I took one look at her, and every feeling I'd had for her a decade ago came rushing back. And when she smiled"—I shake my head, brushing my lips against her knuckles as she stares at me, dumbstruck—"when she smiled, it felt like the earth shifted beneath my feet. I knew in that moment that the only person I could ever marry was my beautiful Lex."

"So then what?" Nick's wife asks, her hands clutched over her heart.

I turn to her, but in my periphery, I can't help but notice that Jackson is about as red as a fucking tomato. Her mother has her hand to her mouth like she doesn't know what to do with her face. Ryder is too damn enamored with Lennox, and Nick is just as captivated as his wife.

"I ended my engagement as soon as the appointment was over."

Nick's wife's eyes light up. "That is the cutest thing I've ever heard."

Her husband nods in agreement. "That's beautiful, man. I've got tears in my eyes."

"So you guys used to date?" Ryder asks, still zeroed in completely on Lennox.

"We were high school sweethearts," I say, my chest puffing out proudly.

"What happened?"

For the first time tonight, my throat grows tight, and I'm left speechless.

Beside me, Lennox tenses. "Oh, you know, college." She shrugs.

I side-eye her, my heart sinking. To this day, I still don't know what the fuck happened.

"I'm actually thirsty. Are you thirsty?" she asks me.

Clearly, she wants to get the hell out of this situation, so I give her a simple nod. It's all I can manage, since words are still hard. With my hand against her lower back, I guide her toward the bar.

"Holy shit, it was like the Spanish inquisition just now," she mutters.

No one is standing in line at the bar, so we order drinks quickly, then I lean against it while we wait.

"Also," she says, her lips turning down, "what the hell was that over there?"

"What the hell was what?" I avoid looking at her. It's taking all my self-control not to ask her what really happened all those years ago. Or to ask why the hell Ryder thinks he has a shot with her.

She straightens, pulling her shoulders back. "The story. The possessiveness."

"What would you have had me do differently? Your father was practically offering you on a platter to skinny pants."

The snort that escapes her is loud. "Skinny pants? Is that an insult?"

Annoyance floods me. Is she seriously defending the guy? "Men who wear cigarette pants are tools. But I'd never get my thighs into pants like that, so you don't have to worry about me wearing them."

Lennox assesses my fabulous thighs and shrugs. "Fine. So we don't like his pants. You know I only stayed to talk to him the other night because I need him to agree to perform at that wedding."

I let out a derisive huff. "That shouldn't be a problem for you now. It seems he'll be happy to make time for anything you ask."

The bartender places our drinks in front of us, and Lennox immediately brings her wine to her lips and takes a sip as she studies me. Her assessment carries on for so long that it feels as though she's dissecting my every thought.

I don't like it one fucking bit. My thoughts are spinning out of control, and if she could see inside my brain right now, she'd know all I think of these days is her.

"You're jealous." She says it like it's just occurred to her. Like she's surprised by it. "Oh my god, you were jealous because Ryder talked to me."

Rather than reply, I keep my mouth shut and force a blank expression.

Scowling, she motions between us. "Aiden, this is fake. You

promised this wouldn't be a problem. That you didn't have feelings for me."

My jaw ticks. "You think that was jealousy? If I were really your boyfriend, how would I be expected to act when your father barters you for business to a man in tight pants who is practically salivating while staring at your tits?"

Lennox's eyes pop. "You're worried about how my father's acting while you're the one practically pissing on me, declaring me yours?"

Angling in close, I grab the finger she's pointing at me. "You *are* mine," I growl, my lips practically touching hers as I say it.

"For fake," she hisses. "I'm yours for *fake*."

I release her hand and lean back against the bar again. "Right. If you were really my fiancée, I'd have done a fuck ton more than just grab your waist and tell your family that we're dating."

Lennox's pupils dilate, and her cheeks go pink. "Like what?"

Fuck.

Something inside me snaps—probably the string that was tethering me to sanity. "You want me to tell you what I'd do if you were really mine?" I loom over her, bringing my mouth to her ear. "Or do you want me to show you?"

When I pull back, anxious to see her reaction, she's got her teeth digging into her bottom lip. Eyes hardening, she lifts her chin, daring me. "*Show me.*"

Rule 1:
Don't fall for
the groom.

Dearest Lennox

Chapter 22
Lennox

AIDEN'S JAW HARDENS, and a mixture of desperation—or is that desire?—and anger darkens his normally warm eyes. The honey color is now as dark as chocolate.

This is Aiden unhinged. Unmasked. I've known him long enough to know that his dopey smile is often nothing more than a mirage.

This man is a stranger to me. When we were together, he was generous with his genuine smiles. Never once was his anger directed at me. Not even when I said it was over. We'd made a promise, and one simple word was all it took. There was no fight. No awkward conversation. There were plenty of tears on my end, but only when I was alone.

But this man right here? He's angry.

And maybe it's because I'd rather have the real version of him than the watered-down one, or maybe it's because the angry side of him is hot. The jealousy? Scorching. My entire body is on fire just waiting to see what will happen next.

I'm pushing him, goading him into reacting in a way that might be our undoing.

I'm not sure if it's because I ache for his touch or if I'm trying to push him to admit that he can't handle this before we both get hurt.

Either way, when he sets both of our drinks on the bar and tugs me toward the black and gold velvet curtains, electricity oozes through my veins.

Somewhere behind us, the evening is beginning. Opening remarks, I suppose. I can barely breathe, let alone focus on what's being said.

Aiden doesn't bother pushing the curtain to the side to look for an opening. He simply bends at the knee and lifts it up from the floor, then nods for me to dip below. I'm only too happy to retreat to the darkness.

"What are we—"

He grips the back of my neck and pulls his mouth to mine. This kiss is nothing like the last one, or the one in my apartment. It's passion and anger, it's want and need, it's lust-filled and brutal. He owns my mouth, his fingers digging into my neck and directing me where he wants me as his mouth demands more and more and more until our chests are both heaving and my clit is aching. He could merely brush against it right now, and I'd combust.

The room erupts in applause, and then live music begins. The voice that cuts in is that of the man that has left Aiden so jealous he's practically unhinged.

Obviously recognizing Ryder's voice too, Aiden pulls back and bites down on my lip, holding me in place with his teeth. His molten eyes tell me everything. *I hate that I want you. I hate that you make me feel this way. I hate that anyone else thinks they have a shot at taking you from me.*

I whimper, though not in pain. I want to tell him that he needn't worry about the man on the other side of the curtain. I want to tell him that there's never been a man who posed any competition for my heart.

But at the sound, he releases me.

Not just my mouth, but my entire body. He holds his hands up, and his eyes bug out like he's shocked by what he's just done.

"Fuck," he mutters, turning away and running his hands through his hair.

"Don't stop," I beg. Seeing him like this, unguarded and real, should scare me, because we promised nothing but fake emotions.

But the fluttering in my belly, the ache between my legs, and the pounding of my heart? This is the realest I've felt in years, and I don't want it to end.

Not yet.

Aiden snaps his attention back to me, and in the darkened space lit only by the window he stands in front of, he's nothing but a shadow. "What?"

"You promised you'd show me." I step closer. "Pretend a little longer."

He laughs. It's a raspy sound, throaty and sexy, and it scratches at the darkest places inside me. "You want me to pretend? Pretend that the way he looks at you doesn't grate on me? Or do you want me to pretend that you're mine and I'm punishing you for even allowing him to speak to you?"

My chest heaves and my panties dampen. "That one."

Aiden hovers close and runs the back of his fingers down my arm. I close my eyes and savor the way it feels to be touched by this man again.

"Pretend that the sight of him looking at you in this top made me want to gouge his eyes out?"

Eyes open again, I nod shakily. Goose bumps skitter across my skin in the wake of his gentle touch. The music gets louder, Ryder's voice almost a taunt in this secret space.

Aiden clamps his teeth down on his bottom lip. "Turn around," he grits out.

Desperate to stare into those soulful eyes and remain in this moment, I don't obey.

Aiden shakes his head, his lips quirking up in a salacious smile. "Always the defiant one." With his hand on my shoulder, he spins me around and forces me toward the curtain, closer to the music. He leads me right up against it, so close that the back of the curtain, which is a rough, muted-gray fabric unlike the soft velvet that faces the crowd, scratches at my skin. "You say it's fake, but you're mine until I say you aren't."

I swallow thickly and hold my head high. "Until *I* say it's over."

His dark chuckle rumbles against my skin as he lifts my hair and drags his nose against the slope of my neck. "It's always you who does."

My heart sinks. *This* is why he's so angry. Why he shut down mid-conversation out there. The breakup. Why we ended. The discussions we never had. "Aiden, I—"

"Shh, Princess, right now, we're pretending. Though I bet there's no pretending how wet you are right now, is there?"

The use of my father's nickname is almost cruel, and yet I like how he's taken the word and made it his. Made it filthy.

Is that deranged?

With the back of his hand, he parts the curtain so that light filters in. A cry threatens to bubble out of me. Dammit. I don't want to leave this space. I want to stay with him. Cling to *us*. Even if we're broken. Even if we're fake.

But when that same hand falls against my breast and he squeezes, all worries fade.

"You hear his voice?" he whispers against my ear.

I nod, the movement jerky, and when he pinches my nipple, I gasp. He releases his hold quickly, then rubs soothing circles. "It's for you."

"What?" I pant as he teases his fingers along the waistband of my skirt. I'm ready to buck up for him, willing to do anything to get his hand between my legs.

"He's singing for you, Princess. He came for you." He bites down on my shoulder as he slips his hand into my panties. Then, without warning, he spears me with one finger. "But you only *come* for me."

A loud moan works its way out of me as I rock against him. The only thing louder is the sounds he makes with his fingers as he fucks me. I'm so wet from all the teasing he's done, and he's working so meticulously.

He suctions that hot mouth to my neck and alternates between biting and sucking. All the while, he works me over, adding another finger and rubbing his palm against my clit, giving me the exact amount of friction I need to grind against to get me so close to the edge I may cry if he doesn't let me come.

"Please," I beg, draping an arm around his neck. I need him to send me hurtling over the precipice. I turn my head, desperate to see his eyes, knowing that's all it will take. It will also serve as a reminder that the man who's acting just shy of cruel is Aiden—*my Aiden*—and he doesn't really mean what he's saying.

But he hooks his chin over my shoulder, locking my head in place so that I'm forced to watch the scene playing out between the slits of fabric. To focus on the man across the room who's to blame for Aiden's anger.

"I want you to watch him. Every time you look at him, I want you to think about *my* fingers inside this greedy pussy. Every time you hear his voice, you'll remember *my* words as I teased this orgasm out of you. You'll remember how it felt to be *mine*."

As I explode, he clamps his free hand over my mouth, muffling my cries. "Now, now, Princess. Only I get to hear you come."

CHAPTER 23
AIDEN

Brooks: Aiden, you still planning on meeting up with us? If not, then I'm gonna head home. War's been staring at his phone all night. Cam and Hall are going shot for shot, and Fitz is flirting hard with the bartender. Parker already left, and Gavin never showed up. 👀

Beckett: Gee, thanks for the invite.

Gavin: Ha, like you would have gone.

Beckett: Doesn't mean I wouldn't appreciate being invited. Where are you anyway?

Brooks: Karaoke bar on 7th. Wanna come?

FUCK, I've been working hard to ignore my phone, instead focusing on my brooding, but not responding is making my hand itch.

> Beckett: Pass.

> Gavin: You can sing I Will Survive. We know that's what you sang in the shower while living in the house of horrors.

I snort, imagining Beckett belting that out in the shower when he first moved in with his wife and her three best friends. Despite what a grump he can be, that is probably an accurate representation of him during that time. Barely holding on while he lived with four women and seven kids in a brownstone that was literally crumbling around them.

When I feel Lennox's eyes on me, I school my expression and push my phone back into my pocket, the many replies I've concocted instantly a distant memory.

"Everything okay?" she asks, her tone tremulous.

She's been that way since I lost my fucking mind and showed all my cards tonight. Kissing her. Fucking her with my fingers. Making her come on command. Any second now, she's going to tell me she's abandoning the plan. Obviously, I can't handle doing this without getting feelings involved.

"I'm fine. Are *you* okay?" I risk looking at her. Despite doing all I can to hide my feelings, I need to know what she's really thinking.

She was quiet for the rest of the night, and as soon as they cut the cake, she was making the rounds to say good night, explaining that she had an early appointment tomorrow morning. Now we're in the back seat of the car that delivered us here, and we've been awkwardly silent.

"Of course." She pushes her hair back behind her ear as the car comes to a stop in front of the elevator bank in the parking garage of our building. She doesn't wait for me to help her out, and I can't make myself feel upset about it. And there's no fucking way I can get in that elevator with her. I'm liable to babble out a string of apologies. If I do that, then I'll have to explain why I acted the way I did, and none of those things are signs of someone who can handle the arrangement we have.

She walks ahead of me, and I force myself not to stare at her ass. At the elevator bank, she presses the button and faces the doors, silently waiting for it to open.

"Will you be okay going up by yourself?" I ask, digging my hands into my pockets to keep from reaching for her.

For the first time since we were behind the curtain, she really looks at me. Fuck, she still looks so perfect. It pisses me off that she cleaned herself up after I had her. That her cheeks aren't still flushed and her lips are barely swollen. Her hair and makeup remain in place, as if I never touched her. Such a fucking perfect princess for her family. Will she do what they ask now that the man they're pushing on her isn't a polo-wearing Chad who golfs on the weekends? Is being with him, maybe marrying him, appealing to her? If she did, not only would it make them happy, but she'd get what she wants.

Brows drawing low, she frowns. "Are you going somewhere?"

I nod toward my car. "It's Camden Snow's birthday. The guys went out to dinner, and now they're at karaoke."

"Aiden, why didn't you mention it earlier? You didn't have to miss your friend's birthday to come to my cousin's."

The elevator opens, and I lean in to hold it for her. "I wanted to. You sure you'll be okay going up?"

With her lip caught between her teeth, she steps closer, pressing her hand to my chest. The heat of her palm sends an electric jolt through me like a defibrillator. "I'll be fine." Her blue eyes hold mine as she pops up on her toes and brushes her lips against my cheek. "Just feel bad I couldn't return the favor. Night, Hockey Boy." With that, she shuffles into the elevator.

I'm only beginning to process her words as I step back. As the doors slide shut between us, she catches my eye and smiles.

I clear my throat, searching for control. "Night, Princess. Sweet dreams."

Even as the doors lock tight, her laughter is audible. "They'll all be about you."

Fuck. I gape at the metal doors, contemplating ditching the guys and running up the sixteen flights of stairs so I can be standing there when Lennox gets out.

But I'm playing it cool. This is a long game.

And if she's dreaming of me, then I'm already a hell of a lot closer to winning than I thought.

"*My boy, my boy, my boy*," Daniel croons into the microphone while Cam sits on a barstool next to him.

The bar is crowded, so it takes a minute to find the rest of the guys where they're recording the disaster playing out on stage.

"Holy fuck, how much have they had to drink?" I ask as I approach. Each of the guys turns and gives me a bro hug.

"Too fucking much," Fitz, our goalie coach, says, bringing his own vodka tonic to his lips. During the season, Cade Fitzgerald keeps his professional distance. He does his best to respect the line between players and coaches. That really could go out the window now that my brother is our coach, but whatever. I understand his desire to keep things professional. But during the offseason, when the unprofessional Cade comes out, he's a fucking blast. He's in his forties, but to my knowledge, the guy has never settled down. He acts more like the old Gavin—out with a different person every week.

On road trips, he can usually be found at a local bar, flirting with the bartender. Man or woman, it doesn't really matter. The guy loves everyone. Though right now, it doesn't appear he's loving our left winger or the birthday boy.

From across the table, Brooks zeroes in on me, his expression going stoic. "How was the night?" he asks. Though it's loud in here—

Hall and Snow are screeching the words to "My Girl" by the Temptations—I can read his lips.

I nod, then throw a thumb over my shoulder, gesturing to the bar. I need a few minutes to figure out how to spin this, and Brooks is the most intuitive guy I know. As a goalie, he's always taking in his surroundings, picking up the smallest details the rest of us miss. That's why he has no trouble stopping a puck hurtling toward his goal at a hundred miles an hour.

The man is one of the best, and he's a good part of the reason I'm the best center in the NHL. I'm not being cocky. My stats speak for themselves, and they look the way they do because I've spent my entire life trying to score goals on my brother. It takes creativity to get through both his mental and physical walls.

How am I going to play this with him?

Lennox is giving me a second chance? Lennox needed a friend? Lennox is the love of my life, so of course I'm going to fake marry her and hope that she falls for me in the process?

"Dude," a voice booms only inches from my ear. "What the fuck is going on with you and Lennox?"

A girlish scream escapes me, and my balls ascend into my body at the decibel. I grip the back of a barstool to steady my racing heart, then whip around and square up with my brother. The words I should say—*dude you scared me*—are replaced by pure idiocy. "I touched her boob."

Brooks is used to his fiancée spouting the most insane things, so I'm not surprised when he tips back his head and laughs.

"What can I get you?" the bartender asks, dropping a cocktail napkin on the lacquered bar top.

I place my order and then turn back to my brother, who is still chuckling.

"I'm so glad that you find me pouring my heart out so amusing."

Brooks coughs out another laugh. "You 'touched her boob' was you *pouring your heart out*?"

"They're great boobs. And it's been over a decade since I touched them. I've missed them. Do you know what perfect pillows they make?"

My brother blinks, his green eyes swimming with confusion. "So you're back together with Lennox?" His words are slow, like he's not sure what to make of it *or* me. Confusing him like this is my secret weapon. It's how I get things past him—hockey pucks normally, though I'm far prouder that he's the one voicing the lie, not me, and it's because he's controlling the narrative now. Though we *are* technically together.

Together meaning we're in a fake relationship, though the details are unnecessary right now. *Bravo, Aiden and your excellent weaving and gliding past the truth.*

I'm giving him a firm nod when the bartender returns with my drink. I order a round to be delivered to our table, along with shots for the birthday boy and then tip my head to our group, silently asking Brooks to follow me rather than asking any insightful Brooks-style questions.

A heavy palm lands on my shoulder, pulling me back like a damn yo-yo. My drink sloshes onto my shirt, but that's not the reason for my grimace. My entire body is working itself up for this conversation.

"You spend a year telling me you aren't obsessed with your ex, then end your engagement and start dating said ex, and all I get is a shrug?" He gives me the stupid, dopey smile he uses when messing with me, mimicking the one I use as a shield, I guess. "And I'm supposed to believe that you aren't bursting at the seams to *sing* about how happy you are?"

My stomach drops and my head spins. Shit. I played this all wrong. He's right. If Lennox and I were truly getting a second chance, I'd be up there with those idiots doing the Macarena *and* the Wobble, blubbering about how Lennox Kennedy is finally *my girl*.

That image dances in my mind briefly, pulling a chuckle from me. *That* would be a good time.

Brooks arches a brow, as if he's caught me in the lie, so I set my drink on the bar and level with him. "Look, I'm trying not to get ahead of myself. Yes, I am excited that Lennox and I are finally spending time together again." *See? No lies to be had there.* "But her father invited the lead singer of Seven, the dude Lennox met last night, a guy she's at least a bit interested in, even if it's only for business." At least that's what I keep telling myself. "Jackson is using her to get the guy to sign with his label, and it pissed me off. Also"—I let out a breath and garner my strength; I'm not used to being this damn vulnerable—"to this day, I still have no fucking clue why she ended things. I worry it's because of her parents. If that's the case, then I'm afraid they'll use this guy to do it again."

My brother glowers, looking like a menacing giant. "Fuck her parents."

The ache in my chest loosens a bit. I shouldn't be surprised by his words. My brothers may be hard on me sometimes, but in the end, we've got one another's backs.

"Thanks. Now, can we get back to the party? I think we're bringing the vibe down. Besides, now that you mentioned singing..."

My brother groans, but he can't hide the smirk creeping up his face. That only makes me smile wider. And this one isn't fake.

Rule 1:
Don't fall for
the groom.

Dearest Lennox

Chapter 24
Lennox

Do you remember that little gelato shop in Positano?
You forced me to go there every day while we were in
town. And while the flavors were dream-worthy, don't
think I didn't catch you staring dreamily at the little
chapel in the square, watching bride after bride marry
her sweetheart. When I asked if you'd ever thought
about your own wedding, you looked me dead in the eye,
chin held high, and told me you were never getting
married. Despite your defiance and the fire in your
eyes, I saw beneath the mask. I saw the hurt girl
who couldn't imagine marrying anyone but the boy whose
heart she broke.

I FOLD up my grandmother's letter again and stick it in my purse as Millie steps out of the dressing room to a chorus of *oh my god*s.

My heart aches at the sight of her. Millie Hall was meant to be a bride. She's more beautiful than every one of those brides my grand-mother and I saw in Positano. Millie is only trying on wedding dresses, makeup free and her curly hair pulled up in a bun, and yet she outshines even my most bittersweet memories.

"This is *the one*," Sara squeals as Liv, Beckett's wife, fixes the train. The sight of the three of them chatting has my throat burning. Each one is married or engaged to one of Aiden's brothers, and they're incredibly close, just like the guys are.

Millie only invited the three of us today. She said her mother would only make it about her. I'm proud of her for knowing her boundaries and implementing them when it comes to the toxic people in her life. I've been keeping my parents at arm's length for years, yet Millie seems more at peace with her decision than I've ever been with mine. Maybe I'm still hoping that one day, my mother will change. That she'll be more like my grandmother—a woman who cared more about me than what I could do for her.

I'm here because I'm Millie's wedding planner, but I wish she'd invited me because I was truly one of the Langfield girls like Sara and Liv. Isn't that a crazy thought, though? They've been nothing but inclusive, and yet I'm on the outside, harboring this sense of longing that makes me want to cry.

"Hockey Daddy is going to lose his mind when he sees you," I say, standing up and swallowing all my insecurities.

Liv laughs. "Hockey Daddy?"

"You don't call Beckett Baseball Daddy?" I tease.

Sara and Liv fall into fits of giggles.

"Could you even imagine?" Sara shakes her head.

Liv twists her lips to the side, her dark eyes dancing. "He prefers Mr. Langfield in the bedroom."

"Oh my god!" Sara screams.

A maniacal laugh bubbles out of me, and Millie shakes with laughter in her gorgeous dress.

Liv merely shrugs. I love how obsessed Beckett is with her. Like me, she's got curves for days and if anyone so much as glances at Liv's, the man looks ready to tear their eyes out.

"What about you, Sar? Does Brookie have a preferred name?" I tease. "Maybe glitter dick?"

Her eyes gleam in challenge. "I don't know, *Lex*. Have you taken Aiden's bedazzled appendage for a ride yet?"

Asshole, using not only Aiden's nickname for me but also taunting me over what has now become my obsession. A bunch of the guys on the team have sparkly peens, and it's killing me not knowing whether that includes Aiden.

Though trepidation over what's going on between Aiden and me swirls with curiosity over the peen situation, I sniff and play it cool. "We're brand-spanking new, and I'm not a hussy, so no, I haven't seen Aiden's anything yet."

Sara eyes me. "He gave you an orgasm, though, didn't he?"

I suck in a harsh breath. What the fuck?

"With his fingers." She beams, so damn proud of herself.

Squealing, Millie bounces, the fabric of her dress rustling. "Oh my god, she's using your magic against you."

She most certainly is. How, though? I possess a special talent that involves sensing the details of my friends' sex lives. It's weird, but I'm irrationally proud of it and annoyed that Sara has turned it on me.

"In public," she adds in a damning tone.

That bitch.

Liv laughs. "What is happening?"

Sara tosses her blond hair proudly. "Oh, just giving my bestie a taste of her own medicine. Was I right?"

With a roll of my eyes, I look away.

"Oh my god, she was? Tell us everything," Millie prods, hopping off the raised platform in front of the mirror.

And that's how I end up telling the three Langfield girls (that's what I've nicknamed them, so deal with it) the story of how Aiden gave me the best orgasm of my life and then refused to let me return the favor.

"This is weird," I whisper as Sara practically drags me up the steps of Liv and Beckett's brownstone. After Millie said yes to the dress and we all teared up, the four of us went for cocktails down by the seaport. While we were there, Beckett texted Liv, informing her that his brothers had come over to hang with the kids while we were out and they were now ordering dinner. Of course it was a given that Sara and Millie would head over, but me? I planned to go home, but Liv insisted I come. So now here I am, about to walk into my fake boyfriend's brother's house, to spend a Sunday night with his family.

I need another cocktail. Or ten.

"Will you stop being weird?" she mutters. Without giving me even a second to collect myself, she throws the front door open and strides in, expecting I'll follow her.

"Hands up! And no quick movements." A kid sporting a fro points a Nerf gun at me as I cross the threshold.

"I'll protect you," Aiden booms as he flies through the air in front of us, coming to rest at my feet. He blinks up at me from the floor, face sweating and eyes filled with wonder. "Hey, Lex."

"Finn, my man, let's try to keep my star player from getting hurt before the season starts, please," Gavin groans as he appears in the hallway carrying his nine-month-old daughter. He ruffles the rambunctious kid's hair and assesses Sara and me. "Where's Peaches?"

I can't help the smile that forms. "Missing your bride already?"

"Always," he says, not even trying to hide his affection for her.

Aiden tugs on my ankle and hits me with a devilish grin.

My core clenches as an image of him looking up at me the other night as he put my shoes on hits. And when a memory of how he touched me last night surfaces, my heart takes off. Shit. I haven't seen or spoken to him since, so I'm glad to see he's still acting so...*hmm how is he acting?*

Flirty? Yeah. He seems back to normal after his jealous insanity.

Not that I exactly hated the fallout from the jealousy.

A teasing smile stretches across his face. Clearly, I've been making googly eyes at my fake man friend for too long. "You gonna help me up, Princess?"

That nickname does it again. My core clenches, and I silently scold my kitty, warning her that she'll be having no playtime. The bitch needs to stand down.

Instead, she purrs and arches her back. The ole girl wants more attention.

I wiggle my foot out of his grasp. "Pretty sure you can help yourself, Hockey Boy."

Aiden grins like he can read all my dirty thoughts. *Ass.*

"Didn't think I'd see you so soon, Lex. Miss me so much you've taken to stalking me?" He jumps up like a human Gumby, practically swaying to his feet.

He's wearing his typical Bolts blue shirt and a pair of jeans. It's unfair how good this man wears a shirt. The perfect way it stretches across his muscles makes me dizzy with need.

"I'm not stalking you. I was dress shopping with the girls when Liv got the call from Beckett, and then she invited me."

He tilts in close, causing the curls on top of his head to fall forward. The urge to yank them is irrational, but I fist my hands to keep from acting on the insanity.

"I'm glad you're here." Then, without warning, his lips are on mine.

When I stand, frozen in place, and don't return the kiss, he bites my bottom lip.

"Relax," he murmurs against my mouth. "We're supposed to be a couple, remember? Play with me, Princess."

Right. I'm *allowed* to kiss him. *Allowed* to want him. Okay, maybe not the last thing, but no one has to know how much I'm truly enjoying this fake relationship, right?

So I kiss him back. And I enjoy it. Melding my lips to his. Licking at the seam of them until he opens and kisses me deeply, making my toes curl and my kitty pulse.

"That's not Auntie Jill." The words are like a record player scratch. I immediately pull back and suck in one harsh breath after another.

Wearing that damn infectious smile of his, Aiden wraps an arm around me and spins me so I'm facing the pint-sized troublemaker. He's lowered his Nerf gun to his side and is studying us with skeptical brown eyes.

"You're right. It's not. This is Lennox. My girlfriend. Lex, this is Liv's son, Finn." There's no hesitation, no sugarcoating. Aiden's voice is strong, and he doesn't squirm, even as the little guy tilts his head, clearly preparing his next zinger.

Fortunately, Millie opens the door behind us, and Finn's attention is diverted. "Princess Peaches is here." He runs straight for her at an unnatural speed.

Millie must be used to this kind of welcome, because she drops down and holds out her arms an instant before the kid crashes into her.

Like he's been summoned with a cowbell, Gavin reappears and steamrolls past us all. As he approaches Millie, he holds out his hand, and she grins at him from the floor.

She straightens, and then she's reaching for Vivi.

Gavin grabs her chin and forces her attention to him. "Missed you, Peaches."

She winks. "Missed you too, Coach. Was she good for ya?"

He leans in, presses a kiss to her lips, then replies quietly.

Aiden pinches my side, startling me. My face heats. Shit. He totally caught me staring at his brother's little family longingly. But how could I not? It's so heartwarming to see Millie get everything she deserves. When I met her a few months ago, she was playing coy, swearing she didn't want Hockey Daddy, but I knew all along this was how the three of them were meant to be. A family.

My smile is wobbly when I turn to Aiden.

His responding one is gentle. "Can I get you a drink?"

"A water would be good."

The two cocktails with the girls were enough. Clearly, they've brought too many emotions to the surface. Tonight, I need to stay grounded, and when I'm around Aiden, I need all the help I can get to keep my feet firmly planted in reality and not up in the clouds where he lives. The fantasies he's concocting of princesses getting their happily ever afters are beautiful, but they're exactly that, fantasies.

Aiden plants a kiss to my forehead, and that feels more intimate than any touch we've shared. "I'm glad you're here," he says again, as if he's reinforcing those words. Like he knows I need to hear them.

I'm wanted. Even if our relationship is fake, he wants me around.

As he disappears into the kitchen, I focus on breathing steadily, allowing that thought to settle my nerves.

The peace is broken quickly, though, when I'm hit square in the head with a Nerf bullet.

Half an hour later, we're seated in the dining room with every takeout option available laid out before us.

"Want some fried rice with your pizza?" Aiden asks as he slides a slice onto my plate.

"Beckett, you know the rules. No phones at the dinner table," Liv says, arching a brow at him.

Beside her, Beckett growls. "Believe me, I'd love to not have to deal with this right now."

"Deal with what?" Gavin asks as he makes a plate for Millie.

She's got Vivi on her lap. Beckett and Liv's baby girls are sleeping, and Finn and his little sister Addie are set up in the playroom with trays. After Finn hit me in the face with the bullet, Liv declared that the adults needed a time-out from the kids.

I've been told they have an older sister, but she hasn't come out of her room.

Secretly, I'm thankful. I like kids well enough, but navigating this fake relationship in front of the adults in Aiden's life is hard enough. Kids are too damn perceptive and ask the important questions—like what the hell happened to Jill?

Though I guess telling Finn that she was a conniving, cheating, awful woman with a big nose probably wouldn't have gone over well with Liv and Beckett.

It's a good thing the kid didn't ask me, because that's what I would have said.

Liv holds up her hand. "No talking business at the dinner table. We have rules, people."

Grasping her hand, Beckett gives it a squeeze. "Sorry, Livy."

She takes a deep breath and sips her wine. "It's fine."

Gavin clears his throat and turns his attention on me. "How are things going on the wedding planning front?"

A little burst of excitement hits me, making it impossible not to bounce a little in my chair. "So good. Millie found her dress today. Your venues are all set. The cake—" My heart lurches. Oh no. The cake. Cringing, I turn to Aiden. "Oh, shoot. I forgot to ask since Aiden is no longer the one getting married—should we stick with the white cake with peach filling or was that disgusting concoction all Jill?"

Sara snorts and Brooks grumbles, dropping his head into his hand.

Millie, mouth agape, scoffs. "It's because Gavin calls me Peaches."

Oh shit.

"I'm sorry. It's probably delicious." The glare I fix Aiden with is icy, even as my face flames. "I just assumed—"

Aiden covers my hand with his and squeezes. "You assumed wrong. I took one look at you and ended it with Jill. Like I told you—from the beginning, we were planning a wedding for them." He nods across the table, but his eyes never leave mine.

"Aw, that really is the sweetest," Liv says.

Beckett puffs up, his dress shirt straining over his solid chest. "We Langfields really are the swooniest, Livy."

Sara coughs out a laugh again. "Permission to make fun of you since we aren't at work?"

"Permission not granted," Beckett grumbles.

"Dammit."

The whole group is laughing when Beckett's phone buzzes again.

"*Beckett*," Liv hisses.

He picks up the phone and holds it out in front of him as he powers it down. "It's not my fault. Hannah is about ready to murder my rookie, and I'm sure there are others standing in line to join her."

"What did Jasper do now?" Gavin asks.

"What hasn't he done?" After a hefty sip of wine, Liv shakes her head. "He was caught with the two strippers last week. The week before that, a woman claimed he fathered her child—"

"She was seventy. She couldn't possibly be pregnant," Sara interjects. "It was bull."

Beckett nods. "The point is that the kid needs a tight leash."

Across from me, Gavin gives a thoughtful nod. "That's why the younger guys on my team live in my building. They aren't getting away with shit."

Sara points finger guns at him. "Nope. We're there to lay down the law."

Chuckling, Brooks cups her hands and lowers them. "Sar, no finger guns."

"No, wait. That's a great idea," Beckett says slowly.

Sara raises them again, making her finger guns dance. "They are very docile fingers. Just ask your brother."

Brooks groans. "How many times have we discussed that we don't talk about sex with my brothers?"

Sara shrugs. "And yet you asked me to marry you? Who's the fool here?"

I can't help but giggle quietly at the way they all interact.

"No," Beckett says, steering the conversation back on track. "The apartment. What's going on with your place now that you're living with Brooks?"

Sara's expression sobers. "Lennox is staying there now."

"I can move out," I offer, shifting uncomfortably in my chair. I shouldn't have been squatting in the apartment in the first place, and now this is just awkward.

Aiden squeezes my thigh. "No way. You have it decorated exactly as you like it."

The grin Sara directs my way is evil. Shit. It's impossible to be prepared for what she might say, especially when she looks like that. "Why don't you put the new guy in War's old place, and Aiden can move in with Lennox?"

Eyes narrowed, I shoot daggers at her. "What?"

Beckett shakes his head. "That's okay. We'll find somewhere else."

Gavin rests his elbows on the table and clasps his hands, pressing them against his mouth. "I think this is a great idea."

Liv snorts, the bun on top of her head bobbing. "You would."

"What's that supposed to mean?" Millie asks, scanning the group. "Am I missing something?"

"Oh, just that Gavin likes to force people to move in together when they aren't ready," Beckett huffs out, glaring at his next youngest brother.

Aiden throws an arm around my shoulder and pulls me close. "Well, that's not us, is it, Lex? We're ready for it all. So sure, I'll move in with my girl, and Jasper can have War's old place."

"You sure?" Gavin asks, his tone full of challenge. "If it's not that serious, you can always get your own place—*not* in the hockey building. Lord knows I pay you enough."

"It's serious," Aiden counters.

I stomp on his foot and twist my heel. What the hell is this guy thinking?

"So serious," he doubles down, hiding a grimace of pain by bringing my hand to his mouth and pressing a kiss to it. "Right, Princess?"

Butterflies flutter in my stomach, even as it sinks. What the hell am I supposed to say to that?

There's only one thing I can say if we want to keep up this ruse. So with a lump lodged in my throat, I whisper, "Right."

Sensing that I'm desperate for a topic change, Millie claps once, garnering the attention of the group.

Gavin fixes his focus on her, his expression oozing affection.

"Sara, Liv," she says, "I was hoping you would agree to be my bridesmaids."

"Really?" Sara squeaks, her eyes welling with tears.

Millie nods. "You'll be my sisters, and I've never had sisters."

"Me neither," Liv replies, swiping at her own misty eyes. "But I'm so happy I'll have you both."

"I want to ask Winnie to be a junior bridesmaid," Millie says.

Beckett wraps an arm around his wife and presses a kiss to her shoulder. The move makes the ache inside me grow. This is just so beautiful.

"That's really sweet," Liv says. "Maybe that'll cheer her up enough to get her out of her room." She lets out a soft sigh. "She's only eleven, and I'm already dreading the teenage years." She's focused on me, likely because everyone else in the room knows Winnie, and I don't.

"I don't miss that age at all," I admit.

Sara lets out a loud sob and clutches her chest. "Me neither."

"Why are you crying?" Millie asks.

"I've never had a sister either," Sara says, hiccupping, and tips her head toward me. "Other than this one. Thank you, Millie. I'd love to be a bridesmaid."

"Perfect." Millie's soft smile grows wide. "For your first duty as bridesmaid, I need you to say yes to my next request."

"Whatever you want, it's yours." Sara bobs her head, her tears replaced with determination. "Even if it's getting this guy to dance at your bachelorette party. He's got a glittery dick, so I can understand why you'd prefer to watch him shake it rather than your fiancé."

"Crazy girl," Brooks bellows, throwing himself back in his chair, his arms tossed in the air.

Gavin roughs a hand down his face. "My penis doesn't need glitter. It happens to work just fine."

Chuckling, Beckett shakes his head. "Thank god we had the kids eat in the other room."

Millie bites her lip to keep from laughing, her eyes dancing.

"Tell them I don't need glitter to keep you happy," Gavin grits out.

With a roll of her eyes, Millie says, "This Langfield brother keeps me more than satisfied." Turning to Sara, she tempers her expression. "What I need from you, Sara, is Lennox."

"Hmm." Sara surveys me for a second and shrugs. "If you'd prefer Lennox dance for us, I could get behind that. Her ass is spectacular. I was just telling her the other day that I'd do her."

"Crazy girl." Brooks covers his face with both hands.

In response, she flutters her lashes and presses a kiss to his cheek. "I'm sorry, Saint. Even your sparkly peen doesn't get me going like her ass does in pink spandex."

Liv shakes beside Beckett, who's got his head tipped back and his eyes closed. "Your future wife is something else," he tells Brooks.

"You hired me." Sara winks at him. "And, according to you, we have you to thank for getting us together."

"What do you need from me?" I ask Millie, steering this runaway train back on track.

Wearing a pensive frown, she looks from Vivi to me. "I was hoping you'd agree to be in my wedding."

My heart pangs as I shake my head. "You don't have to include me just because I'm here tonight. They're family. I get it."

"That's not why I'm asking." She takes an uneven breath and forges on. "You were my first friend when I moved to Boston. I'd only ever been seen as Daniel's sister or Ford's daughter or Gavin's—"

"*Mine.*" The man himself grins.

"I was going to say girlfriend, but yeah, I guess that fits."

He presses a kiss to her head with so much tenderness, I can't help but tear up at the sight.

Millie turns back to me. "But you were my friend just for me."

Nodding, I blink back tears, though the effort is futile. They won't stop. Aiden squeezes my thigh beneath the table.

"So, will you be my maid of honor?" Millie's golden eyes are so hopeful and pure as she asks.

My heart bursts, and tears streak down my face as I nod. "Of course I will."

"Since I'm obviously the best man," Beckett says, "Aiden will have to walk my wife down the aisle." He looks pointedly at the man beside me. "No funny business."

His warning is full of so much heat, my tears turn to giggles. The man is unhinged for his wife. I love it.

"Who says you're the best man?" Aiden counters, crossing his arms over his chest.

Beckett tilts his head, unimpressed. "Please, I'm the match-maker. Not only did I help cover for Gavin and Millie while they hid their damn relationship, but I got the ball rolling for Vivi's adoption."

Gavin nods, his expression solemn. "Sorry, bro. Gotta side with Beckett on this one."

Huffing, Aiden spins to Brooks. "If I'm not your best man, I'll never speak to you again."

Beckett leans forward, his chair creaking beneath him. "I'm the one who stepped in when Gavin almost fired Sara. I even hugged him when he was down and out and worried he'd lose her."

"I *hug*." Aiden slaps the table, making the silverware rattle.

Everyone at the table laughs.

"Listen, we haven't even set a date," Brooks says, pulling Sara close. "But as soon as we do, I'll accept applications for the position."

Laughter echoes around the room, and as we all settle down, the guys launch into a conversation about the current baseball season and then the upcoming hockey season.

Despite how nervous I am at the prospect of Aiden moving in with me, this is one of the best nights I've had in a long time.

CHAPTER 25
AIDEN

"WHY IS MARIO WEARING A RACCOON COSTUME?" I shout over my shoulder.

There's an oversized Super Mario Figurine in the refrigerator. The guy even has raccoon eyes. *Cool.*

"The better question is why is there a Mario in your fridge, Beckett?" Gavin appears in the kitchen doorway, laden with food containers.

The girls are in the living room with a bottle of wine, giggling over the bridesmaid dresses they're perusing on Liv's laptop, so we offered to clean up dinner.

With one hand on the fridge door, I spin to face Gavin. "That's obvious. To protect the orange soda."

Brooks chuckles. "Only you would understand the inner workings of a six-year-old."

"I'm seven, Uncle Brooks," Finn declares.

Crouching to his level, I hold out a fist. "What's with the costume, little dude?"

Finn bumps his knuckles against mine. "It's our week with Junior and the babies."

Beckett's got both hands splayed on the island, his face drawn.

It's got to be exhausting taking care of two infants, an eleven-year-old, a five-year-old, and Finn. The boy on his own is a full-time job. "We share custody of the racoons with Delia and Enzo."

I nod. When Beckett married Liv, she and her three best friends were living in a brownstone down the street, along with a whole horde of kids, so Beckett moved in. They discovered a raccoon living in the house, and Finn declared it his pet. Since my brother is a softie when it comes to the kid—his whole family, really—he created an entire space for the raccoon. Shortly after, they found out the racoon was pregnant, so now they have four racoons. And apparently, they're staying here this week.

Beckett may be crazier than all of us. Though he's currently in the running for my favorite person. The way he forced Lennox and me into living together was nothing short of perfection. Sure, Gavin pushed for it—but it was Beckett's exasperation with his new first baseman that encouraged Lennox to say yes. It's clear my brother has a lot going on—five kids, a baseball team, four raccoons, and his self-declared matchmaking title—who could say no to the guy?

I can't get ahead of myself. Until my Luigi figurine is protecting my coffee milk in Lennox's fridge—listen, it's a great idea; don't judge —she could easily change her mind.

But once I've placed my last pair of socks in a drawer in her bedroom, she'll never get rid of me. I'll koala myself to her and hold on tight until she can do nothing but agree to keep me. I'm cute like a koala, so it *should* work.

"They're here?" I ask Beckett. I haven't seen them in weeks.

He sighs heavily. "Take him to the backyard, Finn."

With a smile, I take the little guy's hand and let him lead me outside. No washing dishes for me tonight. *Suckers.*

Finn and I spend forty-five minutes with the raccoons. These aren't ordinary outdoor raccoons. They do tricks. They dance. They're ducking awesome.

Finn's words, not mine.

Immediately after that comment, he pleaded with me not to tell Bossman.

When we finally come inside, the girls are wrapping up.

Lennox hauls herself off the couch, carefully keeping her gaze averted. As always, she's a flash of pink, brightening the dark wood and dark couch behind her. She's wearing a white and pink wrap dress that cinches her waist and accentuates the ass Sara was going on about at dinner. She's right. My girl's curves are delectable.

I stalk toward her, my movements slow, my intention clear.

"Can you give me a ride home?" Lennox asks Sara.

Sara eyes her best friend and then glances at me. "I figured you'd ride back with Aiden. You know, *your boyfriend?*"

With her lip caught between her teeth, Lennox nods. "Right, of course."

When I reach her, I don't even attempt to hide my knowing smirk. She's nervous about being alone with me.

The question is why.

"You ready to go, Lex?" I tug her close and bury my face in her neck. "Nervous about being alone with your fake boyfriend?" I murmur.

She pulls back and rolls her eyes. "Of course not. I just forgot."

I give her a mock disapproving look. She's so full of it. "You forgot you're mine?"

"You're annoying," she mumbles.

"Mommy says Bossman is annoying in that same tone." Finn stands with his hands on his waist, assessing us. "Then she tells him if he doesn't stop, he'll be sleeping in the doghouse."

"We both know how much I love Deogi," I say, crouching to meet Finn's eye.

My brother's ninety-pound mastiff. When he was a puppy,

Beckett thought he was a mut. Now that he's full grown, the dog is the size of a horse, and he slobbers like it's no one's business, so tonight he's outside with the raccoons.

"You want to sleep over here, Uncle Aiden? Mommy always says she'll be over it by the morning."

Behind me, the girls laugh.

It takes a lot of restraint to keep from joining in. From where I'm squatted beside Finn, I look up at Lennox. "You gonna make me sleep with the dog tonight?"

She rolls her lips together, fighting a smile, but it's no use. Her beautiful face lights up and splits into the biggest grin. "No. I suppose you can come home."

Finn bumps his shoulder with mine and cups a hand over his mouth. "If she changes her mind, you know where I live."

I maintain my best serious face and nod. "Thanks, Huck. See you soon."

"So that was something," I say as I pull out onto the road, desperate to fill the silence on the drive home and incredibly anxious now that we're alone.

"We can't really move in together."

My head whips in her direction.

"Aiden, watch the road."

"Then don't say ridiculous things."

"Ridiculous?" she asks in an almost teasing tone. God, I'd like to turn and look at her. See if she's actually smiling. I keep my eyes on the road, though, because if she is smiling, I won't be able to look away. "What's ridiculous is moving in together when we're fake dating. We barely know one another anymore."

"You want to get to know me better?" I can work with that.

"*Aiden.*"

There she goes with that scolding tone again. It makes my dick twitch. I love riling her up.

"Yes, princess? You want to get to know me? How about we play a few rounds of Never Have I Ever? We can clear out the cobwebs real quick."

"Be serious." Even as she says it, I hear the smile in her voice.

"Oh, I'm incredibly serious. I don't joke about Never Have I Ever. It's sacred."

We pull up to a light, and I finally get my fill of her. She's got her head tipped back against the headrest and turned in my direction. Tendrils of pink glow around her face from the outside lights, and she's smiling. Fucking glowing. I love her like this.

I'd love her even if she was yelling at me, but this? This is so good.

"Never Have I Ever is sacred," she agrees, her teeth sinking into her bottom lip. "Okay, fine. Never have I ever played hockey."

I chuckle as the light changes and return my focus to the road. "You trying to turn this into a game of strip poker, Lex?" I eye her quickly. "Because I can be down for that."

Her lips pop open, her eyes going comically wide. "No! I was just playing the game. Telling you something about myself that feels pretty damn relevant for a boyfriend who plays hockey for a living."

I shrug. "Just saying, seems like you're trying to get me naked."

She laughs. "Fine. There's another one. Never have I ever played strip poker."

"Me neither. Look at that, the game is working. We're getting to know one another again."

Once again, I sneak a glance at her.

She's giving me a coy smile. "Yeah."

"Okay, I'll go. Never have I ever seen a ghost."

"Oh, I totally did!" she squeals.

"Seriously? Fuck, I'm so jealous. When?"

"Sara and I went up to Salem in college. She was so excited to do the whole *Hocus Pocus* thing since she's a movie freak."

"Right," I agree. If there's one thing to know about Sara, it's that she loves pop culture and lazy days on her couch, introducing friends to movies or TV shows they've never seen.

"So I found this gorgeous old house. She was so excited that we could afford such a cool Airbnb. I didn't tell her until we turned the lights off to go to bed that it was because the owner was murdered in the house and he liked to play with the guests at night."

I practically choke on air. "What? You *'played'* with a ghost?"

Irrational as it is, the idea of her playing with anyone makes me angry. Jealousy over Ryder was bad enough. Now I'm fucking ready to fight a ghost.

"*Aiden.*"

"I'm not sure why you're Aiden-ing me. You're the kinky one." I huff out a breath as I shake my head. "Playing with ghosts."

She giggles, and the sound does something to me. Makes me light-headed. Who the hell needs to drink when he's got the girl of his dreams by his side laughing? Greatest thing in the world.

"I've got to be a better roommate than a ghost," I tease her.

She snorts. "You're absurd."

"My game is pretty good, though, right? Now we know that you're a girl who can't play hockey, you like playing cruel jokes on your friends, and you're kinky as fuck. We're a match made in heaven."

Her laughter gets louder. "Yeah, I like this game."

My shoulders grow even more loose as I settle into our easy banter. "I like it too."

And I really like you. That's what I want to say. *God, Lex, I really fucking like you.*

"How's planning for Josie's party going?" I ask, desperate to keep myself from admitting my true feelings. It's too soon. She'll run for the hills and marry fucking Ryder instead.

"Pretty good. Just waiting on Millie to make a call."

"To Lake?"

Every little girl in America is obsessed with Lake Paige, who just so happens to be married to Millie's dad. My guess is the girls want Lake to sign merch for Josie. Even I'm a superfan of the pop icon, so I can imagine an eight-year-old would be obsessed with anything she'd send over.

"Actually, Melina Rodriguez. Lake swears Mel would be happy to come and maybe even sing with Josie."

I shoot Lennox a quick grin before focusing on the road again. "That's amazing, Lex."

Mel is Lake's best friend, as well as a pop star. She's just as incredible as Lake, even if she doesn't have quite the same following. But who does? Lake's fame is on a level I'm pretty sure our generation has never seen. She's as big as the Beatles. I have no doubt girls all over the world cried when she announced that she was taking a break from performing to have a baby, and she wasn't sure when she'd be coming back.

"Yeah, it would be a great surprise. Outside of that, we've got everything set for a pink party in the park."

With a chuckle, I side-eye her. "You are certainly the perfect person to be in charge of that kind of party."

Her gorgeous lips pop open in faux shock. "Are you talking crap about my favorite color?"

I shake my head. "Absolutely not. I love the way you look in pink. Especially when it's a flush on your skin caused by an orgasm I give you."

Squeezing her thighs together, she lets out a soft sigh. "*Aiden.*"

"Hmm?" As the light ahead turns red and I stop, I give her my full attention.

"You can't talk like that."

"That's a pity, because I don't plan to stop."

The light turns green, and I rev the engine. As the car jolts forward, Lennox laughs so freely, my heart does a little tap dance.

Rule 1:
Don't fall for
the groom.

Dearest Lennox

Chapter 26
Lennox

WHILE MY COFFEE PERCOLATES, I pull up my morning playlist and turn on my Bluetooth speaker. For years, I've started my days the same way: dancing around my apartment naked. I can't say I don't get a sick satisfaction out of knowing that my parents would lose their minds if they had even an inkling about what I was doing. And letting my girls hang free while I jam out to Melina, Lake, or Taylor? Heaven.

As I jiggle my sweet booty to the music, I really get down with my bad self. Pretty soon, I'll only get to do this when Aiden is traveling.

It's still unreal. The man is moving into my apartment.

I'm *marrying* him.

And he gave me a freaking orgasm I can't stop thinking about.

God, I wish he'd given me another last night. Instead, he walked me to the door like a gentleman, said "Night Lex," and winked before walking off, leaving me too stunned to speak.

My first instinct was to shout after him, but how could I, when I'm the one who warned him not to get too attached?

Regardless of how unsatisfied I was when I got home, I slept well. Thank god for that, because I'm meeting my father and Ryder for lunch to discuss Seven's tour and to hopefully confirm that they'll play at the Kingston wedding. After I'm finished there, I've got a few last-minute errands to run for Josie's birthday party.

A loud *thump, thump, thump* on the door has me jumping and snatching the robe I keep hanging from the coat rack.

Cinching the pink silk around my waist, I saunter to the door and open it wide, expecting to find Millie. It wouldn't be the first time she's stopped by to ask me to turn it down. Little does she know I turn it up extra loud so she'll come and hang out with me.

It's hard getting time with her now that the Bolts are in the offseason and Gavin isn't traveling. The man keeps her locked in the bedroom—and when she's not being used as his sex toy, she's busy being a mom.

Oddly, it sounds like a perfect little life to me.

"Oh sugarsnap. You're not Millie."

Aiden is dressed in a pair of navy-blue shorts and a Bolts shirt—of course—and he's wearing a confused frown. "Sugarsnap?"

I wave and pull the door open farther so he can come in. "I'm trying something new. I'm not crazy about the duck thing."

Chuckling, he roughs a hand through his messy curls. "Why not just 'oh sugar'?"

I shrug. "It's not enough to get the aggression out, ya know?"

Aiden purses his lips and nods, like he actually gets my insanity. "That's what I said about duck."

With a shake of my head, I pad to the kitchen. "Want a cup of coffee?"

"I stopped by to see if you wanted to join me in the gym."

Coffeepot in hand, I finally take a moment to appreciate the fine-ass specimen that is Aiden Langfield. (Sorry, sugarsnap doesn't work there. I'm telling you, this not cursing thing is a challenge).

His shirt stretches perfectly across his taut chest, but my real weakness is his damn calf muscles. It's got to be the skating. No one on this earth has calves as tempting as this man's.

They're sculpted and pretty. And I don't say it lightly. They're beautiful.

The idea of watching him flex them while he works out? Of bearing witness to the way he'll bend over, causing his calf muscle to protrude even farther? I'd probably fall off the treadmill or drool so much that he'd slip in it, and then I'd be blamed for breaking NHL's golden boy. No thank you.

"I'll pass," I say evenly rather than admitting to the possibility of a drooling disaster.

"Nervous to spend time overheated and sweating beside me?" he challenges, a cocky smirk spreading across his face. "Because as room-mates, we're going to have to share a bed, and things tend to get *hot*"—he practically bites the air when he says the word—"when I'm in bed."

Spinning away from him, I pour coffee into my favorite pink mug. "Obsessed with yourself much?"

"Someone's gotta be."

I've got my head stuck inside the fridge when his words hit me. Does Aiden not know how adored he is? How much his family loves him? How he lights up any room he enters?

I snag the can of whipped cream and straighten, aiming it at my coffee, sweetening it up just like I like it.

Aiden drags his gaze up as I turn toward him. Busted. He was very clearly staring at my ass.

"So gym?" he asks again.

I bring the coffee to my lips slowly. "I recently learned that it takes fourteen muscles to lift a cup of coffee to one's mouth." I wink. "Getting all my fitness right here."

His responding laugh shudders through me. "Come on, Lex. Drink your coffee and then come work out with me. You used to love to come to the gym with me."

"Yeah, because I liked staring at you. You're very pretty to look at."

Propping himself up against the counter on the other side of the kitchen, he waggles his brows. "I'm even prettier now. And I dance between sets. I know how you feel about dancing."

Dammit. I *do* love dancing.

"You can even bring your coffee," he cajoles. "And we can play another round of Never Have I ever." He waggles his brows. "Ya know, get to know one another even better so we're more prepared next time we're in front of one of our family members."

The man slathers it on like butter on a biscuit. My biscuit. And dammit if I don't want to have my biscuit and to eat it too.

"Fine, but only if you promise to do extra squats."

Aiden gives me a thorough once-over. It's only then that I realize how very naked I am beneath the fuchsia silk. "Baby, I'll squat all you want."

My cheeks are likely the shade of my robe, and there's not a whole lot I can do about that. I push him toward the door. "Okay, Hockey Boy. I'll get dressed and meet you down there."

After I take a cold shower.

Where I'll definitely be spending time with my dildo, because, oh sugar daddy, this girl is horny.

Yeah, sugar daddy doesn't work either.

When I walk into the gym, Mariah Carey's "Fantasy" is blasting, and Aiden is lunging across the length of the gym like he owns the place.

When he spots me in the mirror, he purses his lips, his eyes narrowing. In one quick move, he does a jumping spin, and then he stalks toward me, shimmying his shoulders to the beat as he makes up his own lyrics just like he did long ago when he'd drive around with me in the passenger seat. We'd cruise with no location in mind, laughing and singing.

"Oh, when you stalk me every day

Tell me no, then say okay,
My heart goes pitter patter this way,
Mmm, Princess, you're so into me
And if you'd only agree
We could make a sweet symphony,

He steps into my space, his muscles already glistening, his hair damp.

It's not only a—"

I slap a hand to his mouth before he can finish Mariah Carey's line.

"You wish," I say, though there's no fighting the smile that splits my face.

The grin beneath my palm is just as wide, and his eyes dance. Instantly, I'm lost in them, falling into their depths, floating through memory after memory. The songs he'd sing to me, even while we made love.

He nips at my palm, startling me out of my reverie.

Sucking in a sharp breath, I pull back like I've been singed. He's clearly trying to relight the spark between us, so maybe I have. I wish he'd stop. I don't want him to get hurt.

"You going to do reps with me?" Why does every single word out of his mouth sound so seductive? Or is it me? Is it all in my head?

I point at the treadmill. "I'll be over there."

Aiden smirks. "Perfect. That was my next stop."

I can't help the aggravated huff that escapes me. Why is he determined to be so close to me? Doesn't he get that this is a bad idea?

Trying my best to ignore him—which is no easy feat—I step onto the treadmill and set the speed to 3.5.

When the man steps up behind me and rests his hand on my hips, I practically purr. It takes all the self-control I have, but I fight the urge and instead adopt a frustrated tone. "What are you doing?"

"Working out with you," he murmurs into my ear.

"*Aiden.*"

His voice is teasing, his breath tickling my neck. "Yes, Princess?"

I press my ear to my shoulder, forcing his head away. "You're going to get hurt."

He chuckles, his chest vibrating against my back. "You could turn this all the way to the highest setting, and we'd be fine."

I snort. "Thinking pretty highly of yourself again, I see."

"It's called confidence. I'm confident I can keep up. Confident you'll be the first to break."

I suck in a deep breath, and despite my better judgment, I crank the speed up. When it's at 6.5, I'm panting and close to death. Behind me, Aiden strides easily, miraculously not tripping me and still holding my hips. How is he moving his legs so fast without using his arms?

It's probably those damn perfect calves. They're keeping us both going.

"I could do this all day, or you could stop so we can grab lunch and just talk," he sings in my ear. It's to the tune of "Blank Space" by Taylor Swift. I swear to god the man lives in song.

And every time he does it, I feel lighter.

I grab the red emergency tab and pull, causing the machine to come to an immediate stop.

Behind me, the cocky bastard chuckles and gives my thigh a squeeze. "Good girl."

Holy shit, I might hyperventilate. Why are those two words so fucking sexy?

I spin around and push him back, forcing him off the machine. He grins, knowing he's gotten to me.

"I've got plans. Sorry, fake fiancé."

He sticks his bottom lip out in an exaggerated pout. It's ridiculously adorable. The man *pouts* adorably. Come *on.*

Stepping up so close his scent washes over me—clean laundry and a hint of sweat—he clutches my left hand and rubs his thumb along my fourth finger.

"Guess I need to pick up a fake ring," I say, trying to ground us again.

Aiden clenches his jaw and looks from my finger to my face. "I'll handle it. What do you have planned for lunch?"

I do my best to ignore how much I enjoy his touch. "I'm meeting with my father and Ryder."

His grip tightens on my finger, and a scowl forms on his face. "Why?"

With a sigh, I deflate. Dammit. This is the perfect reminder that he won't handle this all well. I may be attracted to Aiden, but he's got feelings. They're big and beautiful, and he's more in tune with them than any man I've ever met. They just aren't directed at the right person. I can't be what he wants.

"You know why. I need to lock his band down for the Kingston wedding."

"Your father wants you to work for him. He wants to control you."

My chest tightens, but I fight the sensation and tip my chin up defiantly. "I can't be controlled."

Eyes softening, Aiden releases my hand and cups my chin instead. His thumb scrapes softly against my skin. "Good." He smiles. "Dinner, then? We can do takeout after I move in."

"You're moving in tonight?" I squeak, instantly assaulted by a flood of nerves.

"That gonna be a problem, Princess?"

There's no stopping the laugh that escapes me at his cockiness. "No problem for me. Just remember the rules, and we'll be good."

Pressing closer, he brings his mouth to my ear. "You set the rules, Princess. I'll do whatever you tell me to."

With that, he walks backward, a smile on his face, and goes back to singing "Blank Space."

Rule 1:
Don't fall for
the groom.

Dearest Lennox

Chapter 27
Lennox

Me: I'm calling an emergency meeting.

Sara: I KNEW you would freak out about the Aiden thing.

Ava: What Aiden thing?

Hannah: What did I miss?

Millie: I'm so sorry Gavin interfered last night. I told him he's not getting into this body for an entire night.

Me: Wow. Thanks for the support.

Sara: Considering she's engaged to a Langfield, that is a punishment. Believe me, holding these men back for even an hour is a full-time job. You'd know if you were really moving in with Aiden.

Hannah: Holy shit, you're moving in with Aiden?

Ava: Wait, isn't he engaged?

> Sara: Keep up. He broke the engagement off as soon as he saw Lennox again because, duh, why wouldn't he? But now they're playing some type of fake-dating game. I don't buy it.

> Millie: I think they're adorable together.

> Sara: Stop being so nice.

> Ava: Are you happy, Lennox?

I STARE DOWN at the last message as I step inside the restaurant. Despite the dread that washes over me as I prepare to meet with my father, I can't say I'm unhappy. Lately, it really does feel like I'm heading in the direction of happy. It's a little scary, since I'm also headed toward a fake marriage with my ex-boyfriend-turned-roommate.

It's delusional for me to think we can pull this off.

Then again, I am the daughter of Jackson and Tia Kennedy.

Delusional might just be my middle name.

I'm halfway across the dining room when my father stands and waves. He straightens his jacket, wearing a scowl. No doubt because my hair is still pink and my clothes are still too tight for his liking. If we're being honest, my curves are too curvy as well. At times, it's as if my entire being offends him. But no matter how much criticism I get, there's no shrinking my body into my mother's petite frame.

He should blame his side of the family, but Kennedys do no wrong.

"Hi, Daddy," I say in the most sugary-sweet voice I can muster.

He leans down and kisses my cheek, murmuring a "Hello, Princess," always keeping up appearances. Once he's pulled out my chair, he takes his own.

"I thought we discussed the hair," he says in a clipped tone, his facial expression never giving away his annoyance.

Rather than let his emotionally stunted tantrum get me down, I remain smiley and bright. "Did we? I didn't realize that what I do or don't do with any part of my body is under your purview."

"Lennox." The single word is a warning.

"Daddy." This one is a taunt. "Where's Ryder?"

With his eyes fixed on his menu, he mumbles, "He couldn't make it."

Annoyed, I scoot my chair away from the table. "Did you trick me into coming to lunch?"

My father's mask slips, and he hits me with a glower. "Didn't realize you'd only agreed to come because of Ryder."

I sigh. "That's not what I meant, and you know it."

The waitress appears, and like a pair of robots who could do this dance in our sleep, we smile and place our orders, keeping our tones polite so no one within earshot would believe we're even the slightest bit agitated with one another.

Once she's gone, my father leans back in his chair. Like he's the chairman in a boardroom—how he approaches basically every interaction in his life—he studies me. "Ryder likes you."

Keeping my expression aloof, I shrug. "I'm dating Aiden."

My father rolls his eyes. "Must I remind you of the trust provision?"

"No, Daddy." Anger bubbles hot and fierce beneath my skin, but I choke it back.

"You're not marrying that boy."

I cough out a laugh. Not that I'm actually surprised that he thinks he has that kind of power over me. "I'll marry whomever I choose." Chin lifted, I sniff. "Or not get married at all."

"Then you won't get access to your trust."

"So you've told me."

The lines on my father's face deepen. "Lennox, be reasonable. Ryder could be an excellent addition to this family. The label has been struggling since we lost Lake to Hall Records."

"You lost her because you screwed her over by refusing to renegotiate her royalties. Ford gave Lake a piece of the pie. The pie *she* brought the ingredients for, then put together and fucking baked. All you did was put it in tin and place it on a shelf. The album sold itself. Try a new tactic, *Daddy*, and maybe you won't lose out next time."

With a grunt, my father throws his napkin down. "He only did that because he wanted to sleep with her."

I sigh, weary. There's no getting through to this man. I've tried, but he's stuck in his ways, and we'll never agree. "I'm not dating Ryder so that you can turn your label around. And I most certainly won't marry him."

"All I'm asking is that you go to dinner with him tonight and talk about our label."

My heart lurches. "Dinner?" This is so like him, and my response is so me. "I can't. I have plans."

He gives me a bored look. He's not surprised by my answer. I rarely say yes. It's our thing. I say no. He makes sure I know how disappointed he is. I go home and stew over whether I said no because I didn't want to do what he asked or because I wanted to spite him. In the end, more often than not, I end up doing what he wants.

He knows he'll get his way if he doesn't push.

It's annoying.

If he pushed, I'd double down and stand my ground.

He hasn't figured out that I'm the one who makes the choice in the end. He assumes he'll always get his way.

In this case, annoyingly, I'll say yes. I need to get Ryder to agree to perform at the Kingston wedding.

But I don't have to be happy about it.

CHAPTER 28
AIDEN

Beckett: What day should I tell Jasper he can move in?

Gavin: The sooner, the better. Right, little brother? We all know how excited you are about moving in with your one true love.

Me: Ha. I'm thrilled. The guys are helping me clear out my apartment as we speak. Then we'll get War's place ready for you.

Brooks: What guys?

Me: Fitz and War.

Brooks: You're hanging out with my best friend and my coach, and you didn't invite me?

WITH A GRUNT, War lifts one side of the couch. My side is still on the floor. "You gonna help with this? There are plenty of other things I'd rather be doing today."

Fitz pokes his head out from my bedroom. "What are we doing with the bed?"

Grinning, I point to the small jar I placed next to the door. "Bed-bugs. I can take care of that, though."

Fitz lets out a howl of a laugh. "Savage."

My phone rings just like I knew it would. Laughing, I tap the speaker button.

"Since when am I not one of your boys?"

"Wow, Brooks. No need to be so desperate. I still love you."

"Seriously," he grits out. "Why are you hanging out with *my* best friend and *my* coach?"

"Because he didn't want to implicate you in this shit. Believe me, it's a good thing," War groans.

Fitz saunters into the living room, shaking his head. "I love this shit. A vindictive ex. Getting revenge. I feel like I'm on my own version of that show."

"What show?" Brooks asks.

"*Revenge*," Sara hollers in the background. "Brooks, how have you not seen *Revenge*?"

"Shit," Brooks mutters. "I know what we'll be watching tonight."

"You're a psycho," War says to me as I drop the phone to the couch so I can lift my end. "Remind me never to get on your bad side."

"That's the thing. He's the fun guy. Never underestimate the fun guy," Fitz reminds us. He was wearing his standard backward Bolts hat when we pulled into the garage but tossed it in the back seat and told us he wanted to go incognito for our little revenge plan. Dude is on my level, and I love it.

"Just get the door so we can load this onto the elevator and get it into storage before psycho Jill comes back," War grumbles.

Sara is still explaining the plot of *Revenge* to Brooks as we pick up the couch. "And then her husband figures it out, and he shoots her. You know what's really cool? They're married in real life."

"Chick is hot," War says.

"Emily Van Camp?" I nod, adjusting my grip on the underside of the sofa. "Yeah, she's pretty."

"Her husband is hot too," Fitz says from the door.

Our laughs echo around the room. "No fair that you get double the dating pool," Sara shouts, her voice tinny.

"Crazy girl, don't hit on my coach," Brooks grumbles.

Fitz smiles wide, his dimple popping. "Don't worry, Sar. I may spend hours with him every day, but your fiancé's ass has nothing on Nick Weschler's."

Over his shoulder, War asks, "Who's that?"

"Hey what's wrong with my ass?" Brooks bites out, clearly offended.

"He's the other guy on *Revenge*. It's a love triangle."

Fitz smirks. "Why have a triangle when you can have a tower?"

The cackle Sara lets out is so loud it startles me, and I fumble the couch. "No wonder he loves us, Fitz. We're the same person. Can we get drinks soon?"

Brooks's voice gets louder as he says, "We gotta go." When the call disconnects, the room goes quiet.

War nods to Fitz. "You're a troublemaker."

With an unapologetic grin, he shrugs. The man loves sex, and he's never hidden it. Doesn't bother me. While I'm a one-woman man, he's an equal opportunist, and it's rare for him to hook up with the same person twice. I like Fitz. We just want different things. I want Lennox Kennedy. I've only ever wanted Lennox Kennedy. But right now, I also want a little revenge.

"You're sure she's coming back? Because that's a really nice mattress. It would suck to infect it if she's not here to be tortured by it," Fitz worries.

"Oh, she's coming back. The woman forgot we still have a shared calendar. I have access to all the events she's put into it, and I can see where she is at all times. This week, it's *vacation with my booboo bear.*" I feign sticking my finger down my throat and make a gagging sound.

War shudders and shakes his head.

"She'll be back tomorrow," I say, walking backward toward the door. "She has dinner with the girls after her hair appointment with Sasha." Sasha comes to our apartment to do her hair. Jill was too important to go to the salon. She complained that women bothered her everywhere she went because she was dating me. *Please.* No one knew who she was when she wasn't standing next to me. But whatever. At least I know she'll be here tonight, and the bedbugs will be waiting for her.

Once, she made a dig about how Beckett's house was probably being infested with them because of his raccoons. My brother is a clean freak. I'm pretty sure Junior and her babies are cleaner than Jill. Who isn't, if she's been spending her time with fucking Vincent Lukov?

As we maneuver the couch out the door, War asks, "You coming down to the house tomorrow?"

War's hosting a barbecue, so we'll finally get to check out his new place.

"It okay if I bring Lennox?"

"Of course." He glances over his shoulder at Fitz. "You gonna bring anyone?"

Fitz shrugs and pulls the door closed behind us. "Eh, I'll see if Dec is around, but he'll probably be at the station. The guy works nonstop."

Fitz and Beckett's brother-in-law, Declan, grew up together. It's wild how small this world can be sometimes.

"I haven't seen him since Finn's first little league game," I say as we make our way down the hall.

"Yeah, guy doesn't know how to relax. I'll probably be solo, but if he's around, I'll try to talk him into coming up for the day."

"Sounds good. Make sure you bring your swimsuits. The lake is nice. If it's hot enough, we can take a swim."

We're still making our way down to the ground floor when my phone buzzes. As the word *Princess* flashes on the screen, my heart takes off.

"Princess?" War teases.

"Shut it," I tell him, itching to swipe the phone off the couch cushion and check the message.

"Things are going well?"

"We're moving in together, so I'd say so."

Fitz tosses his head back and laughs. "I heard that was a Beckett Langfield special."

War frowns. "What does that mean?"

"My brother thinks he's a matchmaker. Though this time, I'm not sure he's the one to blame. He was looking for a place for Jasper. Gavin was the one who offered up Lennox's apartment."

War chuckles. "Your brothers are crazy."

"Certifiable," Fitz agrees.

I shoot them a smirk. "You all just want to be us."

War shrugs, his expression sobering. "Truthfully, you're lucky."

He means it. War's story is tragic, and it's shaped him into who he is now.

"Don't worry, War. You're not getting rid of us. And if you're interested, I'd be happy to convince Beck to match you next."

War scoffs. "No thanks."

I turn to Fitz. "You?"

He rolls his eyes and laughs. "Yeah, that'll be the day."

I'm practically bouncing in anticipation. I forced myself to wait until we'd gotten everything out of the apartment before checking my phone. We loaded several suitcases, mostly with my things, but we grabbed some random things too, knowing she'll spend hours looking, not knowing what I actually took.

I'm not normally a petty person, but I found indescribable joy in the revenge I exacted today.

As I settle in the back seat of War's truck, I pull out my phone and finally unlock it.

> Lennox: Hey, I can't do dinner tonight after all. But I'll leave a key with Gavin and Millie so you can get your stuff moved in. I'll see you when I get home.

My mood instantly sours, and my whole body deflates. I was really looking forward to seeing her.

> Me: Okay, see you then. How did your lunch meeting go? Did Ryder agree to do the wedding?

> Lennox: Still working on it. Meeting him for dinner because he couldn't make lunch.

My stomach knots painfully. Of course the fucker missed lunch.

> Me: That's convenient. Remind him you have a boyfriend, yeah?

> Lennox: Aiden.

> Me: Yes, that's your boyfriend's name. Make sure you use it tonight.

> Lennox: Sounds like you're jealous. Which would be how a real boyfriend with real feelings would act.

Annoyance flares inside me, heating my blood.

> Me: I'm fine. I just don't like people jerking you around. Both he and your father are taking advantage of you, and I don't like it.

Three gray dots bounce on my screen, signaling that Lennox is typing. They disappear, then start again. A heartbeat after they disappear for a second time, my phone rings. *Princess* flashes across the screen, but I ignore the call. If I speak to her right now, there's a good chance that I'll say something I regret.

Long game. I'm playing the long game.

> **Me:** It's fine. I'll see you at home.

Hours later, nothing is fine.

She's still not home, and I'm pacing her apartment like a caged animal. I've color coordinated our closet. Her side is obviously mostly pink and mine is mostly blue. It looks like it belongs in my niece Addie's Barbie Dream House. When that was finished, I stared at the bed, jumped on the bed, realized the bed was a mess and remade it only to freak out thinking about how, tonight, I'll be lying beside Lennox right here.

Which brought my thoughts back to how she's currently out with fucking skinny pants. The guy who's likely trying to get into *her* pants.

So now I'm back to pacing again. Because I have excellent hearing, and I'm listening for any sound that might signal her arrival, I hear when the elevator dings down the hall. Since there are only two apartments on this floor, and Gavin and Millie were already home when I stopped in to pick up my key, there's a damn good chance it's Lennox. I throw myself onto the couch, grab the remote, and turn on the television.

When the door swings open, I glance casually over my shoulder and offer a chin nod. See? I can do casual. Easy. Not insanely jealous and color coordinating our closet like we're Barbie and Ken.

Fuck, I should probably rearrange the closet before she sees it. Once she does, she's totally going to think I'm obsessed and planning our future.

"Hey, sorry I'm so late," she says, shuffling into the room. She zeroes in on my chest before dragging her attention to my face.

Yeah, I'm in nothing but a pair of shorts—I got hot while bouncing on the bed. "Have a good night, Princess?"

In response, she licks her lips like she's parched.

I fight a smirk, but it's pointless, because my pecs do it for me. They flex and dance to the rhythm of "We Belong Together" by Mariah Carey.

Lennox's blue eyes ignite. There's no hiding the cocky smirk now.

With a huff, she shakes her head and strides toward the bedroom.

Looks like I'm not the only one desperately losing their mind.

Rule 1:
Don't fall for
the groom.

Dearest Lennox

Chapter 29
Lennox

OH, he wants to play. We'll mother-freaking play. I kick my shoes into my closet and remove each article of clothing piece by angry piece.

All night, I was tormented by the knowledge that he was in my apartment and I was at dinner, fending off pass after pass from Ryder. Because, of course, Aiden was right. The man wasn't interested in hearing my pitch for the wedding. He wanted to just "get to know" me.

I said Aiden's name more tonight than I did in the entirety of our relationship all those years ago, trying to drill into the imbecile's head that I have a boyfriend.

Fake fiancé, really. Once we get a ring. And make the announcement. But whatever. The point is, I'm a taken woman.

Ryder didn't get the message.

I left dinner without a yes for my boss. Instead, I reluctantly agreed to having lunch with Ryder next week "to discuss."

I thought that was what dinner was for.

Clenching my fists, I do a jumpy dance and bite back the scream just begging to be let loose. The frustration coursing through me was only compounded when I walked into my apartment to find Aiden acting totally casual, like he isn't the least bit fazed by the prospect of sleeping beside me tonight. Oh, and the ass was freaking shirtless.

I'm horny, and I'm agitated. Some people get hangry, but I get *hagitated.*

And there is only one thing that will cure this.

I stalk out of the bedroom in all my naked glory, head held high. "Want something to drink?" I call to him as I head to the kitchen.

He's lying on the couch, pretending to watch TV. As I peer over my shoulder at him, he looks up. His eyes practically bug out of his head, and he shoots up to sitting when he realizes he's staring at my bare ass.

"*Lex.*"

I spin, giving him a full frontal. "Yes?"

Catapulting off the couch, he slaps a hand to his face, covering his eyes. "You're...*naked.*"

"And you're shirtless," I say. "Thought we were getting comfortable since it's our apartment. This is what I wear when I'm at home. Can you not handle it? Ready to admit you're catching feelings, Hockey Boy?"

Aiden's chest rises with a heavy inhale, drawing my attention to the defined pecs, then the cut abs on full display. "Come on, Lex. You can't walk around naked and expect me to stay over here."

"Who said you have to stay over there?"

He pulls his hand away from his eyes, only to fist it and bite down on it, clearly using all his restraint to keep his eyes focused on mine. But I see the longing there. The want. The desire. It fuels my next words.

"We should probably set some rules."

With a thick swallow, he nods and drops his hands to his sides, fists still clenched tight. "Right. Rules. Yes, I know I got carried away the other night, but I get it. We're just friends, and I can apparently look"—he gives me a once-over, his lips parting—"but I can't touch."

My heart lurches. "What? No."

Aiden frowns. "What do you mean *no?*"

I put a hand on my hip. "There was no mention of forced celibacy while we're living in this charade. For all we know, this could take a freaking year. No sex for a year? No thanks."

He scratches at his face, trying so hard to keep his focus fixed on my face rather than my plentiful assets. "So you want to, what, have sex with other people?" He grimaces, a vein in his forehead pulsing.

Ah, unhinged Aiden has finally made an appearance. It's a relief to see behind the polite, unaffected mask he's so good at wearing.

Glaring, I step closer. "You touch another woman, and I'll cut your pretty dick off."

His brows shoot to his forehead, and he coughs out a laugh. "You think my dick is pretty?"

Teenage Aiden's dick sure was. I have a feeling adult Aiden is going to rock my world and ruin me.

"I have no idea. It's been years since I've seen it. Played with it. *Sucked it.*"

Aiden stares at me, eyes wide and unblinking. "You want to fool around?" His voice is hoarse, thick. "Just us, no one else, for as long as we're pretending?"

I arch my back, forcing my tits higher. Aiden's Adam's apple bobs in response. And in those athletic shorts, there's no hiding that he's just as turned on as I am. The outline of his erection is prominent.

"Yes. Fiancés with benefits. All the sex. All the fucking. All the orgasms. All the time." I smirk. "*None* of the feelings. Can you do that, Hockey Boy?"

Aiden's chuckle is dark, almost angry. "You set the rules, Princess. I abide by them, right? So yeah." He crosses the room so we're toe to toe. "I can handle them."

For a heartbeat, I think he's going to lean in for a kiss, like he's going to give us what we both want. Instead, he brushes past me and saunters to the kitchen. "What are you doing?"

Aiden returns quickly, holding a can of whipped cream, his eyes blazing.

Excitement courses through me, lighting up my nerve endings.

"You have your rules, and I have mine." He pops the cap off the whipped cream, letting it clatter to the floor, and rests his finger on the nozzle. "I always have something sweet before bed."

My pulse quickens, and my knees tremble in anticipation. "Okay?"

His grin is wicked, his dimple popping. "And I always have whipped cream on my dessert."

He stalks forward, the abrupt movement sending me stumbling back until he has me pressed against the wall. With sin in his eyes, he presses the cap down. The whipped cream explodes all over my tits, the sputtering sound of the can drowning out my gasp.

Then Aiden's mouth is on me, sucking hard, making me arch in surprise.

"Holy shit." The words are breathless, desperate.

He swipes his tongue against my nipple, circling and sucking and then teasing me with his teeth. With each nip, heat pools in my core until I'm a puddle of need.

"Please, Aiden."

"So you do know the name of the man you're dating," he teases without looking up.

"I need your cock," I whimper, grasping his waistband.

Before I can yank his shorts down, he shuffles back. He's still sucking on my tits, but he's backed up far enough to keep his hips out of reach.

"First," he grits out with a lap over one nipple, "I want you on the bed, on all fours, ass up. Once I get my fill of you, maybe I'll fuck you like you so desperately need."

"Yes, I'd like that," I pant, so dizzy with desperation, my vision goes dark.

He finally looks up at me and leans in so his lips are pressed against mine. "You may be their princess, but I'm not your pet." His voice is rougher, darker than I've ever heard it. "In bed, your rules go out the window. I'll fuck you rough when I want to, and soft when I need it. Do you understand?"

Swallowing past the boulder in my throat, I nod. Speaking is impossible. Hot, fiery need radiates from him. His eyes are molten, and he's practically vibrating with the effort it takes to hold on to his control.

It's clearer now than ever that the hurt I inflicted years ago has changed him, molded him, from the boy who wore his heart on his sleeve to the man who's got it locked in its rightful place, out of reach. He's protective of himself. As much as I hate that I broke his heart, I can't help but be relieved that he's not taking my shit. That he's pushing back. If he didn't, I'd be worried about us moving forward. But for the first time since we started this dance, I'm not. Aiden's in control now, so I'll let him stay that way.

With a pinch so fierce it pulls a shout from me, he presses his mouth to mine, swallowing the sound and kissing me brutally. Yes, I think I like this version of Aiden very much.

CHAPTER 30
AIDEN

MY MOUTH WATERS at the thought of eating her for hours. Lennox doesn't have the first clue what she's in for. She wants a fuck buddy. Entertainment. I'll show her that fucking her is my ultimate hobby. Eating her, a delicacy.

But I like my food prepared a certain way. I want to watch her arms tremble as I steal orgasm after orgasm from her body. By the time she finally gets to feel the head of my cock inside her, when she gets to experience what it's like to ride the barbells there for *her* enjoyment, she's going to be so overstimulated she'll see stars.

With a final kiss to her lips, I step back and motion toward her bedroom door. Her movements are slow, dazed, as she passes me. Jaw tight, I smack her ass, leaving a bright red mark on her pale skin. She yelps, but she picks up her pace, headed straight for the bed. Fuck, I can't wait to finally taste her.

As soon as she walks into the room she pauses, her attention on the floral arrangement beside her bed. "Are those peonies?"

"Um what?"

"*Aiden.*" Even naked and ready to be devoured by me the woman manages to make my balls curl up into my body with that tone.

The *we aren't supposed to be doing sweet things* tone. The *you're not my real fiancé* tone.

I shrug like it's no big deal, because honestly, it's flowers, not a diamond ring. "They're your good-night flowers. Do you not like them anymore?"

Her lips fold over as she tries unsuccessfully to hide her smile, and then she shakes her head. "I love them."

I smirk. "Good. Now get on the bed so I can have my good-night snack."

She stares at me for one more second before shaking whatever hesitations she has from her mind. Then she obeys. Impossibly hard and ready for what comes next, I look away from her and focus on our surroundings, rather than allowing my heart to take over.

Predictably, her room is all whites and pinks. I give it a quick scan, smiling, as I wait for her to get into position on the bed. On all fours, she peeks back at me, her pink hair falling over her shoulder.

I hand her a pillow. "Make sure you're comfortable. You'll be in this position for a while."

Her lips form a surprised O, but she does what I ask without argument.

Inhaling deeply, I study every inch of her, then settle on her face. "Can I take a picture?"

A laugh bubbles out of her. She's surprised again. I love that I keep surprising her. "Why?"

"Because you're perfect. Because I don't want to forget the moment you gave over all control to me. It'll help me to behave out there," I tease, nodding toward the bedroom door.

With her teeth pressed into her lip, she dips her chin. "Okay."

I work quickly, making sure to get her blue eyes focused on me, her hair falling around her, the sultry pout she wears without even trying. I snap one quick picture. From the angle and the pose, it's impossible to tell she's naked. This isn't a picture I'll share with anyone, but this isn't about sex. It's about this moment, where she's soft and sweet and giving in to me. Now that I've documented it, knowing I can return to it when I'm away from her and need this reminder that this moment was real, when my thoughts get the best of me and insecurities run wild, I can return my focus to pleasing her.

"Never have I ever wanted a woman in the way I want you, Lex."

Pressing her forehead to the mattress, she whimpers.

I kneel on the bed behind her, settling my hands against her round ass, squeezing and kneading her curves, relishing her softness. I pull her cheeks apart and take in how beautifully pink and wet she is for me. "Perfect." Hovering closer, I flatten my tongue against her sex.

She sighs and whimpers, pushing her hips back, seeking more.

"Don't you worry, Princess. I plan to eat this pretty pussy until you're crying for me to stop."

And then that's what I do. I take her to the edge over and over again with my tongue and with my fingers, and I send her hurtling over it. She thrashes and pulls at the sheets and squeezes her thighs to try to stop me. I lick and suck and finger her until her arms and legs are shaking. Until she's pulsing around me, sucking my fingers into her body. Pulling moans and pleas and whimpers from her until she's coated in a sheen of sweat and tears run down her face.

I soak up her orgasms, loving the taste of her pleasure, until my cock is so hard it pulses.

"Please, Aiden, I need you to fuck me," she babbles.

Quickly, I haul myself back and get to my feet. "Not yet."

The alarm in her eyes as she looks back at me is almost comical. "Please don't leave me like this."

I slide my shorts down and finally let her see what she's been begging for. Gripping myself firmly, I stroke, then roll my thumb over my head, giving myself just enough pressure to ease the ache.

"Holy shit," she murmurs, locking her arms and angling her head so she can get a better look.

"Stay how you are. Stick out your tongue."

Her blue eyes blaze with heat. "Yes, sir."

A hot zap of desire shoots up my spine at her response. *Fuck.* I stroke myself again. "Good girl."

I settle on the bed, once again on my knees, though this time I'm in front of her, and then I feed her my cock. "I want you to count each barbell as you feel it hit your tongue, Princess. Imagine how good it's going to feel when I finally let you take me for a ride."

She moans around me, her blue eyes blazing with need. I take that as permission and push in, barbell by barbell. She grunts each time one slips between her lips. Counting unintelligibly.

When she gets to four, I push in all the way, making her gag. "Fuck, you sound so good with my cock in your mouth." I cup her cheek, stroking her with my thumb. "But you feel even better."

She licks the underside of my shaft, her warm, wet heat more incredible than anything I've ever experienced. Eyes locked on mine, she teases each barbell with her tongue, pushing them back and forth.

Head thrown back, I shudder. The piercing was worth every ounce of pain, if just for this moment. "Fuck, Lex, I'm not going to last if you keep doing that."

She grins around my cock without stopping, the expression sending tingles through my extremities.

With a hand buried in her hair, I pull her back. "There's no fucking way I'm coming in your mouth the first time. Slow down, Princess. I want to enjoy every second of this."

Eyes dancing, she licks her lips. "Fine. Fuck me from behind. I want to feel each one of those barbells."

Tipping closer, I kiss her mouth. Then I settle beside her on the bed. "No way am I taking you from behind right now. Climb on top of me."

She lowers her gaze and shakes her head. "You should be on top."

Frowning, I cup her chin, forcing her to look at me. "Why?" Why the fuck is she still over there? Why am I not already inside her?

"Aiden, I love my shape, but I'm a big girl."

All the air leaves me. I've never known Lennox to be insecure. Though I hate that she's even thinking like this, I can't help but appreciate that she's not hiding herself from me. I want all of her. The fearless Lennox and the insecure girl hiding inside.

More than all of that, I'm turned on by her shape. And I want her to know that.

"You think I can't handle you? Think the idea of you moving above me, tits bouncing, doesn't turn me on?" I rough a hand down my face and suck in a breath. "For more than a decade, every time I've fucked someone, I've thought about you. When I got this piercing, it was with you in mind. Fantasizing about your reaction to it. And I've dreamed about these curves." I pull her closer and cup her ass. "So if you think for one second that I won't have you above me, looking down at me while you ride my cock, then you've lost your damn mind."

"*Aiden*," she chides, her tone soft, full of emotion.

"In this room, I'm in control. You agreed to that, right?"

Lips twisted into a smile, she exhales a long breath.

I pat my thighs. "Your throne awaits, my queen."

Her pupils dilate in response to that term.

"That's right, Lex. Out there, you're a princess, but in here, you're *my* queen."

What I don't tell her is that when I say *in here*, I don't mean in the bedroom.

I mean in my heart.

Rule 1:
Don't fall for
the groom.

Dearest Lennox

Chapter 31
Lennox

I'M in so much trouble. It's official. I really like my fake boyfriend-slash-fiancé.

And I *really* love his tongue.

I'm weighed down, my body spent after all the orgasms he's doled out. Still apprehensive. But this is what he wants—me on top—and I won't hurt him.

The man is a walking piece of art, down to his blinged-out penis. Fuck, was it satisfying to finally know for sure, to finally get to play with it. The way those silver barbells slid as I twisted them with my tongue and the sounds he made when I did? This is going to be so much fun.

"Condom?" he asks. "I've been tested since Jill—"

A bolt of unease courses through me. How I hate that those words have to be uttered. Not because I don't appreciate a good safe-sex talk, but because she cheated on him. Because she treated Aiden, one of the kindest men to ever exist, so poorly.

Rolling to my side, I snag one from the drawer beside my bed. "I'm good with or without," I say, tossing the foil square onto his chest. "I'm on the shot, and I'm negative."

With a nod, he studies it. We never used them when we were in high school. We were idiots. But I've used them with every person since. I do not want to ask what his situation with Jill was.

Aiden drops it to the bed beside him. "I want to feel you."

My heart trips over itself. God, I want that too, and it feels so damn good to know he trusts me enough to know I'd never put him at risk. I'd never trap him. Though I'm sure plenty of women would try. He's a catch in every sense of the word.

Without another word, Aiden pulls me on top of him, and suddenly, I feel like I'm sixteen again. We've both changed so much, but our hearts are the same. And right now, I'm looking down at the man who would do anything for me. The man who would take on my father, pretend to be engaged to me, and break his own damn heart, just to keep me happy. I vow right here and now to do all I can to keep from breaking it again.

I talk a big game, but it's been a long time since I've shared my bed with a man, so I suck in a breath and hold it as I position him between my thighs. When I look up at Aiden's face, he's fixated on my hand and how it's wrapped around his dick, his brows furrowed and his lips pressed together. He's so focused.

When I don't move, he licks his lips and drags his gaze up to my face. "Put me in, baby. Put me out of my misery."

With a soft smile, I obey, notching his head at my entrance, then sliding down slowly. In unison, we gasp, eyes locked, as I slip down one barbell after another, my body stretching to take him.

"Holy shit, that feels amazing," I whisper.

Jaw locked tight, Aiden grits out, "So good."

On instinct, as if we were never apart, I plant my hands on his chest, lower myself, and take his mouth. Aiden moans against my lips, like that was the last thing he expected. Like the sensation is more satisfying than anything else we've done tonight. His tongue melds with mine as I glide my hips against him, teasing my sensitive, swollen clit.

"Holy shit, Aiden, this—fuck."

"I know," he murmurs, cuffing my neck with one hand and pulling me back in for another drugging kiss.

We stay like that, mouths fused, as I grind down on him, and he pistons up into me, fucking like we can't get enough.

I feel whole in an indescribable way. Full. Complete.

I pull back. This is too much. *He's too much.* But of course in my effort to break his spell on me I see the pink peonies he bought me.

He bought me my favorite flower.

And they're beautiful. Bold vibrant pinks, wide open and fully bloomed. There's not just a bushel, no there are at least two dozen. Too many, if we're being honest. They take over my nightstand. Force you to notice them. Just like he does.

His deep growl does just that. Forces my eyes back on him. "That's right Lex, eyes on me while I'm inside of you. Don't hide from me pretty girl, not when we're like this." He fucks up into me, the sensation taking me over the edge, as he wraps his fingers around my throat, squeezing gently, and pulls my mouth back down to his.

"Shit, shit, shit." Warmth flows through my body, followed by a tingling sensation signaling that I'm seconds from tumbling over the edge into bliss.

"That's it, Lex. Squeeze me," he whispers against my mouth.

As my orgasm crests, washing over me, I bite down on his bottom lip. In response, he goes rigid, his cock swelling and filling me. Our breaths are heavy as we float back down. Then we're kissing again. Did we ever stop? I don't know, but I don't want to. I want to prolong the moment. Make this time between us last.

As he softens inside me, I pull back and smile. "Sit tight. I'll be right back." I swing my leg over his hips and hustle to the bathroom. Quickly, I clean up, then I wet a washcloth with warm water and head back to the bedroom.

Aiden is still lounging, one arm behind his head, a lazy smile on his face. When he spots the washcloth in my hand, his gaze narrows. "What are you—"

"Taking care of you," I say, hovering over him to clean him off.

Aiden grabs my wrist, holding me in place for a moment, his dark eyes so sincere. "You're perfect."

My cheeks warm under his praise.

"But if you think I want to be clean of you, you're crazy."

I choke back a giddy laugh, playing it cool. "But you'll be all sticky."

"Then let's shower together," he suggests, hauling himself up to sitting.

Neither of us is ready for this moment to end. Because if we're still in it, then we can still touch, and it won't mean anything. It's just sex.

These lies I'm telling myself are dangerous. There will never be enough distance between us to keep us safe, and yet I can't get close enough.

With my heart in my throat, I whisper, "Okay."

A half hour later, we're snuggled beneath the covers, facing one another.

"This isn't how I thought tonight would go," Aiden admits.

"Really? You don't frequently christen new apartments with whipped cream, followed by multiple orgasms? What a pity. Welcome to the wild side."

He lets out a loud laugh. "I figured it'd be awkward. Thought you'd disappear into the bedroom, and I'd be sitting on the couch wondering if I should come in here or not. I'd probably have waited until I thought you were asleep to avoid this moment."

"I can't imagine you ever feeling awkward. You're always so chill about everything."

"Nah, I'm just good at pretending."

He continues, but I get hung up on that single sentence. It tells me more about him than anything he's said to me since that day in my office. It hits the nail squarely on the head. This is what's been bothering me about Aiden. He's sunshine, but he's not genuinely happy. He hides behind a persona, the louder version of himself, in hopes that the people who care about him won't dig too deep to find the quieter one. But I want that quiet side too.

No. No, you don't. Do you hear yourself? This is temporary. Fake. Don't go falling for your temporary fiancé. It will only end in heartbreak. A complete disaster for the both of you.

"And the whole one bed thing."

Finally forcing myself to tune into the conversation again, I frown. "What about it?"

"Just figured you'd set up a pillow wall or something. Tell me that while I may be allowed to sleep in here, I definitely can't touch."

I grasp his hand and press it against my hip. "You can definitely touch. In fact, I like when you do."

The silence around us is deafening as he regards me, his expression a mix of wonder and disbelief. Then, as if he's finally accepted my words, he pulls me close and embraces me. "I like it too."

"Speaking of the fake stuff," I say, my stomach twisting at that word. *Fake.* "We're going to have to take things up a notch in public."

Aiden reels back a little, watching me, his lips pressed in a firm line, not giving away his thoughts.

"My father doesn't buy that we're in a relationship. Says it couldn't be that serious, considering you just broke off your engagement."

Aiden scans my face, silent, like he's biting his tongue to keep from saying uncouth words about my father.

"So I was thinking," I say as I tiptoe my fingers up his chest. "We really need to sell this relationship in public. Public dates, lots of PDA. Basically, I need you to act like you're obsessed with me everywhere we go."

Aiden's lips tip up, and his eyes dance. Like the idea of faking it with me—an idea that sets my blood on fire and makes me giddy beyond belief—is the greatest thing he's ever heard. "And when we're in private?"

My toes curl at the huskiness of his voice. At the desire that floods through me even after spending the entire night being worked over by him.

"In private, we're us. If you want to play, I'm game. There's no faking orgasms."

Aiden chuckles. "Oh, Princess, there's no need for you to ever fake with me. Pretty sure I've already made that clear."

Heart pounding in my chest, I close my eyes and smile. Visions of the next year play out in front of me. Laughing with Aiden. Dates with Aiden. Hanging out at home with Aiden. And sex, so much sex, *with Aiden.*

I clear my throat and tamp down on the euphoria sweeping through me. Playing it cool like he does. "So what do you say?"

With his teeth pressing down on his lip, he strokes my hair softly and trails his hands down my body. "To summarize, when I'm not by your side in public, worshiping you, waxing poetically about your beauty, showing the world that I'm crazy about you"—he squeezes my hip and sucks in an excited breath—"you want me to be in this bed." With one finger, he traces a line across my stomach, then lower "Between these thighs." He presses inside me without warning. "Working you over until you're too tired to think, let alone worry about what anyone else thinks?" Still spearing me with one finger, he rolls my clit with his thumb.

I suck in a harsh breath. "Yeah, you think you can do that?"

With a low laugh, he continues to finger fuck me, reaching a spot inside me I can never quite get to myself. "Oh, Princess, I was made for this job. Forget Hockey Boy. The princess's sex slave is a much more fitting title."

"It does have a nice ring to it," I pant, riding his hand.

He sinks his teeth into my shoulder, then laves at the spot, easing the sting. "You can test it out while I make you come."

CHAPTER 32
AIDEN

Gavin: Did you sleep all right in your new living quarters, princess?

Me: Slept like a king. Don't call me princess.

Brooks: What makes you think he was referring to you? Maybe he was talking to Beckett.

Beckett: Ha. Like anyone would ever call me princess.

Gavin: Way too much of a duckhole for that name.

Beckett: Duck you.

Brooks: It's getting a bit rowdy for 8 a.m., bros. Sara's giving me the side eye.

Me: Want to ride to War's together today?

Brooks: Yeah, Sar has been talking nonstop about how she and Lennox will be sisters soon.

Brooks: Don't F this up.

Brooks: Sorry, Sara stole my phone.

Me: LOL. I don't intend to F anything up.

Beckett: What's at Wars?

Gavin: Aw, were you not invited?

Beckett: The Revs are playing today anyway. Can you take the older kids? That way, Liv only has to deal with the twins while I'm gone.

Gavin: On it.

Brooks: Gav, you pick up the older kids. I'll bring the big kid with me.

Me: Haha, you're all so funny.

"AIDEN," Lennox shouts from the closet. "Did you color coordinate my clothes? It looks like Barbie and Ken's Dreamhouse closet in here."

Ah, shit. I knew I forgot to undo something last night.

Me: Gotta go. See ya in a few hours.

"Shotgun!" Sara screeches as soon as we approach Brooks's truck.

When she and I reach for the back door in unison, I pull back, confused.

"I meant bestie shotgun. You live with her, so I get her to myself for the next forty-five minutes."

Lex flips her pretty pink hair over her shoulder and winks at me. "Sorry, Hockey Boy. Chicks before bedazzled dicks."

Sara throws her head back and cackles. "You hear that, Brookie? She's finally seen it."

"Crazy girl," Brooks huffs. "No talking about my brother's dick."

Lex doubles over, clutching her stomach, and laughs.

Today's already shaping up to be perfect.

Forty-five minutes later, we're pulling up to an oversized house on a wooded lot.

"This is so not what I pictured," I admit, surveying the sprawling lakeside home.

Brooks shrugs as he shifts the truck into park. "I can see it. He hasn't had a place to call home since his mother died."

Instantly, the mood turns somber. As always, I shift to keep everyone upbeat. "Well, then let's make sure we make it a good day for him."

Brooks appraises me, his expression softening. "Yeah, let's do that."

I'm out of the car quickly and opening Lennox's door.

Her blue eyes light with surprise when I hold out my hand to help her down from my brother's monster of a truck. "Such a gentleman," she teases.

"Just following your rules, Princess," I murmur, tugging her close. "Ready to be worshipped?"

Her cheeks go pink as she peeks over at Sara, as if she's checking to see if she overheard.

Of course, Sara isn't paying us any attention. She's too busy flinging herself straight from her seat into Brooks's arms. He catches her easily and spins, his mouth pressed to her ear, probably whispering words neither of us wants to hear.

Gravel crunches under the weight of a car slowly rolling down the long driveway. It's followed by incessant honking that cuts through the peacefulness of the neighborhood.

"Party's here!" Daniel hollers out the window.

Fitz is driving, and Camden and Jorgenson, a new addition to the Bolts, are in the back.

I love rookies. While McGreevey is an incredible captain, I take it upon myself to bring the new guys under my wing. Especially during the offseason, when McGreevey goes home to Canada. I love witnessing the joy and terror that war inside them during their first game. The high of it all. It reminds me of why I love it all so much. Keeps me grounded.

Gavin's oversized SUV rolls up behind Fitz. He's barely come to a stop before Finn is leaping out and running in our direction.

The front door swings open, and War appears. "Wow, when I said noon, I didn't expect you'd all be so punctual."

With a huff, Finn puts his hands on his hips and looks back at Gavin. "You didn't tell me we were coming to this clown's house."

War throws his head back and laughs. "Wait till you see the setup in the back before you decide whether you want to be friends."

I crouch so I'm eye to eye with Finn. "Hey, Huck, do me a favor— be nice to War. I can't have him all bent out of shape on the ice. He helps me score."

Finn lets out a loud sigh. "Fine, but you better tell him to watch his language. There's babies here."

Biting back a snort, I give him a nod. "Want to race me to the back?"

Finn's little brown eyes grow two sizes. "You got it." He's already digging his feet into the ground, but before he can take off, I grab him by the back of his shirt and lift. His feet are still moving, but he's not going anywhere.

"Need a good luck kiss from the princess first," I say, grinning at Lennox.

Finn scrunches up his face. "Ew, gross. I don't want one."

Lennox sticks out her tongue. "Wasn't offering you one." With her hands pressed to my cheeks, she smiles so big my heart nearly trips over itself. "Laying it on thick today, Hockey Boy."

"I'm very good at taking orders. And exceptionally competitive," I remind her.

Her eyes dance as she angles in and kisses me. It's soft. Gentle.

Sweet. If not for the little boy groaning about how gross it is, I'd be liable to lose myself in her.

Confident that we got our point across, I step back and wink at her. I set Finn down, then take off. "Last one to the backyard jumps in the lake!"

Within seconds, I'm not the only one racing my nephew. Daniel buzzes past us, followed by Fitz, who shouts at the rookie to keep up.

I'm laughing too hard to stick with the guys. There's no way I'm winning, but I definitely won't let Finn lose.

Another runner catches up. Brooks. As he gets close, he snatches Finn off the ground and takes off. "Come on, Huck. We're going to beat all of them."

We spend the afternoon outside, enjoying the beautiful summer day. War's property is outrageous. A long, rolling green hill leads down to a small lake with a single dock. His dock. His *lake*. He's got a powerboat, a Jet Ski, and a paddle board. We try out all of his toys, and Brooks and I take turns taking Finn and Winnie out on the Jet Ski.

I can't stop looking at Lennox, where she's settled with the girls, along with Addie and Vivi. Her laughter and smiles have me practically floating off the ground all day. I'm attentive, as a good boyfriend would be, making sure she has a drink at all times, bringing her plates of food, and once an hour, I go over to lather her in sunscreen.

"I think they believe it," she whispers as I rub the lotion over her shoulders for the third time.

"Believe what?" I say as I press a kiss to her neck.

"That you're obsessed."

I nuzzle into the crook of her neck. She thinks I'm doing this for others, but this is all me. Though I'll let her believe I'm doing it for show. It's freeing, giving in to my obsession without being called out for getting too attached. It'd be too late if she warned anyway.

"What's Ava doing here?" Sara asks, pointing at the redhead making her way across the yard on the arm of a man I don't recognize.

She's in a white sundress and sunglasses, but even from here, I can see her face scrunching in confusion.

"Doesn't look like she expected to be here either," I offer.

Sara is already on her feet and striding toward Ava. When Lennox sits up to move, I hop to my feet and help her off the grass. She gives me an appreciative smile, and I take her hand—keeping up appearances and all that.

"Not going to lie. You are the last person I thought I'd see today," Sara says as we approach her and the newcomers.

Ava looks at the man beside her. "I'm confused. I thought I was meeting your stepbrother."

She introduces the man beside her. Xander.

I bite back my choked laughter. Shit. War is gonna lose it. He hates his stepbrother. And he has some sort of weird obsession with Ava. Though he'd never admit it, I can read my winger. It's my job to. When he and Ava are in the same room, despite the way he pretends he can't stand her, he tracks her every move. His eyes are always on her when she's not looking.

"He just bought this house," Ava says, "and he invited Xander for a barbecue."

My gut clenches. Damn, this is going to be a shit show.

"Come on, Lex." I tug her toward the lake, keeping my voice low. "We don't want to be here when War realizes that his evil stepbrother is dating his obsession."

Rather than stick around and wait for the fallout, Lennox and I take the Jet Ski for a spin around the lake. The feel of her hands around my waist, her squeals in my ear when I rev the engine and take off, and the heat of her pressed up against me leave me smiling and happy.

Genuinely happy.

So happy that I don't want it to end.

When I spot a small alcove on the other side of the lake, I pull the key out of the ignition, bringing it to a stop, and spin around on the seat so I'm facing her. "You having a good day?"

The smile on her face says it all. "One of the best."

"Any way I can make it better?" I waggle my brows suggestively.

Her responding laugh is bubbly and light. "What do you have in mind?"

"Never have I ever fucked on a Jet Ski."

The hitch in Lennox's breath tells me she's interested. "How's your balance, Hockey Boy?"

Cocky as shit, I jump up and shake, rocking the vessel from side to side, easily maintaining my balance.

Lennox lurches forward, her fingers digging into my thighs like she truly believes I'd let her fall. "*Aiden.*"

Looming over her, I shoot her a wink. "Take out my cock."

Her eyes dart to the shore. We're well hidden in the alcove behind a copse of large spruce trees, so there is no way they can see us.

"What did I tell you about when we're alone?" I grasp her chin, pulling her focus back to me. Her lips part in shock. "In public, you're in control, but here—" I press my thumb against her bottom lip with a little more force than necessary. "Here, you are all mine to play with."

She grazes my thumb with the tip of her tongue, making my dick jump.

"Now take out my cock and show me that you know how to listen."

This time, she remains focused on me.

We're wearing life vests, but considering the water is shallow in this cove, I unbuckle mine and nod for her to take care of hers. As she unzips the neoprene jacket, her nipples pebble against the fabric of her hot pink bathing suit. "Pull the straps down and let me see how beautiful you are."

Lennox has never been shy a day in her life, and today is no exception. So now that she's been reassured that it's just us, she pulls both straps down. "Now what?" The way she says it, so obediently, as her eyes sparkle, her pink hair blowing in the light breeze, has me growing harder by the second.

"Suck my cock until you're so wet that I can bend you over this Jet Ski and fuck you. I want you whimpering around me and humping that seat. Think you can do that?"

Her face hardens in determination, and then she's scrambling to pull me out of my shorts. When she's got my hot, hard length in her hand, she licks her lips in anticipation. The first swipe of her tongue pulls a groan from my chest and has me clenching my ass cheeks.

"Yes," I groan. "Just like that."

The Jet Ski rocks as she bobs, and when she grinds against the seat like I asked, water sloshes up both sides.

"Good girl, listening so well. You getting that pussy nice and wet for me? Gonna slide all over my cock until you come."

Moaning, she drags her gaze up to mine. The connection is visceral. A jolt that courses all the way to my toes. The way I feel about this woman? Fuck, it's indescribable. She's every dream I've ever had. Having her here, where it's just us, knowing she's doing this because she wants to, not because we're playing our parts, is enough to have me teetering on the edge of losing control.

Gripping her chin, I force her to stop. I drop my forehead to hers, panting. "I need to be inside you."

I flip my leg over to one side and drop to the seat behind her. "Push up, baby. Grab those handlebars, ass in the air for me."

Over her shoulder, she shoots me a wicked grin. "Starting to think that's your favorite position."

"The view of your ass is hard to beat."

Once she's in place, I rise up behind her and slip her bathing suit bottoms to one side. With my fist around my cock, I rub my head through her lips, drenching myself, then press in slowly. She's so wet I slide in with no problem.

Her moan echoes my own. "Dammit, Aiden. Why is this so good?"

Draping myself over her back, I brush her hair over one shoulder and press a kiss to the other. "Because it's us, Princess. Because it was always meant to be us."

Before she can object—or think too much about my confession—I slide out and slam back in again.

She grips the handlebars so tight her knuckles go white as we rock, creating a wake.

Within minutes, my legs are shaking and the telltale tingling starts at the base of my spine. "Shit. Sit on my lap, baby."

"*Aiden.*"

"If you say a goddamn word about being too heavy, I will lift you up, wrap your legs around my hips, and fuck you while standing. I love your body, Lex. It's the body of my dreams. So please, sit the fuck down on your throne and let me worship you."

With her head dropped back against my chest, I lower us both to the vinyl seat, grinding my pelvis against her ass once she's seated fully. Water sloshes in rhythm with our movements. I snake my hand around her waist, working her clit.

"Holy shit. That—yes," she babbles.

"That's it, Lex. Ride me until you come. I'm going to fill you up and then lead you back to the party. You'll smile at our friends, and I'll play the doting boyfriend just like you want, but we'll both know you're dripping with me."

She digs her fingernails into my thighs as she cries out, her orgasm coming on so quickly that it takes me by surprise. When she spasms around me, the tingles surge, going straight to my balls, and I tumble over the edge with her, biting down on her shoulder to keep from growling like a caveman.

"Shit." The word scrapes out of me. It's far from what I really want to say, but if I voiced my true thoughts, I'd ruin everything. Because I'd confess my undying love. I'd beg her to tell me why she'll never get married for real. Why she doesn't believe in real relationships. Why she left me...

So when she turns her head and grasps my face and presses those gorgeous lips to mine, relief washes over me. Once again, she's stealing my breath. I'd gladly give her my last one. In fact, that's just another dream of mine.

Rule 1:
Don't fall for
the groom.

Dearest Lennox

Chapter 33
Lennox

DESPITE AIDEN'S ORDERS, I run for the bathroom as soon as we get off the Jet Ski. There is no way I can spend the rest of the day with his family, friends, and teammates with his cum dripping out of me.

For a moment, I press myself up against the locked door and just breathe. When I'm a little more grounded, I step in front of the bathroom mirror and study myself. I look wild. Carefree and happy.

Beautiful.

My cheeks are flushed, my lips are plump, and my eyes are brighter than they've been in years.

I look like a woman falling.

For all my concerns about Aiden, I'm the one at risk of getting in too deep.

With a shake of my head, I push the thoughts aside and take a few moments to fix myself so that my slutty, slutty ways aren't so obvious and change into a pair of shorts and a tank.

As I'm stepping into the hall, voices echo against the empty walls.

"This place is seriously beautiful." *Aiden.*

"Thanks." That must be War.

"What's up with your brother and Ava?"

War is grimacing as I turn the corner and find them standing in front of another closed door. When he sees me, his eyes light up and he lets out a relieved sigh, like he's happy he doesn't have to answer that question. "Need anything?"

"I'm good, and I agree with Aiden. This place is truly gorgeous. Are you going to miss being in the city, though?"

War shrugs. "Maybe, but then I can pull an Aiden and crash on your couch."

Aiden dons his signature dopey smile. "No more couch surfing for me. Right, Lex?"

I lean into him and allow myself to sink into his hold when he wraps his arms around me. It's far too comfortable. Far too easy to slip back into being his.

"What's in this room?" Aiden asks, pointing to the shut door.

War shrugs, though his eyes dart from side to side. "Nothing. The previous owners left a bunch of furniture."

With a curious hum, Aiden pushes open the door. When the beautiful pink room covered in music lyrics and little purple birds comes into full view, we suck in matching sharp breaths.

"Holy crap, it's like my dream," I whisper.

Aiden nudges War. "You got a secret family you aren't telling us about?"

With a roll of his eyes, he shoves his hands into his pockets. "I told you, it came this way. But, uh—" He squeezes the back of his neck and eyes me, wearing a look of concern. "It's nice, right? Like if you were a little girl, you'd like it?"

I cough out a laugh. "As an almost thirty-year-old, I like it. As a child, this would have been my dream."

War's cheeks have gone a shade of red that can't be blamed on the sun today. Something is going on, and if I didn't have a million other things to worry about, I'd be dying to find out.

Aiden is like a dog with a bone, though. He steps inside, hands on his hips, and spins slowly. "You sure—"

"Lennox!" Sara shouts from downstairs.

War heads straight for the bedroom door. "Coming," he hollers. Without turning around, he books it down the steps.

"That was weird, right?" Aiden says to me.

I nod, surveying the room again. "Yeah. So weird."

He slips his hand into mine and tugs me out into the hall, closing the door behind us. "Let's see what your crazy friend wants."

Downstairs, Sara is standing in front of War, arms crossed over her chest, interrogating him about our whereabouts.

"They're right behind me," he says, thumbing over his shoulder.

"Guilty," I mutter as we step into the kitchen.

Ava, Xander, War, Daniel, Fitz, Brooks, and Sara are all standing around the oversized island. It's butcher block and covered in an array of cheeses and crackers, fruits and salads. The ceiling is vaulted, with a huge wooden beam down the center of it that's stained to match the chocolate brown cabinets.

Beyond the kitchen is a view of the lake. In the yard, Millie and Gavin are chasing Winnie, Finn, and Addie in what looks like a game of tag.

"Where's Vivi?" I ask, scanning the yard for our littlest bestie.

Sara points to the stroller in the living room. "Napping, but the better question is where were you?"

I squirm under her scrutiny, my thoughts instantly turning to our activities. Dammit. I will my mind to focus on something, anything, but where we were. On the Jet Ski. Practically naked. Writhing beneath his touch.

In my periphery, Aiden smirks. Fuck.

Sara points at me, her mouth popping open. "On the Jet Ski. Bedazzled penis. In the mouth."

War, who has just shoved a cracker into his mouth, sputters and coughs. With his fist over his mouth, he asks, "Is this a sick version of Clue?"

I glare at my best friend. "Do not use my superpower against me."

Head dropped forward, Brooks groans. "Crazy girl, how many

times do we have to go over this? No talking about my brothers' schlongs."

Our friends all watch our interaction with amused smirks, clearly used to Sara's ridiculousness. Xander, on the other hand, is wearing a concerned grimace. Beside him, Ava is pressing her lips together to keep from laughing. Clearly, he still believes she's a demure thing. I mean, she is, but we're working on corrupting her.

"It's not my fault your brother is dating my best friend," Sara throws back. "Pretty sure I get to talk about Aiden's dick as long as I'm talking about it in the context that he is Lennox's boyfriend."

Brows lowered, Brooks shakes his head. "No."

"Wait, you're brothers?" Xander asks, pointing between Aiden and Brooks.

"They're practically twins," Sara says, frowning at the guy. Her tone is laced with an irritation she rarely exudes. Clearly, she doesn't like him.

"No, we're really not," Brooks says.

"I'm definitely better looking." Aiden puffs out his chest and grins in a way that makes his dimple pop.

While they have similar features, Brooks has inches on his brother, along with pounds of muscle. He's practically a giant. And his hair is much longer. Aiden is tall and muscular. His curly hair is well-trimmed yet long enough for me to tug and run my hands through. As I survey them, I suppose they do look a lot alike, but Aiden is always so smiley in comparison to his stoic brother.

"And you're dating best friends?" the guy asks, flattening his palms on the quartz top of the island.

"Wild, right?" Sara replies. "Gavin is one of their older brothers, and Millie is a close friend too. These two, though, were high school sweethearts." She sighs, hearts dancing in her eyes. "Aiden was actually engaged to someone else, and then he saw his one true love again—"

My stomach twists as she embellishes our story. "That's not exactly how it went."

Aiden pulls me against his chest. "It was, actually. When I discovered Lennox was our wedding planner, I dumped my fiancée on the spot. A week later, I asked this one to be mine again."

Despite the decade apart, I know Aiden better than I know anyone else. I know when he's lying. His genuine smile turns stiff, brittle, and his voice takes on a more authoritative tone—he turns into Aiden Langfield, star center of the Boston Bolts, the persona he and his PR team have spent years perfecting.

Right now, though, his smile is that dopey one I've been seeing more and more of. His voice is warm, and his eyes are gooey, like a chocolate sundae, as he gazes at me.

My heart pangs. Because suddenly, I'm wondering how close he is to speaking the truth.

Sara rubs her hands together, drawing our attention again. "Since we all agree that when asking about Lennox's boyfriend, I'm allowed to ask about his bedazzled peen—"

"We don't agree," Brooks mutters.

Sara ignores him, instead zeroing in on me. "Did you get the scoop on what Aiden's truth was? What he wouldn't admit that led to him being forced to Lisa Frank his peen?"

Ava's face contorts in confusion. "Lisa Frank?"

"Ya know, because it's colorful," Sara explains, like this conversation isn't the least bit bizarre.

"Jesus Christ," Aiden mutters, covering his mouth and eyeing his brother. "Do you tell her everything?"

Brooks chuckles. "Aiden wanted to get pierced because War and I had already gotten ourselves roped into it. War asked him an easy question, and Aiden chose not to answer because he wanted to be like us."

Aiden is vibrating beside me. "That's not what happened."

Bothered by the uneasiness in his tone, I study him. His brow is furrowed and he wears a frown that looks foreign on his face. "Then what did happen?"

War rolls his eyes. "All I asked was why he hated shamrocks."

A lead ball settles in my throat. I can't speak. I can't look at Aiden, even as the heat of embarrassment, humiliation, and maybe anger radiates off him.

"It's weird, right?" War goes on, absolutely clueless to the turmoil rolling through Aiden. "The man nicknamed the Leprechaun getting quiet every time a fan gives him a shamrock as a gift. Almost as dumb as his fear of bunnies."

"It's their eyes," Aiden grits out, his body rigid.

Though my heart is pounding loud in my ears, I school my expression and shrug. "I had a bunny when we were growing up. It bit him. Let the kid live."

I grip Aiden's hand and squeeze. When he doesn't immediately squeeze back, my heart sinks. I need to get the both of us out of this conversation stat, then figure out how to make him smile the way he was only a few minutes ago.

That's only a Band-Aid, though. To the outside world, we look perfect. The second chance everyone thinks we deserve. But the truth is, if this were a real relationship, we'd have to have some serious conversations before we even had a shot at forever.

Is that even what I want?

Divine intervention does its thing in the form of a phone call.

"Oh," Ava says, "it's the hospital."

My heart lodges itself in my throat. Across from me, Sara is instantly wringing her hands, looking concerned.

"I gotta take this," Ava says, stepping out onto the deck.

We all watch as she paces across the wooden planks, practically holding our breath. She nods a lot, bites her finger, nods some more, and stops and takes a few deep breaths. Eventually, she comes back inside, her eyes welling with tears.

Worry settles like a blanket over the room as Sara and I rush her.

"What's going on? Is Josie okay?" Sara asks.

Nodding, Ava blinks tears from her eyes. "Yeah, it's good." She swipes at her damp cheeks. "They found Josie's birth mother." Her words are choppy, broken up by sniffles. Closing her eyes, she takes a deep breath, then continues. "I guess she was sixteen when she had her. She gave her up for adoption, figuring Josie would have a better life. She never imagined—" She shakes her head, pressing her lips together.

She doesn't need to go on. I can guess. Josie's mother never imagined someone would care for her child for years, only to put her back into foster care when she became seriously ill. It's tragic, and it's haunted all of us for months and months. This beautiful little girl deserves all the love in the world.

I pull her into my chest. "It's okay, babe."

Ava sniffles against my shoulder. "It's good. I shouldn't be crying. Why am I crying?"

Sara eyes me over Ava's head, rubbing circles against her back. "Because you wanted to be her mom. And because you love her. But this is a good thing."

"I'm going to miss her so much." Ava pulls back and wipes her tears with the back of her hand. She sucks in a ragged breath. "She's still coming to the party tomorrow, but then Maria is taking her to meet her mother. I guess the mother hired Maria to help with the transition. As a nanny or something."

"Wow," Sara says, that single word echoing my thoughts.

Ava nods, lowering her gaze. "So tomorrow has to be amazing."

There's no doubt I'll make that happen. "It'll be the best birthday party any little girl has ever had."

Rule 1:
Don't fall for
the groom.

Dearest Lennox

Chapter 34
Lennox

You can do anything you set your mind to. You just need to be pushed and supported. I think there was a time in your life when you believed it. When you would look at something the rest of the world might pass by and find joy. Find beauty in the unexpected. Now you just keep walking. You're too young to be this jaded. Too young to not believe in yourself. Instead of running away, take a moment to really sit and think. What do you want to do with your life? If you could have everything—if you could do anything—what would it be?

I KEEP my promise to Ava. The party is a huge success. The guys helped us set up, but then they disappeared to their secret underground bar. I'm making it my mission to score an invite. Sara and Hannah have been there, and they swear it's nothing to go crazy about, but the secretive nature of it and the exclusivity have me chomping at the bit.

"Look at how happy she is," Sara squeals beside me.

She's right. Josie is sitting between Melina and Ava, wearing the brightest smile. Millie came through and got in touch with Melina, who, from what I've seen today, is down to earth for a pop star. She showed up equipped with two bodyguards who are hovering on the outskirts of our party, on high alert. Fortunately, she's incognito, wearing a blond wig over her dark brown hair. She's even more gorgeous in person.

Millie, who's bouncing Vivi on her lap, nudges my shoulder. "This is an absolutely gorgeous setup. I can't wait to see what you do for my wedding."

My boss is on the other side of the table, talking to Josie's nurse, Maria. When I told her Melina Rodriguez had agreed to attend, she suggested she come to help out.

She's probably never worked a child's birthday party, but I wasn't going to argue, and when she arrived, she seemed genuinely impressed by the setup. A low, long table has been set up on the grass in the shade of a nearby copse of trees. Sequined pillows in varying shades of pink line it on either side, serving as comfy seating for guests. The place settings are light pink and the cutlery is gold. The cake Aiden and I picked has been cut, and Josie and her crew are digging in, enjoying themselves.

And then there are the three crystal bowls that line the table which are filled with water and pink floating peonies which Aiden dropped off right before the party was set to start. God, just the sight of them sends me into a tizzy. There hasn't been a day since Aiden moved in that I haven't received my 'good night' flower.

The carousel is to our right. There's just something whimsical about the colorful horses on the old-fashioned ride set in the middle of a park in Boston. It's unexpected.

Find beauty in the unexpected...

My grandmother's words whirl around in my head like patterns in a kaleidoscope until suddenly, they stop and form the most perfect picture. Aiden and me on that carousel. A pink wedding dress beside a striking tuxedo. A bouquet of peonies in my hands. Each of us growing a little older year after year as we return to this spot to celebrate our anniversary.

Little hockey players who look just like him.

Kids. My kids. *Our kids.*

That image steals all the breath from my lungs. I've never thought about children. Not in any serious way.

I've always sworn that I wouldn't have kids, because once again, it's what's expected of me.

Marry a man my father approves of, give him a few heirs to choose from...

I shudder at the thought.

Nope. No kids for me. My father's controlling enough with me. I'd never put that on another person, let alone my own child.

"Len," Sara says, her voice raised like maybe it's not the first time she's called my name.

I pull in a deep breath, relishing the way my lungs burn. "Sorry, yeah?"

"Maria has to get Josie back to the hospital so she can meet her mom. Why don't we get one more picture in front of the carousel together?"

Ava is standing beside her, doing all she can to put on a brave face. She's doing a terrible job. Her green eyes glisten, and just as a tear falls, she slides her sunglasses on.

After half a dozen pictures—including a goofy pose, one where we all smile nicely, and then a couple where we're probably all a bit somber, knowing it's the final one and that this is our last Sunday with Josie for a while—we say our goodbyes.

Fortunately, my boss approaches and signals that she'd like to have a word, distracting me from the tearful farewells. I give Josie a big hug and remind her that pink is always the answer, then I head back to the table so I can oversee clean-up.

She walks beside me, her heels sinking into the soft ground. Even as they do, she manages to remain completely at ease. I wore flats for that exact reason. Had I worn heels, I surely would have twisted my ankle, taken out the table, and landed squarely on the cake.

"It was a good event. What's the status on Seven?"

My stomach sinks. *Right. Ryder's band.* "Ryder asked to meet again this week to go over it further."

She furrows her brows. "Is he giving you the runaround?"

I shake my head. The last thing I want is for her to think I can't handle this. "He was preoccupied when we met last week"—with my breasts, though I don't tell her that—"Probably because of the record deals they're considering."

Her expression smooths out, instantly sending a wave of relief through me. Aiden won't be happy, but there's no avoiding meeting with Ryder again. I need him to say yes to this wedding gig.

"Just let me know if you don't think they're interested so I have time to come up with a plan B. This bride is"—cringing, she scans the park, then angles in closer—"very demanding."

"As she should be. We're the best, right?" I say brightly.

With a nod, Serena turns and heads off toward the street, apparently heading out. I, on the other hand, stare at the mess of a table like the answer to my problem is hidden somewhere in the cut-up cake.

"Were you talking about Ryder Sinclair?"

I jump, surprised by the proximity of the voice. Spinning, I slap a hand to my chest and come face to face with Melina. "Sorry," I breathe. "You scared me."

She doesn't smile. Nor does she apologize. "Were you?"

"Um, yeah." I swallow past the lump suddenly lodged in my throat. "My boss wants Seven to perform at a wedding, and if not them, then another big talent. I think he's jerking me around, though. He probably doesn't want to do the wedding, but rather than say that, he keeps stringing me along, inviting me out for drinks and dinner to "discuss," then conveniently veering the conversation off topic. My boyfriend isn't happy," I add, grimacing, because it's true, and also, I should mention Aiden, right? For the sake of our fake relationship?

Or maybe I just like referring to him as my boyfriend.

Ugh. I have issues.

Without hesitation, Melina pulls out her phone. "When's the wedding?"

"August eighteenth, why?"

She slides a finger across her phone screen, then taps away. When she finally looks up at me, she's wearing a soft smile. "I'm free. I'll do it. Send me details, and I'll make it happen."

Disbelief leaves me staring at her, speechless.

"Does she have her heart set on Seven?" Melina asks, tilting her head and frowning.

"What?" I straighten, forcing air into my lungs. "No. I don't think she's even heard of them. Her parents mentioned them, but they're open to other options."

"Listen, the band performed at my birthday party last year—Lake's surprise." She smiles at the mention of her best friend. "And while I've never interacted with Ryder outside of that event, I know his type, and I've heard stories. I've dealt with plenty of men like him in the industry. Stringing you along until they get what they want." She screws up her face in disgust. "I'll do the event. You can do dinner with Ryder if you want. Or skip it. But at least you won't *owe* him anything."

It takes more effort than it should not to pump my fist in the air and scream girl power, but I manage. Though there's no stopping me when I grab Mel by the shoulders and pull her in for a big hug.

Her bodyguards immediately shift closer, though they settle when they see she's hugging me back.

"Thank you so freaking much."

Mel shrugs like it's no big deal, and I decide in that moment that I'm going to buy every single one of her albums for all my friends and the entire hockey team.

CHAPTER 35
AIDEN

"HONEY, I'M HOME," I yell in my best Ricky Ricardo voice. Lennox is on the couch, curled up with her Kindle.

She tips her head and smiles at me. "How was your game?"

"Skate," I say, reminding her of the lingo again.

With a grin, she goes back to her book. The move is comforting. Because we've fallen into a routine. She knows precisely what I'll do next. I'll saunter up to her and drop a kiss to her forehead, then throw myself over the couch and snuggle with her while she reads. She'll make it another few pages before I finally annoy her enough that she can't concentrate, thus she'll pay attention to me. From there, we'll figure out what we want for dinner.

This is what we've done every night since I moved in a few weeks ago. Dinner at home some nights, restaurant hopping on others, ensuring we're being seen fawning over one another. Though the fawning doesn't end when we close the door to the apartment. She's just as affectionate.

Most nights, we barely make it back home before she's ripping my clothes off and talking me into trying something new. Toys, plugs, ass play—you name it, and the girl wants to do it. And I'm all about it.

I pull her feet onto my lap and dig my thumbs into one heel. "What are you in the mood for tonight?"

With a moan, she leans back, eyes closed. "I was thinking we could try anal tonight."

I cough out a laugh. "I meant for dinner."

She gives me a lazy smile and shrugs. "Oh, I guess steak is fine."

I drop her foot and pull her onto my lap. "Nah. I like your first suggestion better. We're staying in, and I'm having your ass for dinner."

Licking her lips, she holds my gaze. Captivated. That's what I am when she looks at me. "Takeout it is, then."

Grasping her face, I pull her in for a deep kiss. It's intoxicating. She's intoxicating. Doing this whenever I want is heaven. There's no pressure to force a smile, to force joy, when I'm with her. I can simply exist. Be myself. I should probably be worried that I feel most at ease with myself when I'm 'faking' with my 'fake girlfriend' but I'm not going to think about that right now. With one final chaste kiss, I pull back and smooth out her hair. "Did you see the article *Jolie* published on their website that mentioned Josie's party?"

I'm so fucking proud, my heart is bursting.

Lennox rears back, wearing a confused frown. "What?"

Shifting, I pull my phone from my pocket. "They did a piece about kids' birthday party ideas, from simple to extravagant." I eye her. "Clearly, yours was deemed extravagant."

Her cheeks are as pink as her hair, and her blue eyes shine with excitement. "You're not fucking with me?"

I tip my head as I hand her my phone. "You think I'd do that?"

As she reads the article, surprised delight takes over her expression. "Holy shit, Aiden, this is amazing!"

"Your boss even sang your praises." I point to the section where Serena talks about how they'd never considered children's parties before, but that Lennox had a vision. She went on about how they'd be happy to create memories like this for more of the children of Boston.

Clutching my phone to her chest, Lennox beams so brightly it's hard to look at her. "I can't believe this."

"Why? The party was spectacular. You should be recognized for all you did. And after Gavin's wedding this weekend, everyone is going to be talking about you again. This is only the beginning, Lex."

She bites her lip, a hint of uncertainty flashing in her eyes. "You really believe I can do this?"

"Of course I do. You can do whatever you put your mind to."

She blinks at me, her lips parted.

"What?"

Ducking, she lets out a slow breath. "It's just rare to have someone believe in me."

Fuck, the genuine hurt in her tone eats at me. Has anyone ever believed in this girl? Is that why she's so flippant? I guess I can relate. I can look back now and see how oblivious I was to some of what Lennox went through when we were in high school. I had hockey, my brothers, and Lennox. I had everything I needed.

But maybe she only had me.

Was I so distracted by my own wants that I failed at supporting her? Clearly, I made mistakes, because one minute, we were happy, and the next, she was gone.

I'm still lost in the past when she continues. "The only person who ever believed in me, besides you, was my grandmother."

I angle in closer, eager to digest every morsel Lennox is willing to share with me. I want every detail of her life while we were apart. If I could crawl inside her brain, I would. "How so?"

She leans back against the cushions and lets out a long exhale. "After graduation, she knew I wasn't ready for college."

I nod. "And then you decided to spend the year in Europe."

For years, we'd planned to go to college together. I had to report early for hockey, but her plan was to follow me that fall. The life we imagined was far different from this reality. We'd probably be married by now, with kids.

I choke back the devastation threatening to swamp me and press on. This is as close as we've come to a discussion about the breakup. "Are you glad you took that year off?"

Lennox laughs lightly, though there's nothing funny about this conversation. Because what I'm really asking is this: Does she regret ending things? Does she regret our breakup at all?

"I should probably have taken two years. Maybe ten. I still have no idea what I want to be when I grow up."

"I thought you loved what you do?" I ask, genuinely perplexed.

Her smile quickly morphs into a frown. "Aiden, I plan parties for a living. It's nothing, really."

"You bring joy to people." Unlocking my phone screen, I hold the device up, showing her the picture *Jolie* published along with the article. "You see Josie's face right there? You did that."

She shakes her head, even as her eyes brighten. She wants it to be true. She wants to matter. If only she could see herself the way I see her. She'd know she matters so much that it makes it hard for me to breathe. Hard for me to contemplate anything other than how I can show her she matters. With my hands. With my lips. With my heart.

"That was a good day," she says softly, studying the photo of Josie and the girls in front of the carousel.

In this moment, I know with absolute certainty that I'm in trouble. Because as much as I love loud, bubbly Lennox, the one who teases and sasses me—the one who walked naked through this apartment to taunt me into admitting I couldn't handle faking with her—I love this Lennox too. The one she hides beneath the loud. The one she doesn't let anyone see. And this Lennox, just like every other version of her, feels a hell of a lot like mine.

I vow here and now to use these next few months, while she's mine, to prove to her how good we are together. I vow to use this time to help her fall in love with herself. To fall in love with this city. And hopefully, if I'm lucky, to fall in love with me.

Rule 1:
Don't fall for
the groom.

Dearest Lennox

Chapter 36
Lennox

"FIRST MELINA RODRIGUEZ, now a *Jolie* article? Should I be worried you're going to get all the good projects now?"

I eye Rayna, a single mom I share coffee with every morning in the office, checking to see if her words hold any malice. The brunette merely smiles at me.

Odd. Every other place I've worked has had a competitive culture. A toxic one at that. Where men talk down to women and women cut one another with their words. But I haven't experienced that here once.

"Beginner's luck, I'm sure," I reply, reaching for the whipped cream in the fridge. I hold it out to her, but she shakes her head, so I cover the top of my coffee with the sweet treat and then return it to the shelf.

"Don't downplay how hard you've been working," Serena says as she strolls into the break room, salad in one hand and a water bottle in the other. "There's no luck about it."

My face heats. I've never actually been good at anything. It's one thing to have Aiden tell me he's proud of me, but my boss too, and co-workers...

"Knock, knock."

At the sound of that familiar voice, I spin toward the door, my lips lifting. Aiden wears one of his easy, happy-go-lucky smiles as he hovers outside the breakroom.

"And who do we have here?" Rayna teases, blatantly checking him out.

I do the same. How could I not? He's wearing a pair of light blue shorts and a black T-shirt that molds to his body so perfectly it makes my mouth water. His hair is lightly gelled, making the natural highlights in his curls appear almost golden.

"Hey, Hockey Boy, what are you doing here?"

"Gavin mentioned wanting a waffle bar in the bridal suite, and I know the perfect place to order them from. Figured you could help me since you *are* the wedding planner." He waggles his brows suggestively.

God. How is it possible for this man to be so damn adorable and irresistible at the same time? Two weeks ago, I told Sara that my life isn't a movie and that I shouldn't be kissing the groom. Yet I've done an awful lot of kissing this man these last few weeks. Thankfully he is no longer *the groom.*

"Oh, let me know what you think of the place, Lennox. The Kingstons were just asking for brunch ideas for their event," my boss says. She gives Aiden a nod, then heads back into the office.

"Will do," I reply happily. "Just give me a second to put this in a to-go cup," I tell Aiden.

As I'm transferring my coffee, Rayna leans over and mumbles, "First, you're a rockstar at work, and now I find out you're dating that hot hockey player?" She wears a teasing smile as she adds, "Some girls have all the luck."

"Hungry?" Aiden pulls a candy bar from his pocket and dangles it between us.

Laughing, I shake my head. "I thought we were going to the farmers' market for waffles."

Aiden opens the Hershey's wrapper and takes a bite. "Just a snack to hold us over."

"Do you always carry around snacks?"

Due to the uneven bricks of the cobblestone street, I've had to reach for Aiden's arm more than once. Though I can't say I mind. Naturally, the man came prepared. I'd only wobbled two or three times when he pulled a pair of flip-flops from his back pocket. With a flourish and a grin, he kneeled in front of me and traded them for my Louboutin heels. Now, I'm steadier on my feet, though it doesn't stop me from linking my arm through his. With his other hand, he holds my heels, letting them dangle from his fingers.

"Did you know the microwave was created in Boston?"

I giggle. "Where did that come from?"

"It's about my snacks. Just follow along." He eyes me as he takes another bite of his candy bar. "So there was this guy—"

"Ah, the beginning of all good stories."

"Nah, he wasn't a stalker, and we know that's how all your good stories start."

I don't even try to fight my smile as butterflies flap wildly in my belly. I love flirting with this man, and I love our banter. Since we moved in together and started doing whatever it is we are doing, I love it all even more. "So there was this guy..." I prod.

Aiden smirks. "Yes. He worked for Raytheon, and he was in the lab running tests when he noticed that the candy bar in his pocket had melted."

"So he had a sweet tooth like you?"

"Nah, he liked to feed the animals during his lunch break."

"Ah, a Good Samaritan, then. Not a candy addict."

Aiden chuckles, his eyes boring into mine as his smile stretches across his face. "Yeah, Princess. *Anyway.*" He stretches the word out, and I blink out of the daze his eye contact alone puts me in. "He ran a few tests the next day to see if it was just a coincidence. First, he used an egg, and it exploded. Then he tried popcorn kernels, and they popped. That's when he realized that the device he was working on had food-heating capabilities, and they started to work on the microwave."

"That's pretty cool."

Aiden nods. "So don't make fun of my chocolate-carrying ways. You never know, maybe I'll discover the next big thing."

"Got it. Never doubt Aiden Langfield."

Chuckling, he guides me across the street toward Boston Common.

"I love this spot," I tell him.

"Did you know that this is America's oldest public park?"

Warmth spreads through me as I assess him. "You're just full of fun facts today. Got anything else?"

Aiden smirks. "Did you know the first subway system in the US was right here in Boston?"

What is with this guy and all his Boston facts? It's like he's trying to sell me on the brilliance of the city. Internally, I roll my eyes. That's so something I've read in a book. Big Boyfriend Energy right there. But that's not what we are. We're...God, who knows what we are.

Almost-fake-engaged exes who like to fuck and have fun together?

Now that's a mouthful.

Either way, what we aren't is a real couple, so Aiden has no reason to feel the need to woo me. And even if he were turning on the charm, spewing facts about Boston would be a silly way to do it. I love this city. Not because of the history—*the place where the microwave was invented?*—yeah, that's definitely not romantic. Though the idea does make me giggle.

This is just Aiden being Aiden. Who wouldn't smile at that?

"The waffle stand is on the other side of the park," he says, interrupting my insane thoughts.

"Great, let's go order some waffles."

Despite being convinced that he's not trying to get me to fall in love with Boston, we spend the next few hours doing very touristy things in my favorite city.

For lunch, he takes me to Sugar Factory, which seems like overkill. "Aiden, we couldn't possibly need more sugar."

With a simple shrug, he orders the sugar factory sliders, which come on mini buns in a variety of colors and with a toy.

"Finn is going to love this," he says, snapping a picture of the yellow duck that sits beside our burgers. Seriously, what are the chances? This ducking family.

He also orders a Cookie Monster milkshake for himself and a Barbie one for me. When our server drops them off at our table, I can't help but laugh. His is practically Bolts blue, and mine, of course, is pink.

With a grin, he says, "They match our closet."

After lunch, I feel like I could use a nap, but according to Aiden, we have places to be, so he leads me toward the seaport and straight to a large bus-like vehicle.

I can't help but chuckle at the sight. A Duck Tour? It's such a Langfield activity. The tour bus is a military-grade vehicle created during World War II to operate on land and in the water. Here in Boston, the DUKW, which was used on the beaches in Normandy on D-Day, as well as many other locations during the war, is used to bring tourists through the city and then down the Charles River and yes, it quacks.

We sit up front, and about halfway through, Aiden steals the mic from our guide and serenades the lucky tourists. He lists fact after fact about Boston to the tune of Billy Joel's "We Didn't Start the Fire."

By the time we hit the Charles River and he's started on "The Downeaster 'Alexa,'" the entire group is singing along.

It's amazing how this man can make even strangers fall in love with him. How the hell do I stand a chance of walking away from this with my heart still intact?

It's dusk by the time we make it to the park where we met up all those weeks ago. It's only a few blocks from our apartment. Aiden is now carrying a bag full of several souvenirs he's purchased throughout the day, including a Boston Duck from the Duck Tour company, which he says he'll store next to Luigi, who guards the coffee milk in the fridge. I don't understand that one at all, but I just smile and nod.

As we come upon the crowded carousel, Aiden points to the grassy area where I envisioned his wedding taking place. "Looks like they're having an outdoor movie night."

Silently, I take in the scene before me. There's a large blank screen set up where I imagined the ceremony would take place. Families sit on blankets in the grass, and picnic baskets litter the ground.

I sigh. "God, I always wanted to go to one of these."

Aiden grabs my hand and tugs me forward.

"Where are you going? We don't have a blanket."

Without a word, he guides me to a large blue Bolts blanket spread out on the ground beneath a willow tree. There are lanterns dangling from the branches above, creating a romantic scene.

"Aiden Langfield, what did you do?" I can't hide the surprise in my voice, and I can't pretend to be unaffected. Because this? This is just...I have no words.

He drops his bag of souvenirs to the ground and holds out his hand. "Dance with me."

Butterflies flap wildly in my belly, and my heart pounds so loud I can barely hear the music playing from speakers nearby. Even so, I take his hand and let him pull me close.

"I honestly had no idea they did this. Is it, like, a weekly thing?" I rest my head on his chest as he spins us around our little spot.

"It is now," Aiden murmurs.

I straighten and look up into his beautiful brown eyes. Maybe it's the magic of the day, or the lighting from the movie screen, but they're glowing with happiness. "What do you mean, *it is now?*"

With a secretive smile, he presses a kiss to my lips. "I brought peanut M&M's for you. But I'm keeping all the blue ones."

A movie night on the lawn. Dancing under the stars. M&M's.

"Aiden, why does it feel like we're in *The Wedding Planner?*"

He ducks his head, burying it in my shoulder.

"Aiden—"

His chest rumbles as he laughs. When he pulls back, his smooth smile steals my breath. "Don't ask questions you don't want the answer to."

"Did you—"

He silences me with a kiss, though I'm pretty sure I already know the answer.

Aiden Langfield spent the day trying to get me to fall in love with this city. And tonight, he recreated one of teenage Lennox's favorite movies, a movie we've quite literally been living for the last month.

I can't help but wonder, if what we're doing is all still fake, why would he go to all this trouble?

And if it's all still fake, why do I love every moment of it so much?

CHAPTER 37
AIDEN

Me: Who came up with the puffin idea?

Beckett: I made it happen.

Brooks: LOL. Of course Matchmaker Beckett is to blame.

Beckett: Haha. Laugh all you want. You're all happy because of me, and now we have puffins walking down the aisle. I'm clearly the best man in this group.

Gavin: Why do I have a feeling I should have picked you as my best man?

Me: Who me?

Brooks: Definitely me.

Gavin: Honestly, either. It would surely be better than listening to Beckett drone on about how amazing he is.

Me: I can switch boutonnieres and be in the groom's suite in five. Just say the word.

> Gavin: Aiden, I need you on bird duty.
> Brooks, can you make sure Sara knows not
> to let Vivi touch the puffins? Avery says
> they're friendly, but I'm not taking any
> chances.

DAMMIT. I push my hair back and head down the beach toward Christian Damiano, the Boston Revs' infamous pitcher, and his fiancée, Avery, also his coach's daughter, who are guarding the little penguin-like birds. Damiano is crouched beside one, having a full-on conversation. When he finishes speaking, I swear the bird fucking nods. Then Damiano pats the thing on its head.

Strange.

"Hey, guys. I've been told to hang with the puffins." I hold a hand out to Damiano.

Instead of shaking it, he stares at it and grimaces like it's diseased. I know the guy is a germaphobe, but he literally just touched one of those birds, and now he's worried about my hand?

Avery takes my hand instead, side-eyeing her fiancé. "Hi, Aiden. The birds are ready. Don't you worry."

Her eyes are lit up with infectious excitement. It's exactly the vibe I need. I've been nervous all day. Not because my brother's getting married—and definitely not because of the puffins, though the way one is looking at me right now, like he might be hungry, has me keeping one eye on him as I talk. No, I'm nervous because this is Lennox's first solo wedding, and I want it to go well for her. I want her to be confident in herself. I want to make sure she's happy, content, settled, before I'm forced to make hockey my primary focus for the next month.

The last few weeks with her have been perfect. Lunches out, hangouts with my family, double dates with my brothers and their women, more nights like the one we had in the park, watching movies from the early 2000s, like *Fever Pitch* and *13 Going on 30*—some of our old favorites.

Now, though, it's almost time for Gavin and Brooks and me to shift our focus. If Lennox is confident in her business, content in this life, maybe I won't fail her again.

Because the more I think about it, the more I realize I did fail her all those years ago. At least a little. And that's likely why she ended things.

I was so obsessed with making it to the NHL that I didn't see what really mattered. I didn't see how lost she was. Being with someone so focused, so sure, and so supported couldn't have been easy.

As the music starts, I nod at the puffins and then head down the aisle with my brothers and Daniel, who's joining us as a groomsman since he's Millie's twin.

In the sand on either side of the aisle, white chairs are set up, facing the water. As we make our way past each row, I note one familiar face after another. It's a small wedding—only our family, Millie's family, some of our teammates and their families, as well as a select few friends.

Lake sits beside my mother, holding her two-week-old son Nash. It's a wonder she's here, but it was important to the whole family. She and Millie got off to a rocky start, but in the last several months, they've grown close.

Gavin kneels in front of the women and presses a kiss to our mother's cheek. He runs a soft hand over Nash's head, then gives the new mom a quick peck too. The way Lake beams up at him makes me tear up. I truly do *love* love.

The sun is bright, but the breeze off the water makes the temperature almost bearable as we wait for the music to begin.

I eye the birds hanging with Avery and Damiano, and a bad feeling washing over me. Involving flying creatures in this wedding may not have been Beckett's best idea.

I tilt to one side and whisper, "How well-behaved are the puffins?"

Beckett runs a hand down the front of his suit coat and surveys the beach. "I don't know. Probably better behaved than you."

I scoff. "Right."

Brooks nudges me. "Will you two be quiet and stop fidgeting? The photographer is taking pictures. If you ruin them, Lennox will kill you. And if Lennox kills you, Aiden, then I'll somehow be in trouble with Sara, and no one wants to face Sara's wrath."

Gavin chuckles. "Yeah, your girl is nuts."

Brooks points at him. "I'll let you get away with that, but only because it's your wedding day."

Gavin winks. "Sorry. I'll be good. What is taking the girls so long? It's ducking hot out."

As if he's summoned them, the music starts.

Instantly, his eyes light up. While everyone here will be watching the ladies—and I'm anxious to watch Lennox as she comes down the aisle—I keep my focus trained on the man of the hour. It's the most beautiful thing, watching him get everything he's ever wanted.

Sara is the first one down the aisle. Her blond hair is swept to one side, and her peach floor-length chiffon gown flutters around her. When she sees Brooks, she winks. Then, with her focus set on Gavin, she shoots finger guns, making her bouquet bob. "Your bride is beautiful. You're going to cry."

Next up is Liv, who remains calm as she makes her way toward us, her long brown hair in loose curls.

When she smiles at Beckett, he shakes his head. "Luckiest ducking guy in the world."

Winnie, Finn, and Addie are next. Winnie is wearing a peach dress like the bridesmaids, and though she's wearing a smile, it's forced.

I make a mental note to drag her out onto the dance floor tonight. I haven't seen her light up in a while, and I miss the easy smiles she gave out so freely when she was a little girl.

Five-year-old Addie is in a white dress with some kind of tutu. She's very seriously tossing flower petals as she goes, keeping her focus trained on the basket she's clutching.

With her next toss, Finn, who's beside her, gets a face full of petals. Scowling, he yanks the basket from her hand. As they reach the end of the aisle, he pulls back like he's going to toss it at her. He's decked out in a tuxedo and looks adorable, save for the attitude. Just as he's ready to let the basket fly, my father grabs it.

In unison, every one of us up front lets out a relieved sigh.

That could have gone so much worse.

Next up is my sister, Sienna, the youngest Langfield and Millie's former boss, who is carrying Vivi girl. My niece is wearing a poofy white dress with a peach sash tied around the waist.

It's in this moment that my joy takes over, and I break out in song. It's a Jack Black tune. My Millie song, of course. "Peaches, peaches, peaches, peaches, peaches." I throw a hand up and really lean into the bravado, channeling the opera singer inside me.

Finn tugs on my jacket and stomps on my toes. "Not the time, Uncle Aiden. Bossman says we have to behave."

Holding one hand out and the other to my chest, I cough out a laugh. "Sorry, guys. The moment got the best of me."

Gavin tips forward and glares at me around Beckett. Lake is giggling quietly behind her hand in the front row.

Sara is full on chortling.

I straighten my jacket, position Finn in front of me, and keep my head down. I've finally settled when the music transitions and Lennox comes into view.

I practically swallow my tongue at the sight of her.

She's stunning. Her pink hair is styled in some fancy updo with braids and curls. She's beaming. She outshines her surroundings, which is saying something, because she did an incredible job on everything today.

God, I hope she can truly take a moment to appreciate how gorgeous the ceremony is and recognize that *she* did this.

When her blue eyes meet mine, the music fades, as does my concern for the birds. All I see is my future.

I see the park where Lennox and I met up when we began planning this wedding. The one with the carousel and the setting sun. I see her walking down the aisle to me, our eyes connecting, my heart bursting with love.

My knees wobble, and for a second, I think I'm going down.

Brooks grabs my shoulder and squeezes. "Breathe, brother."

I don't look away from Lennox to acknowledge him, but I inhale through my nose. I work hard not to blink, not wanting to miss this. It may be the only time she ever walks toward me like this. But with every step she takes, my resolve grows. I'll do everything in my power to make sure it isn't.

It isn't until the birds have made it down the aisle behind Lennox that I come out of my stupor.

Sienna must have passed Vivi to Gavin when I wasn't looking, because she's now in his arms, pointing at the waddling puffins and shouting, "Duck, duck!" entertaining the crowd.

The music shifts again, and we all fall silent. I should have known there'd be no traditional wedding waltz today. On Ford's arm, Millie stands at the end of the aisle, radiant. Two musicians play a saxophone rendition of "Witchcraft" by Frank Sinatra.

The first time Gavin set eyes on Millie, she was playing a piano and singing this song.

Millie's dress is simple silk that hugs her curves. Her curly auburn hair blows loosely in the wind.

Gavin sniffles, catching my attention. With tears in his eyes, he whispers to his little girl, "Look how beautiful Mommy is."

The waver in his voice only makes me more emotional.

When Millie and Ford finally reach us, Millie gives Vivi a kiss on the cheek.

Ford pulls her in for a tight hug, pecks her cheek, then hands her off to Gavin while simultaneously scooping Vivi into his arms.

As the pastor welcomes us all, Vivi points to the puffins and screams *duck* again. Ford pulls her to his chest, whispering in her ear, instantly settling her.

All eyes turn back to the bride and groom. My brother squeezes Millie's hand, and as a tear slips from his eye, she swipes at it with her thumb. He grasps her wrist and kisses her fingers, then holds her hand to his lips as the ceremony continues.

My eyes get misty again, and my heart aches at how beautiful this moment is. The pastor's words are moving, and as the sun sets, the sky is a vibrant red. I couldn't imagine a more perfect day for my brother to get everything he's ever wanted.

The perfection is stained a bit when Vivi screams *duck* again, because in the next instant, the sound of flapping wings drowns out the pastor's voice.

I throw my arms over my head as the startled birds flap over our heads. It only makes Vivi squeal louder.

Beside me, Beckett hollers at Damiano. "Get the ducking ducks out of here!"

It's too late, though, because the bald pastor's head is already coated in an oozing brown and white goo.

"Oh, I'm going to throw up," Gavin mutters, backing away and pulling Millie with him. Gagging, he points to the pastor. "Someone help him. And get him away from me." He bends at the waist and clutches his knees. "Oh, it's so bad."

"Whoa, Uncle Gav is going to barf," Finn yells, bouncing on his toes in front of me.

"Damiano," Beckett yells.

The poor pitcher is corralling the puffins, using some type of whistling call, and thank fuck, they're all waddling in a line down the aisle.

Avery cringes, clutching her hands in front of her. "I'm so sorry. I think the crowd made them nervous. But good news," she says as she approaches, pulling a towel from her purse, "the applesauce consistency means the birds are healthy. You shouldn't need any shots."

"Oh my god. You need to go," Gavin groans.

Lennox's face has gone white. Shit. I need to fix this for her.

"Can someone get the groom a water?" I yell.

"And a wet cloth," Lennox hollers, finally kicking into gear.

It takes a good fifteen minutes, but once everyone is hydrated again, and the smell of the birds dissipates, we're all back in position. All of us but the pastor, that is. Though Beckett has taken over the ceremony.

"I knew being ordained online was a good idea," he says with a wink.

The crowd breaks into a chorus of chuckles and whistles and full-out guffaws as he begins.

"We're here today because one of the best people I've ever had the privilege of knowing met my brother."

More laughter.

"No, seriously. Millie, if it weren't for you, Gavin never would have known true happiness. He never would have settled down, and he may not have been ready to be a father to Vivi. The three of you are living a beautiful story full of family and love, showing the world that following your heart, no matter the cost, will always be worth it."

As Beckett goes on, I can't help but watch Lennox. She's misty eyed, with bright cheeks and that dazzling smile.

By the time Beckett finally announces that Gavin can kiss his bride, I swear he's coming out of his skin, dying to touch her.

"It is my great honor to pronounce you man and wife. You may now kiss your bride."

Gavin grasps Millie by the neck and pulls her close. "Peaches," he mutters, his lips against hers.

It's not a chaste kiss. No, he goes all out, dipping her back.

She giggles against his mouth when he brings her back to her feet. "That's Mrs. Peaches to you."

Beckett stands behind them, chest puffed out proudly. Just as the happy couple goes in for another kiss and the photographer steps up to snap a picture, a black bird flies overhead and lets its bowels loose on Beckett's suit.

"Ducking shit," Beckett yells up at the sky.

Vivi claps. "Duck!"

Finn shakes his head, peering up at his dad. "I got bad news,

Bossman. That is not the consistency of applesauce." Then, in a quieter voice, he adds, "Also, that'll be a thousand."

The reception is a blast. It's impossible not to feel the love radiating off Gavin and Millie, even from across the room.

When Beckett gets up to give his speech, we hop up for a surprise flash dance mob, boogying to "I've had the time of My Life." Daniel plays Johnny to my Baby. My brothers and I shimmy our shoulders and walk toward him, dancing to the beat. Millie and the girls are laughing so hard, tears stream down their cheeks. Gavin is grinning wide. When it comes to the lift scene, I give the crowd an exaggerated wink, then sprint toward my Johnny.

Just like I knew he could, my left winger lifts me into the air and spins.

It's a highlight of my life.

It's almost as great as the text message I receive only moments later, while Lennox is in my arms and we're swaying to the music.

> Jill: Hi. Did you buy your mattress from a discount store? Because I am covered in bites from some type of bedbug, and I must be allergic. I tried calling the mattress store, but they said because the order was in your name, you would have to make the claim on my behalf. I'm forwarding my medical bills, my lost wages (since I can't post on social media looking like this), and my therapist's bills. I can't sleep, Aiden. Every time I close my eyes, I picture the little terrors biting my skin. Do you have any idea how awful this is? Here are the pictures that the company needs for the claim. You need to deal with this NOW!

<PICTURES OF JILL'S BODY COVERED IN RED
SPLOTCHES AND HER HIDEOUSLY ANNOYING
RASH-COVERED FACE>

With a guffaw, I show Lennox. Then I shoot Jill a text.

Me: New phone, who dis?

Before she can respond, I block her for good.

CHAPTER 38
AIDEN

THE MORNING LIGHT filtering into the bedroom is bright. We clearly forgot to shut the curtains last night when we stumbled in like two drunken elephants doing a mating dance. If the streaks on the glass are anything to go by, I must have had Lennox up against the window at some point.

It was a great night. And it's a beautiful day. Lennox is lying in bed next to me, her face relaxed and her light pink hair spread across my pillow since she's a bed hog and sleeps on top of me.

While I love that, along with every moment I spend with her, I can't blink away the very empty feeling that settles inside me as I wake fully.

This happens sometimes. No rhyme or reason. I see the sun and count out all my blessings, yet the heaviness in my chest remains.

Like every good thing I have could be ripped from me because I don't appreciate it enough.

The darkness consumes me in these moments. Rather than sucking Lennox into my misery, I slip my arm out from beneath her and face the wall, shutting out the sun. It's a taunt. The people around me are happy, and outside, it's shaping up to be a beautiful day. Yet here I am, stuck in my brain, practically suffocating in my emotions.

Will I ever get over this? I've always hoped that not having Lennox in my life was the issue. But even with her beside me, even after the greatest night with my family, I'm back in this place again.

It's been over a month since I felt this way...I really thought I was past this.

"Morning, handsome." Lennox's voice is raspy. Innocent and easy. Sexy and delicious.

I blow out a breath, trying to summon the happy guy she enjoys so much. I'd been doing so well. Showing her a good time. With my family. With our friends. In Boston. In our bedroom. Everything had been so damn good. "Hey, Lex."

Soft fingers press against my back and then slide across my side, sending a shiver down my spine as she settles them around my stomach and pulls her warm body against mine. "Last night was fun." She drops a kiss to my back.

I try so hard to focus on the way her lips feel. Search for the pleasure in this moment. This is quite literally my dream. Having her all to myself. Her soft, naked body against mine. *Having her*. And yet...

I feel nothing.

Well, that's not completely true. I feel empty. Morose. Heavy. And my frustration leaves me loathing myself. The darkness threatens to swallow me whole.

"It was," I reply, my voice a distant echo of nothing.

She nuzzles against the back of my neck. "Sar said everyone is heading to the beach at ten to continue the festivities. Want to get a quickie in before we shower or while we shower?"

Both. That's what I wish I could say. I want to force a smile. Take her into the shower and do very bad things to her. But I can't summon the energy to move. If I tried, my dick probably wouldn't even show up. That would be so much worse than lying here, letting her think I'm uninterested.

But I care about her too much to do that. She asked for honesty, and if I can't give her bright and shiny Aiden, the least I can do is give her the real me.

"I can't." My voice is devoid of emotion, like a robot has taken me hostage.

She slides a hand over my hip and grips me. "Was I too rough last night? You need me to kiss it better?" Hooking her leg over mine, she pushes me to my back and straddles me.

My expression, or lack thereof, maybe, has her backpedaling almost immediately. "Sorry." She pushes off my chest, ready to dismount.

I grip her thighs and hold her in place. Her fallen expression makes it clear she believes I'm irritated by her, or maybe not attracted to her. That's the farthest thing from the truth, but she won't know that if I won't fucking talk.

Some days, fighting my demons for myself feels futile. But for her, I'll walk through hell. Even if it's a hell of my own making. I'll give it all I've got.

"Sometimes, after a really good day, I feel off." Pressing my lips together, I study her, forcing myself to hold eye contact, begging her to hear my innermost thoughts and ignore the robotic tone. "Like I should be happy. I should walk through life with the biggest smile on my face. Because I've got everything, Lex." I squeeze her thighs again, signaling that she's the everything I'm referring to. "But all that smiling. All the energy it takes to garner smiles from everyone around me." I take a steadying breath. "It just—"

"It costs you," she whispers, her blue eyes swimming with emotion.

"You too?" I say, hope worming its way into my heart for the first time today.

She shakes her head, and I deflate. "I don't give of myself like you do, Aiden. You make everyone you encounter smile, but it's at the expense of your own mental health."

Eyes closed, I blow out a breath. My body is weak. My mind is weak. My heart hurts. I hate that I can't just put on a smile for her. I hate that I can't be normal. That these dark moments plague me the way they do.

"You should go to the beach with everyone. I just need—" I roll my head to one side, looking out the window into the bright day. Forcing my eyes shut again, I exhale. "I just need darkness."

The loss of her is instant, but I'm too numb to feel the pain of rejection when she slides off the bed and walks away from me.

She's going to leave. She should. I told her to. Rather than watching her go, I survey the ceiling and muster the courage to tell her to have a good day. When the room is suddenly shrouded in darkness, the ache in my head begins to ease.

The bed dips, and then her warm hand is on my abdomen and she's curling herself against me, holding me tight.

"What are you doing?"

"Holding you."

I still beneath her, my breath catching. "What?"

"Just relax." She presses a kiss to my chest.

"You don't have to sit here with me. I'll be fine. I just need a few hours."

"That's fine. We'll lay here together in the dark."

"Lex." This time, my heart pangs, and emotion clogs my throat. "Go. Have fun. Don't let my depression ruin your day."

She nuzzles into me and squeezes me tighter. "I'm right where I want to be, Hockey Boy."

Rule 1:
Don't fall for
the groom.

Dearest Lennox

Chapter 39
Lennox

"I REALLY THINK we need something to set us apart from the Kingston wedding." Across the desk, I meet Rayna's eye. Then I assess our boss, Serena, who sits beside her. The bride on the phone has been obsessed with one-upping the Kingstons after Melina's performance at the reception went viral on TikTok.

Serena nods to me, signaling that I should reply, since the bride isn't aware that she's on speakerphone. We were in the middle of an office meeting when the woman working up front told us the bride was on the phone, in a tizzy and demanding to talk to me. "I understand where you're coming from, but your wedding is this weekend. What exactly are you thinking?"

"Elephants."

The snort that escapes my lips can't be avoided. I clear my throat loudly, hoping like hell I can recover before she notices and come up with a tactful response. But all I've got is "Elephants?"

"Yes, there was that exhibit at the Newport Mansions this summer." She launches into a monologue about how, if they're good enough for the gilded town, then they should wow her guests.

Serena is snapping her fingers at Rayna and mouthing for her to pull up the exhibit.

She taps at her phone, then, with a frown, Rayna turns the screen my way. And once again, my surprised squeak can't be avoided. "They're not real."

The bride scoffs. "What do you mean they aren't real? I heard all about these damn elephants and how magnificent they were from Missy Tomlinson at the club just yesterday."

I study the statuesque elephants on the lawn in Newport, tilting my head one way, then the other, trying to figure out what they're made of and ascertain just how heavy they are. Transporting them could be a bitch. "I mean they're not real. They're art. Made from—" I snatch Rayna's phone and scroll so I can read the description out loud. "The sculptures were created by The Coexistence Collective, a community of two hundred indigenous artisans in the Nilgiri Hills of South India. They're made from lantana camara, an invasive weed that encroaches on wildlife habitats."

The bride harrumphs. "Well, that's ridiculous."

I'm not sure her request for real elephants three days before her wedding is any less ridiculous than these being sculptures, but I don't argue with her.

Serena leans down and speaks into the phone. "Would you prefer real elephants?"

While my eyes would love to bug out of my head at the question, the bride doesn't even seem to realize I'm not the one speaking.

"Maybe. What do you think? A real elephant would definitely be cooler than a singer, right?"

Cooler? Maybe. Smelly? Most definitely. Impossible to arrange? Probably.

Once again, Serena replies. "Oh, absolutely. You'd be the talk of the city."

Rayna covers a snort with a fist to her mouth.

"Yes," the bride says slowly, as if she's really thinking about it. "Yes, absolutely. Although...do you think we could find an elephant that doesn't poop?"

I fold my lips in, doing everything I can not to burst at the seams.

No, we can't find an elephant that doesn't poop. "That might be why the mansions brought in statues instead."

"Yes, right. Do you think we should do the statues?"

According to the website, they're traveling across America this year. It's an art exhibit. I doubt it'll be as easy as requesting them, but I can figure out how to let her down once we're off the phone and I have some time to think about what I can offer instead. "Let me look into it, and I'll get back to you this afternoon."

As soon as the bride disconnects, I let out the loudest sigh. "Elephants? Seriously?"

Serena purses her lips, fighting a smile. "Not every event is as glamorous as a child's birthday party."

I cough out a laugh. "Yeah, I guess not. What should I do?"

My boss stands up and shrugs. "Horses?"

"Horses poop." I shake my head. "No animals. Even the puffins pooped on the pastor at the Langfield wedding."

Both women are chuckling as they head for the door. At the threshold, Serena turns and winks at me. "You'll come up with something spectacular. I have faith in you."

At least one of us does.

My instinct is to call Aiden, so I pick up my phone and start to pull up his number. He'll help me come up with something great.

Before I can tap on his contact icon, it occurs to me that I shouldn't be bothering him with this. He's traveling for the preseason, and to be honest, I'm not even sure which city he's in today. I'm trying to be a big girl, reminding myself that while yes, we are friends who fuck, and I'm really, really enjoying that part of our relationship, I shouldn't be this attached.

Obviously, the sex is blurring the lines. And his swooniness. He's just so damn adorable. And nice. Every night since he's moved in, he gives me another pink peony.

Does he have a stash of them hidden in a fridge somewhere?

Is he growing them on the roof?

Who the hell knows. But even while traveling, he somehow manages to have one delivered daily.

What will happen when that stops? When we get married, and the lawyer turns over the family trust, and we can divorce and move on from this insanity. Will we stop fooling around? Stop kissing? Stop...everything?

Yes.

Obviously, that's what's going to happen.

I'll move out, and he'll keep the apartment. We'll remain friends, but it's not like I can date my ex-husband, so...

Yeah, we'll be...over.

My chest tightens, and I rub at the ache I can't ignore.

Thinking about the future is a bad idea. I can't change any of it, but I can come up with a plan for this wedding. I drop my phone and settle back into my chair. I've got a lot of work to do and a lunch date with my mother in—I glance at the clock. Shit, I'm already late. As I'm scrambling, my phone vibrates.

> Mom: Can't wait to see you! Just finishing up a round of tennis with Tacky, so I'll meet you at the bar.

Awesome. Sounds like I may make it on time after all. I grab my things and hustle toward the door. I'm slightly overwhelmed, but for the moment, I'm feeling upbeat. Right now, my personal life and my professional life are going well. They're both sources of pride. Even if my relationship is fake. Also, if anyone can think of over-the-top displays of events for a wedding, it's my mother.

I sit beside my mother and try not to squirm. Across from us is her friend Tacky and Tacky's son Harvey. For the past five minutes,

Tacky has been droning on about Harvey's latest acquisition. To be fair, he seems about as interested in this obvious setup as I am. The blond tech trader has checked his phone no less than ten times, and we've only just placed our lunch order.

While my mother's meddling is nothing new, this time feels especially devastating. For once, I was actually looking forward to having lunch with her. I was looking forward to spending time with her.

I should have known better.

Short of marrying someone who helps my parents' social status, nothing I do will ever make them proud.

I'll never be enough for this woman as I am, and I'm tired of continuously trying to please her.

"Could you excuse me?" I say before Tacky can start on another tangent. Quickly, I remove myself from the table and head for the bathroom. Halfway there, I decide that I need fresh air and make a left toward the lawn.

As I breach the stuffy building, I suck in a breath of fresh air, and without thinking, I pull out my phone.

I said I didn't need him. Convinced myself that I should stand on my own two feet. But right now, he's all I want.

I pull up our text thread and immediately type out *I miss you.* But before I hit Send, that tightness in my chest returns. Should I be texting that? Am I supposed to admit that I miss him? Is this against the rules? We promised that if either of us developed real feelings, we'd say *shamrock* and it all would end. What if he calls me out on it?

As I'm deleting the message, heels clack against the composite boards of the deck.

"What are you doing out here?"

My mother's voice grates on me in a way that feels particularly cruel at this moment. I came out here for a break, for the comfort that I'm beginning to realize only Aiden can provide. Instead, I'm about to get a lecture.

"Why did you invite me to lunch?"

My mother swipes at a nonexistent hair on her face and gives me a perplexing glare. "Because I wanted to spend time with you."

"Then why did you invite Tacky and her son? Why couldn't we have lunch alone? Why am I never enough?" The last question comes out as almost a whisper. A hiss of emotion I wish I could hide. My mother has never approved of showing vulnerability, so I shouldn't be surprised by her response.

"You're making a scene over nothing. Tacky's son is a wonderful young man, and I'm sure he's less than impressed after you up and walked away from the table like that. We watched you walk out the door. I—" She shakes her head, as if I'm the one in the wrong. "I just don't understand you."

Frustration oozes like a festering sore. "I'm not trying to impress Tacky's son. I have a *boyfriend*, mother."

"Please. You're not really going to marry that hockey player. Be serious, Lennox."

"His name is Aiden, and I would be so lucky to marry a man like him." Truer words have never been spoken. I'd be the lucky one if Aiden really wanted me. If what we were doing wasn't a sham.

With a roll of her eyes, my mother points toward the door. "This is not a topic we're going to discuss here. I'm going inside. I expect you to follow." She doesn't even wait for me to acknowledge her statement. Like my father, she knows I'll do what I'm told.

For now, at least.

Too weak to stop myself, I unlock my phone and send Aiden a message, confessing to what I truly need at this moment.

> Me: I could really use one of your hugs right about now.

Then I go inside, knowing full well that I won't get anything I want today.

It's only four o'clock, but it feels like the longest day of the year. After an unbearable lunch, I spent the afternoon researching last-minute wedding surprises and actively ignoring the fact that Aiden has yet to respond to my text. As I walk into the apartment I share with him, though, I can't help but feel let down and foolish.

If anything, today is a reminder that I need to pull back from whatever we're doing. Sex has obviously complicated our arrangement. It's probably for the best that today happened. Now I can—

I'm pulled from my thoughts by the sound of my phone ringing. I dig it out of my bag, and my heart stumbles when Aiden's name flashes across the screen.

"Hi," I say with a sigh, trying to ignore the way just his name has my stomach doing flips.

"Hi, baby. How's my girl doing?"

Tears blur my vision as relief, along with another emotion I can't quite put my finger on overwhelm me. I blink a few times. "I'm okay. Just had a shitty day."

"Tell me about it?"

I drop my purse on the counter and pull a bottle of water from the fridge. When I spot Luigi and the duck guarding the orange soda and coffee milk, my chest warms with affection. "Just a bride with an impossible last-minute request and my mother being herself."

"I'm sorry about your mother. As far as the bride goes, I'm sure you'll figure it out. But if there's anything I can help with—"

I cut him off. "Aiden, don't you have a game?"

"Tomorrow. We finished up early today. I'm sorry I couldn't reply to you sooner."

"It's fine. I shouldn't have bothered you. I'm not sure why I let my mother get to me like that."

The doorbell rings, startling me so badly I bobble the phone.

"Oh," I say as I bring it to my ear again. "Someone's at the door. I hope it's Millie. I could really use one of her wine breaks right about now."

Aiden chuckles. "Go on, answer it. You can call me back."

Even as I walk to the door, I don't want to hang up. But that's precisely why I should. Relying on my friends is one thing. Needing Aiden to make me feel whole is another.

"All right. Good luck tomorrow," I say wistfully.

When I pull the phone away from my face, I realize that Aiden's already gone. My stomach sinks. That kind of stings. The door is barely cracked when I catch a glimpse of the pink peonies. I pull it open wider and discover the sweetest surprise: Aiden Langfield, wearing a smile. It only gets better as I take him in. He's holding my favorite flowers and a bottle of wine.

"What are you—" I shake my head and blink back tears. "I thought you were—" Swallowing, I try to catch my bearings. "What are you doing here?"

He holds his arms open, the bouquet in one hand and the bottle in the other. "My girl said she needed a hug."

"Aren't you supposed to be in—wait, where are you supposed to be?"

"Cincinnati."

"*Aiden.*"

"C'mere, Lex. I only have an hour before I have to get back to the plane if I want to make it to the hotel before curfew."

I throw myself into his arms, forgetting every hesitation I've been stewing over. Fuck it. I'm so far gone for this man already. He got on a plane and flew home so he could give me a hug. He brought my favorite flowers, my favorite rosé, and flew home. For me. The least I can do is say the words I typed but was too afraid to send. "I really missed you today."

"Good Morning, Boston. This is Colton, and I'm here with Eliza to bring you the Hockey Report."

"I can't believe it is finally time," Eliza chirps.

"Yes, game one is tonight, and our boys will be facing off against New York on their ice."

"For those of you living under a rock for the last year," Eliza starts, "the Bolts fired their head coach, Sebastian Lukov, last year after it was discovered that he was having inappropriate relationships with the staff while still married to Zoe Langfield. So not only is this a vicious hockey rivalry, but it's also a personal one for the Langfields. Though Lukov is no longer coaching his nephews Brooks and Aiden Langfield, he's now coaching another. And Vincent Lukov has quite the reputation. He's been known to get into fights with Aiden Langfield on the ice. It will be interesting to see how that all plays out tonight."

"Let's not forget," Colton says, "that we've had quite a roster change this season. After Bolts' captain James McGreevey announced his retirement days before training started, we have a new defenseman in Jensen Jorgenson."

"Yeah, can't wait to hear the nickname they come up with for him." Eliza laughs. "I'm sure it will be a good one."

"*The choice for new captain has been announced as well. Though I think most of us assumed it would be the Leprechaun, Aiden Langfield, Coach announced that Tyler Warren would be wearing the C.*"

"*We'll see if the instigator can keep his temper in check in New York tonight. All right, we'll be back to discuss the team's stats after a word from our sponsor, Hanson Liquors.*"

CHAPTER 40
AIDEN

THE MUSIC in the locker room is turned up loud, and the guys are getting into the zone. For years, my pregame routine has been to dance and sing and get the team pumped up.

Brooks couldn't be more different. He slips on a pair of headphones and ignores every one of us while he goes through every play he thinks could occur on the ice.

Our lineup isn't the only thing that is different this year.

I'm changing up my routine. Sitting against the bench, I focus on my phone, reading each word as Lennox does. The last two months have been nothing short of everything I've ever dreamed of, despite the normal dips in my mood. Hockey during the day, Lennox in my bed at night. Scratch that. Me in Lennox's bed every night. Fulfilling every one of her desires. Making her come until we're both sweaty and exhausted. Until her guard has lowered and she spills every thought that enters her brain. Every wish. Every desire.

I absorb every word. Using them as a play map to win her back. To keep her.

I study her every move, her every desire. Like right now. My girl is reading a stalker romance about two men who are obsessed with the same woman. Naturally, I'm cataloging every detail, running through ways I can make this little fantasy play out for her. Without anyone else touching her, of course. I'm crazy *about* her, not plain crazy.

"What are you doing? Did you manage to get New York's play sheet?" Daniel's question pulls me from my deep thoughts.

I lock my phone. The pages have stopped flipping anyway, which means Lennox has stopped reading. My guess is that she's getting ready to head to the arena with Sara. *In my jersey.*

My cock swells at the mere thought of it. I begged her to put it on last night. Told her I'd get a chubby during the game if she didn't give me a preview.

She refused.

And here I am, hard at just the thought.

I'm so fucked.

"Just a book." I tip forward and stretch, ready to move through the rest of my routine. No more fucking around. Tonight is going to take all my focus and attention.

Not only is it the first game of the season, but it's the first time I'll be up against Vincent Lukov since I found out he'd been fucking my girlfriend for years behind my back.

Scumbag.

I've already gotten my revenge on Jill. Tonight, I'll take down Lukov for good. And then I'll move on.

"Since when do you read?" Camden chirps, earning him a swift hit in the back of the head from our new captain.

"Don't be an ass." War has been different the last few weeks. More focused. More serious.

"I see the C hasn't eased that aggression," I tease.

He folds his arms over his chest and lifts his chin. "Fine. Be an ass, Camden. Ask him what he's reading."

The knowing tone has the back of my neck heating. Does he know?

No. He couldn't possibly know what I did.

Camden runs his hands through his hair with a grimace. "I feel like I'm walking into a trap."

Eyes narrowed, I study War. "What do you know?"

He doesn't move a muscle. His stare hardens.

Brooks must sense the tension. He slides his headphones down, letting them fall to his neck, and surveys all of us. "What's going on?"

War raises a single brow. "Waiting for Aiden to tell us what he was reading."

A bead of sweat drips down my spine, and my throat gets tight. Feigning a cool I don't feel, I shrug. "Why are you all being weird?"

"Okay, now I'm intrigued," Daniel says, swinging a leg over the bench so he's facing me. "What's on that phone of yours?"

My brother swipes it from my hand and clutches my chin, forcing me to look at the screen. "*Ow*," I yell as the phone unlocks, and my home screen appears.

He tosses it to War before I can grab it from him.

"What do we have here?" War mutters as he thumbs across my screen. My ogre of a brother holds me in place with just his damn hands on my cheeks. It's embarrassing, if I'm honest, but even his muscles have muscles. There's no competing with them.

"Holy shit," War groans, dropping his head back. "This is worse than I thought."

Stomach sinking, I close my eyes. Shit. I've been outed.

"You cloned her phone?" he hisses. "This is psycho-level shit, Aiden."

Brooks's grip on my face tightens. "He *what*?"

"It's not what you think," I say, though since I can barely open my mouth, the words are jumbled.

"Let him go. We need that pretty face to take on New York," War mutters, tossing the phone back at me. "Now speak."

I roll my eyes as I lock my phone and toss it into my bag. Nothing to hide now. "It's not a big deal. I just like knowing what Lennox is reading so I can act out her fantasies for her."

Brooks scowls. "Does she know you do this?"

Biting back a grimace, I shrug. Okay, some may call it stalkerish to clone a person's phone, but I don't read her text messages or anything. I just follow along with what she's reading using her Kindle app. Makes me feel closer to her when we're apart. And we're going to be apart a lot now that the season has started.

"That's fucked," Camden murmurs.

War nods, but his look is appraising rather than condemning. "Truly fucked."

"Is it because of Lukov?" Brooks says, his tone soft. "Trust issues after what Jill did? You know Lennox isn't like that. It's clear she's crazy about you."

It's clear she's done a great job of making everyone *believe* she's crazy about me. Sometimes she even has me convinced.

"I don't read her messages. I'm not stalking her," I defend, gripping my phone tight.

Brooks cocks a disbelieving brow.

"It's like *half* stalking," I amend.

War snorts and kicks at the bench leg closest to him. "Half stalking. I like it."

"You should tell her how you feel," Brooks offers.

My chest tightens again. He means well, but Lennox and I aren't like him and Sara. They were best friends when they started fake dating. She never rejected him.

If I tell Lennox how I feel, she'll call the whole thing off. Then she'll marry someone else to get her inheritance—someone who isn't hopelessly in love with her—and I'll lose my chance at convincing her that we could be more than fake. That we could be forever.

"I will," I lie. "I do. All the time. Seriously, this isn't about Jill. I do it to feel closer to her. But I'll tell her I did it. She'll probably find it hot. She loves stalker romance." I grin, hiding my emotions behind my go-to funny guy mask. "Now, it's time to unveil the new team song I've been working on."

War's lips twitch. "New song?"

"Yeah, I figure new captain, new season." Hopping up onto the bench, I raise my hands. "New song!"

"Fuck yeah." Camden and Daniel launch themselves up onto the bench on either side of me.

The room grows quiet. Why wouldn't it? This is a sacred part of our game prep.

I start with the beat, stomping my foot twice and following it with a clap. Camden and Daniel catch on quickly, mimicking the movement and sound. It only takes a couple of heartbeats for the rest of the team to catch on to where we're going with this and break out in cheers as I start my own personal rendition of Queen's "We Will Rock You."

"Brooksie, you're our guy, make a big save,
Defense got your back, gonna be a great game today
With Halls to my left and Cap to my right
Sliding the puck right into the net, chanting
The Bolts will, Bolts will win it.
The Bolts will, Bolts will win it."

The chants grow louder as I lead the team in our new anthem, giving each man attention, calling to their strengths, reminding them that, as a team, we've got this.

By the time Gavin comes in to give his pregame pep talk, we're energized, focused, and ready to take New York down.

Starting the season playing on another team's turf isn't ideal, but it happens. Tonight, though, is so much worse than any old away game. New York fans hate us. They've welcomed Seb with open arms, seeming not to mind that he's a cheating asshole who cares about no one but himself.

I keep my eyes averted from New York's bench so that I don't inadvertently make eye contact with the fucker. I try my best to stay grounded during warm-ups as Daniel and I circle one another, slapping the puck back and forth, then as we move into stretches. The music in the arena is loud, but War is quieter than normal, his gaze drifting to New York's bench often. Unlike me, he'll gladly make eye contact with Seb, and every time he does, he shoots daggers.

Brooks skates out of the crease and taps me on the back. "You ready for this?"

I throw my weight into him, wrapping him and his bulky gear up. The guy doesn't even budge. "I'm good, bro. Let's fucking do this."

Brooks releases me with a laugh and skates backward, gloved hand pointed at me. "Let's go."

War is by my side an instant later. "Remember, let him come after you first. You can't make the first move."

"You can't either," I remind him.

War's grin is devilish. "Don't you worry."

"You remember your lines, right?"

War rolls his eyes. "To the wall—yeah, I got it."

I smack him against the chest. "Don't fuck with the songs, War. It's how we win games."

He skates away from me. "No. We win because I toss you the biscuit, Lep."

I'm readying a quip when I catch a glimpse of pink behind his head. "Move," I yell, waving wildly and tilting to one side to look around him.

He does a little dance, blocking my view, but when I charge toward him, he skates out of the way.

She hasn't spotted me yet, so I speed toward the plexiglass and stop with a twist of my ankle, icing the boards. When she still doesn't see me, right the fuck in front of her, I bang on the glass.

Lennox finally turns my way, her pink lips turning up in a big smile. "Hey, Hockey Boy. Fancy seeing you here," she yells.

With a twirl of my finger, I motion for her to turn around, but she just raises her eyebrows coyly, as if she has no idea what I want.

Tease.

"Princess," I growl. I need to see my name on her back. Though I'm loving the way the jersey fits snugly across her breasts. How the Bolts blue makes her irises more vibrant. As I take her in from head to toe, my jersey, a pair of white jeans with slivers of her thighs peeking out beneath the ripped fabric, I catch on a flash of blue in her hair. Amidst the pink, she's got a tiny blue braid on each side of her head. As she slowly turns, she reveals that the braids meet at the back of her head with a blue ribbon. And she's wearing my fucking name and number. As I take it all in, the *Langfield* emblazoned across her shoulders and the 12 beneath it, my cock thickens beneath my gear.

Just as my gear gets a little uncomfortable, she turns around and winks. "Now go win the game. If you're lucky, I'll still be wearing this when you get back to our room tonight."

I'm a simp for this girl. Despite how focused I am on winning tonight, it's incredibly hard to skate away. So I don't. I watch her continue on to find her seat until War literally drags me by the back of my jersey to center ice.

I'll probably be a meme tomorrow, and I couldn't give two fucks.

My girl's in my jersey, I'm smiling, and we're about to kick New York's ass.

Rule 1:
Don't fall for
the groom.

Dearest Lennox

Chapter 41
Lennox

"SORRY, WAGS COMING THROUGH," I sing as I shimmy my shoulders, practically dragging Sara through the arena.

She apologizes to each person I push past. I'm obnoxiously excited. It's my first game as Aiden Langfield's side piece—I'm testing out different titles; I suppose that one doesn't work—and it's the first time I'm wearing his Boston Bolts jersey. I've heard all about the magical things that happen to women when they wear these things—orgasms on desks, sex on pianos—I can't wait to see what the orgasmic jersey fairy will grant me.

Sara tugs on my arm. "Lennox, slow down."

I practically growl in my pursuit of getting to the ice. The team traveled to New York last night, so Aiden and I spent the night apart. I haven't seen him in twenty-four hours, and I haven't had an orgasm in like twenty-four and a half hours. Your girl is *hagitated*.

Since Gavin and Millie's wedding, Aiden and I have barely gone a night without fucking. Most of the time, more than once.

Practicing, training, studying, and all the other *ings* he has to participate in have kept him busy, but the man still has the stamina to fiddle my skittle every night.

Except for last night, of course. And it's been a shock to my system.

The guys are finishing warm-ups when we find our seats. I haven't even settled in, though, before Aiden is banging on the glass. It's like he's got a tracker on me. The mere idea of something so psychotic has my blood heating and my skin flushing.

Clearly, I'm sick in the head.

I tease him by acting nonchalant. As if I have no idea why he's so excited about what I'm wearing. I love him like this. The unhinged puppy.

Sara laughs as we make our way to the seats Gavin scored us. "You're evil."

I shrug. "No idea what you're talking about."

"Sure you don't." She lets it go, though, because she's working today and has to focus on the game and the goings-on both off and on the ice so she can anticipate what questions the media will ask, prepare the players, and intercept if necessary.

Though once we're settled, she turns to me, and suddenly, it feels like she's the media. I can practically see the list of questions spinning through her mind. "Excited to be back in New York?"

Humming, I survey the ice and the guys getting ready to play. "It's not that different from Boston, to be honest."

In my periphery, Sara is watching me. "So you don't miss it?"

I take a moment to reflect on the time I spent living here. By myself. Going from job to job, man to man, friend to friend.

My life in New York was the opposite of consistent. Before I moved back to Boston, I would have sworn that was the dream. I didn't owe anything to anyone, and that meant I was free to do whatever I wanted.

What I didn't allow myself to see was that in return, I was owed nothing from anyone, leaving me living a sad sort of existence.

Since I returned to Boston, I've created routines. Sunday brunch with the girls, coffee dates with Millie, movie binging sessions with

Sara. Genuine friends who want to see me, who care about me and expect me to be there for them too. I love it.

And that says nothing of the time spent with Aiden. He brings me coffee in bed every morning—with whipped cream swirled on top. He understands and shares my love for everything sweet. We learn TikTok dances together, then force his teammates to do them. We ride bikes in the gym after practice, just so we can talk. Twice a week, we attend couples' dance classes at the studio we found for his fake wedding.

My life is full and busy and bright.

I look back at my friend and answer honestly. "No, I don't miss it at all."

Sara hums. "You've been in Boston for seven months." Though it's a statement, it feels a lot like a question.

"Okay?"

Her eyes dance. "You never stay in one place longer than six."

The buzzer sounds, announcing the game is going to begin, and we shift our focus to the ice. But her words keep playing in my head, even after the puck has dropped.

CHAPTER 42
AIDEN

VINCENT LUKOV IS A BULLY. Like that kid in high school who doesn't get enough attention, so he just keeps chirping, hoping someone will look in his direction. He's mean, miserable, and too dumb to realize that no one cares what he thinks.

I'm focused on the puck in the ref's hand. New York's center is vying for it with his stick, just like I am, so Lukov's taunts don't even register.

The sound of the crowd is deafening, but the moment the puck drops and I slice, the dance begins. My skates grind into the ice as I push forward, but Lukov is right on my heels. He slices at my skates, coming after my scraps like he always does, but my vision tunnels as my body takes over. I could play hockey with my eyes closed.

"What? You can't face me now that I stole your girl?" he jeers behind me.

I just hum my tune, ignoring him.

"Now dip, War, dip," I holler.

War nods and does just that, dipping behind, luring the defenseman trailing his ass to circle back toward him.

"To the left," Daniel shouts. The idiots around us think he's talking to me, rather than singing the lyrics to our next play, and they almost leave enough room for me to slide my stick in that direction. But it's War who appears to the left of me now, jutting out his stick, tearing between Lukov and me as I break away. The plan is that Lukov will either trip or be delayed, but I'm too focused on the net and the man who stands between me and my goal to worry much about it.

A muffled "fuck," followed by a thud sounds behind me, and I assume he's gone down. Then my teammates are pressing forward and into position.

"To the right," I hum, almost coming to a stop in front of the goalie, Matteo Rodego, who is braced for my shot. The rest of his team is almost caught up now.

I fake it right, and then slash the puck over his left shoulder and into the goal.

"Didn't expect you to dance with us, Rodego," I yell, laughing, as Daniel and War tackle me in celebratory hugs.

Less than a minute into the game, Boston has a goal on the scoreboard. My heart pounds, and adrenaline courses through me. While I've scored hundreds of goals in my career, none have felt better than this one. Because she's here, and she's wearing my name on her back.

Every guy has their celly, their celebration after a goal. Some dance, some have a signature move, some just enjoy the thrill of hugging their guys. Me? In high school, my move was all for her. I did it after every goal because she was always there to cheer me on. First as my best friend and then as my everything. Today, she's once again both.

My moves are slick like Michael Jackson doing the moonwalk. It's instinct. Like my body has been waiting years to do this again. Not once have I had the opportunity since I hit the NHL.

Turning to the camera, I put my hand on my heart, then bring my fingers to my lips and blow Lennox a kiss. If I knew where she was sitting, I'd point right at her. But in the general direction of where she was headed before the game will have to work.

She knows exactly what that move is. Wherever she is, she's

catching the kiss and smiling. Fingers on her lips, knowing that this goal, like all my future goals, is for her.

With a smile still on my face, I turn, only to find Lukov coming straight for me.

Motherfucker.

"You're a little late to the block," I call, skating past him.

He grabs me by the jersey, clearly looking for the fight. "I'll let you have that one since I stole your girl."

With a shove, I scoff. "From the way she tells it, you didn't steal her. You pawned her off on me, hoping I'd pay to keep her. Joke's on you, though. I'm not Blockbuster. I don't keep rentals."

Jaw clenching, he yanks his gloves off and throws them to the ice. Looks like I've hit a nerve. He wants this. Joke's on him again. I'm too fucking happy to fight.

He's just another bully seeking attention, and I have no interest in wasting any of mine on him.

Unfortunately, the hate he spews next is impossible to ignore.

I spin on him, tossing my gloves too. From the look on his face, shock mixed with fear, he knows he's taken this seventy thousand steps too far. I rear back and slam my fist into his throat, aiming for his vocal cords, hoping to do enough damage to keep him from ever speaking again.

Rule 1:
Don't fall for
the groom.

Dearest Lennox

Chapter 43
Lennox

"HOLY SHIT," Sara hisses as we gape at the scene playing out on the ice. Only moments ago, she was screaming about Aiden's breakaway. During the first play of the game, the Bolts scored, and Aiden blew me a kiss, just like he did when we were in high school. Though I'd love to focus on what that means and maybe even process how it made me feel, I'm sitting on the edge of my seat, clutching my thighs, because some guy just rammed into him from behind.

Sara grabs my hand and squeezes. "It's going to be okay."

"It doesn't look okay."

I bite my lip as Aiden throws his gloves down and punches the other guy square in the throat. As the man goes down, his helmet flies, and then his head is hitting the ice.

Screams echo around the arena. These aren't cheers for Boston. They're a battle cry. The fans want Aiden to pay for the guy's injury.

"Who the hell is that?" I whisper as we watch to see what happens next.

Rather than climb to his skates, the guy lies on his back on the ice, and as one second bleeds into another, my nerves fray.

"Vincent Lukov," Sara murmurs, her eyes trained on the ice. "As in the guy Jill was cheating with."

The tether that held my nerves together snaps, and a heavy weight slams against my chest.

Vincent Lukov. Jill's boyfriend. As in Aiden's ex fiancée's current boyfriend.

Fuck.

My stomach rolls. Aiden rarely fights. He's the happy guy on the ice. But even from all the way up here, the rage radiating off him is palpable.

Why did he fight him? What did Lukov say to provoke this kind of anger from the easiest-going guy I know?

My stomach twists at the thought. It's not hard to figure out. The man slept with Aiden's fiancée. A woman Aiden spent three years with.

I'd have to be a fool to think Aiden is over it. He told me as much when we came up with the fake marriage farce.

I'm offering this as a friend.

I won't fall in love with you.

Aiden's on top of the guy now, and New York's players are descending. It's a melee. Blue and black jerseys blend together as fists fly.

Trembling, and with my heart in my throat, I search for Aiden amid the chaos.

I made him promise he wouldn't catch feelings. He swore he'd be fine. He promised he could fake it. Clearly, he was right. Apparently, our friends and family weren't the only ones who were fooled.

CHAPTER 44
AIDEN

EVERY MUSCLE ACHES when I finally walk into the hotel where Lennox and I are staying for the night. The rest of the team is headed back to Boston now, but since we don't have practice tomorrow, I got the okay to stay behind. Lennox promised to spend a few hours in the dark with me in the morning, and then, if I'm up for it, take me to her favorite lunch spot before we take the train back. Then I'm off to Seattle for our next away game.

Even after the ten minutes I spent in the sin bin, we pulled off a win. I rarely get penalties, but this one was worth every minute.

No one talks about Lennox.

Unlike in Boston, the people I pass in the hotel lobby aren't happy to see me. Anyone who recognizes me practically scowls with hatred. Especially after tonight.

By the time I make it up to our room, my head is pounding, but the thought of the woman on the other side of the door—*in my jersey*—has renewed energy coursing through me.

I push open the door to our oversized suite. "Lex?"

I loosen my tie as I stride across the main area in search of her. The door to the bathroom opens, and she appears. Her sullen expression registers first. Her face is devoid of makeup, like she scrubbed every bit of it off, but her skin isn't smooth and glowing like it normally is after she finishes her nightly routine. It's splotchy and red.

She's been crying.

She's also *not* in my jersey.

My jaw ticks, and tension knots in my shoulders. It was literally all I asked for. All I wanted. And after tonight, after everything that happened, it's what I needed.

"You're upset," she says plainly, turning off the light in the bathroom.

As she steps into the room, I can't help but state the obvious. "You're not in my jersey."

With a huff, she rolls her eyes. "I'm not wearing your jersey after you got into a fight over another woman."

I reel back. "What?"

"Vincent Lukov. He's the guy Jill was cheating on you with."

Shrugging, I get to work unbuttoning my shirt. Might as well get comfortable if we're having a discussion. "Yeah, so?"

Lennox's breasts rise and fall under an oversized pink T-shirt that reads *I am the fun.* Her cheeks redden and her blue eyes go hard. "You're obviously still hung up on Jill. Otherwise, why would you beat the shit out of him?"

My fingers halt on the third button of my shirt, my heart thumping hard against my sternum. "Because he said your name." My voice comes out sharp. *Angry.* Because I am. Lukov went too far tonight.

Her eyes go wide. "What?"

Keeping my focus fixed on her, I continue unbuttoning my shirt. "I couldn't give a flying fuck about Jill. Which I told him. He can have her. Or get rid of her. Whatever. But no man will mention your name the way he did and not end up breathing out of a tube."

"Holy shit, that's hot." Her pink lips are parted, her eyes searching mine. With a sharp intake of breath, she covers her mouth and shakes her head like she can't believe she said that. "Aiden—"

I pull the tie from my neck and wrap it around my hand, then point it at her. "No. I'm sick of everyone telling me how I feel. I haven't cared about Jill since the moment I saw you again."

She rolls her eyes, the action so sassy I'm tempted to bend her over my lap and spank her. "Maybe once you found out that she cheated."

I eat up the space between us in two strides and get right up in her space. "No," I grit out. "Since long before that. I walked into that meeting dreading it. Knowing I wasn't supposed to marry her. I was miserable, Lex. And then you walked in there like a damn ray of sunshine and I..." I force a long breath in and hold it in my lungs before releasing it. Finally, my anger dissipates. This woman in front of me changed everything that day. "I knew right then and there I couldn't marry her. The elevator hadn't even made it to the ground floor before I ended it."

Frowning, she whispers, "After she told you about the affair." It's not a question, yet the statement is filled with doubt. She's unsure.

I don't want her unsure. I want her to know. Fully. The whole truth.

"No."

Her blue eyes cloud with confusion and disbelief. "What?"

I huff out a breath, garnering my courage. It's time to lay it out there. "Not after. *Before*. I told her it was over. That I couldn't give her my heart when it still belonged to someone else."

"*Aiden*," she whispers, bringing a hand to her heart.

"You've had it since we were fourteen, Lex. Whether you wanted it or not, my heart's always been yours. I'm not jealous of Vincent Lukov. I couldn't give a fuck about him or Jill." I cup her jaw, brush at the lone tear that slips down her cheek. "I've been miserable since the day you walked out of my life without telling me why. Don't pretend you don't know it. You may not want me the way I want you, and that's okay. I'm okay with our situation. I've made peace with it. But don't pick a fight with me over someone who doesn't matter. Don't play dumb. We both know where we stand. Me on my knees, *always* worshiping you."

"You're rewriting history," she hisses, backing out of my hold. Then louder, angrier, she adds, "You haven't been miserable for the last decade. I've seen you, Aiden. You dated. You're going to be in the freaking hall of fame. *You* got engaged."

"I *survived*," I yell, my voice far too loud, the agony that's plagued me for a decade coursing through my veins. "I put one foot in front of the other. What choice did I have?" I point to her chest. *"You left."*

"Yes," she hisses. "I left. I had to. Because you threatened to follow me."

All the air leaves me. Mouth agape, I can do nothing but stare at her. "I what?"

With a deep inhale, she turns and shuffles toward the window. "You don't remember?" She glances over her shoulder but doesn't wait for my response. "I didn't know what the hell I wanted from my life. Obviously, since I still don't. But back then? *God*, my parents were on me *every day*. They had all these plans for me. You had plans for me—"

My heart cracks open. Fuck. To be lumped in with her parents? It's like a knife to the chest.

She turns back, her expression softer. "I wanted our plans. But I was eighteen, and I wanted to experience life too."

"You ended it because you wanted to experience *other* things?"

Other people. That's the first thing that comes to mind. She wanted to see what else was out there. I figured as much. It's what my friends all told me I should do when they found out I was still hung up on Lennox years later.

"No. I wanted to experience life, period. You were so secure in your knowledge of what you wanted. It made me feel lost. So when my grandmother suggested the gap year, it seemed like the answer."

"But why couldn't we do long distance?" Desperation pricks at me. The years I spent wondering, questioning myself, bleed into my every word. "Why couldn't you travel, figure out what you wanted, while I worked to get to the NHL? Why did you just leave me behind and act like our time together meant nothing to you?" Emotion stings behind my eyes. My chest is flayed open for her to see. "Like *I* meant nothing to you."

Blue eyes sparkle, full of tears, and regret laces her words. "You meant *everything* to me, Aiden. You meant so much that I broke my own heart and gave up my dream to make sure that you didn't give up on yours."

My exposed heart sinks. I'm empty. Lost. "What are you talking about?"

"You called me after I told you I was going to Europe."

"No." I drop my head and give it a shake. "I didn't. You said shamrock, and I respected the pact."

She huffs out a watery laugh. "That wasn't the pact. We agreed that if one of us said shamrock, then we'd go back to being friends. *Nothing changed. That* was the pact."

I throw my hands out, aggravation getting the best of me. "I was eighteen and pissed off that my girlfriend dumped me for no reason. I'm sorry. I was an asshole." I suck in a breath, trying to rein in my emotions. "Why did you say shamrock? *Why* did you end it?"

I plead for the truth. Desperate to understand. Because I want this. I want us. But I don't know that we can ever truly make it if I don't get these answers.

"You called me," she says, her mouth turned down. "You were drunk and sad because I'd told you I was going to Europe instead of joining you at school. You'd already left for training camp. I told you I wasn't coming. That I was going to Europe."

My heart stutters at the vague, blurry memory. "Yeah, I remember."

She runs her hands through her hair, parting it to the side. "You said you would leave camp the next day. That you'd come back and spend the rest of the summer with me. That you'd take a gap year too."

Lips pursed, I study her sincere expression, the crease between her brows. She doesn't look like she's making this up, but that's ridiculous. I couldn't do that. I'd have lost my spot on the team.

She points at my face, drawing her finger in a circle. "See? You get it now. You were willing to throw away your career because you loved me. And I loved you too much to allow you to do that."

With my hands on my head, I tip it back and blink up at the ceiling. *Fuck*. She's right. I would have done it. I was so head-over-heels in love with her that I would have done anything for just a little more time with her. Hell, I still would. Look at me, planning a wedding so I can spend time with her, conning her into agreeing to marry me in the hopes that she'll fall for me in the process, cloning her damn phone so I can read along with her because I miss her when we're apart. It's not rational. I'm downright insane when it comes to her.

"I was miserable without you," I say. That's the simple truth. I straighten and exhale. "I played like shit for months. Didn't talk to anyone. Hell, it took me two years to go on a date."

And it was a horrific experience. Touching another person never got easier. Yet I had no choice. She left me. Didn't want me. That's what I thought.

She sucks in a breath. "I went the opposite direction. Kissed all the wrong people, hoping I'd forget you. Hoping it would hurt a little less. But I—" She shakes her head. "I don't think I ever did."

"I know I never did."

She shakes her head and whimpers. "Aiden," she says, the word a plea. "You were engaged."

I sigh, but it's not in aggravation anymore. Or sadness. I'm exhausted. Tired of the lies. Tired of holding it together all the time.

The truth spills out of me like an old, rusted faucet. It spurts ugliness and then gushes, purging the years of half-truths and lies until nothing but clear, pure honesty flows through.

"Because my brothers wouldn't stop bothering me about my obvious crush on you. I ran into the damn wall the first time I saw you back in Boston. The second time, I threw up. They were onto me, but after the devastation I lived in when you broke up with me, I figured it would be easier to marry someone I didn't feel that way about. She couldn't hurt me if I didn't love her, right?"

Tears well in Lennox's eyes. "You really didn't love her?" she whispers. There's hope laced amidst the sadness.

"How could I when my heart still belonged to you? I've never loved anyone but you. If you'd stayed, I would have only ever kissed you. If you'd have let me, I would have been your one and only, and I'd have worn that title proudly." I smile ruefully. "Hell, I probably would have been insufferable about it. Matching T-shirts and everything."

The tears fall then, rolling down her cheeks, even as she breaks into a smile. "Idiot."

I move closer, cupping her face and brushing away the tears that continue to fall. "I'd be your idiot any day of the week. Forever. I'm stupid in love with you, Lex. I always have been. There's no reason for you to ever be jealous or insecure. You're the only person I see. The only person who truly makes me smile. Even in the darkness. And though I can't be your only kiss, I'll take being your last. I think I could wear that title proudly."

Eyes shining, she gives me a watery smile. "I'd really like that kiss now, Hockey Boy."

With her cheeks still cradled in my palms, I tilt her head back and press my lips to hers. It's electric, our connection. It always is. But in this moment, it feels like we're sharing our first kiss. Like a beginning and yet also like coming home. There's a comfort in knowing the truth. In laying it all on the line and opening up my heart.

No longer do I have to hold back and pretend that I'm not head over heels for her. I don't have to play a game or act in any sort of role. We're living in this moment, and though I have no idea what the future holds, I know that we have right now. And right now, she's mine completely.

"I have another confession," I whisper against her mouth, holding her in place.

She exhales, her breath skating over my lips.

"I stole your phone and cloned it. I've been following along with your stalker romance as you read it."

Her lashes flutter and her brows dip. "What?"

"I'm crazy. Yes." I shrug, going for nonchalant, even as my heart rate kicks up with a mixture of fear and excitement. "But you find crazy sexy, right? At least in your books?"

"Are you a little stalkerish?" Her tone is raspy and filled with wonder.

"Mildly." I hold my thumb and forefinger an inch apart. "Just a little."

Her breathing has quickened, her pupils dilating. "Fuck, why is that hot?"

"'Cause I'm a friendly stalker?" I surmise, with a slow grin. "Kind of like Casper."

She huffs a laugh. "He was a ghost."

"That your kink?" I tease. "I'm sure I could figure out how to do that too."

I'd do anything for her. Be anything for her. Even if, deep down, I hope that I'm enough on my own. Every day, I'm a little more confident that it's the truth.

Lennox sucks in a breath. "Are you saying you want to make my book fantasies come true?"

Heat coursing through me at the excitement in her tone, I lick at the seam of her lips. "Is that something you'd want?"

"Maybe," she whispers. Her words are a little hesitant, but the hope in her eyes as she catalogs my reaction is enough of an answer for me.

"Did you bring any toys with you, Princess?" I run a hand up her side, to the curve of her breast. When I reach her nipple, I give it a pinch.

Her eyes fall closed, and her breath goes ragged. "Like what?"

Smiling, I pinch again. "Whatever you have."

She rubs her thighs together, clearly as excited about the prospect as I am.

With my hands on her shoulders, I spin her around and push her toward her suitcase, smacking her on the ass as she goes. "Come on, Princess. Grab everything you've got. Let's see what we're working with."

With a quick peek over her shoulder, she opens her suitcase. Then she pulls out the selection she's brought with her.

I sidle up beside her and take the toys. When she straightens, I brush a kiss to her lips. "I'll take these. Can you go grab some ice down the hall?"

Her eyebrows furrow adorably. She's already worked up, and now she's frustrated that I'm sending her on an errand instead of getting her naked. "Ice?"

I give her hips a squeeze and nod to the door. "Play along, Princess. I promise you'll enjoy it."

Her blue eyes glaze over. "Okay." Ice bucket in hand, she pads to the door.

"Try not to scream too loud tonight," I say as she steps out into the hall. "Wouldn't want the hotel staff to find the Kennedy princess getting fucked like the little whore we both know you are."

The door clicks shut, cutting off her gasp, and I get to work. Tonight, I'll give Lennox Kennedy every fantasy she's ever had. She deserves it and so much more, because that woman is every fantasy of mine come true.

Rule 1:
Don't fall for
the groom.

Dearest Lennox

Chapter 45
Lennox

MY BRAIN CAN'T COMPUTE what's happening right now. How we went from angry to truthful to loving to *this*...whatever this is.

For now, I ignore the war of emotions raging inside me. I'll have plenty of time to analyze the confessions that finally broke free from both of us and how it feels like a turning point—whether I'm ready or not—later. For now, I'll focus on the words he spoke as I left the room.

Try not to scream too loud tonight. Wouldn't want the hotel staff to find the Kennedy princess getting fucked like the little whore we both know you are.

Why the hell do I love it so much when he talks to me like that? It should feel degrading. Should make me want to punch him in the face. If he were anyone else, I'd slap the words right out of his mouth.

But when he treats me like his dirty whore, it sets me ablaze in the best way. When he calls me Princess, like the word is filthy, it empowers me.

Because despite the vulgar words, he worships the ground I walk on.

And I know for a fact he'd never hurt me.

I press the button for ice, and as the bucket fills, I can't help but imagine all the ways we might use it. Pulling in a few ragged breaths,

I try to calm my pounding heart. It's no use. I'm wet, excited, and desperate for his touch.

There's no tempering this emotion.

So I hustle back to the door. Excitement and nerves spark inside me when I find it ajar, the bolt holding it open just a smidge. The room is dark as I step inside, the silence ramping up my anticipation.

As the door shuts behind me, there's suddenly a hand clamped to my mouth. Then I'm pulled back into a thick, hard chest. "Don't scream, Princess, and you'll make it out of here alive."

Holy shit. As my pulse skyrockets, arousal floods my body.

"Cover her eyes," he says, the rough tone making my kitty flutter. His breath ghosts over my ear as he leans close. "I'm going to take my hand off your mouth. If you scream, I'll have to shut you up, and I promise you *won't* like it." His words come out harsh, like he's truly angry.

The temptation to test him, to find out what tricks he has, is hard to ignore. But for the moment, I obey, nodding against his fingers.

Just as my eyes begin to adjust to the darkness, they're covered, and I'm doused in complete darkness again. The fabric is satiny smooth. Probably the silk tie he removed while we were arguing. He tugs twice, then nods against my shoulder. "Good girl."

Shivers cascade down my spine at his praise. Why does it feel so good to know I please him?

"I want her on all fours," he says, once again talking to *someone else.* With his hand on my shoulder, he guides me forward. When my knees hit the bed, he pushes me onto my stomach with his palm to my back and holds me down.

"First I need to prep her," he replies to himself, his tone slightly deeper.

"Spread your legs, Princess," he mutters in a voice more like his own. He yanks my pants down, groaning when he finds me bare beneath them. "Look at that, easy access. It's like you want this. Like you were waiting for us to sneak into your room and fuck you until you can't remember your name."

I whimper, suddenly starved for air. I'm dizzy with lust, bucking against the bed, needing his touch. He laughs behind me, still pinning me down with a hand to my back.

"Look at you, humping the bed. You need release?"

"Yes," I rasp.

The sound of his hand cracking against my bare ass registers before the stinging sensation.

"Too bad," he grits out. "We're going to have you soaking these sheets before we give you what you need, Princess."

"And we know what you need," he adds in that darker timbre. "'Cause we've been following you. Watching you. *Stalking* you."

My chest rises and falls, my breathing ragged. Aiden removes his hand from my back, the loss of him so acute, it makes my chest ache. Cold liquid hits my ass, startling a gasp from me. Then warm fingers massage slowly between my cheeks. When he presses his thumb inside my tight hole, I flinch.

"Breathe, Princess. I promise this will make you feel so good."

With a deep breath in, I will my body to relax.

Aiden caresses my back, silent assurance and praise, as he works his thumb in farther. Then more liquid is poured onto my ass, and his thumb is replaced by a cool metal object.

"Holy shit," I hiss, recognizing the feel of the anal plug.

"Stay," he mutters. That single word is followed by the loss of his heat.

Seconds tick by, my clit pulsing more fiercely as the anticipation builds. I'm not sure I've ever been so turned on in my life.

The bed dips. "Fuck her throat until her ass is ready."

Desire ignites in my veins as his voice transitions to that stern tone again.

"On all fours," he instructs, guiding me with his hands on my hips. When I'm in position, he tilts my chin up. "Open." He grasps my jaw with the slightest force, and I eagerly oblige. He feeds the head of his cock into my mouth, my lips against his hot, hard length, my tongue laving over the barbells. I gag almost immediately.

In response, he grips my throat and squeezes lightly. "You'll take this cock all the way to here without complaint." He presses against my vocal cords.

I hum in anticipation as he sinks deeper, the cool metal of each barbel warming against my tongue. When his tip is touching the back of my throat, when my eyes are stinging and I'm fighting for air, he squeezes my neck again. "Now swallow."

I do as he says, and when I don't gag this time, his hold on my throat becomes a gentle massage. "I can feel myself right here."

"She's doing so well." His voice is deeper again. The way he transitions between soft and hard makes me wetter. My every fantasy floods me until they blend together, leaving me throbbing with need. "Now fuck her throat until she comes."

I couldn't. He couldn't...

But I'm already so close, there's a throb between my legs. Is it possible? Could giving him pleasure be enough to make me come?

Fisting my hair, he thrusts, his pace relentless. I'm whimpering and tearing up from the intensity. Without the ability to see my surroundings, I'm hyper-focused on every sensation. I can only rely on him to control me so I don't fall forward or choke. Every move is more intense.

Without slowing, he pinches my nipple. The move has me flexing around the plug, and then my entire body bursts into tingles, and I moan around his cock. He pulls out quickly, jerking my head back as I cry out his name.

"Holy fuck, Aiden. I'm coming."

The next thing I know, he's sliding beneath me, sucking my clit into his mouth.

"Yes, you are. You're dripping all over my face. Fuck, you're so sweet," he rasps between sucking and licking and nipping at my clit. When he impales me with his tongue, my eyes practically roll to the back of my head. "I think she's ready." He punctuates the observation by sucking my pussy fiercely, like he's trying to inhale me.

He slides from beneath me and replaces his body with a pillow.

"Lean on this. If it gets to be too much, bite down on it so we don't wake the entire hotel."

"Cocky much?" I taunt.

Instantly, he lands a sharp slap to my ass, pulling a squeal from me. I'm not sure how he got there, but now he's behind me, and already, my body is raring to go again.

He presses a soft object to my clit, and at the familiar tugging sensation of the massager, I moan, recognizing the rose he's latched to me.

"Sit on his face, Princess," he mutters. "He can take it."

Obediently, I press my weight against the toy and relish the way the delicious pressure mounts.

Then the head of his cock is between my thighs, and without warning, he thrusts inside me. The force makes me bite down on the pillow to muffle the curse that escapes me.

"Oh, she likes your tongue on her pussy while I stretch her," he says in that cold tone again.

Yes. Yes, I do. There isn't a thing Aiden could do that I wouldn't like.

"But she needs more," he taunts. "Right, Princess? One cock isn't enough for you. You need to be filled in this hole too." He presses his thumb against the plug, teasing me.

"Yes," I pant.

He pulls the plug out without slowing his movements, still thrusting in and out slowly, still rocking my hips against the rose that's suctioning my clit perfectly.

I bury my face deeper in the pillow and release the cries building inside me.

By the time the buzzing starts, I'm already dripping with excitement. In anticipation of what's coming next.

"Wet his cock so he can fuck you properly." Aiden, voice harsh, wraps his hand around my throat and lifts me up, guiding the vibrator into my mouth.

I suck on it good, imagining it's him. I'm so into everything he's doing that he has to pull it from my mouth, the move creating a loud *pop*.

"She loves having your dick in her mouth," he grits out. "She's gushing around me right now."

I moan, grinding against him, not embarrassed in the slightest by how needy I am. When he presses the vibrator against the tight ring of muscle, I tense.

Aiden puts a warm palm against my back, and in a steady tone, he talks me through it. "You love this, don't you? You love feeling him sink inside you. Want to know a secret, Princess?"

Whimpering, I wiggle my ass, desperate to make the burn subside.

"I love it too," he groans. "Love the feel of the vibrations against my cock. I can feel him working himself deep inside your asshole right now. You're so fucking wet. Being shared like this turns you on, doesn't it?"

I love every second. But what I love the most is that I'm with Aiden. That he cherishes me so much that he's giving me this. Playing this game.

I'm lost in that thought when a switch flips. All of a sudden, he's fucking me roughly, giving me exactly what I crave. The vibrator hits me exactly where I need it as the clit simulator sucks and his piercing massages perfectly. It only takes seconds for him to send me skyrocketing into an abyss that has the darkness consuming me. My limbs are boneless, my body humming with desire. When he swells, his movements jerky, and lets out a low groan, coming in hot waves inside me, I ride him into my third orgasm of the night, my body lighting up like a fireworks display.

Gripping one hip, he holds me up as my knees shake. "I got you, Princess." He gently removes the vibrator, then pulls himself back, murmuring soothing words the whole time. Carefully, he adjusts me so I'm on my side. "Stay," he murmurs, dropping his lips to my hip. Then he's gone. With shaky, tingling hands, I turn the rose off and toss it, heeding his request to lie here and catch my breath rather than slip the blindfold off.

He returns moments later, first removing the tie covering my eyes. He follows the move with a tender kiss to my lips, then my cheeks. I blink my eyes open, but the room is still shrouded in darkness, and all I can make out is his silhouette. He presses a warm, wet cloth between my legs, cleaning me, and when he's finished, he pulls the blankets up and tucks me in. He joins me a few seconds later, water bottle in hand. "Drink."

I obey. I'm far too gone to think for myself.

After he confirms I've had a sufficient amount of water, he pulls me to his chest and strokes my hair.

I'm pretty sure I fall asleep within seconds.

Deliciously sore, I wake up with a smile on my face. Last night was...intense.

The sex. The emotions. The confessions.

Despite the way my body aches, I feel lighter than I have in years. I never realized how much our breakup weighed on me. Questioning whether I did the right thing. Wondering if he'd hate me forever for how I handled it all.

Telling Aiden the truth of why I walked away, watching his face register the shock and then acceptance, was cathartic in a way I never would have expected. Because he understood. That understanding reinforced my belief that I made the right decision for us back then. He's incredible on the ice, and he would have come to regret walking away. He'd have resented me eventually. We wouldn't have made it.

But as I lie in bed with him now, relishing the way he holds me and his even breaths against my neck, a different future for us forms in my mind. One I never thought was possible. One I've wanted so badly for years. It's the reason I gave up on the idea of happily ever afters, because if it wasn't with him, I didn't want it.

With a sleepy groan, he presses a soft kiss to my shoulder, making my heart flutter.

Spinning so I can face him, I survey him and quickly get lost in his warm, sleepy brown eyes. "Hi, Princess."

"Hi Hockey Boy."

He slips his hand down my backside and squeezes. "How are you feeling?"

"Like I got fucked by a pair of stalkers."

Chuckling, he brushes his lips against mine. "Must be my many dazzling personalities and huge cock."

Circling his length, I give it a firm squeeze. "It's positively massive." I thumb each bar along his shaft, twisting them as I go.

He closes his eyes, and a guttural moan escapes him. As I slide my thumb over the head, smoothing his arousal over him, he shifts his hips closer. I'm adjusting, ready to slide down his body and show him precisely how much I enjoy his massive dick, when my phone dings.

That specific sound is a bucket of ice water on a hot fire. It's the ringtone I set for my parents so that I'm always prepared before picking up the phone. Even a text message from them can sour my mood, though I didn't realize until now just how badly that simple sound could ruin a moment.

I wince and drop my hand, a niggle of worry hitting me. I hate to disappoint him, but the moment is lost.

His face doesn't fall. He doesn't even look disappointed. No, concern swims in his eyes, but that's the extent of it. "What's going on in that pretty head?"

I groan into his chest. He's so warm. I could easily get lost in him if I breathe deeply enough.

"Lex," he says with more urgency. "What's wrong?"

"It's my parents. That's their ringtone. Ignore it. They'll just ruin today."

Warm lips press against my forehead. Once, twice, three times.

Then he tips my chin, forcing me to face him. "We can't keep running. Let's face it head-on. Together."

His words fill me with a strength I didn't know was within reach this morning. So with a hum of agreement, I pick up my phone and look at the message.

> Mom: I've booked the club for your thirtieth birthday. Could you send me a list of people you want me to invite?

My stomach rolls at the thought of my birthday. Especially when a second text pops up, this one in a separate thread.

> Dad: Just over a month until your deadline. How about we turn the party into a wedding reception? I've already spoken with Donald. He thinks it's a great idea.

With a loud groan, I throw myself onto the mattress. "He's such an asshole."

Aiden's eyes narrow. "Who's Donald?"

"Donald Sparrow. Of Sparrow Holdings. He plays golf with my father."

"What would he have to do with your wedding reception?"

Oh, sweet Aiden. He still doesn't get it. My father will never stop making deals. He'll use every advantage, every situation, to increase his fortune and his standing. Despite how little we need either. "I guess my father thinks he should be the groom."

Aiden's jaw hardens.

The almost imperceptible reaction makes my heart lurch. I drop the phone and press my hands against his face, anxious to soften him. "He's never going to give up on this."

"That's why we have this plan, isn't it?"

My stomach flips. "You still want to do this? It feels wrong now that things are—" I sigh. I'm not even sure what things are, but they're complicated. That's for damn sure.

"They're what?" Aiden asks, his tone perfectly calm.

"I still don't know what I want to do with my life. Hell, I don't even know if I really ever want to get married. Or if I want kids. My parents have always dictated my life. I'm only now learning what I like. For so long, I've made choices just to spite them. Finally, I'm taking into consideration what I actually want."

He studies me, his lips pressed together in earnest consideration. "Do you want to be with me?"

"Yes." There's no hesitation in that answer. "But you want—"

Aiden presses his finger to my lips. "*You.* I want you. We can figure out the rest along the way. You don't want kids? Fine. I'm an awesome uncle. Not sure marriage is for you? That's okay too. I make an excellent roommate, and I'm pretty sure I proved to you last night that I'm an amazing lover."

He presses his lips against mine, and I relax against him. How is it that my mind and my body settle so easily when he's near?

"There's no rush for me, Lex. I love you. I'm not going anywhere. Years ago, you gave me what I needed by walking away. Let me give you what you need by staying. You have me by your side for as long as you want me—fake weddings, real ones. I'm down for it all."

My heart floats in my chest as I think of all the possibilities. Of all the fun we could have. A lifetime of it. "We'll need to really sell the engagement."

Aiden's smile is blinding. "You leave that to me. Just promise me one thing."

"Anything," I whisper.

"You'll be in my jersey at the home game on Friday night."

CHAPTER 46
AIDEN

> Robert: Just confirming our session for this evening.

I WINCE at the text from my therapist. For once, my life is going perfectly. I don't want to focus on the bad right now. And every time we talk, that's where the conversation leads. Plus, I'm busy tonight. But it's a good thing. A great thing, really.

> Me: I've got to get ready for my game.

> Robert: I understand, but this is the second time you've canceled. I would love to help you process what happened at your last game.

> Me: Tomorrow. I promise.

I switch over to my family text.

> Me: I need everyone at the game tonight.

> Brooks: Wouldn't be anywhere else. LOL.

Me: Ha. I'm serious.

Gavin: Why text all of us? Beckett's the only one you need to confirm with. Obviously, I'll be there too.

Me: Because I mean everybody. Millie, Sara, Liv, the kids. Team meeting at the game.

Beckett: Whoa. Only I get to call team meetings.

Me: So call a damn team meeting.

Beckett: You could ask politely.

Me: Just ducking be there. All of you.

Brooks: Everything okay?

Me: I'm good. Very good. And for some reason, I want my annoying-ass brothers and their families there to see how good.

Beckett: We'll be there.

Brooks: Like I said, I wouldn't be anywhere else.

Gavin: if you need anything...

Me: I need you to find a reason to get Lennox in the box during warm-ups.

Gavin: On it.

Me: Thanks.

Beckett: Is this what I think it is?

Brooks: Holy shit, Sara's gonna lose her mind.

Gavin: It's about damn time.

I sigh as I read my brothers' messages. They couldn't be more right. It is about damn time.

"Good Morning, Boston. I'm Colton, and this is my co-host Eliza. We're here to bring you the Hockey Report."

"After two away games, our boys will finally play on home ice for the first time this season," Eliza says.

"Despite the rough way game one started," Colton chimes in, "with the fight between Vincent Lukov and Aiden Langfield, the guys have had a great start."

"Yes," Eliza agrees. "Lukov is still out due to his injuries. We're fortunate that he was the one to take the first swing. Otherwise, our star center would have likely been suspended for a few games."

"The new D-line is incredible. Parker and Jorgenson play together like they've been doing it for years. I was worried there'd be hiccups after McGreevey's retirement, but so far, the two have great chemistry. Let's see if they can keep it up tonight against Denver."

"Yes, tonight's game will include a ceremony to celebrate last year's Stanley Cup win, so I imagine McGreevey will be in attendance. I'm sure the guys will appreciate seeing him there."

"Yes, the puck drops at seven thirty, so make sure you tune in. We'll be back tomorrow to recap what will likely be another exciting night on the ice."

Rule 1:
Don't fall for
the groom.

Dearest Lennox

Chapter 47
Lennox

Go into this with an open heart. I promise I'm doing this with only the best of intentions. You're floundering and missing out on life because you're too scared to go after what you want. I hope you take this as the push you need rather than as another excuse to hide. Pick someone you could love. Maybe someone you already do. A person you can laugh with. Who enjoys the same things you do. A man you care about. One whose loss would be palpable if you didn't take the leap with him. Stop surviving and start living.

I FOLD the letter up again. I'm still not ready to finish it. I've been savoring her every word. Sometimes the brutal honesty is painful. And there are times I despise the control she's wielding—something she never did while alive. But I savor every sweep of the pen because it's the only thing I have left of her. I've spent months reading it slowly. Knowing there are only two more paragraphs makes my stomach roil with unease. I'm not ready to let her go.

I slide the paper back into my jewelry box, grab my purse, and head for the door. It's odd how the words feel like they were written for the game Aiden and I are playing.

Nervous anticipation skitters through me as I head to the arena, and it stays with me as I wave and smile at each person I recognize in the concourse. I'm wearing Aiden's jersey as requested—the question is, what does my Hockey Boy have planned for me?

Sara jogs up to me as I head toward the suite. Threading her arm with mine, she gives me a tug. "The boys are about to start warm-ups. Wanna ogle them with me?" She waggles her brows and breaks into a bright smile.

I point at her, giddy, because it hits me now that my senses are back. "Oh, you just got naughty in the supply closet."

Sara's jaw falls slack. "Bitch."

"A BJ too. Way to go, Brookie."

She snorts. "Unreal." She narrows her eyes, scrutinizing me. This time I'm the one making my brows dance. "Dammit," she huffs. "I'm not getting a read on you."

"Because I'm not a slooty sloot who gets sloppy in the closet."

With a shake of her head, she turns toward the ice. "Whatever."

Music blasts through the speakers, then the guys are skating out one by one. Beyoncé's "Crazy in Love" is playing, which is...*odd*. This was our song in high school, and it's about the last song I would expect hockey players to warm up to before a game.

Also, their warm-up routine looks completely different. Like they're moving in a synchronized way. Like it's choreographed. Like its...*planned*.

"What is happening?" I whisper as Aiden skates closer. He doesn't have his helmet on, and he's wearing a big smile.

Gavin opens the gate to the box and waves us in. "Need your help with something, Lennox."

When I don't move, Sara pushes me forward.

"Seriously, what's happening?" I ask as the guys skate into a line behind Aiden and come to a stop, spraying ice as they do.

The arena lights flash, and the announcer comes over the system. "Please rise and give a warm welcome to our Boston Bolts."

The stands are only about half-full, but as the fans stand, the noise level cranks up a notch. The speakers crackle as "Crazy in Love" transitions to "Single Ladies." As it starts, the guys lined up behind Aiden shimmy their shoulders back and forth. Aiden launches himself into a series of complex dance moves on his skates that mimic Beyoncé's movements in the music video.

It's a flash mob of hockey players on the ice.

My body swims with joy, my pulse racing and my cheeks aching because my smile is so wide.

When Aiden starts to sing, I realize he's mic'd.

"All the hockey players, all the hockey players,

All the hockey players, all the hockey players,

Put your sticks up,

It's been a few years, quite a few tears, I got tired of doing my own thing,

Almost picked wrong, though I knew all along, only Lennox Kennedy was for me.

I looked at you, you looked at me

No one else ever had my attention

You've owned my heart, right from the start, and now I'm gonna get down on one knee."

I clap a hand over my mouth as the entire team breaks into the chorus, their shoulders dropping down as they slide their skates back and forth, doing the moves perfectly.

"I really like it, so I'm gonna put a ring on it,

You're my dream girl, so I'm gonna put a ring on it."

Then he's skating toward me, and Sara is pushing me through the gate and out onto the ice.

Before me, Aiden drops to a knee.

"Just marry me and I'll put a ring on it."

The team sings the chorus as Aiden opens his palm and looks up at me, revealing a gorgeous oversized pink diamond. He covers his mic with his free hand and whispers a challenge. "Never have I ever gotten married."

His brown eyes twinkle, and I swear they say *I told you I had a plan.*

In response, my heart asks, *Is that all this is, though? Part of the plan?*

But as he looks at me with nothing but pure love, his warm smile says, *You know it isn't.*

"Marry me, Lex," he says out loud.

I lean into him, needing to be closer so that he knows my answer is genuine and just for him. So he knows that I want this. I want to take the leap with him. I don't want to just survive the next few months so I can gain access to my trust. I want to live this life. I want to enjoy it. I want him. Us. *This.*

"Yes, a thousand times yes." My words echo throughout the arena, startling me. A laugh bursts from my chest when I remember that he's mic'd.

"She said yes," he yells to the guys who are still dancing to the music, making him proud.

When he turns back to me, the brightness of his smile has tears pricking at the backs of my eyes. With both hands cupping my cheeks, he presses his lips to mine. The diamond digs into my face, making him pull back quickly. "Shit. You need this."

I hold up my hand and allow him to slide it onto my finger. "It fits perfectly."

He smiles. This time he mouths his response, letting me know it's just for me. "I know. I measured your finger while you slept."

I snort. "Stalker."

He shrugs. "A friendly one, though."

Pulling me in close, he kisses me again, this one soft and languid. The crowd is watching, and the cheers around the arena are deafening. Though Aiden has created a giant spectacle, none of it feels like it's for them. This is for us. As he releases my mouth and drops his forehead to mine, I study my ring. He absently strokes over the band with a thumb, like he just needs to be reminded that it's there.

"Is this real?" I whisper, still shocked.

Cupping my cheeks again, he ducks down and locks eyes with me. "This is whatever you want it to be, Lex. You have me, in whatever capacity you want, forever."

My heart swells as the gravity of his words hits me. "You've got a game to win, Hockey Boy."

He nods and presses another kiss on my mouth.

Sara taps on my shoulder and directs us to smile at a photographer who's appeared out of nowhere. We take picture after picture, the team even getting in on some. Then, still lost in a whirlwind of emotions, I follow Sara upstairs to the owner's suite.

"Holy shit," Sara breathes. "You're getting *married*." She spins and takes me in, wearing the biggest smile I've ever seen. "We're marrying brothers. We're going to be *sisters*."

My chest splits open then, and I swear butterflies pour out. "Holy shit. That's wild."

"Brooks has always been my favorite, for obvious reasons but Aiden just nudged him out of first place."

I snort. "You realize that we also have Brooks to thank, right? He's gotta marry you in order for us to become sisters."

Her eyes darken. "Are you trying to insinuate there's a world in which he changes his mind and doesn't marry me?"

"No. Definitely not." I grip her arm and stretch my hand so she refocuses on the sparkly ring and not dark thoughts. "Come on, we need a picture of our hands together."

"We do," she squeals. Then she's pulling out her phone and throwing herself into the task. Fifteen hand pictures later, we head into the suite.

When we step inside, the whole Langfield crew is here, along with our friends, cheering and clapping and rushing me.

Then, with a glass of champagne in hand, I watch my guy play one of the best games of his life. Between the second and third periods, Beckett appears by my side. "I take it Aiden hasn't made a terrible roommate?"

I bite my lip. "He's been very respectful of my space."

Beckett nods, though his gaze remains trained on the ice, like he's actually interested in watching the Bolts mascot skating around and making a fool of himself. "He wants a dog, you know."

"Huh?" I shift in my seat and scrutinize the incredibly confusing billionaire. He's known as a demanding grump to the press and his employees, but I've never seen that side of him.

He gives me a calming smile. "Not now. But eventually. There's a brownstone on my street. Plenty of space for a dog to run in the yard. Kids in the neighborhood. It's not for sale yet, but it will be by the end of the year."

My heart lodges itself in my throat. I'm thoroughly confused by this cryptic conversation. "Okay?"

"Liv tells me that Josie's party was incredible. And Ava mentioned that she could use some help with charity events for Langfield Corp."

I nod, chest growing tighter, still confused about where this is going.

"Is that something you'd be interested in?"

I peer over my shoulder, searching for who could be putting him up to this. Sara is preoccupied with Millie and Vivi, dancing in front of the glass and pointing down at the mascot. Liv isn't even in the room. She and Winnie dipped out to use the bathroom. Winnie has been withdrawn all night again, despite the festivities. No one else is watching us, so I turn back to the peculiar Langfield brother. "Did Aiden put you up to this?"

Crossing his arms over his chest, Beckett frowns. "What? I don't run business decisions by my brothers."

"This seems like a stalker thing Aiden would do. A way to get me to his away games like Brooks has with Sara."

Beckett scowls. "I assure you, I have nothing to do with my brother's *stalker* plans." He clearly doesn't get the implication in that word.

Thank god. Even so, my cheeks heat. "You'd actually be very busy. The events are all held in Boston, so you'd rarely have to travel, and you definitely wouldn't be accompanying the team. You'd be planning parties for sponsors and investors. Sometimes players, I suppose, but those would all be local. The charity work we do would be a large part of it."

"So you, what, heard I'm good at this and are offering me a job?" I'm still so confused. I've never been good at anything. If Aiden didn't ask Beckett to do this...

"Yes. I make a point to hire the best. Name your price, and we'll make it work."

I appreciate that he assumes it's a done deal. Like I'd be an idiot to say no. The truth is, I would. This is what I've been waiting for. A career I love. One I'm good at. One with a purpose. Sure, weddings are fun to plan, but Josie's party was far more rewarding because it brought joy to a little girl who doesn't regularly experience it.

"I'll think about it."

Beckett nods evenly, like he has no doubt I'll say yes. "Get with Liv and set up a time to come in this week. We'll get you into the Langfield system and make it all official."

"I appreciate it, Beckett." I hold out a shaky hand. Between the engagement and the job offer, my nerves are a mess.

Rather than shake my hand, he pulls me in for a hug. The man truly is a conundrum.

As he releases me, he adds, "And think about the brownstone. There's a park across the street, so Aiden would have plenty of room to run."

I snort. "You mean the imaginary dog you've selected for us would have room to run?"

With a tilt of his head, he furrows his brows. "No. Have you met my brother? He's the one who needs a field." Without another word, he slides his hands into the pockets of his dress pants and strides away.

I, naturally, burst into laughter.

This really has been a strange day.

The crew is all smiles, mingling and snacking and goofing around. All except for Beckett's son—the troublemaker. He's got his arms crossed, and he's staring me down.

Glutton for punishment that I am, I head in his direction. "Hey, Huckleberry. You going to congratulate me?" I crouch down to his level and look him in the eye.

The kid squares his shoulders and eyes me up and down. "The last girl he proposed to didn't make the cut. You going to be nicer to him?"

Appreciation sweeps through me. There's no hiding my smile. This kid. He's seven and already watching out for Aiden. It's official —he's my favorite. "He's my guy, Huck. Don't you worry. I'll work to make him smile every day, just like he does for me."

And I mean it too. Standing in this room, surrounded by our friends and family, waiting for the man of my dreams to play his dreams out on the ice, is everything. It makes all the difficulties in my life seem inconsequential.

My job. My parents' demands. The trust. None of it compares to the way I feel about this man.

After another incredible win, Aiden joins us in the suite to celebrate. From there, he tells me to pick a place to move our celebration. I request the underground bar. His responding laugh is raucous. Because while I could choose any place in Boston, I picked the team's sports bar. What he doesn't get is that where we go doesn't matter. Being with him is all I care about.

And tomorrow, we'll wake up together, close the blinds and sit quietly in the dark.

Together.

Rule 1:
Don't fall for
the groom.

Dearest Lennox

Chapter 48
Lennox

DESPITE THE BURNT orange and yellow leaves adorning every tree flanking the street as I walk down Langfield Way toward the corporate offices, the warm sun is decadent on my skin.

Beside me, Sara is wearing a smile that rivals mine. Her hair is now Bolts Blue because the season is officially underway.

She bumps me with her shoulder. "We could do this every day, you know."

A warm laugh bubbles out of me. "You are at the arena or traveling for like half the year."

"Okay, not *every* day. But still," she says, growing quieter. "This is huge, Len. An engagement and a new career? Are you freaking out?"

I give myself a moment to mull over her question. Not even a year ago, I was single and living in New York. I didn't have a career; I had a job. I owed no one anything.

We're approaching Langfield Corp so that I can discuss the potential new job. Accepting it would mean I'd be tethered to the Langfield family not only through our marriage, but for work too.

I'd be going all in.

A breeze kicks up, causing fallen leaves to ghost past us. That swish of wind feels like magic. Like Boston's way of luring me into accepting. Reminding me of its beauty in the simplest of moments.

Fall in New England.

A walk to work with my best friend.

Bliss warms my cheeks and brings a smile to my face. "Not freaking out even a little bit."

"Good. Liv's awesome. Not just as a future sister-in-law, but at work. And she keeps Beckett in line." She snorts. "Well, as much as anyone can keep that man baby in line."

"He really is hard to figure out. One minute, he's aloof and glaring, and the next, he's on the ground, wrestling with Finn."

Sara nods, a big smile spanning her face. "Exactly. At work, he's a lot more reserved." She grips my arm. "Unless he's with Cortney Miller. He calls him Man Bun. Jeez. I can't even tell you how excited I am to talk to you about all this insanity."

"Man Bun?"

She smiles. "He's the GM for the Boston Revs, and he's married Liv's best friend Dylan. You'll love her. They're neighbors too."

Beckett's comment from the other night comes tumbling back to me. The house on his street with lots of room for Aiden to run. I can't help but giggle at the suggestion. For a moment, I force myself to really picture it. A home with Aiden. Family nearby. My best friend turned sister in the same city. Millie, Liv, all their kids.

A full life. One that almost makes up for the lackluster response from my own parents after I texted them both, asking if we could get together this week so I could talk to them in person about my engagement.

My mother told me she could possibly fit me in next Friday.

Next Friday.

She only has one child, and she can't make time for me until a week from now, and that's not guaranteed.

Why am I even bothering? They'll only ruin my joy. They never liked Aiden, and they'll never accept the engagement. My mother will pout, and my father is probably already scheming ways to break us up.

Outside Langfield Corp, I tip my head back and take in the skyscraper. The hundreds of floor-to-ceiling windows make it look like a hunk of blue ice standing amid the standard brick of Boston.

Is that why they chose the design? The family is obsessed with the color, with the sport—at least Aiden is—so it wouldn't surprise me in the least.

I eye my reflection, then Sara's. My faded pink hair is pulled low and to the side in an elaborate braid. My darker pink sweater cinches at my waist. Beside me, Sara is wearing a black skirt and black boots, just like I am. She leans into me, also taking in our reflection. For a long moment, all we do is breathe.

"I'm so proud of you," she says.

My heart squeezes. I'm proud of us both. For going after what we want. For taking a risk after being hurt. For being true to ourselves.

"Come on," I say, tugging her inside. I'm ready for the next big thing.

As Sara leads me through the offices, she introduces me to every person we pass. She's obviously well liked. It isn't even slightly surprising, since she's my favorite person.

Hysterical, kind, and generous with her time and affection. She's always been all of those things. For years, though, she saved those parts of herself for only the people closest to her. In college, she was closed off, and I made it my mission to help her make friends. Dragging her to parties. Forcing her to flirt.

It was all in an attempt to be so loud that no one ever truly got to know the real me.

Except for Sara. But even with her, I hid my softer side. Aiden may be the only person who's ever known the whole of me. It's fitting, since I only feel whole when we're together. When I'm his and he's mine.

Sara practically drags me toward her office, but we stop short when we hear giggles from the door beside hers.

"Beckett, stop. Not here."

"Can't. Need you."

That phrase is followed by a loud, low growl.

My best friend and I look at one another, eyes wide, and burst into laughter.

"Holy shit. Beckett can get it," I whisper.

Sara drops her head and gives it a shake. "You have no idea," she mouths. "I've walked in to find our future sister-in-law fixing her lipstick too many times to count."

I waggle my brows. "Get it, Liv."

Grasping my hand, Sara pulls me through her door. "I'll just email her that we'll be ready for her when they're done."

With a chuckle, I settle into the couch in her office. I'll never get over how nice her space is. It always smells like fall in her office because of the diffuser she keeps going. There's also an entire book-shelf filled with pictures of her family and friends.

My personal favorite is a picture of her sitting on Brooks's back as he does one hundred push-ups on the ice while in full gear—their pregame ritual. She's got this big smile on her face that only comes out when she's around her fiancé.

A light tapping has us turning our attention to the door.

When Ava tentatively peeks in, I squeal. "Oh, hi, girlfriend."

Ava is still pretty quiet around us, and it's probably a good thing. I'm not sure our group of friends could take another loudmouth like Sara and me. Hannah is sarcastic and a badass boss babe, but she's not loud. Millie is quieter, though not timid in the least.

Ava seems like she's always one wrong move away from breaking. Like a beautiful piece of blown glass created by a difficult situation that has left her incredibly delicate.

"Liv asked me to be around for the meeting, but I can wait in the hall until it's time, if you girls are catching up," she says in her soft way.

"Stop it." Sara scowls. "We've been over this. You're one of us girls."

With a deep breath, Ava sets her shoulders and floats into the room. Her long, thick red hair is probably the heaviest thing about her. Other than her personality. She's constantly surrounded by sadness. The only time I've seen it lift is when she's around Josie.

And she hasn't seen Josie in weeks. Since the little girl went to live with her mother and her mother's fiancé, all she's gotten is a few photos and vague updates here and there. But we do know that Josie is healthy and happy. It's hard to ask for anything more.

"How are things with Xander?" I ask.

Ava clutches her iPad to her chest. "Still pretty new, but good."

Sara chuffs out a breath. "I still can't believe you're dating a guy who's related to War."

Ava's grip on the iPad tightens further, her knuckles turning white. "Yeah."

Curiosity has me leaning forward. Aiden is close with War, especially now that War is captain, because Aiden has always been invested in helping his teammates, the rookies more than anyone. I like War. He's got a rough exterior, but like with Ava, I think there's more to his story.

"How's he been?"

Ava shrugs. "They aren't close, so I see him more at work than when I'm with Xander."

Sara perks up. "Brooks mentioned that."

Ava nods, pressing her lips together. "Xander is close with his stepfather, but I guess War isn't. After his parents' divorce, War chose to live with his mom and really didn't visit his dad. The guys had barely met before they were in high school, even though they'd been stepbrothers for years and years." She lowers her gaze to the floor between us. "I don't know. Family is difficult, I suppose."

I snort. Truer words have never been spoken.

"That's why we have each other," Sara says.

"That we do," Liv chimes in from the doorway.

I practically jump out of my chair, straightening my skirt, my heart suddenly pounding. It's strange, feeling like I have to make a good impression while simultaneously knowing this woman is about to become family. "Hi, Liv."

As she steps into the office, her cheeks are flushed, and the tie on her wrap dress is askew.

Behind her, Beckett strides in wearing a smile, looking perfectly presentable.

Liv glances back at him, and in response, his eyes settle possessively on her lips. God, I love them.

"Stop," she hisses, obviously seeing what we all see.

Beckett merely smirks, then turns his attention on the rest of the room. "Good morning, ladies. Ava, thank you for joining us for this meeting."

"Nope," Liv says, turning and pushing him toward the door.

Confusion pulls at Beckett's brows. "What do you mean *nope?*"

"I can talk to Lennox about the job. You will just get in the way, Mr. Langfield."

Sara and I eye one another, rolling our lips to keep from laughing. Liv did say that's what Beckett likes being called in the bedroom. That knowledge instantly turns us into schoolgirls, ready to throw ourselves down on the floor in a fit of giggles.

Ava must be used to this, because she doesn't blink over their interaction.

"Fine, but you owe me a date night," he says to his wife.

"We don't have a sitter," Liv says, her shoulders deflating.

Beckett turns to the rest of us. "We haven't had a night out since before the twins were born. She refuses to let any of my brothers watch the kids. Thinks they can't handle all five of them by themselves."

Sara straightens. "We'll do it."

Every head in the room whips in her direction.

"Right, Len? The guys don't have a game on Friday. Between the four of us, we can handle them."

My chest gets a little tight at the prospect. The older kids, maybe.

BOSTON BOLTS HOCKEY: HOCKEY BOY   385

But twin babies? I've spent almost no time around children, especially babies. This is the definition of being thrown into the deep end.

Then again, Beckett's words from the other night replay in my mind. Aiden's need for a place to run and play. He'd be such a good dad. Maybe spending time with his nieces and nephew would help me figure out whether I could ever see myself wanting kids of my own.

"Yeah, we can do it," I say, my tone firm. Aiden will be thrilled with this idea. And it'll give me a chance to check out this neighborhood a little more closely.

"I knew hiring you was a good idea," Beckett says proudly.

I chuff out a laugh. "I haven't accepted the job offer."

Beckett adjusts his suit jacket and smirks. "You will. All right, ladies, if Livy has this covered, I'm going to find Cortney. We've got a bet going, and I'm totally going to win, so I've got to up the ante." He presses a kiss to his wife's cheek and mutters in her ear. Whatever he says has her swatting him away and makes her cheeks flush.

"You guys are so freaking adorable," I say as I settle on the couch again.

Liv rolls her eyes. "He's incorrigible most of the time."

"And you love it," Sara sings.

Ava, who's still standing, shoulders pulled up to her ears, watches the three of us with a small smile on her face.

I pat the space next to me. "Come over here and tell me why I should accept this job. And what we'll be doing."

As she settles beside me, she quietly asks, "You really haven't accepted yet?"

I give her a wink. "I like to keep the Langfield men on their toes."

But the truth is, I already know my answer. I'm going all in. With Aiden. With Langfield Corp. With his family.

And maybe with one of our own.

The realization has me excited to share it all with Aiden. But because we never do things easily, through a conversation, my mind is spinning with ideas. With grand gestures—because if anyone deserves an over-the-top gesture, it's my guy.

CHAPTER 49
AIDEN

"HE'S BENDING his ankles too much," I tell Gavin as we watch Andrew Keegan, the center we just drafted, practice with Camden Snow and Daniel Hall. Switching up lines is never a bad idea. That way, if one of us gets hurt and he has to change things up, the chemistry is already there and the change will be seamless.

My brother doesn't even glance in my direction before shouting a correction.

"Cam needs to slow down and give Keegan a second to catch his bearings," War notes from beside me. We both watch, arms crossed and assessing, as the guys continue running drills over and over before my brother calls in the next group and heads their way.

"I was thinking we should have a team dinner soon," War says without taking his focus off the ice.

I can't help but study him for a few seconds and really take in his posture.

Over the last few months, the right winger has changed in big ways. Becoming captain has settled him, making it clear that Gavin made the right decision by giving War the title. Though I do miss my aggressive winger every once in a while, his level-headedness has the potential to be a stronger asset for us this season than any of his fights have been in the past. Even if he instigated them to protect me or Hall.

I lift my chin. "Sounds like a plan. You going to do it at your place?"

"Fuck no. That's my sanctuary," he mumbles. "Team dinner, your place." He turns and levels me with a commanding stare.

I merely grin. "It'll be tight, but I'm sure we can make it work."

War groans. "Fuck. Coach will probably suggest we do it as his place because it's bigger, and don't get me wrong, I love your brother, but we should do it somewhere that isn't littered with baby toys."

That's an apt description of Gavin's place. For years and years, he was the bachelor of all bachelors. Now, his apartment is all baby toys and feminine touches.

"We could set something up in the common area. Or Ground Zero?"

War's eyes light up. "Common area. We can make it a potluck. Everyone brings a dish."

Before we can hammer out details, Gavin calls us out for one-on-one drills, and then I lose myself in my second favorite thing: hockey.

Practice was grueling. Though I had no trouble assessing my teammates' strengths and weaknesses, I couldn't put my finger on what was slowing me down today. Gavin promised/threatened me with additional time on the ice tomorrow so I'd be prepared for our next game.

Brooks offered to join me.

The idea of getting out on the ice with my brothers lit me up inside. I was tempted to text Beckett and ask him to join like the old days, but he'd only remind me that a family skate isn't what I need, even if it sounds like a blast. When the Hanson brothers are in town,

Gavin and Beckett get together with them for morning skates. It's an activity I wish I could be part of, but risking injury for a pickup game would be unwise.

I shake off the disappointment that plagues me when I think about it. I play with Brooks every damn day. That should be enough to satisfy me.

"Honey, I'm home," I say, imitating Ricky Ricardo as I step into our apartment.

The smell of sugar and fried dough instantly hits me, and the tension from practice begins to melt from my body. The apartment is bathed in a warm glow from electric candles set up on every surface. The television is on, but it's paused on the opening credits to a movie. The couch has been pushed to the side and in its place is a cozy pillow fort. There's a sheet draped over a few chairs, with Christmas lights strung beneath it. On the floor below is a pile of blankets and what looks like every pillow in the apartment.

"Lex," I call out, my heart thumping against my chest.

The surprise itself lifts me up, but the overwhelming calm that settles over me even when I step into our home is because of Lennox.

She gives me a peace that can't be replicated—there is nothing, including hockey, that settles me the way she does.

I drop my bags at the door and saunter inside.

"Hey, Hockey Boy." Lennox's sweet, teasing tone eases another ache inside me.

Warmth starts in my chest and works its way through me as I take in the hypnotizing sway of her hips as she peeks at me from where she's bent over with her head in the fridge. Black spandex molds to her curves, making my mouth water. As she straightens and then finally turns to face me, my grin only grows.

"C'mere, baby," I mumble, holding out my arms.

She doesn't make me wait. In a heartbeat, she presses her soft body against mine and wraps me in a strong hug. No one hugs like Lennox. She puts her whole self into it. Her breasts press against my chest, and her heart beats against mine, matching its rhythm. Her warm breath ghosts against my neck as she sighs, like the embrace is just as comforting for her. Head tilted back, she kisses my chin. "Missed you."

Fuck, coming home to this woman is the greatest thing in the world.

Every worry, every concern, every ounce of stress, evaporates when she's in my arms.

Makes me wonder if she's all I needed all these years. If she could cure my darkness...

"How did your meeting with Liv go?"

Lennox cuffs the back of my neck and forces her lips to mine, taking me in a rough kiss. As our tongues tangle and our breaths mingle, I get lost in her.

When she pulls back and smiles, swiping my lips clean from what I imagine is her lip gloss, I breathe out a curse. "Fuck, Lex. This is some way to come home."

Her rosy cheeks lift, and her blue eyes sparkle. "Hopefully it'll always be like this," she says with that mischievous glint in her eye.

"You won't find me complaining about that."

Linking her fingers with mine, she leads me toward the fort she's created. "Relax while I grab our dinner."

I arch a brow. "You cooked?"

Her soft responding laugh has my cock growing impossibly hard. "Cooking would be grossly overstating what I did."

I chuckle as I watch her walk away, craning my neck until she's completely out of view. Then I lean back against the pillows she's pulled from our bed and make myself comfortable.

"How was practice?" she calls from the other room.

My phone buzzes in my pocket, reminding me that it was blowing up as I was rushing to get home. The screen is filled with text notifications from my brothers, but for once, I don't rush to read them. I have no doubt that whatever they're talking about would make me laugh, but I just want her. I hit the power button, turning it off completely, and toss the phone onto the couch. Everyone else can wait. The outside world can fade away for all I care. Everything I need is in this room.

"It was good. I'll probably need to get some extra time in with the rookies this week, but I just wanted to come home to you tonight."

When Lennox reappears, a tray in her hand and a knowing smirk on her face, I know I made the right decision. "I appreciate that."

As she approaches, I take the tray so that she can settle beside me. "Orange soda and sandwiches," I muse as I take in the spread. Even as I tease her, my chest squeezes again, my heart trying to find a way out while my body pulls it right back in. I'd hand it to her on this platter if it was possible.

When Lennox is settled beside me, she turns those blue eyes on me. They're tender rather than teasing.

"I thought that keeping things surface level with men would keep me safe. I knew I couldn't survive another us, so I hid my true self behind my sass and loud personality. It was better that way. The only person who ever really got past the walls I'd put up was Sara, but she had her own walls—her own secrets. It was easier to sit atop them together than to break them down. So I flitted from job to job, casually dated, kept in touch with family and friends through text messages rather than making time for real connections, all because I thought that if I got too close, a man might worm his way into my heart, and I'd risk being broken again."

I watch Lennox silently, understanding precisely what she means. Maybe I let more people in because I had—*have*—good relationships with my brothers. My sister and parents too. Teammates I'd fight for who'd also fight for me. I've allowed myself relationships, but like Lennox, when it came to love, I never truly gave myself to anyone else. Never let them see the broken pieces of me—or the real parts.

I gave the world a sugared version of myself, but for different reasons than she did. I did it because I was afraid if they saw the real me, they'd be disappointed. Different reasons, same outcome: we kept everyone on the outside.

"I don't want to do that anymore. I want to feel. I want to risk. I want to *love*. And I want to do it all with you by my side." Lennox takes my hand. "I'm going to take the job with your family's company. I'm all in, Aiden."

This declaration feels a hell of a lot more permanent than even her acceptance of my proposal. Unconsciously, I stroke her engagement ring. It should be one hell of a sweet reminder that she's mine. If not for the timeline imposed by her family trust, I'm not sure she would have said yes. But right now? It sounds like she's saying yes to us.

Whatever that entails.

And in the meantime, she'll become my wife, and hopefully one day she'll be happy about that too.

"That's good, because I've been all in since day one."

With a soft laugh, she angles in to kiss me again.

"I like the spread," I say, grabbing one half of a peanut butter and Nutella sandwich and handing it to her.

Lennox hums as she takes a bite. "Figure we have a lot of movie nights to make up for."

I perk up in excitement as I pick up the other half of the sandwich. "Oh yeah? What are we starting with?"

Lennox just grins and nods at the remote control. "Have at it, Hockey Boy. Figured I'd start with one of our favorites."

When I hit play and Bridget Jones's voice filters through the space, I bark out a laugh. "Yes!" I pump one fist.

Beside me, Lennox giggles and snuggles closer. With a deep inhale, I sink into this feeling. Into the past and into the present. Into the good.

And I say a prayer that this feeling never ends.

CHAPTER 50
AIDEN

> Beckett: Are you sure you don't want me to force Man Bun to watch the kids? He's good with babies.

> Brooks: We'll be fine.

> Gavin: It's only a few hours. And there are four of them.

> Beckett: And I have five kids.

> Gavin: If you can handle them, I'm pretty sure Brooks, Sara, and Lennox have this covered.

> Me: Hey! I'm in this chat.

> Gavin: Just making sure. You're awfully quiet over there.

ACROSS FROM ME, Robert clears his throat. "Am I keeping you from something important?"

I pocket my phone, trying to ignore the instant FOMO. When I walk out of this appointment, they will have had an entire conversation without me. And I'll have had an entire conversation with my therapist.

This morning, I woke up and felt nothing again. After spending a night laughing over Bridget Jones and sinking inside my gorgeous fiancée, I felt morose and tired, and I didn't want to get out of bed.

The one woman I've wanted my whole life gave me everything last night—her heart, her body, and her future—and still it was a struggle to get up. And at practice, I was basically useless.

I didn't want to be there. I *never* don't want to be there. Hockey has always been the one thing that settles my mind, but today, even shuffling forward on the ice took effort. My brother practically ripped my head off and told me that if I acted sluggish like this again, he'd enact a curfew.

I should have felt embarrassed. Angry, even. Instead, I felt a whole lot of nothing.

So I called my therapist and told him I needed to see him. And here we are.

"Sorry. Just my brother confirming that I can babysit tonight."

He crosses his leg and nods. "I take it you enjoy babysitting?"

I smile, thankfully feeling better than I did this morning. "Why do you say it that way?"

"Your face lit up when you mentioned it."

I am an open book like that. But what can I say? I like what I like. My family. Lennox. Hockey. For the most part, I'm a simple man.

"My brother's kids are awesome," I say. "My fiancée and I are watching them with Brooks and his fiancée. The girls are best friends, so it makes it even better."

Robert's smile is warm. "Things are going well?"

The question is a simple one, but it makes my heart race, none-theless. Like it's a trick. Robert has told me time and again that there are no trick questions. But I find that hard to believe. The man's job is to dig around in my head, to probe for things he believes I'm hiding.

And though he's not wrong, because I'm constantly trying to put on a façade, pretend life is great when I'm outside this office, I'm truly not hiding anything right now.

"Things are good." And because I just promised myself that I would be honest, I add, "I've told Lennox about my struggles with depression, and when it gets to be too much, she understands what I need."

Robert's brows rise. "And what's that?"

"To sit in the dark. Silence. You know, the usual."

He nods, his expression thoughtful. It irks me. Once again, it feels like he's trying to figure me out like I'm a puzzle, rather than just listening to my words.

"How often do you have these episodes?"

I grip my thigh, relishing the bite of pain. "They aren't episodes."

He's labeled them as such in the past, but he's got it wrong. I just overdo it sometimes. I'm too loud, and I use too much energy. He thinks I'm like the rest of his patients, but he isn't with me day in and day out. His other patients haven't been blessed the way I have. They probably have good reason to be depressed. Me? I'm just in my head.

"I just need the quiet sometimes. Especially after an exciting day. After having to be 'on' so much."

I just need him to help me figure out how to avoid falling into the dark moments during hockey season. I have a job to do, and if I don't do it, my brother will have no choice but to replace me.

Across from me, Robert pulls his glasses from his face, cleans them with a cloth he pulls out of a drawer, then sets them on the desk between us. "Aiden, you have depressive episodes. Depression is an illness, but it's not like cancer or the common cold. We don't treat it with the expectation that it will be eradicated. We find ways to deal with it. Coping mechanisms so that we can handle the episodes when they occur. But as I've told you before, one of the first and most important steps is to recognize the illness for what it is."

My throat goes tight, making it hard to breathe. "I know what it is." I slide my hands up and down my legs, willing myself to remain calm. "What I'm trying to say is that Lennox knows as well, and she doesn't mind."

He nods. "I'm glad you found someone who loves you and makes you happy. Genuinely. But if you are having more episodes, then maybe we should discuss medication—"

I shake my head before he can finish his sentence. "I don't want that."

"I know you don't want that. But if things are escalating—"

"I've got it handled."

That may not be totally accurate, but if I have to choose between medication and figuring it out myself, I'll figure it out myself.

I'll stick with my routines. Do the things that make me happy. If I can keep from fucking it all up, I can maintain all the good things in my life. My career. Lennox. My family.

But if I have to go on meds, I'd have to tell the team doctor and Gavin. He's my coach. What would he think if he knew that his star center needs fucking medication to smile? Would he trust me to do my job?

It's absurd. I've got everything. There's absolutely no reason I should feel this way, so I'll keep it under control.

"Hello, Langfields. Your favorite uncle is here!" I yell as I open the door to my brother's brownstone. Immediately, a baby cries and the dog howls.

Brooks barrels past me. "Nice job, favorite uncle. I call dibs on the older ones."

Sara giggles as she passes me, her blue ponytail swishing back and forth. "I promised Addie we'd have a tea party, so you boys are on baby duty. Come on, Len. Let's find the girls."

When Beckett appears on the stairs with a screaming baby in his arms and a glare on his face, I wince.

"June Bug, you can scream in your uncle Aiden's ear, since he's the one who woke you up."

Fortunately, his wife—my favorite sister-in-law at the moment—follows behind him with a quieter baby. "Beckett, you will not hand off our daughter until she's back to her happy self."

Beckett sighs down at the miserable baby. "It's gonna be a while."

At the top of the stairs, Winnie walks past the steps and heads down the hall without even a hello. *Ouch.*

"Tough crowd," I grumble as I hold out my hands for the screaming baby.

"Are you sure you can handle this?" Beckett asks, pulling June into his chest.

Brooks has already disappeared with Finn, so it's just Beckett, Liv, the twins, and me.

I so don't have this, but I'll never admit it. Friday nights have always been date nights for Beckett and Liv, and I've done plenty of babysitting, but since the twins were born, they've had nights in. My brother has been chomping at the bit to take his wife out again, and I refuse to disappoint them. Especially because Liv's birthday is this weekend. Knowing my brother, he's got some big thing planned. When it comes to Liv, he spares no expense.

Liv settles Maggie Mae in a walker—it's terrifying to think that another one of Beckett's kids is close to walking—and Beckett finally hands June over. After they're gone, I glance down at her and smile. "Let's see what kind of trouble we can get into, kid."

Lex and Sara reappear with Addie, swinging the five-year-old between them from step to step. She giggles the entire way down, and once they hit the ground level, she darts at me. The little ball of energy has really come into her own personality. She's got two pigtails, though one is lopsided.

"Let me guess. Auntie Sara did your hair?"

Addie shakes her head and rolls back and forth on her heels, which leaves her belly peeking out of her T-shirt. "I did its myself," she says proudly.

I pull on one side, evening it out a bit. "Perfect, little one. You did a great job."

"You want to join us for a tea party?" Lex asks, holding up two pink plastic teacups.

Beside her, Sara is holding the coordinating purple cups.

I glance up the stairs, hoping Winnie will appear. She's eleven and may be a little too old for tea parties, but with all of us here, I'm surprised she hasn't even come to say hi. "Winnie coming down?"

Sara shrugs. "She said she was tired."

Tired? It's seven on a Friday night. Sure, she's allowed to be tired, but still...

My stomach knots with concern. It's not like her to hide away like this.

"You mind?" I say to Lex, who's already reaching for the baby in my arms.

When my niece settles against her with her head on her chest, a warmth like I've never experienced rolls through me.

"You're beautiful," I say, sliding her pink hair behind her shoulder and then pressing my lips to her forehead.

"Oh my god, could you guys get any cuter?" Sara lifts Addie in her arms and spins her in a circle, as if she's spreading the joy through the room.

I march up the stairs, hoping some of her joy makes the journey with me. I have a feeling Winnie needs a little extra today.

Pictures line the hallway upstairs. I rarely come up here, so I take a moment to look through them. In one photo, Beckett and Finn are wearing Boston Revs jerseys and standing on the field. Finn is missing his two front teeth, but the damn smile on his face has one tugging on my lips.

The one beside it is of Liv, Winnie, Addie, and Finn. It looks like before she even married Beckett. Back before they found themselves married in Vegas and he moved into the house with her and her friends and their kids. Finn was only four, Addie two, and Winnie was eight.

Back then, Winnie was quiet. But that all changed the day Beckett set a container filled with beads on the table and asked if she could help us make friendship bracelets for a fundraiser. That afternoon, as we made bracelet after bracelet, Winnie opened up to her stepdad's brothers. I'm sure we were intimidating. Brooks is a massive hockey goalie, and Gavin was in his broody phase, since he and Millie were on different continents. But Winnie bonded with all of us as she taught us how to make bracelets.

Rather than going straight to Winnie's room, I pop into the playroom at the end of the hall where Liv keeps the bracelet-making kit. We break it out often. I find it kind of relaxing stringing the beads together, and I like to add ridiculous sayings to them and give them to the guys on the team.

The closet in the playroom is stuffed with toys. The sight of it makes me grin. I can only imagine how badly this annoys my brother. He likes things so orderly, and yet he moved into a house filled with chaos because living without Liv was never an option.

I suppose the four of us brothers are all the same. Utterly obsessed with the women in our lives. Only happy when they're happy.

And right about now, it's clear that Winnie is not happy. That means I have work to do. I spot the beads and string up at the top and pull the container down carefully. I have no intention of spilling all these beads—the stress of worrying that the twins could choke would eat me alive.

Then I head to the tween's door. There's a pretty drawing on the outside with her name on it. It's flowery and colorful, and if I had to guess, I'd say she drew it. Rapping my knuckles against the door, I call for her, knowing better than to just walk in. "Hey, Bear."

"I'm fine," she calls from the other side.

"I need your help. Any chance you have a minute? I know you're a busy girl."

The snort she lets out makes me smile.

"I suppose I can make time for you," she says drolly as she peeks out into the hall. When she spots the goods in my hand, she eyes me. "Bringing in the big guns?"

I shrug as I enter. The way her room is shrouded in darkness sends tingles down my back. "No idea what you're talking about."

Head lowered, she settles down on her canopy bed. Her room is oversized, with pops of color everywhere. Purple comforter, teal walls, light pink furniture—Beckett surprised Liv with the house, but he brought Winnie with him for furniture shopping.

In the corner is a desk littered with art supplies and books.

The room is every girl's dream, and yet the feeling inside it is morose. The lights off, the curtains closed, her face blank.

"Wanna help me make a bracelet?"

"Sure." Winnie nods at the mattress beside her.

Obediently, I set down the supplies and sit opposite her. Without looking up, she opens the bin and grabs beads in several shades of pink. She settles them on the comforter, then selects a pink string. "What do you want it to say?"

Tongue in my cheek, I try to hide my grin. "Why'd you pick those colors?"

She rolls her eyes. "Please, Uncle Aiden, this is obviously for Lennox."

"I'll go with Princess."

She sighs like she's disappointed in my choice, and I try not to take offense. It is an awful nickname, but I didn't pick it. I just stole it from her father. Silently, Winnie digs through the compartment filled with lettered beads, so I take the opportunity to chat with her.

"So what's new?"

"It's fine, Uncle Aiden. We don't have to talk. I'll make the bracelet for you."

My heart sinks at her sullen tone and her brush-off. She's always been happy to have silly conversations with me. "But what if I want to talk?"

Her focus remains on the beads, her fingers still rooting around for the correct letters. "You can talk," she says with an exaggerated sigh.

Pushing away the unease, I ask, "You been working on any new drawings?"

This sigh is more forceful, but it's the only reply I get.

Maybe I'm being overly sensitive, but she's definitely off. And maybe that's why I find myself wanting to open up to her. "Sometimes I find it hard to do the things I love."

Winnie peers up at me. "Huh?"

"Hockey, singing." I twist my lips. "Smiling. Sometimes it's hard to do it, even though I love it. Ya know?"

She shrugs, back to sorting beads for a moment. But then she bites her lip and glances at me. "You always seem so happy." She picks up a bead and slides it onto the bracelet.

I follow suit, grabbing a string of my own. It's easier to talk when I'm doing this. It's an odd form of therapy, but I guess we do what works. "Sometimes it's easier to fake it than to talk."

Her response is another heavy breath.

"I can imagine this house can get pretty loud and busy."

Winnie's watching me now, her stare weighted. Like she thinks I'm an idiot. Probably because it's obvious that a household of seven would be loud.

Maybe I am an idiot. But I continue anyway. I feel like she needs to hear this. "When things get loud for me, I like to sit in the dark. My therapist thinks that if I do that too much, it may mean I may need something more." I swallow, leaving it at that rather than mentioning antidepressants. I'm not ready to deal with that yet.

With a hum, she continues stringing the beads. I follow suit, working hard to remain silent. She lets out a heavy sigh as she ties off her bracelet and hands it to me.

I smile down at the word *princess* on the pink bracelet. Mine says *wifey*. I'm already imagining my girl's likely reaction—it'll be epic. I snap the lid of the bead kit closed, taking the hint that I'm being dismissed, but before I can hop up, Winnie's tiny hand grips mine.

"Would you maybe—"

She hesitates, so I settle my other hand over hers and squeeze. "Anything, Win. I'll do anything you ask."

Brown eyes blink up at me, going misty, and her look of apathy morphs into sadness. Her voice hitches as she rasps, "Sit with me? For a little longer?"

Hours later, I'm lying in the dark with my girl, my mind still a jumbled mess. Winnie and I finally left her room when the pizza was delivered. She shyly asked me if she could give Lennox the bracelet— and I lit up when Lennox's surprised squeal at the gift made Winnie smile.

For the rest of the night, she seemed more present, happier. I hope it wasn't all an act. That she wasn't hiding beneath a mask. That I'd given her enough peace to get her through the night. Though I'm struggling with how to move forward. Would it be wrong to talk to Liv and Beckett about my suspicions? Would it be wrong not to?

Depression is hard enough for me as an adult. I can't imagine having to navigate it as a kid. In some way, though, I suppose I always did. I just didn't have the tools to understand the way the pendulum of my moods swung.

Out of my depth, I turn to Lennox and pour it all out. "I just wish I could help her," I say quietly after sharing my thoughts.

Lennox plays with the bracelets on her wrist. "I think you did."

My heart aches as I study her, looking for the lie, the placation. I certainly don't feel like I did much of anything.

Lennox cups my chin. "Sometimes people just need to know that they're not alone. That what they're going through is normal."

My skin itches at that word. *Normal.* What even is normal? Whatever it is, I know I'm not it. But I do want Winnie to know that she's not alone.

"It's not normal, Lex. That's why it's called a disorder."

She frowns. "You'd be surprised. A lot of people suffer from depression. You're not abnormal, Aiden. You're just in tune enough with your emotions to seek help. And now, because of you, Winnie will be too."

She curls her body into me and relaxes. Within minutes, she's asleep, but I lie on my back, staring at the ceiling, replaying her words long into the night.

"Good Morning, Boston. I'm Colton, and this is my co-host Eliza. We're here to bring you the Hockey Report."

"How is it already November? This season is flying by."

"It absolutely is, and although the Bolts have suffered their fair share of growing pains, the guys are looking good," Colton surmises.

Eliza hums. "The new center is something else too. I know we always say Aiden Langfield is Boston's lucky charm, but Andrew Keegan is showing us that the future is bright for this team."

"Yeah. I'm sure Coach Langfield is thrilled with how both his first and second strings look, especially when Aiden has an off game like he did last week."

"He was a little slow against LA, but they had been on the road for ten days—"

CHAPTER 51
AIDEN

LENNOX SLAMS the radio dial in the back of the limo, and the car goes silent. "They don't know what they're talking about."

I affect an easy smile. "They aren't wrong. I was slow. And Keegan is awesome. We're lucky to have him."

"Aiden Langfield, you are the best center the game has ever seen. There is no comparison. Keegan is good because you've been putting hours in on the ice with him, training him, working out with him, studying with him. All so your team will be better."

I grip her thigh and squeeze, chuckling. "Love when you get all protective of me, Princess, but I promise, my ego can take a little ribbing from commentators."

She doesn't want to let it go. She's assessing me, a line between her brows, trying to surmise if I really am okay. Since we're headed to her birthday bash right now, and because I have big plans for afterward, I focus on those things, keeping my thoughts light, hoping she can sense it and let this go.

It's been one hell of a month since I proposed on the ice. Our friends were supportive, and my family was ecstatic, but her parents were ambivalent. So tonight will be interesting.

We've been too busy over the last few weeks to focus on them. To focus on anything but all the good in our lives. When Lennox told me about the job offer from Beckett, I couldn't help the surprised chuckle that left me. My brother, always making things happen for his family. And this move wasn't just for me—though I'm grateful he's giving her this chance. No, this was for Lennox. My brothers have welcomed Lennox back into the fold without so much of a blink of an eye, and that means everything to me. For so long, I've felt like I was making my way alone. That I was merely here for their entertainment. But as always, Beckett showed me that he'd been watching.

He showed up, and along with the pure joy the rest of my siblings exuded when I proposed to Lennox, it's clear they've all got my back. So despite the mounting pressure in my chest over her parents' disapproval and the commentators take on my performance, I'm choosing to keep the positive at the forefront of my mind.

Lennox loves her new job. When she gave her notice to her boss, she was at peace. For the first time, she realized she wasn't running from one job to the next. Instead, she was settling into a career. She seems calmer now. Happy.

When the two of us aren't working our asses off, we're together. The way it should be.

I squeeze her hand. She's glowing tonight. There's some type of shimmery blush on her cheeks, her hair is twisted back in a long pink braid, and she has on a deep pink gown that hugs all her curves.

"Do you remember our first date?"

Lennox's face scrunches adorably in confusion. "The pizza shop?"

I laugh. "Not when we were kids." I squeeze her thigh again. "Though I love that you remember that. No, I'm talking about at the park."

"That was *not* our first date," she huffs.

"Oh, it was. You just didn't know it yet."

"We were planning your wedding to another woman."

Her annoyance shouldn't make me smile. "No, *you* were planning my wedding to another woman. *I* was envisioning you walking down that aisle to me."

The limo comes to a stop in front of the club, which means I only have a few minutes more of her all to myself. So I cuff the back of her neck, pulling her to me.

"I can't wait to marry you," I whisper against her mouth.

Hers tips up in a smile. "You catching feelings for me, Hockey Boy?"

I bite her lip and murmur, "Something like that."

Ten minutes in, it's clear that this is going to be a bad night. First off, her parents have gone with a black and silver color scheme. Not even remotely Lennox's style.

Second, Ryder and his band are set up on the stage. It appears Jackson Kennedy will stop at nothing to push that man on his daughter, even two days before her wedding.

Ruthless.

My blood heats, and I break into a sweat as I work to tamp down the pressure building inside me.

When Sara appears out of nowhere, screaming "Bitch, it's almost your birthday," I guide Lennox toward her best friend, grateful to have a few minutes to stew without ruining Lennox's night.

"Ready for tomorrow?" Brooks asks as the girls disappear into a throng on the dance floor.

The happiness radiating off her helps ease the pounding of my heart.

Tomorrow, we play New York for the first time since my fight with Vincent Lukov. He didn't end up with a breathing tube like I'd have liked, so he's slated to play. That means there'll be drama. It's all he knows. After our last altercation, one would think that rather than professional athletes paid to win a game, we're Roman fighters meant to fight to the death.

I'd win. There's no question.

Without taking my eyes off Lennox, I promise, "I'll be fine."

"That's not what I was asking."

Irritation runs up my spine. How the hell is he so calm all the time? The Lukovs didn't just fuck with me. Our uncle fucked with him too.

"I could ask you the same thing." I turn and study his reaction. I want him to get angry. For his heart to beat wildly out of his chest like mine does.

Am I really the only one of us Langfields who has to live with these overwhelming swells of emotion?

Sure, my brothers have snapped before. But in general, they remain steady under pressure. I, on the other hand, handle it by getting loud. By singing. Anything that keeps me from having to feel the buzzing within my body that makes me want to jump out of my own skin.

Brooks turns his attention to the dance floor. "If he lays a hand on you, then yeah, I'll be ready."

My throat gets tight. I was not expecting that kind of response. "I can fight my own battles."

He squeezes my shoulder. "But you shouldn't have to. Your future father-in-law is headed our way, though, so tell me—you fighting this one on your own, or am I sticking by your side?"

I flex my hands, then button my jacket, feigning cool even as my heart takes off again. "I'm good."

With a terse nod, Brooks heads to the bar where our brothers and their wives have congregated.

On the dance floor, Lennox is laughing and smiling with Hannah, Sara, and Ava. It eases my mind a little to know she's having a good time. I can handle her asshole father, so long as she's smiling.

As he approaches, I turn my attention to him. His blondish hair is slicked back, and his black tuxedo is impeccable. Everything about him screams money and misery.

The complete opposite of his daughter.

"Enjoying yourself?" he mumbles, rather than giving me a true greeting.

"Of course. My fiancée is smiling. That's all I need."

With a grunt, he shoves his hands into his pockets. "She won't be your fiancée for long."

I can't help but smirk. "True. Soon, she'll be my wife." I pull at the sleeve of my tuxedo jacket, exposing the face of my Rolex. It's Bolts blue, of course. Langfield Blue, as Beckett likes to call it. "In approximately thirty-six hours."

Scowling, Jackson steps back so he's elbow to elbow with me, his focus turning to the dance floor. "That won't be happening once I tell my daughter the deal is off."

I will my heart to beat steadily and swallow past the lump in my throat. "Deal?"

He's the one smirking now. He knows he has me. The man can smell the blood in the water. Fuck. His shoulders shake as he silently chuckles. "You think I don't know this is all a sham? My daughter had no interest in marriage until I laid out the terms for her trust. Then, suddenly, she's dating the ex she dumped without even a backward glance."

The words hit me in the gut, just like he hoped, but I don't let it show. "Or we reconnected and realized what a mistake we made. Realized that we don't want to wait another minute to start the rest of our lives together."

Jackson leans in close and clasps my shoulder. "I guess we'll see which of us is right. I'll let my daughter know she doesn't have to marry you to get her trust. Have a good night."

Anxiety twists my stomach so fiercely I worry I might throw up right here on my shoes. With a deep breath in, then back out, I focus on Lennox again. Before Jackson tells her she no longer has to marry me, I need to tell her why she does. And hope like hell that I'm enough for her.

Rule 1:
Don't fall for
the groom.

Dearest Lennox

Chapter 52
Lennox

All I want is for you to be happy. To choose joy. To chase it, really. Do me a favor. Think of the last time you felt true joy. Do you have it? Do you remember? If I'm right, and I think I am, you know what you need to do.

MY GRANDMOTHER'S words swirl in my head as I stand in the middle of a party filled with miserable people. I could practically feel the tension radiating off Aiden as we walked in tonight. We've been going nonstop for the past few days. Between games and practices, he hasn't gotten a break. We have to survive the rest of this party, then endure the game against New York before we head to the courthouse to make this marriage official.

Typically, Aiden takes it easy the night before a game. If not for this party, he would have gone to practice today, then holed up in our apartment watching movies. He needs that downtime to preserve his energy. So he can be the Aiden Langfield the world expects him to be, on and off the ice.

Instead, we spent the afternoon getting ready for the party, and now we're here. He hasn't complained a single time. All because he loves me. I know it with every fiber of my being, and I can't wait to tell him I love him too.

I'm not sure what's held me back. Maybe it's the not knowing where this was going. Or how the marriage would work. And then it morphed into wanting to do something epically special for Aiden, since he's always the one doing epic things for me. I've talked the moment up so much in my head that now I'm nervous about uttering the words. What if the simple phrase is a letdown for him?

"You okay?" I ask, even though I know he's not, and hold out my hand.

He squeezes it and gives me his dopey grin. The expression isn't genuine. I know him well enough to see it. He's placating me, tiptoeing since this is my birthday celebration, and he wants me to enjoy it. It makes my chest ache to look at him like this.

When Aiden's stressed—when he's truly uncomfortable—there's no hiding the rapid pulse in his neck.

I press my palm there and step up close so that I'm all he can see. "Let's have one more drink, then I'll feign an illness, and we can go."

Cupping my face, he drops his forehead to mine. "Princess, you are the belle of this ball. No one is going to allow you to leave, least of all me. It's your night. I'm here. I'm good, I promise." He kisses me, easing my worries, which is exactly the opposite of my plan.

Dammit, the man is too perfect.

"What do you want to drink?" he asks as he holds up a hand to signal to the bartender.

Beckett, Gavin, and their wives have just said their goodbyes, and the crowd on the dance floor is getting rowdier. By *crowd*, I mean Sara. She kept me dancing for almost an hour while Aiden hung back with his brothers. After we'd worked up an appetite, we sat with our guys and had dinner. The guests all sang "Happy Birthday" as the caterers brought out a boring white cake. It's late enough now that most of my parents' friends are filtering out, leaving only the drunkest of people. With the Bolts playing tomorrow, Brooks and Aiden really should be heading out soon.

"I'll have one more prosecco, then bed."

Aiden taps my ass. "Go dance. I'll bring your drink to you."

Sara is already hollering for me and making a scene, so I give in without a fight. As I make my way toward her, Ava is heading off the dance floor.

"No way," I say, clutching her arm. "If I have to go out there, then so do you."

Ava throws back her head and groans. "I have to be up early for the charity breakfast. Take pity on me."

With a shake of my head, I pull her along. "Hey," I say, tilting in close so she can hear me over the music. "Beckett mentioned that fire-fighter fundraiser. Should we get together this weekend to plan?"

Beckett's brother-in-law is the fire chief in a town where a string of fires has destroyed multiple businesses, as well as depleted a lot of the fire department's resources. Apparently, the town is known for their Christmas celebrations, and since his brother-in-law won't accept straight-up donations from the Langfields, Beckett has tasked us with coming up with an event that will include Bolts players and firefighters. An auction or something along those lines. He's left the details up to us. I'm thinking a calendar with shirtless firefighters and hockey players would make a killing. Not sure how Beckett will feel about that, though.

"Yeah, he mentioned it. Millie mentioned that since Lake and her father live in that town, she can probably get Mel to come and sing at it too."

I grasp her arm, grinning. "Now we're talking."

We've almost made it to the dance floor when my mother sweeps in and stops us. "Lennox, I'd like you to meet someone," she says.

I offer Ava a shrug, but she merely smiles, probably happy that she can make her way back to the bar where her boyfriend is waiting.

Xander is quiet and seems to make Ava happy. That's all that really matters to me, though he gives off a vibe I'm not sure I love.

"You remember Kara's son, Thomas," my mother says, bringing me back to the present.

I force a smile at my mother's "friend," a woman from the club that I've encountered a few times at events like these, and yes, I remember her son. He's made a comment or two under his breath about my weight.

"How could I forget Thomas? Your hair is looking spectacularly thin tonight."

The man who's always running a hand through his dark, wavy hair grins like the comment hasn't quite sunken in.

My mother, on the other hand, hisses. "Lennox!"

I shrug. "Sorry, mother. I gotta go." I point toward the dance floor and book it in Sara's direction. When I get to her, I snatch her by the arm, then grab Hannah too and rush toward the front door. I need a little fresh air, and slipping out will help me avoid any more run-ins with my parents and their "friends."

All night, my father was trying to have a serious conversation with me, catching my eye from across the room and popping up everywhere I go. But Sara has stayed on me like peanut butter on jelly, so he hasn't had the chance to ruin the night.

"Everything okay?" Hannah asks as we step out into the cool air. Fall is in full effect. I can practically see my breath.

"Yes, just had to get away. I swear my parents are getting extra desperate with my wedding creeping up."

Sara sticks her bottom lip out. "I still can't believe you won't let me throw you a bachelorette party. Tomorrow is your last night of freedom."

I fold my lips in to stifle a giggle. "Doesn't feel like that at all. I honestly can't wait to be his wife."

Hannah rubs her arms aggressively, already chilly. "Leave her be. She's in love."

"Yeah, me too," Sara says with a shrug. "But I don't get the rush. Are you hiding something?" Her eyes dip to my stomach.

This time, I don't hold back my laughter. "I'm not pregnant, you psycho. I'm just excited to be Mrs. Aiden Langfield. He makes me happy, and we don't want to wait."

"If you say so," she mutters, giving me another once-over.

I shove her to the side, making her teeter on her heels. "Stop staring at my fat!"

"You're not—" Both girls are hissing at me, but their words are cut off when a van pulls up in front of us, the tires screeching to a halt.

"What the—"

The back door swings open, and a handful of men in masks jump down and rush us.

"Holy *shit*," Sara screams.

My throat has closed up, surprise leaving me speechless. When a pair of strong arms circles my waist and lifts me with little effort, I suck in shallow breaths.

Don't scream. Don't draw too much attention. Maybe then everything will go as planned.

We're shoved into the van carefully, and as the door slams shut, we're shrouded in darkness.

"Oh my god," Hannah cries. "We need to bang on the doors. Make as much noise as we can before we get too far from the city."

She crawls to the back of the cargo area and pounds her fists against the door.

While she wears herself out, I slump back against the leather seats. "It's a fancy van for a kidnapping," I muse.

Hannah turns around. "What are you doing? *Help* me."

Across from me, Sara's features are barely visible. She looks perplexed, but not panicked.

"The way the tall one grabbed me," I whisper. "So hot."

"*Lennox*," Hannah hisses over her shoulder.

"This is hardly the time," Sara mutters.

"Don't get your panties in a wad. I'm sure Saint Brooks's bat signal is going off as we speak. And you." I point at Hannah. "You write stalker romances. You know this is hot."

"I don't write stalker romances. I write men who are obsessed."

Tilting my head, I blink at her.

With a sigh, she slumps against the seat. "Fine, stalker romances can be hot. Real-life kidnappings are not."

Sara moves closer to Hannah. "Wait, you write books?"

"Oh my god, that isn't what's important right now! What is wrong with the two of you? We've been kidnapped. They probably want ransom money because she's a Kennedy. Or maybe because you're both marrying Langfields. It's all well and good for you. No one kills the ones worth money. But me—"

I can't help but giggle. If they don't realize that the boys are our kidnappers, I'm not going to ruin it.

"Why are you laughing?" Sara demands, her brow creasing in confusion.

I arch a brow at her. She has to know. Even if she didn't immediately recognize Brooks's body, there's no way he didn't whisper something in her ear to let her know she was safe. He'd never scare her.

"I laugh at inappropriate times. You know this about me."

As the van comes to a smooth stop, I tap my Manolo Blahniks in anticipation. I can't wait to see what Aiden has up his sleeve.

The van door swings open, startling us. I almost feel bad when Hannah grips my hand with all her strength.

"You girls ready for your surprise?" Aiden asks, his smooth voice sending a shiver down my spine.

"Oh my god," Hannah screams. "I am going to kill you guys." She shoves me off her. "And you? You *knew*?"

There's no use trying to temper my laughter as I scoot down the leather seats.

When I'm close enough, Aiden pulls me into his arms and settles my feet on the ground. The cold immediately hits me like an arctic blast. "Come here, Princess. I've got a blanket for you."

I feel bad leaving Sara and Brooks to placate a fuming Hannah, but when Daniel and Camden head in her direction, I relax and let Aiden lead me to the front of the van. Hannah has a major crush on Daniel. There's no way she'll stay mad once she realizes he's here.

Aiden pulls a pink chenille blanket from the floorboard and wraps it around me, then pulls me to his chest. "You all right?"

"You know I am." My cheeks hurt from smiling. "You kidnapped me," I whisper.

Aiden presses a kiss to my lips. "My kinky girl loves it, doesn't she?"

I angle back and clutch his lapels. "I'm so wet."

"Come on, Lex." He spins me around, then grasps my hand. "Walk with me."

"Don't you want to take me home and benefit from how turned on you've made me?" I tease.

He tugs me to his side and drapes an arm over my shoulders, leading me away from the group. For the first time, I take in our surroundings. "Where are we?"

"You don't recognize it?" he muses.

I focus harder, noting the trees on either side of us and the heavy moon that hangs above us. None of it registers until we get to a clearing, and the carousel comes into view.

"*Aiden*," I whisper, emotion making it come out as a rasp.

"In two days, we'll be married at the courthouse, but I wanted to do something a little more fitting for you and me. Tonight we had the party, and tomorrow, I have to play, and—" He takes a deep breath. "Lex, you deserve the wedding you imagined for us. Even if marriage isn't what you want, I'd like to stand in front of that tree over there and pledge my love for you, and then I'd like to take a ride on the carousel together. Just like you planned."

Tears well as I envision the wedding I described the day we met here. The wedding where we'd finally get our happily ever after. I dreamed of it even when I had no right. Even when he belonged to someone else. Only the truth is, Aiden has always been mine, and I certainly have always been his.

His face blurs in front of me as the tears crest over my lashes and keep coming. "Aiden, it's closed, baby. But the sentiment is beautiful. We can still get a picture."

Like magic, the carousel comes to life. Bright lights in the middle of darkness, followed by "Crazy in Love" blasting from the speakers that typically stick to cheerful carousel tunes.

"Sure about that?" he teases.

"*Aiden.*" I bury my face in his chest. "What did you do?"

"I did what I had to do to make you happy. I always will. Come on, Princess." He tugs me toward the carousel. "Never have I ever ridden a carousel at night with my future wife."

An airy laugh bubbles from my chest as I let go of our past and spring into the future with this man I love so much. Our friends join us, and although the guys are having a blast jumping from one horse to another, Aiden remains by my side the entire time. We take pictures that I can't wait to frame and hang all over our apartment. We laugh. We kiss. And I experience a joy I never thought was possible.

Then, under the light of the moon and in front of our friends in the middle of the park, Aiden pledges to love me for the rest of his days.

CHAPTER 53
AIDEN

FROM THE MOMENT we woke up, I knew this would be a bad day.

"Don't go."

"Aiden," Lennox whispers, studying me in the dark. "You have morning skate. You won't be here anyway."

I sigh. She's not wrong, but from the instant she got the message from her family's lawyer, saying he needed to meet with her, I've been suffocating. The lead weight in my chest is making it impossible to get out of bed.

They're going to tell her she doesn't need to get married to have access to her trust. She's going to call off the wedding.

Will I lose her completely? Will she decide that since the marriage is no longer necessary, she'd rather we go our separate ways? Originally, we agreed to a temporary union. That's it. So why would she stay with me now that she doesn't have to?

Unless she wants to.

Just as the light is brought into my thoughts, darkness settles again.

Why *would* she want to? She didn't want to get married. She was doing this to gain access to her trust. That's it. Sure, she's enjoyed the last few months. Lennox makes everything fun. She took a bad situation and was determined to enjoy it. But I can't forget her one rule. Don't catch feelings. The rule she knows I've completely ignored, because I've told her as much.

But she hasn't told me she's fallen for me.

I've tried to be everything Lennox could ever want, but I'm out of time. If she hasn't fallen yet, then why would she marry me?

"Of course," I rasp, forcing a smile.

"And just think," she says in that light, happy tone that makes even my dark mornings brighter, "tomorrow, I'll be your wife, and then we can lay in bed together all weekend."

I cling to that idea—and to the belief that once she has options, she'll still choose me—and pull her in for a kiss I pray won't be our last.

When the front door closes behind her, I'm hit with a sense of finality that weighs me down. I need to get up, take a shower, and head to the arena. The music, the team, the feel of my skates against the ice, the sound of it, will ground me and pull me out of this gray funk that I'm drowning in.

I slide my phone off my nightstand, ready to put on my game day jams, refusing to wallow, and stumble upon a text from a number I don't recognize.

> Unknown: Thought you should know you aren't as irreplaceable as you thought.

Below is a screenshot of a text message. My stomach sinks as I begin to read, and as I go on, it twists and cramps and rolls.

> Unknown:

Gavin: If he keeps this up, I'm not going to have a choice but to bench him.

Beckett: You need to think like a coach, not his brother.

Brooks: I hate to say it, but I agree.

Gavin: I thought that when he wasn't named captain, he'd wake up. But with how well Keegan is playing and how badly he is, I might not have a choice but to drop him down to second line.

Fuck.

I don't make it to morning skate. It isn't until a loud banging startles me that I realize how badly I've fucked up.

It's like wading through mud as I pull myself out of bed and shuffle to the door.

War pushes in without waiting to be invited. "Are you sick?"

With a long breath out, I stumble to the kitchen. I need to have a game-day smoothie and turn this day around. "I'm fine."

"You didn't show up for morning skate. Coach is livid."

I peer into the fridge, searching for ingredients. "You mean my brother is livid."

Behind me, War scoffs. "I have no idea what the hell is wrong with you, but whatever it is, get over it."

Shame washes over me. Fuck. Straightening, I roll my shoulders. "Sorry. I will. I just—I needed a few hours."

"Get your head on straight or sit tonight. Choice is yours."

"Okay, Captain," I grit out.

"Stop that shit. I'm here as your friend. If something is wrong—"

"Nothing is wrong." I focus on breathing evenly, doing everything I can to ignore the stabbing pain in my chest. "Like I said, just needed a few hours."

War stares at me, really fucking stares at me, for so long that I almost break down and spill my guts. But just as I'm working up the nerve, he nods and heads for the door.

"Head in the game, Lep," he shouts over his shoulder. "We need our lucky charm tonight."

The weight of that title hits me, stealing all the oxygen from my lungs. When the door snicks shut, I crumple to the floor, taking the light with me as I go.

The noise level inside the arena is almost as intense as the pounding in my head.

Lennox texted me that she wouldn't be back before I had to leave for the game, but that she had big news.

I already know the news, and the dread of it all keeps me from looking for her in the suite where she usually sits with Sara. I waited to hit the ice until the last possible moment, and while I was doing that, I got reamed out by my brother for missing morning skate.

"Being a Langfield doesn't give you the right to pull that shit. Do it again, and I'll bench you and put Keegan in."

I nodded. What the fuck else was I supposed to do? They all know I'm off, but it's nothing new, I guess. For the last few weeks, I've been slower. Sloppier. Like I'm skating through a fog.

It makes no fucking sense. I have everything I've ever wanted. I should be happier. That thought only sends me spiraling further.

I take my place at center ice, stick in hand, attention locked on the puck gripped tightly in the ref's fingers, ignoring the entire line in front of me, including Pochenko, New York's center, who hasn't stopped mouthing off since he skated up to the line.

"Figured I'd be facing off against Keegan. This should be easy."

Ignoring him, I wait for the whistle, and the moment the puck drops, I'm slapping it toward War.

I barely keep my balance when Pochenko shoulder checks me even though I no longer have the puck. With a grunt, I push the asshole away, determined to focus on the game and not the tingling in my fingers.

"Whoop, there it is!" War hollers, signaling our next move.

I lunge to get in position, but when the puck flies my way, I'm three seconds short, and Vincent Lukov takes control of the biscuit.

"Your brothers should have benched ya," he jeers as he skates by me.

Dots dance in front of my eyes. They only clear when the buzzer signaling a goal for New York rings through the arena.

I'm trying to blink back to reality when War appears in front of me and practically drags me to the boards. "Second line's coming in. What are you doing?"

In a jerky motion, I jump out of the way so the game can continue.

A water bottle hovers in front of me, so I snatch it and pour it over my face. Despite the frigid temperatures in the arena, I feel like I've been in the Sahara for days.

I flex my fingers beneath my gloves, desperate to regain sensation in my extremities, and will myself to focus on the game.

"You okay?" Hall asks from my left.

I nod, though I keep my attention on the ice.

The next period is much the same, though near the end, I'm on a breakaway one second, and in the next, I'm on the other side of the rink, having no memory of scoring a goal.

War and Hall jump on me, jostling me so roughly I nearly tumble to the ice. The crowd is screaming, chanting, though I can't make out their words.

Gavin slaps me on the back as I come in for the change-out. "That's what I'm talking about."

Finally, energy surges through me, and breathing comes a bit easier.

Keegan and Camden weave down the ice, and using a technique I taught him last week, Keegan sails the puck into New York's net. We're on our feet, screaming, and then it's back to the center for faceoff.

"Heard about the trade rumors," Pochenko taunts.

"Fuck you, Potato," War sneers. "Lep, head in the game."

"Yeah, listen to your captain," Lukov sings.

I shake my head, tuning them all out, and blink away the black spots dancing in front of me again.

When the ref drops the puck and I scoop it out from beneath Pochenko's stick, my toes dig into my skates, powering me forward.

"Slide to the left," Hall calls.

Following Hall's command, I send the puck to War on my right and quickly duck as War sends it flying over my head to Hall, who's now on a breakaway. We're all rushing down the ice, Lukov on my toes, constantly going for my skates with his stick.

I almost stumble, but I right myself, and with my chest burning, I rush forward again.

"Where's the fucking penalty, ref?" War shouts from my side.

"Can't stay up on your skates. Can't keep a fiancée to save your life," Lukov taunts as New York's goalie blocks Hall's first attempt.

I ignore Lukov, but I'm hit with an intense need to see Lennox. I look to the box where the girls sit, only to find Sara, Hannah, and Ava sitting side by side. No Lennox.

My head swims, and dread builds, weighing me down.

Of course she's not here. Why would she be? Her father told her he'd turn over the trust. She doesn't need you.

I'm still skating forward, but the play in front of me is nothing but a blur.

"Lep," War calls, that single word far away and garbled.

Then I'm hit from behind and crumpling to the ice. And finally, I welcome the darkness.

Rule 1:
Don't fall for
the groom.

Dearest Lennox

Chapter 54
Lennox

My dearest Lennox,

I know you are probably very angry with me. But please know I have only the best intentions, and I love you.

Do you remember that little gelato shop in Positano? You forced me to go there every day while we were in town. And while the flavors were dream-worthy, don't think I didn't catch you staring dreamily at the little chapel in the square, watching bride after bride marry her sweetheart. When I asked if you'd ever thought about your own wedding, you looked me dead in the eye, chin held high, and told me you were never getting married. Despite your defiance and the fire in your eyes, I saw beneath the mask. I saw the hurt girl who couldn't imagine marrying anyone but the boy whose heart she broke.

You can do anything you set your mind to. You just

need to be pushed and supported. I think there was a time in your life when you believed it. When you would look at something that the rest of the world might pass by and find joy. Find beauty in the unexpected. Now you just keep walking. You're too young to be this jaded. Too young to not believe in yourself. Instead of running away, take a moment to really sit and think. What do you want to do with your life? If you could have everything—if you could do anything—what would it be?

All I want is for you to be happy. To choose joy. To chase it, really. Do me a favor. Think of the last time you felt true joy. Do you have it? Do you remember? If I'm right, and I think I am, you know what you need to do.

If you still haven't figured it out, I've left another letter with my attorney. He'll call you the day before your birthday. Make sure you get over there in time.

All my love,
Grams

Dearest Lennox,

I know you probably think this plan was wacky. But I remember the games you and Aiden used to play in high school. The dares. You always wore a smile when you'd tell me about them. Our relationship is a special one, Lennox. Not many grandmothers are fortunate enough to have a granddaughter who shares all about her first kiss, her first love.

You are special. And when you walked into my

apartment last week and told me you'd seen Aiden Langfield again—how butterflies flapped in your belly wildly, how upon seeing you, he ran straight into the plexiglass—I couldn't help but laugh. I watched the clip on YouTube later, and it was clear as day that the boy was smitten.

So I devised this little plan. Force you into a marriage with the hope that you'd seek Aiden out to make that happen. Forgive me, my darling, if my plan didn't work. I just love you so much. But if this isn't what you want—if Aiden Langfield isn't up for this next adventure with you, I've enclosed an amendment to my trust. Give it to my attorney, and he'll turn the trust over to you, no questions asked, no marriage needed.

I love you. You have always been the sunshine of my life and the brightest light in this family. Don't let anyone dim your sparkle.

All my love,
Grams

WITH A LAUGH, I fold the letter and slip it into my pocket. Then I rush down to the ice. While I was up in the box with the girls, Beckett texted that Melina was here and sitting with Lake. He wants me to go over the plans for the firefighter fundraiser with them both.

Although I hate missing even a second of Aiden on the ice, I take the elevator down. Once I'm rink-side, I'll be even closer. Despite the goal early on in the game, his stress is palpable. Likely from traveling, then partying last night, when he really should have been resting. More than anything, I wanted to stay in bed with him this morning, but the message I got made it clear that my presence at the attorney's office was mandatory.

Truthfully, I think Aiden needs more than darkness, and I plan to broach the subject after the wedding.

He needs more than quiet. More than rest. He's clinically depressed, but he's too scared to speak the words out loud, and he's too scared to ask for more help.

He prefers being the one doing the helping. Hell, that's why the commentators are going on and on about the rookie. The kid is so good because of all the work Aiden has been doing with him.

Once we're married, once he finds out that my father no longer holds the control, at least one measure of stress will be removed. I'm hopeful that from there, he'll agree to try antidepressants.

I still can't believe my grandmother's trickery. My father called this morning to tell me he'd agree to turn over the trust if I promised not to marry Aiden. I told him to go screw himself. That I was done playing his games. Then, when I walked into the lawyer's office, I realized why my father had been so desperate.

Not only did the amendment give me access to my trust at the age of thirty, regardless of my marital status, but it gave me control of the entire Kennedy Trust. As in, I am the sole trustee for all the Kennedy Assets, including Kennedy Records, Kennedy Diamonds, and Kennedy Properties.

I snort at the thought of how Aiden will react when he finds out that I now have the power to tell my father to jump and how high.

For Aiden's birthday, I just may make him my temporary proxy. He'd get a kick out of bossing my father around for a day.

I sober as soon as I make it through the tunnel and see the guys lining up. Aiden's hunched over, anxiety radiating from him. When the puck drops and the play starts, I stand stock-still. I don't want to miss even a second more of him on the ice. It's like a dance, the way the Bolts play hockey. Normally, it's a fun dance. They glide around, laughing, smiling, and joking, even when they're grunting and getting slammed into the boards. Today is vastly different. The air is thicker, the lights dimmer. As if New York, Lukov especially, has brought the gloom along with them. Aiden is all out of sorts, as if he feels he has to prove that he's worthy after all the Chads and Brads on the internet said his lucky streak is ending.

He doesn't have a lucky streak. The man has talent.

I hate everyone who dares to utter a word against him.

Hall misses the shot, and the crowd breaks out into groans.

"Shit," I mutter.

Aiden gets into position, but then freezes, staring out at the fans. Lukov is headed for him, and so is War, skating in from the other side. The two men look like they're on a collision path, and Aiden is the target.

"Move!" I yell, willing Aiden to skate forward or sideways. Even a couple of inches would save him from being clobbered.

It's like slow motion as the two men barrel into him. Aiden doesn't react. He doesn't try to steady himself. He merely crumples, dropping to the ice.

And then I'm running.

Shouts echo around me as I stand near the back of the players' box, desperate to get to Aiden but unsure of whether I should step out onto the ice. The refs and War hover around him, then Gavin is running onto the ice, his face a mask of panic.

A hand gently grasps my elbow, then Beckett is at my side. "Come on. Let's see if we can get closer." He guides me past the bench where the team is congregated, watching the scene play out.

"I think he's crashing," the ref says as Gavin waves us over.

"My heart will go on," Aiden sings, albeit slightly out of tune.

The medic pulls back. "He's talking."

"Get his heart rate," Gavin mutters.

"The power of love," Aiden croons, his eyes still closed.

Tears stream down my face as I get closer. "You need to help him, *please.*"

Aiden's lashes flutter open, and he locks eyes with me. "Because you loved me." His eyes fall shut again.

"Is he singing a Celine Dion medley?" Beckett kneels beside him. "Aiden, *please* wake up."

"It's all coming back to me." His lashes flutter again, but he doesn't open his eyes.

"Dammit, Aiden," I sob. "I can't do this again. *Shamrock.*"

His eyelids snap open, so I say it again. "Shamrock. Shamrock. *Shamrock.*"

The cold leaches through my pants as I crawl past the medic and clutch Aiden's hand. I pull off his glove and press his palm to my heart. "I love you, Aiden. Please don't do this to me. I can't lose you again."

He pulls his hand from mine and cups my chin.

Another tear crests my lashes at the sheer decadence of his touch.

Voice hoarse, he says, "Catching feelings for me, Princess?"

I laugh out a sob and fall against his chest. "Something like that."

"What the fuck was that?" Gavin growls.

It seems we're all finally breathing now that Aiden is conscious.

"That was a cheap fucking shot that could have cost him his career," he yells at Lukov, who's standing beside Sebastian and the ref.

"He's fine," Sebastian scoffs. "The boy's just getting slow in his old age. Wouldn't have happened if you were a better coach—"

"Fuck you," Beckett yells, getting in Sebastian's face. "You don't deserve to breathe the same air as any of my brothers, let alone talk about them."

"I want him tossed from the game," Gavin shouts, pointing at Lukov.

Aiden clears his throat, and I bolt upright. Shit, I'm probably making it hard for him to breathe.

"It was me," he rasps.

As the guys keep yelling, Aiden tugs on my hand. "Tell them it was me."

I shake my head. "What?"

"It was *me*," he says louder, finally garnering the attention of the guys fighting around us.

"What was you?" I whisper.

"I had a panic attack," Aiden says softly, searching my face like he expects to find judgment. "I froze." With a sigh, he lowers his gaze. "I had a panic attack."

"Fucking pansy," Sebastian jeers. "Told you he's not fit for the game anymore."

"And you're not fit to be a coach," War hollers, cocking his arm back and slamming a fist into Sebastian's face.

In seconds, a full-on brawl breaks out on the ice. Fortunately, the medics get Aiden up, and in his concern for me, he guides me off the ice while the refs work to break up the fight.

"You okay, Princess?" he asks as his focus shifts from me to the action on the ice and back again.

He wants to be out there helping his teammates and his brothers, but there's no way I'm allowing him to go.

My heart beats rapidly in my chest as I throw my arms around him. "Just stay with me," I beg.

Aiden loops his arms around my waist and squeezes me tight. "Always, Lex. I'm not going anywhere."

CHAPTER 55
AIDEN

"WHO ELSE NEEDS ICE?" the team trainer, Rory, asks as she holds up another pack.

Beside me, Beckett raises his hand. His black suit is rumpled, and his tie is missing, as are some of the buttons on his shirt.

With a *tsk*, she presses the packet against his face. "Liv is going to be pissed."

Gavin laughs, but it's cut short when he winces and clutches his ribs. "Fuck, that hurts. But yeah, Liv is going to kill you."

Brooks leans against the lockers across from us, shaking his head. "A bunch of grown men throwing fists. Idiots."

I snort in response, taking in the sorry sight around me.

Beckett hits me with a glare. "We did it for you."

My heart sinks, and my face heats. "I'm sorry."

Beside Brooks, War is sporting a swollen lip, but he grins. "Don't apologize. That was the most fun I've had all season."

"Cap misses the fights," Brooks muses, his tone light. In the next heartbeat, though, he's staring me down, his mouth a flat line. "You going to tell us what the fuck happened out there?"

Once again, my heart rate spikes. I flex my hand, searching for some semblance of control. "I had a panic attack."

"Yeah, we got that part. But why?" Gavin asks, his brow furrowed in concern.

Every eye in the room is trained on me as I take a heavy breath. "I have anxiety and depression. I've been working on coping skills, but today, they just weren't enough."

"You're the happiest person I know," Daniel says from the corner, his tone far more subdued than usual.

"Means nothing," Fitz says, running a hand down his face. "I've been on antidepressants for years."

War nods. "Same."

My heart stumbles as I look from Fitz to War. "What?"

He shrugs. "Sometimes we can't do it on our own."

"But," I stammer, grappling with the reality I've been thrown into, "doesn't it affect how you play?"

"Some meds can affect some people that way," Fitz says. "But honestly, it's more likely to have a positive effect than a negative one. So long as you take the medication regularly and *check in with your coach*"—he hits me with a look laced with a heavy dose of reality— "and you're regularly monitored by the team doctors, as well as your own."

Shame washes over me. Slumping, I hang my head. "I really fucked this up. I get why you were considering benching me."

Gavin scoffs. "We were *what*?"

"Somebody sent me a screenshot of your texts," I say, keeping my focus locked on my lap.

"What texts?" Brooks shuffles up to me so we're standing toe to toe.

Still avoiding eye contact, I nod to my phone on the shelf in my locker.

Brooks snatches it and grasps my face to unlock the screen. Then he's sucking in a breath and tossing the device to Gavin. "That's not real. This has Sebastian written all over it."

"That motherfucker," Gavin growls as he hands the phone to Beckett.

Beckett grunts. "We'd never."

My mind swims. What the fuck? Clearly, I no longer know what's real and what's not.

Though one thing is for sure. I let my team down by keeping secrets.

War takes a step forward and points at me. "Don't."

Forcing myself to look at him, I frown. "Don't what?"

"Blame yourself. You cannot control your depression. All you can do is control how you handle it. Now that we know that you're struggling, we can help you. In fact, as captain, I'm enacting a new rule. Everyone sees a therapist weekly. It's good for all of us. Consider it team bonding."

"Thought we already bonded over the glitter dick," I say on a dry laugh, trying to make light of the situation. I can't believe this is happening right now.

War scans the room, wearing a stern expression. "Pierced dicks and therapists. It's our new motto. New guys, make sure you're taking notes."

Jorgenson swallows audibly. "You want me to pierce my—" He doesn't say the word, like just saying it out loud will hurt.

"Yeah. Team-building activity. You're up first, followed by Keegan. Then we'll have a team therapy appointment."

With a shake of my head, I raise my hand. "I appreciate it, man. But no one else has to get pierced."

Hall lets out a massive sigh. "Dammit, I was really hoping—"

War glares at him. "You need help, man. Seriously."

Gavin drops onto the bench beside me. His shirt is tattered, and there's a cut on his cheek. Body angled in, he stares me down, his brown eyes full of affection. "You are the heart of this team. I should have seen that you were struggling. I'm sorry I missed it." He grips my shoulder and squeezes. "We're going to get you the help you need. But Aiden, you have to know, the three of us love you and only ever want to support you. I'd never discuss your career with the two of them behind your back."

I take a shuddering breath, fighting back the tears threatening to fall. "I should have known that. You're a great coach. I was just in a dark place. *Am* in a dark place. And...I need more help."

"Sorry to interrupt," Sara says from the doorway, a hand over her eyes.

"Everyone's dressed, crazy girl," Brooks says, already striding to her.

"Press is waiting. I've told them that Aiden won't be speaking tonight."

Standing, I shake out my hands. If I don't do this now, I might lose the courage. "No. I won't be taking questions, but I will be speaking." I scan the guys around the room, and when all I find is support, I look back at Sara. "But can you grab Lex for me? I could use her there."

Sara gives me a small nod. "Of course."

"What are you going to tell them?" Gavin asks as he follows me out of the locker room. We're a mess, but there's something fitting about that.

"The truth."

"Good Evening, Boston. This is Colton, and I'm here at Bolts Arena to bring you a special edition of the Hockey Report. We've just been told that Aiden Langfield will be making a statement."

"Yes, Colton. All four Langfield brothers have funneled into the press room, and it appears that the Bolts have decided to skip the showers and game-day suits. I'm not sure I've ever seen Beckett Langfield look so disheveled. What's even more strange is that he's smiling."

"Good evening, everyone," Sara Case, head of Bolts PR, says into the mic. "As I mentioned a few moments ago, Aiden Langfield will not be taking questions. But he does have a statement. We ask that you refrain from interrupting him. Thank you."

"Thank you, Sara. And thank you to the press for giving me the opportunity to say a few words," Aiden starts. "Most of you probably know me as a generally happy guy. I strive to always have time to talk to the press, to give you guys some good clips and funny moments. For years, I've used those instances, when I've pushed myself to portray the happy-go-lucky guy Boston expects, as an excuse for how I felt afterward. Because what you all don't see is that more often than not, the day after a game or another big event, I feel empty. Sad. Depressed.

"It's always bothered me, because let's be honest, how could a guy who has everything—an amazing career, a supportive family, the best damn fiancée he could ask for—be unhappy?" Pressing his lips together, he takes in the crowd. "But sometimes I am, and because I haven't been effectively treating my depression, I had a panic attack on the ice tonight. You're probably wondering why I'm telling you all this. It's not to excuse my poor performance. It's because I want to help others. Here I am, an adult with unlimited resources, and even I was too scared to ask for help. Ashamed to admit that I wasn't 'normal.'

"But my fiancée reminded me that there are a lot of people out there like me, and there's a chance that, like I was, they're too afraid to speak up. Worried about how the stigma of suffering from a mental illness will affect their career. How people look at us. How we look at ourselves.

"Because I want to make my fiancée proud, and because my niece said to me the other day that she couldn't believe I felt this way because I always 'seem so happy,' I want to say this out loud, to all of you: I suffer from depression. I see a therapist, and I will continue to do so. I'll also seek out a professional opinion regarding medication." He lets out a sigh. "And I'm going to be okay. Sara tells me that we will be updating our social media pages with resources to help those of you who suffer from depression and need someone to talk to. I hope you take us up on this. I know I'm glad I finally spoke my truth. Thank you."

The room erupts, reporters shouting questions, but Sara returns to the podium. "As we said, we will not be taking questions at this time. We'll have more information for you tomorrow. Thank you all and have a good night."

"Wow," Eliza whispers.

"I think we owe Aiden Langfield an apology," Colton says, his voice gruff.

"You never know what someone is going through," Eliza muses. "We'll be back after a word from our sponsors..."

CHAPTER 56
AIDEN

"HOW DO YOU LOSE A RACCOON?" I grumble into the phone as I pull up to Beckett's house.

"Slick is missing," he says. "Not my raccoon. *Junior* is my raccoon."

As I climb out of my car, he approaches, sporting a nice shiner.

"Liv pissed?" I ask, pocketing my phone.

He does the same, chuckling. "You trying to say my wife controls me?"

I grin. "You know she does. As Lennox controls me. Speaking of which, I have to meet her soon."

Beckett smiles. "For your wedding."

My heart skips at the sound of that single word. "Yeah, my wedding."

It feels like a miracle that we're still getting married today. The last two days have felt more like a lifetime. The birthday party, her father's threat, her appointment with her family's attorney, the shit show that went down at the arena, and then my confession to the world.

Needless to say, we're still reeling, but she stood beside me, told me she loves me. And I can't wait for her to be my wife.

"Bossman, he ran in here," Finn hollers from across the street. He's standing in front of a brownstone that looks almost identical to theirs.

"How'd he get over there?" I ask, trailing behind Beckett as he crosses the street, headed toward the house that Finn's just disappeared inside. "And whose house is that? It belongs to one of Liv's friends, right? Or did your kid just break into a stranger's home?"

Beckett grumbles. "It's not one of ours."

The neighborhood is lined with trees, most of which are bare this time of year. The brownstones that stand side by side are standard red brick with black doors, and they're all beautifully maintained. It hasn't always been this way. Maybe my brother has formed an association that has imposed rules and compliance. It wouldn't surprise me.

I follow him up the steps, and as he opens the door and walks in without hesitation, I wince.

"Nice house," I comment. "Though it's a bit bare." There's a fireplace in the corner, and on the floor in front of it, a blanket is laid out. Beside it is a champagne bottle stuck in a bucket of ice. Clearly, someone has plans to celebrate. Maybe they just bought it.

Beckett continues down the hall, his shoes clacking loudly against the hardwoods.

"Aren't you worried someone is going to call the cops?" I call after him.

I take in the dark wood cabinets, the oversized island, the double fridge. It's a dream, really, especially when I note the television hanging in the corner. It'd be convenient to watch ESPN or a rom-com while making dinner. Hell, a kitchen this big would be perfect for team dinners.

That gets my mind spinning. Would Lex ever consider a house like this?

When Beckett storms out the back door, I take off at a jog to keep up. Jeez, his legs aren't any longer than mine. Must have big feet. And you know what that means.

I chuckle to myself as I open the door. I barely make it two steps down when a dog comes barreling toward me. Not just any dog. It's a puppy. He's white and bouncy, like his body is too small to contain all his energy.

At the sound of Finn shrieking "giddy up, Bossman," I scan the yard. Beckett is running through the grass with Finn on his shoulders.

"What the—" I mutter as they disappear out the back gate. *Where the hell are they going?*

The puppy jumps up on my leg, distracting me from my thoughts. In its mouth is a piece of green fabric. It takes a minute for it to register, but when it does, my stomach bottoms out. "You didn't," I mutter as I tug at the Luigi costume. The last time I saw the racoons, they were dressed in costumes—Mario, Luigi, and a Princess Peach.

He wouldn't. He didn't.

"Duck." I pull on my hair as panic races through my veins like ice. Finn is going to lose his mind. *"Duck."*

"Nah, his name's Goose."

I shriek like a teenage girl and jump a good foot in the air when Lennox pops out from behind the bushes.

"Holy shit, Lex. What the—what are you—" My jaw goes slack, and my tongue rolls out like a cartoon character as I take her in. With my jersey over a white dress, she is absolute perfection. "I thought..." I shake my head, at a loss, because I have no idea what I'm thinking.

Lennox lights up, breaking into a pretty smile. "What do you think of our puppy?" she asks as she saunters toward me.

Holding my breath, I study her face, trying to find the joke, but she seems sincere.

"Our puppy?"

"Yeah. And the house. It's nice, right? Beckett mentioned that there's a park around the corner. It'd be a great place for you to run around in. Ya know, to get the zoomies out?"

I nod, as if any of the words leaving her make sense.

"So what do you think?"

My heart stutters. "About the house with the dream kitchen and the puppy that I've always wanted?"

She grins. "And the girl of your dreams to come home to every night? What do you say, Hockey Boy? Never have I ever grown up. You want to do it with me?"

I lunge for her and pull her into my arms, holding her tight, like if I can bring her in close enough, this dream won't disappear. Because that's what this is. My wildest dream. A life with Lennox. *Forever with Lennox.*

I pull back and cup her face, staring into her pretty blue eyes. "I love you so much. Of course I want to do this with you. Did you really think that was a question?"

She shrugs and shows me her wrist. "I had a plan to get down on one knee and give this to you—" She slides a blue and white friendship bracelet over her hand and dangles it between us. "Marry me, Aiden. Not because of some trust, and not because you think it's what I need. Marry me because you can't imagine spending another day without me. Because I know I can't imagine going another day without being your wife."

"Oh, I'm going to marry the shit out of you," I say, taking the bracelet from her. The beads spell out *husband*, coordinating perfectly with the *wifey* bracelet on her wrist.

"Made it with Winnie before I came over," she says softly. "She's really proud of you, ya know. Liv let her listen to the Hockey Report. She heard everything you said."

"Yeah?" I smile, my throat going tight. At least I got that right. Hopefully she's one of many kids who heard me. Who realize that it's okay to not feel "normal" and that she's comfortable talking about it, whether to me or her parents or a therapist.

"I got matching T-shirts for us too," she teases, tugging the hem of her jersey up. It's like those *I'm with stupid* shirts, with arrows that point to one side, but this one is emblazoned with *His Last Kiss.*

I drop my head back and bark out a laugh. The sound makes the puppy whimper at our feet. "I fucking love you, Lex."

She leans in and brushes her lips against mine. "I love you. And full disclosure, I get the trust whether we get married or not. My father *did* offer it to me if I agreed not to marry you, but I turned him down. Then I discovered that my grandmother had the trust amended, removing the marriage clause. But with or without the money, I want to be your wife."

My chest practically bursts with affection for this woman. "Lucky for you, your bank account balance is the least attractive thing about you."

She grins. "Right back at you."

"Did you really buy this house?"

She bites her lip and lowers her gaze.

My stomach dips with a disappointment I'm ashamed to feel. Of course she only used it for the proposal. Damn, I really did like it.

Tipping her chin up, she gives me a rueful smile. "It's a wedding gift, actually."

Brows pulled low, I frown in confusion. "From who?"

"Your brother. Though it comes with a few strings. I may have agreed that we'd watch the kids on Friday nights when we can."

Laughing, I bring my forehead to hers. "Fucking Beckett."

"Ducking," she murmurs.

The dog yelps again, eager for attention, so I crouch down and pet his soft fur. "Goose?"

He barks like he knows his name.

She shrugs. "Beckett."

I groan, annoyed that he came up with such a great name without me. "I can't believe he named our ducking dog Goose."

She smiles down at us. "I don't know. I think it's kind of perfect."

Popping up, I throw my arm around her.

The puppy instantly darts into the house, streaking mud across the gorgeous hardwoods.

"Nothing's perfect," I say. "It might even be a disaster. But so long as I'm with you, Lex, it will be everything I've ever wanted."

Rule 1:
Don't fall for
the groom.

Dearest Lennox

Chapter 57
Lennox

Aiden: May I present to you Mr. and Mrs. Aiden & Lennox Langfield <picture of us wearing matching His Last Kiss/Her Last Kiss Bolts blue T-shirts as we stand outside city hall with huge smiles on our faces>

Sara: OH MY GOD. STOP IT! YOU'RE ADORABLE. ALSO, I'M GOING TO KILL YOU FOR GETTING MARRIED WITHOUT ME.

Me: Don't worry, you'll all be invited to our wedding this summer in the park. I just couldn't wait to make this one my husband.

Beckett: Congrats, guys. I think I'm officially ten for ten when it comes to matching couples. You're welcome.

Gavin: LOL. And now you're living across the street from him instead of next door to me. Good luck with that.

Millie: So happy for you guys, but I'll miss having you next door.

Sara: Brunch Sunday?

> Aiden: We just got married. You aren't having boozy brunch and leaving us guys out.

> Brooks: I'm with Aiden. I want to come.

> Sara: All you had to do was ask Brookie. I'll take care of you.

> Brooks: CRAZY GIRL!

> Sara: 😘

> Liv: Welcome to the family and the neighborhood. Just let us know where and when we're celebrating, and we'll be there. (Preferably without kids. Mama needs a break)

> Me: Thank you. Love you all! We'll see you Sunday!

"I CAN'T BELIEVE we did it," I whisper, dropping my phone to the floor.

Beside me, my husband lies on his back on the pillow-covered floor in front of the fireplace, wearing the sweetest smile.

Aiden takes my hand in his and holds them above us so I can see our rings. There's something about seeing the gold band wrapped around his left finger.

Mine.

He's all freaking mine.

"Wouldn't have wanted to do it with anyone else." He presses a kiss to my knuckles.

"Says the man who was engaged to another woman when this all started."

Aiden props himself up on his elbow and tickles my side. "Take it back."

I squeal with laughter as I fight him off. "Never."

With his lip caught between his teeth, he hovers over me, oozing happiness. "I love you so much, wife."

"Love you too. But do me a favor, Hockey Boy."

Aiden grins that dopey lovestruck grin. "Anything."

"Fuck me like you hate me."

"Yes, ma'am." He perks up. "You want stalker Aiden or ghost Aiden?"

I run my hand across his cheek, mesmerized by this man. "I just want Aiden."

He eases in close, his lips brushing against mine. "Then I can only make love to you."

I bite his bottom lip, pulling him closer. When he hisses, I let go and smile.

"Fine," I huff teasingly. "You can be my stalker."

He winks. "Like Casper, the friendly kind."

The End

EPILOGUE

Aiden

"THAT'S RIGHT, Princess. Slurp it like the dirty wife you are."

I smack her ass and pull her thighs closer. She's being a tease, tempting me by putting her sweet pussy in my face. She's just far enough away that I can't taste her while she goes to town on my cock, and it's driving me to madness. I thrust up into her hot mouth and groan when she moans around me. My wife loves it rough.

Sixty-nine is an extremely underrated position, in my opinion. There is nothing better than eating her and getting my dick sucked at the same time.

But right now, she's not letting me snack, and I'm getting frustrated. Knowing what my girl likes, I suck my thumb into my mouth. When it's nice and wet, I slide it across her perineum, then push into her tight hole. Lennox whimpers and pushes back, right where I want her.

"Aha," I say. Fuck yeah. While I continue to work my thumb in out of her, I dive in, sliding my tongue inside her.

She pushes back farther, grinding against me, her efforts to blow me almost forgotten.

It's fine. I'm not coming anywhere but in her pussy. Or maybe her ass. Only time will tell.

"Shit, Aiden. That's so—" Her words turn into a moan as her first orgasm hits.

I spear her with my tongue again, relishing the way she pulses around it, then I lap up every drop of her pleasure until she's collapsing to the side of me.

"Hands on the headboard," I order. "I need you to sit on me, baby." I lean back, waiting, but I'll only be patient for a few seconds.

"Give me a minute to catch my breath," she gasps. "You just stole all the air from my lungs."

"Welcome to my life, wife. You leave me breathless daily. Now get on my face."

"*Aiden.*"

Even as she scolds me, she straddles my neck. Chin tucked, she watches me, her expression a mix of need and affection.

Her tits make an incredible sight, but I can't play with them the way I love in this position. I want to eat her ass, but she gets weird about me kissing her after. Strange, I know. So I slide my thumb back into that tight hole, then I suck her clit into my mouth. The sounds she makes as she rides me have me leaking and bucking up, desperate for friction. Fuck, I need her to come again.

"Ass or pussy?" I grit out, pulling away.

"Oh god." Head tossed back, she moans.

"Not God, baby. Your husband. Now tell me. After you come again, am I shoving my cock into your ass or your pussy? The toy goes in the other hole, so choose wisely."

"Ass."

I press that thumb deeper, stretching her. "Good answer."

Knowing what's in store for us both, I suck her clit back into my mouth and allow her to use my chin to get herself off. She grinds against me until she's crying out and dripping down my face.

She's still blinking back to reality as I pull the toy and the lube out of the bedside drawer. I can't wait any longer. I've got to be inside my girl. She's my home.

An hour later, I rush back to our old apartment to grab Lennox's good-night flowers. So what if I had a greenhouse installed on the roof of the building? I have to ensure my wife gets her favorite flowers on the regular. While we've started construction on a greenhouse for the brownstone, it won't be finished until spring.

Tomorrow we're heading to Bristol for the fundraiser for Liv's brother's fire department, but for one more night, Lennox is all mine. The three days since our wedding at town hall—not exactly a honeymoon, but I'll take it—have been some of the best of my life. How could they not be, when it's just been the two of us?

I take the stairs of the brownstone two at a time. These days, I'm always rushing toward my life with Lennox. There will never be a moment that I don't run toward her, full steam ahead, excited for what's next. Even if it's just another movie night in bed with my girl and Goose.

Speaking of our puppy, when I step inside, he's not sitting at the door waiting for me, which means he's cuddling with Lennox. After our late afternoon sexcapades, we showered, and then I left her curled up and sleepy.

The giggles that echo down the hall are the first sign that this night is not going in the direction I planned. Even so, I make my way toward our bedroom, pink peonies in one hand and a pizza box in the other.

I push the door open, then freeze on the threshold. "What are you doing here?"

Okay, I know I sound like Beckett. I may have even growled, but seriously. Seriously. It's our honeymoon. Why is Sara lying in my bed with my dog at her feet and her head on my boobs?

Fine. They're Lennox's boobs, but now that we're married, they belong to me too.

It's the law.

My law.

And a great one at that.

"*Aiden,*" Lennox chides.

"Don't you Aiden me," I tell her, holding out her favorite flowers. "I was promised more sex and cuddles and the second Bridget Jones movie."

"Oh my god, that's my favorite one," Sara squeals.

"Of course it's your favorite. It's the best," I reply with a huff. Damn, Beckett is rubbing off on me.

"And he brought pizza," Sara says. "Best husband ever. Don't tell Brooks I said that," she adds, completely ignoring me. She pops up on her knees and reaches for the box. I gladly hand it over. Lennox is what I want. I couldn't care less about the pizza. Hell, I don't even need the movie night or the sex, but I'm putting my foot down. This is our honeymoon.

"We're married. Bedrooms are for married people," I tell Sara. "Take your pizza and go."

Lennox's mouth drops open.

Sara, who's already pulled a greasy slice out and taken a bite, doesn't bother to swallow before she counters. "Nah, best friend trumps husband."

Irritation zips up my spine. "Best friend does not trump husband. Tell her, Lex. Best friend does *not* trump husband." I sound like a whiney bitch, but there's no stopping it.

My pink haired bride tosses her head back and cackles. "No. Not doing this. I love you both," she says, eyes fixed on me now, "but Aiden—"

Now I'm the one gaping, jaw slack and everything. "*Excuse* you?"

She giggles, cupping a hand over her mouth. "Let me finish my sentence," she says when she's composed herself.

I fold my arms over my chest, teeth gritted, daring her to continue.

She folds her lips, this time keeping herself in check. "Remember when you said you were sad that you were leaving the hockey building so soon after finally living near your brothers?"

I nod once, the move succinct. Yeah, I love this house, but I didn't experience the full effect of popping into Brooks's or Gavin's apartments whenever I wanted in my short time at the Pad. I'll definitely be stopping in at Beckett's—though I'm not sure my presence will be noticed; fuck, there are a lot of people living there—but it's not the same.

"And you mentioned that you wished more athletes could talk directly to the media like you got the chance to last week. Set the record straight and all. Remember that?"

Now Sara has set her pizza slice in the box and is watching me closely. Huh. Maybe her presence here has something to do with whatever Lennox is tiptoeing around.

"Yeah?"

Sara presses her hands together in a prayer pose and then claps them quietly, bouncing on her knees.

"Then you're in luck," Lennox chirps. "Because all your brothers are currently in Beckett's basement, getting ready to record the first episode of the Langfield brothers' podcast."

I jut out my hip and drop a hand to it. "I get my own podcast?"

Lex giggles. "Well, you have to share it with your brothers."

"This is—" Excitement rushes through me, arcing like electricity. "I mean, I always knew I was meant for big things—"

Sara cackles. "Get out of here, you lunatic."

"Was this your idea?" I ask her.

She points at Lex, who's wearing the biggest smile. "This was all your wife."

Of course it was. Because Lennox Langfield knows me better than anyone. She's perfect for me. She always has been.

I launch myself onto the bed, almost sending the pizza box tumbling, which has Goose scrambling to his feet. As I drape myself over my wife, Goose gets up in our faces, covering us both in doggy kisses. It's yet another of the greatest moments of my life.

Then again, I have a feeling that life is going to be this good from now on. Every day will be better than the last. There's no more living in the past for me. And when things get dark, I know this woman will be by my side, giving me exactly what I need.

Lennox

"Come on, Becks. It's for a good cause," I say, ribbing my brother-in-law.

"I am not taking off my shirt. And for the sixtieth time, don't call me Becks."

Aiden, who's shaking with laughter, pulls me back against his chest. Across from us, Sara and Brooks are chuckling too. Liv is also laughing, though when Beckett glances at her, she presses her lips together, doing a poor job of hiding it.

We're in Bristol, raising money for Liv's brother's fire department.

Like Beckett, Chief Declan Everhart is scowling, though his expression is directed at his best friend, Fitz, who's trying to get him to take off his shirt too.

I wink at Fitz. We had a plan. Get the hockey players and fire-fighters shirtless for a few photos, and we'll sell them to raise even more money. We're basically in the middle of man Candy Land here. How could we not take advantage?

The town is decked out for Christmas, making the small town feel even cozier. And I'm feeling all sorts of festive.

"It was a mistake to bring the girls in on this episode," Beckett mutters.

It's their second one. They recorded their first episode last night —they did it live and unscripted while Sara and I ate pizza and giggled and listened to our four favorite guys talk about hockey, sports, and each other. I think what people will like the most is the banter between the brothers. I certainly do.

"Please, everyone is going to love this episode. How could they not, when we're coming to them live from Bristol, Rhode Island, where both Lake Paige, *now Hall*, and Melina Rodriguez are going to serenade us with Christmas tunes?"

I convinced the guys to do this, with Ava's help, of course. It was an easy sell to Beckett. He's determined to get his brother-in-law to like him. It's kind of hysterical how much the grumpy fire chief reminds me of Beckett.

We're set up in front of the Christmas tree, ready to record, when I notice that Melina has stepped between Fitz and the chief.

Fitz shuffles in closer to her, as well as his best friend, his smile infectious.

"Hey." I nudge Sara, who's now standing at my side.

"I don't think we're going to get Beckett naked," she says with a laugh.

I shake my head. "No. Look." I nod at the three people hovering close together. Their chemistry is so palpable it's practically swamping the crowd. "Do you see what I see?"

Head tilted, Sara studies them, then turns to me and smiles. "One in the front, and one from behind."

I shimmy my shoulders and grin. "Looks like Melina is going to have a good time."

"You two are terrible," Ava whispers from my other side. "We're supposed to be working."

I turn to the angel on our shoulder—we're so clearly her devils—

and shrug. "Twenty bucks says Melina is going to have a very merry Christmas."

Sara bounces on her toes. "With lots of balls."

Brooks glares at us both. "I told you no talking about balls."

"But they aren't your brothers," Sara whines, her shoulders slumping.

Beckett clears his throat, garnering our attention, and when we've quieted, he leans into the microphone. "Good evening, Boston. This is Beckett Langfield, and I'm here with my brothers, Gavin, Brooks, and Aiden—"

"And their wives," I shout.

"And our wives," Beckett finishes, his green eyes narrowed on me, clearly signaling me to be quiet. "And we're here to bring you another episode of the *Langfield Love Stories*..."

Wondering if Beckett will play matchmaker again with his grumpy brother-in-law, Chief Declan Everhart? Find out what happens between the Chief, Fitz, and Melina at the Christmas fundraiser in Trouble! *Available to preorder NOW.*

ACKNOWLEDGMENTS

This one is hard. Writing the last of the Langfield brothers feels a bit surreal. This family feels like my family. I've laughed more writing these four men than anyone else, I've swooned harder, and I have felt every dark emotion as well. But I'm not going to lie, writing Aiden was tough and I couldn't figure out why until I wrote the dedication. While I was walking down the bike path as I often do when I'm blocked, it occurred to me that I am a lot more like Aiden than I realized.

But here's the thing...just like Aiden has his brothers, so do I. These characters will continue to show up because we all know I love to write easter eggs into my books and I love to develop rich worlds that intertwine. So while the Langfield Brothers officially all have their happily ever afters, I'm going to keep them and continue to share bits and pieces of their lives with you because they bring me joy just like Lennox brings Aiden light in his darkness.

So thank you for loving these characters so much so I can continue to do the thing that keeps me bright and shiny too.

This series would not have been possible though if not for some really amazing people. If you know me, you know without Sara none of this would be possible. She continues to take on more responsibilities when it comes to my books and this one is no different. From plotting, to listening to my bad renditions of Aiden's songs, to formatting, to cover design to marketing to...I think you get the point. Without her, none of this would be possible. So thank you! Most of all thank you Sara for your friendship.

To Jenni who helped me create this world and who loves it as much as I do—this job is fun because of you. I'm so excited for our next adventure and I know our readers will be too.

To my lovely editor Beth, I know on an almost monthly basis I am asking you to squeeze in just a few more words and you always do it with a smile. My books wouldn't be what they are without you.

To my street teams, I truly appreciate each and every one of you. I love our conversations and our tangents. Every release gets better because of you!

To my beta readers, Glav, Becca, and my lovely sensitivity reader Jill, this book is what it is because of your comments. Whether I was laughing along with you, or digging deep to make the necessary changes, I was smiling because of how much you all care.

And to my amazing readers, thank you for all of your messages, your Tiktoks, your dms, your posts and your rants. There is nothing I love more than hearing from each of you how a character affected you, or a storyline made you laugh. I love your reviews, your anecdotes, and the notes you send to me.

If you want to follow along on my writing journey and have sneak peeks into all the characters in Bristol, follow me on Instagram, join my awesome Facebook group, sign-up for my newsletter and follow me on TikTok.

ALSO BY BRITTANÉE NICOLE

Bristol Bay Rom Coms

She Likes Piña Coladas

Kisses Sweet Like Wine

Over the Rainbow

Bristol Bay Romance

Love and Tequila Make Her Crazy

A Very Merry Margarita Mix-Up

Boston Billionaires

Whiskey Lies

Loving Whiskey

Wishing for Champagne Kisses

Dirty Truths

Extra Dirty

Mother Faker

(Mother Faker is Book 1 of the Mom Com Series, but is also a lead in to the Revenge Games alongside Revenge Era. This book can be read as a Standalone, or after Revenge Era and before Pucking Revenge)

Revenge Games

Revenge Era

Pucking Revenge

A Major Puck Up

Boston Bolts Hockey

Hockey Boy

Standalone Romantic Suspense

Deadly Gossip

Irish

Made in the USA
Las Vegas, NV
26 December 2024

15404850R00272